Julia Quinn started writing her first book one month after finishing college and has been tapping away at her keyboard ever since. She is the author of the *New York Times* bestselling *Bridgerton* series which begins with *The Duke and I*. Other titles in this series are: *The Viscount Who Loved Me*, *An Offer from a Gentleman*, *Romancing Mr Bridgerton*, *To Sir Phillip, With Love*, *When He Was Wicked*, *It's In His Kiss* and *On the Way to the Wedding*. She is a graduate of Harvard and Radcliffe colleges and lives with her family in Colorado.

Please visit her on the web at www.juliaquinn.com

Also by Julia Quinn:

The Secret Diaries of Miss Miranda Cheever
The Lost Duke of Wyndham
Mr Cavendish, I Presume
Splendid
Dancing at Midnight
To Catch an Heiress
How to Marry a Marquis
Everything and the Moon
Brighter than the Sun
What Happens in London
Ten Things I Love About You

Bridgerton Series:

The Duke and I
The Viscount Who Loved Me
An Offer from a Gentleman
Romancing Mr Bridgerton
To Sir Phillip, With Love
When He Was Wicked
It's in His Kiss
On the Way to the Wedding

The Smythe-Smith Quartet:

Just Like Heaven
A Night Like This

Minx

Julia Quinn

PIATKUS

First published in the US in 1996 by Avon Books,
An imprint of HarperCollins, New York
First published in Great Britain in 2008 by Piatkus Books
This paperback edition published in 2008 by Piatkus Books
Reprinted 2008 (three times), 2009 (twice), 2010, 2011, 2012

A CIP catalogue record for this book
is available from the British Library.

ISBN 978-0-7499-3914-4

Data manipulation by Phoenix Photosetting, Chatham, Kent
www.phoenixphotosetting.co.uk
Printed and bound in Great Britain by
Clays Ltd, St Ives plc

Papers used by Piatkus are from well-managed forests
and other responsible sources.

Piatkus
An imprint of
Little, Brown Book Group
100 Victoria Embankment
London EC4Y 0DY

An Hachette UK Company
www.hachette.co.uk

www.piatkus.co.uk

For Fran Lebowitz—
a wonderful agent, a wonderful friend.

And for Paul, even though he kept asking,
"Where are all the minks?"

Dear Reader,

It's always a little daunting to write a book for a character you've established in previous novels. Especially when that character is a devil-may-care, wickedly handsome rogue who has readers everywhere clamoring for more. But after William Dunford (almost) stole the show in my first two novels, *Splendid* and *Dancing at Midnight,* I knew that I had to make him the hero of my third, *Minx.*

The question was—who would be the heroine? Who could take the ordinarily suave Dunford and ruffle his feathers until he didn't know which end was up? The answer turned out to be surprisingly easy. Henrietta Barrett, better known as Henry, practically flew off the pages, charging forth with de-termination and charm and a stubborn streak that left Dunford reeling. And I, the author, happily realized that it was an awful lot of fun to bring London's smoothest and most unflappable bachelor to his knees.

I hope you enjoy reading *Minx* as much as I did writing it!

With my warmest wishes,

Julia Q.

Prologue

London, 1816

William Dunford snorted with disgust as he watched his friends gaze longingly into each other's eyes. Lady Arabella Blydon, one of his best friends these past two years, had just gotten herself married to Lord John Blackwood, and now they were looking at each other as if they wanted to eat each other up. It was revoltingly cute.

Dunford tapped his foot and rolled his eyes, hoping they would be able to tear themselves apart. The three of them, along with Dunford's best friend, Alex, the Duke of Ashbourne, and Alex's wife, Emma, who happened to be Belle's cousin, were on their way to a ball. Their carriage had met with a mishap, and they were presently waiting for a fresh one to be brought around.

At the sound of wheels rolling along the cobbles, Dunford turned. The new carriage pulled up to a halt in front of them, but Belle and John didn't appear to notice. In fact, they almost looked as if they were ready to throw themselves into each other's arms and make love on the spot. Dunford decided he had had enough. "Yoo-hoo!" he called out in a nauseatingly sweet voice. "Young lovers!"

John and Belle finally tore their eyes off one another and turned, blinking, to Dunford, who was making his way toward them.

"If the two of you can stop making verbal love to each other, we can be on our way. In case you hadn't noticed, the fresh carriage is here."

John took a deep and ragged breath before turning to Dunford and saying, "Tact, I take it, was not emphasized in your upbringing."

Dunford smiled merrily. "Not at all. Shall we be off?"

John turned to Belle and offered her his arm. "My dear?"

Belle accepted his gesture with a smile, but as they passed Dunford, she turned and hissed, "I'm going to kill you for this."

"I'm sure you'll try."

The quintet was soon settled into the new carriage. After a few moments, however, John and Belle were gazing rapturously at each other again. John laid his hand on hers and tapped his fingers against her knuckles. Belle let out a little mewl of contentment.

"Oh, for God's sake!" Dunford exclaimed, turning to Alex and Emma. "Will you look at them? Even the two of you weren't this nauseating."

"Someday," Belle said in a low voice, her finger jabbing at him, "you're going to meet the woman of your dreams, and then I'm going to make your life miserable."

"Afraid not, my dear Arabella. The woman of my dreams is such a paragon she couldn't possibly exist."

"Oh, please," Belle snorted. "I bet that within a year

you'll be tied up, leg-shackled, and loving it." She sat back with a satisfied smile. Beside her, John was shaking with mirth.

Dunford leaned forward, resting his elbows on his knees. "I'll take that bet. How much are you willing to lose?"

"How much are *you* willing to lose?"

Emma turned to John. "You seem to have married a gambling woman."

"Had I known, you can be sure I would have weighed my actions more carefully."

Belle gave her new husband a playful jab in the ribs as she leveled a quelling stare at Dunford and asked, "Well?"

"A thousand pounds."

"Done."

"Are you crazy?" John exclaimed.

"Am I to assume that only men can gamble?"

"Nobody makes such a fool's bet, Belle," John said. "You've just made a wager with the man who controls the outcome. You can only lose."

"Don't underestimate the power of love, my dear. Although in Dunford's case, perhaps only lust will do."

"You wound me," Dunford replied, placing his hand dramatically over his heart for emphasis, "assuming I am incapable of the higher emotions."

"Aren't you?"

Dunford's lips clamped together in a thin line. Was she right? He really had no idea. Either way, in a year's time he'd be a thousand pounds richer. Easy money.

Chapter 1

A few months later Dunford was sitting in his salon, taking tea with Belle. She had just stopped by to chat; he was glad for this unexpected visit since they didn't see quite as much of each other now that she was married.

"Are you certain that John isn't going to come barging over here with a gun and call me out?" Dunford teased.

"He's too busy for that sort of nonsense," she said with a smile.

"Too busy to indulge his possessive nature? How odd."

Belle shrugged. "He trusts you, and more importantly, he trusts me."

"A veritable paragon of virtue," Dunford said dryly, telling himself he was not the least bit jealous of his friend's marital bliss. "And how—"

A knock sounded at the door. They looked up to see Whatmough, Dunford's unflappable butler, standing in the doorway. "A solicitor has arrived, sir."

Dunford raised a brow. "A solicitor, you say. I cannot fathom why."

"He is most insistent, sir."

"Show him in then." Dunford turned to Belle and gave her a what-do-you-suppose-*this*-could-be shrug.

She smiled mischievously. "Intriguing."

"I'll say."

Whatmough ushered the solicitor in. A graying man of medium stature, he looked very excited to see Dunford. "Mr. Dunford?"

Dunford nodded.

"I cannot tell you how glad I am to have finally located you," the solicitor said enthusiastically. He looked at Belle with a puzzled expression. "And is this Mrs. Dunford? I was led to believe that you were not married, sir. Oh, this is odd. Most odd."

"I'm not married. This is Lady Blackwood. She is a friend. And you are?"

"Oh, I'm sorry. Most sorry." The solicitor took out a handkerchief and patted his brow. "I am Percival Leverett, of Cragmont, Hopkins, Topkins, *and Leverett.*" He leaned forward, adding extra emphasis when he said his own name. "I have very important news for you. Most important indeed."

Dunford waved his arms expansively. "Let's hear it then."

Leverett glanced over at Belle and then back at Dunford. "Perhaps we should speak privately, sir? Since she is not a relation."

"Of course." Dunford turned to Belle. "You don't mind, do you?"

"Oh, not at all," she assured him, her smile saying she would have a thousand questions ready when they were through. "I'll wait."

Dunford motioned toward a door leading to his study. "Right through here, Mr. Leverett."

They left the room, and Belle was delighted to note they did not shut the door properly. She immediately stood up and moved to the chair closest to the slightly open door. She craned her neck, her ears pricking up right away.

A mumble of voices.

More mumble.

And then, from Dunford, "My cousin *who?*"

Mumble, mumble.

"From *where?*"

Mumble, mumble, something that sounded like Cornwall.

"How many times removed?"

No, that couldn't have been "eight" that she heard.

"And he left me *what?*"

Belle clapped her hands together. How delightful! Dunford had just come into an unexpected inheritance. She rather hoped it was something good. One of her friends had just unwillingly inherited thirty-seven cats.

The rest of the conversation was impossible to decipher. After a few minutes the two men emerged and shook hands. Leverett shoved a few papers into his case and said, "I'll have the rest of the documents sent over as soon as possible. We'll need your signature, of course."

"Of course."

Leverett nodded and exited the room.

"Well?" Belle demanded.

Dunford blinked a few times, as if he still couldn't quite believe what he'd just heard. "I seem to have inherited a barony."

"A barony! Goodness, I'm not going to have to call you Lord Dunford now, am I?"

He rolled his eyes. "When was the last time I called you Lady Blackwood?"

"Not ten minutes ago," she pointed out pertly, "when you introduced me to Mr. Leverett."

"Touché, Belle." He sank down onto the sofa, not even waiting for her to seat herself first. "I suppose you may call me Lord Stannage."

"Lord Stannage," she murmured. "How perfectly distinguished. William Dunford, Lord Stannage." She smiled devilishly. "It *is* William, isn't it?"

Dunford snorted. He was so rarely called by his first name that they had a long-running joke that she couldn't remember it. "I asked my mother," he finally replied. "She said she thinks it's William."

"Who died?" Belle asked baldly.

"Ever brimming with tact and refinement, my dear Arabella."

"Well, you obviously cannot be grieving overmuch over the loss of your, er, *distant* relative, since you didn't even know of his existence until now."

"A cousin. An eighth cousin, to be exact."

"And they couldn't find anyone more closely related?" she asked disbelievingly. "Not that I begrudge you your good fortune, of course, but it is quite a stretch."

"We seem to be a family of fillies."

"Nicely put," she muttered sarcastically.

"Metaphors aside," he said, ignoring her jibe, "I am now in possession of a title and a small estate in Cornwall."

So she had heard correctly. "Have you ever been to Cornwall?"

"Never. Have you?"

She shook her head. "I hear it's quite dramatic. Cliffs and crashing waves and all that. Very uncivilized."

"How uncivilized could it be, Belle? This is England, after all."

She shrugged. "Are you going to go down for a visit?"

"I suppose I must." He tapped his finger against his thigh. "Uncivilized, you say? I'll probably adore it."

"I hope he hates it here," Henrietta Barrett said, taking a vicious bite of her apple. "I hope he really hates it."

"Now, now, Henry," Mrs. Simpson, the housekeeper of Stannage Park, said with a cluck. "That isn't very charitable of you."

"I'm not feeling terribly charitable at the moment. I've put a lot of work into Stannage Park." Henry's eyes glowed wistfully. She had lived here in Cornwall since the age of eight, when her parents had been killed in a carriage accident in their hometown of Manchester, leaving her orphaned and penniless. Viola, the late baron's late wife, had been her grandmother's cousin and graciously agreed to take her in. Henry had immediately fallen in love with Stannage Park, from the pale stone of the building to the shimmering windows to every last tenant who lived on the property. The servants even had found her polishing the silver one day. "I want everything to sparkle," she had said. "It has to be perfect, for this is truly a perfect place."

And so Cornwall had become her home, more so than Manchester had ever been. Viola had doted on her, and Carlyle, her husband, became a sort of distant father figure. He didn't spend a lot of time with her, but he always had a friendly pat on the head ready when she passed him in the hall. When she was fourteen, however, Viola died, and Carlyle was desolate. He retreated into himself, letting the details of running the estate flounder.

Henry had immediately stepped in. She loved Stannage Park as much as anybody and had firm ideas on how it should be run. For the past six years she had been not only the lady of the manor but the lord as well, universally accepted as the person in charge. And she liked her life just fine.

But Carlyle had died, and the estate and title had passed on to some distant cousin in London who was probably a fop and a dandy. He'd never been to Cornwall before, she'd heard, conveniently forgetting that she'd never been here either before she'd arrived twelve years before.

"What was his name again?" Mrs. Simpson asked, her capable hands kneading dough for bread.

"Dunford. Something-or-other Dunford," Henry said in a disgusted voice. "They didn't see fit to inform me of his first name, although I suppose it doesn't matter now that he is Lord Stannage. He'll probably insist that we use the title. Newcomers to the aristocracy usually do."

"You talk as if you're a member of it yourself, Henry. Don't be turning your nose up at the gentleman."

Henry sighed and took another bite of her apple. "He'll probably call me Henrietta."

"As well he should. You're getting too old for Henry now."

"*You* call me Henry."

"I'm too old to change. But you're not. And it's high time you lost your hoydenish ways and found yourself a husband."

"And do what? Move off to England? I don't want to leave Cornwall."

Mrs. Simpson smiled and forbore to point out that Cornwall was indeed a part of England. Henry was so devoted to the region that she could not think of it as belonging to any greater whole. "There are gentlemen here in Cornwall, you know," she said instead. "Quite a few in the nearby villages. You could marry one of them."

Henry scoffed. "There is no one here worth his salt and you know it, Simpy. Besides, no one would have me. I haven't a shilling now that Stannage Park has gone off to this stranger, and they all think I'm a freak."

"Of course they don't!" Mrs. Simpson replied quickly. "Everyone looks up to you."

"I know *that,*" Henry replied, rolling her silver-gray eyes. "They look up to me as if I were a man, and for that I'm grateful. But men don't want to marry other men, you know."

"Perhaps if you'd wear a dress . . ."

Henry looked down at her well-worn breeches. "I do wear a dress. When appropriate."

"I can't imagine when *that* is," Mrs. Simpson snorted, "since I've never seen you in one. Not even at church."

"How fortunate for me that the vicar is a most open-minded gentleman."

Simpy leveled a shrewd gaze at the younger woman. "How fortunate for you that the vicar is overfond of the French brandy you send over once a month."

Henry pretended not to hear. "I wore a dress to Carlyle's funeral, if you recall. And to the county ball last year. And whenever we receive guests. I have at least five in my closet, thank you very much. Oh, and I also wear them to town."

"You do not."

"Well, perhaps not to our little village, but I do whenever I go to any other town. But anyone would agree that they are most impractical when I'm out and about overseeing the estate." Not to mention, Henry thought wryly, that they all looked dreadful on her.

"Well, you'd better get one on when Mr. Dunford arrives."

"I'm not completely daft, Simpy." Henry chucked the apple core across the kitchen into a bucket of scraps. It fell squarely in, and she let out a whoop of pride. "Haven't missed that bucket in months."

Mrs. Simpson shook her head. "If only someone would teach you how to be a girl."

"Viola tried," Henry replied cheekily, "and she might have succeeded if she'd lived longer. But the truth is, I like myself just fine." Most of the time, at least, she thought. Every now and then she'd see a fine lady in a gorgeous gown that fit her to perfection. Such women didn't have feet, Henry decided. They had rollers—virtually gliding along. And wherever they went, a dozen besotted men followed. Henry would wistfully stare at this entourage, imagining them mooning after her. Then she laughed. That particular dream wasn't likely to come true, and besides, she liked her life just fine, didn't she?

"Henry?" Mrs. Simpson said, leaning forward. "Henry, I was talking to you."

"Hmmm?" Henry blinked herself out of her reverie. "Oh, I'm sorry, I was just thinking about what to do about the cows," she lied. "I'm not sure we've got enough room for all of them."

"You should be thinking about what to do when Mr. Dunford arrives. He did send word that it would be this afternoon, didn't he?"

"Yes, blast him."

"Henry!" Mrs. Simpson said reprovingly.

Henry shook her head and sighed. "If ever there was

a time for cursing, it's now, Simpy. What if he wants to take an interest in Stannage Park? Or worse—what if he wants to take charge?"

"If he does, it will be his right. He does own it, you know."

"I know, I know. More's the pity."

Mrs. Simpson shaped the dough into a loaf and then set it aside to rise. Wiping off her hands, she said, "Maybe he'll sell it. If he sold it to a local, you wouldn't have anything to worry about. Everyone knows there's nobody better to manage Stannage Park than you."

Henry hopped down from her perch on the counter, planted her hands on her hips, and began to pace across the kitchen. "He can't sell. It's entailed. If it weren't, I daresay Carlyle would have left it to me."

"Oh. Well, then you're just going to have to do your best to get along with Mr. Dunford."

"That's Lord Stannage now," Henry groaned. "Lord Stannage—owner of my home and decider of my future."

"Just what does that mean?"

"It means that he's my guardian."

"What?" Mrs. Simpson dropped her rolling pin.

"I'm his ward."

"But . . . but that's impossible. You don't even know the man."

Henry shrugged. "It's the way of the world, Simpy. Women haven't brains, you know. We need guardians to guide us."

"I can't believe you didn't tell me."

"I don't tell you everything, you know."

"Just about," Mrs. Simpson snorted.

Henry smiled sheepishly. It was true that she and the housekeeper were much closer than one would expect.

She absentmindedly twirled her fingers around a lock of her long, brown hair, one of her few concessions to vanity. It would have been more sensible to cut it short, but it was thick and soft, and Henry just couldn't bear to part with it. Besides, it was her habit to wind it around her fingers while she was thinking hard about a problem, as she was doing now.

"Wait a minute!" she exclaimed.

"What?"

"He can't sell the place, but that doesn't mean he has to live here."

Mrs. Simpson narrowed her eyes. "I'm not certain I understand your meaning, Henry."

"We just have to make sure that he absolutely, positively doesn't want to live here. Chances are it won't be difficult. He's probably one of those soft London sorts. But it certainly couldn't hurt to make him slightly, er, uncomfortable."

"What on earth are you thinking of, Henrietta Barrett? Putting rocks in the poor man's mattress?"

"Nothing so crude, I assure you," Henry scoffed. "We shall show him every kindness. We shall be politeness personified, but we shall endeavor to point out that he is not suited for country life. He could learn to love the role of absentee landlord. Especially if I send him quarterly profits."

"I thought you poured the profits back into the estate."

"I do, but I'll just have to split them in half. I'll send half to the new Lord Stannage and reinvest half here. I won't like doing it, but it will be better than having *him* in residence."

Mrs. Simpson shook her head. "Just what exactly are you planning to do to him?"

Henry twirled her finger in her hair. "I'm not certain. I'll have to give it some thought."

Mrs. Simpson looked over at a clock. "You'd better think fast, because he'll be here within the hour."

Henry walked over to the door. "I'd better wash."

"If you don't want to meet him smelling like the great outdoors," Mrs. Simpson retorted. "And not the part with flowers and honey, if you know what I mean."

Henry shot her a cheeky grin. "Will you have someone fill a bath for me?" At the housekeeper's nod, she dashed up the back stairs. Mrs. Simpson was right: she smelled rather unsavory. But then, what could one expect after a morning overseeing the construction of a new pigpen? It had been messy work, but Henry had been glad to do it—or rather, she admitted to herself, to supervise it. Getting knee-deep in muck was not exactly her cup of tea.

She stopped suddenly on the stairs, her eyes lighting up. It was not *her* cup of tea, but it was just the thing for the new Lord Stannage. She could even bring herself to get more actively involved in the project if it meant convincing this Dunford fellow this was what country lords did all the time.

Feeling much enthused, she bounded up the rest of the stairs to her bedroom. It would be several minutes before the tub was filled, so she picked up her hairbrush and walked over to the window to look out. Her hair had been pulled back like a pony's tail, but the wind had whipped it into snarls. She untied the ribbon; it would be easier to wash detangled.

As she pulled the brush through her hair, she stared out over the green fields surrounding the house. The sun was just beginning to set, tinting the sky like a peach. Henry sighed with love. Nothing had the power to move her as these lands did.

Then, as if timed just to spoil her perfect moment,

something glinted on the horizon. Oh, God, it wasn't . . . It was glass, glass from a carriage window. Damn and blast—he was early. "Stupid wretch," she muttered. "Deuced inconsiderate of him." She glanced back over her shoulder. Her bath wasn't ready.

Pressing closer to the window, she peered down at the carriage that was now rolling down the drive. It was quite elegant. Mr. Dunford must have been a man of some means even before inheriting Stannage Park. Either that or he had wealthy friends willing to loan him a conveyance. Henry stared at the scene quite unabashedly, brushing her hair all the while. Two footmen dashed out to unload the trunks. She smiled proudly. She had this house running like clockwork.

Then the carriage door opened. Without realizing it, she moved even closer to the glass of her window. A booted foot emerged. A rather nice, manly boot, Henry observed, and she knew her boots. Then it became apparent that the boot was attached to a leg that was every bit as manly as its footwear. "Oh, dear," she muttered. He wasn't going to be a weak sissy. Then the owner of the leg hopped out, and she saw him in his entirety.

She dropped her hairbrush.

"Oh, my God," she breathed. He was beautiful. No, not beautiful, she corrected, for that would imply some sort of effeminate quality, and this man certainly had none of that. He was tall, with a firmly muscled body and broad shoulders. His hair was thick and brown, slightly longer than was fashionable. And his face . . . Henry may have been looking down at him from fourteen feet up, but even she could see that his face was everything a face ought to be. His cheekbones were high, his nose straight and strong, and his mouth finely molded with a slight wry quality to it. She couldn't see what color his eyes were, but she had a sinking feeling they would be filled with shrewd intelligence. And he was much, much younger than she'd expected. She'd been hoping for someone in his fifties. This man couldn't be a day over thirty.

Henry groaned. This was going to be much harder than she'd anticipated. She was going to have to be very crafty indeed to fool this one. With a sigh, she reached down for her hairbrush and walked back to her bath.

As Dunford was quietly inspecting the front of his new home, a movement in an upstairs window caught his eye. The sun was glinting off the glass, but it appeared to be a girl with long, brown hair. Before he could get a better look, however, she'd turned and disappeared into the room. That was odd. No servant would be standing idly by a window at this time of day, especially with her hair unbound. He wondered briefly who she was, then let the thought drift from his mind. He'd have time enough to find out about her; right now he had more important things to attend to.

The entire staff of Stannage Park had assembled in front of the house for his inspection. There were about two dozen altogether—a small number by *ton* standards, but then Stannage Park was a fairly modest home for a peer of the realm. The butler, a thin man named Yates, was taking great pains to make the process as formal as possible. Dunford tried to humor him by adopting a slightly austere manner; it seemed to be what the servants expected of the new lord of the manor. It was hard to suppress a smile, however, as maid after maid bobbed a curtsy in his honor. He had never expected a title, never expected lands of his own or a household to go with them. His father had been a younger son of a younger son; God only knew how many Dunfords had had to die to put him in line for this inheritance.

After the last maid had bobbed down and up, Dunford returned his attention to the butler. "You run an excellent house, Yates, if this introduction is any indication."

Yates, who had never acquired the stone-faced facade that was a prerequisite among London butlers, flushed with pleasure. "Thank you, my lord. We do try as hard as we can, but it's Henry we have to thank."

Dunford raised a brow. "Henry?"

Yates gulped. He should have called her Miss Barrett. That's what the new Lord Stannage would expect, him being from London and all that. And he was Henry's new guardian, wasn't he? Mrs. Simpson had pulled him aside and whispered that particular tidbit in his ear not ten minutes before. "Umm, Henry is . . ." His voice trailed off. It was so hard to think of her as anything *but* Henry. "That is to say . . ."

But Dunford's attention had already been captured by Mrs. Simpson, who was assuring him that she had been at Stannage Park for over twenty years and knew everything about the estate—well, at least about the house—and if he needed anything . . .

Dunford blinked as he tried to focus on the housekeeper's words. Dimly, he sensed she was nervous. That was probably why she was rattling on like a . . . like a something. What, exactly, he didn't know, and what was she saying? A flash of movement in the stables caught his eye, and he allowed his gaze to wander in that direction. He waited a moment. Oh, well, he must have imagined it. He turned back to the housekeeper. She was saying something about Henry. Who was Henry? The question formed on his tongue and would have rolled off his lips if a giant pig hadn't suddenly exploded out through the partially open door of the stables.

"Holy, bloody . . ." Dunford breathed, unable to complete his curse. He was mesmerized by the sheer ludicrousness of the situation. The creature was hurtling across the lawn moving faster than any pig had a right to. It was an enormous porcine beast—surely that was all one could call it—this was no ordinary swine. Dunford had no doubt it would feed half the *ton* if taken to a proper butcher.

The pig reached the assembly of servants, and the maids shrieked, running in every possible direction. Stunned by the sudden movement, the pig stopped, raised its snout, and let out a hellish squeal—and then another, and another, and . . .

"Will you shut up!" Dunford commanded.

The pig, sensing authority, didn't just shut up—it actually laid down.

Henry did a double take, impressed in spite of herself. She had dashed downstairs the minute she saw the pig emerge from the stables, and had arrived in the front drive just as the new Lord Stannage was trying out his new lordly imperiousness on barnyard animals.

She ran forward, forgetting she hadn't managed to take that bath she knew she needed, forgetting she was still garbed in boys' clothes. Dirty boys' clothes.

"So sorry, my lord," she muttered, offering him a tight smile before leaning down and grabbing the pig's collar. She probably shouldn't have interfered, should have let the pig get bored of sitting on the ground, should have laughed when it came forward and did unspeakable things to the new Lord Stannage's boots. But she took far too much pride in Stannage Park not to try to salvage the disaster in some way. There was nothing in the world that meant as much to her as this smooth-running estate, and she couldn't bear that someone might think that free-roaming pigs were a common occurrence, even if that someone were a London lord of whom she heartily wanted to be rid.

A farmhand ran up, took the pig from her, and led it back to the stables. Henry straightened, suddenly aware of the way every last servant was gaping at her, and wiped her hands on her breeches. She glanced over at the darkly handsome man standing across from her. "How do you do, Lord Stannage?" she said, curving her lips into a welcoming smile. After all, there was no need for him to realize she was trying to scare him away.

"How do you do, Miss, er . . ."

Henry's eyes narrowed. He didn't realize who she was? No doubt he'd been expecting his ward to be a trifle younger, a pampered and spoiled young miss who never ventured out of doors, much less ran an entire estate. "Miss Henrietta Barrett," she said in a tone that said she expected him to recognize the name. "But you can just call me Henry. Everybody does."

Chapter 2

Dunford raised a brow. *This* was Henry? "You're a girl," he said, realizing how stupid he sounded even as the words left his mouth.

"Last time I looked," she said cheekily.

Somewhere in the background someone groaned. Henry was fairly sure it was Mrs. Simpson.

Dunford blinked a few times at the bizarre creature standing in front of him. She was wearing a pair of baggy men's breeches and a serviceable white, cotton shirt which, if the number of muddy streaks on her person were any indication, had recently been serviced. Her brown hair was unbound, freshly brushed, and flowing down her back. Rather beautiful hair it was, very feminine and somewhat at odds with the rest of her appearance. He couldn't quite decide if she was attractive or merely interesting or if she might even be beautiful if she weren't wearing something quite so shapeless. But there was no way he was going to make a closer inspection anytime soon because the girl smelled decidedly . . . unfeminine.

Quite honestly, Dunford didn't want to get within three feet of her.

Henry had been wearing eau de piglet since morning and had grown quite used to it. She saw the new Lord Stannage frown and figured he was probably reacting to her rather unorthodox attire. Well, there was nothing to do about that now, thanks to his early arrival and the giant pig's untimely appearance, so she decided to make the best of it and smiled again, wanting to lull him into thinking she was pleased to see him.

Dunford cleared his throat. "Forgive my surprise, Miss Barrett, but—"

"Henry. Please call me Henry. Everybody does."

"Henry, then. Please do forgive my surprise, but I was told only that someone named Henry was in charge, and so naturally I assumed . . ."

"Pay it no mind," she said with a wave of her hand. "Happens all the time. It often works to my advantage."

"I'm sure it does," he murmured, discreetly taking a step away from her.

She put her hands on her hips and squinted across the lawn at the stables to make sure the farmhand was securing the pig properly. Dunford watched her surreptitiously, thinking there had to be another Henry, that this girl couldn't possibly be in charge. For God's sake, she didn't look a day over fifteen.

She turned back to him with a rather sudden movement. "This is not a common occurrence, I have to say. We're building a new pigpen, and the pigs are in the stables only as a temporary measure."

"I see." She certainly sounded as if she were in charge, Dunford thought.

"Right. Well, we're about halfway done." Henry grinned. "Famous that you arrived when you did, my lord, for we could use another pair of hands."

Somewhere behind her someone coughed, and this time she was certain it was Mrs. Simpson.

Fine time for Simpy to get an attack of conscience, Henry thought, mentally rolling her eyes. She smiled again at Dunford and said, "I'd like to see the pigpen done as soon as possible. We don't want a repeat of this afternoon's unfortunate incident, do we?"

This time Dunford had no choice but to acknowledge that this creature was indeed running the estate. "I understand you're in charge here," he finally said.

Henry shrugged. "More or less."

"Aren't you a little, er . . . young?"

"Probably," Henry replied without thinking. Darn, wrong thing to say. That would only give him an excuse to get rid of her. "But I'm really the best man for the job," she quickly added. "I've been running Stannage Park for years."

"Woman," Dunford murmured.

"Excuse me?"

"Woman. The best woman for the job." His eyes glinted with humor. "You are a woman, are you not?"

Henry, completely missing the fact that he was teasing her, blushed painfully pink. "There's not a man in Cornwall who could do a better job than I do," she muttered.

"I'm sure you're right," Dunford said. "Pigs notwithstanding. But enough of this. Stannage Park looks quite splendidly run. I'm sure you're doing a good job. In fact, perhaps you should be the one to introduce me to the estate." Then he let loose what had to be his most lethal weapon: his smile.

Henry tried very hard not to melt at the sheer force

of his grin. She'd never had occasion to meet a man who was quite as much of a . . . of a *man,* really, as this one, and she didn't like the way her stomach was fluttering one bit. He didn't look the least bit affected by her presence, she noted with irritation, other than that he obviously found her quite odd. Well, he wouldn't see her swooning all over him. "Certainly," she replied smoothly. "I'd be happy to. Shall we start right now?"

"Henry!" Mrs. Simpson said, rushing over to her side. "His Lordship has just traveled all the way from London. I'm sure he'll want to repair himself. He'll be hungry, too."

Dunford flashed them another one of those deadly smiles. "Famished."

"If I had just inherited an estate, I'd want to see it right away," Henry said loftily. "I'd want to know all about it."

Dunford's eyes narrowed suspiciously. "To be certain, I do want to learn all about Stannage Park, but I don't see why I cannot begin tomorrow morning after I have eaten and rested." He turned back to Henry and inclined his head just a fraction of an inch. "And bathed."

Henry's face burned beet red as she realized the new Lord Stannage was telling her as politely as he could that she stank. "Of course, my lord," she said in a glacial tone. "Your wish is, of course, my command. You are the new lord here, of course."

Dunford thought he might throttle her if she inserted one more "of course" into her speech. Just what was she up to? And why was she suddenly so resentful of him? She'd been all smiles and welcomes just a few minutes earlier. "I cannot tell you how delighted I am to have you at my disposal, Miss Barrett. I'm sorry, er, Henry. And from your rather pretty speech, I can only deduce you *are* at my complete disposal. How intriguing." He smiled blandly at her and followed Mrs. Simpson into the house.

Darn, darn, darn, Henry thought wildly, resisting the urge to stamp her foot. Why on earth had she let her temper get the better of her? Now he knew she didn't want him here and would be suspicious of her every word and action. He was no corkbrain, this one.

That was her first problem. He was supposed to have been stupid. Men of his sort usually were, or so she'd heard.

Problem number two: he was too young. He wasn't going to have any trouble keeping up with her tomorrow. So much for exhausting him into realizing he wouldn't like it here at Stannage Park.

Problem number three, of course, was that he was quite the best-looking man she'd ever seen. She hadn't seen too many men, that was true, but that didn't diminish the fact that he made her feel like . . . Henry frowned. What *did* he make her feel like? She sighed and shook her head. She didn't want to know.

Her fourth problem was obvious. Despite the fact that she didn't want to admit the new Lord Stannage could be correct about anything, there was no way around the truth.

She stank.

Not even bothering to conceal a groan, Henry returned to the house and stomped up the stairs to her room.

Dunford followed Mrs. Simpson as she led him to the master suite. "I hope you find your rooms comfortable," she was saying. "Henry's done her best to keep the house modernized."

"Ah, Henry," he said enigmatically.

"She's our Henry, she is."

Dunford smiled at her, another one of those devastating combinations of lips and teeth that had slain women for years. "Just who *is* Henry?"

"You don't know?"

He shrugged and raised his brows.

"Why, she's been living here for years, ever since her parents died. And she's been running the place for . . . let me see, it must be at least six years now, since Lady Stannage passed on, God bless her heart."

"Where was Lord Stannage?" Dunford asked curiously. Best to find out as much as possible as soon as possible. He'd always believed that nothing could arm a man like a bit of research.

"Mourning Lady Stannage."

"For six years?"

Mrs. Simpson sighed. "They were quite devoted to one another."

"Allow me to assure myself that I understand the situation correctly. Henry, er, Miss Barrett has been running Stannage Park for six years?" That couldn't be possible. Had she taken over the reins when she was ten? "How old is she?"

"Twenty, milord."

Twenty. She certainly didn't look it. "I see. And just what is her relation to Lord Stannage?"

"Why, *you're* Lord Stannage now."

"The former Lord Stannage, I mean," Dunford said, careful not to let any of his impatience show.

"A distant cousin of his wife's. She had no place else to go, poor dear."

"Ah. How generous of them. Well, thank you for showing me to my rooms, Mrs. Simpson. I think I'll take a short rest and then change for supper. You do keep country hours here?"

"It's the country, after all," she said with a nod. Then she picked up her skirts and left the room.

A poor relation, Dunford thought. How intriguing. A poor relation who dressed like a man, stank to high heaven, and had Stannage Park running as smoothly as the most posh London household. His time in Cornwall certainly wouldn't be dull.

Now, if he could only find out what she looked like in a dress.

Two hours later Dunford was wishing he hadn't wondered. Words could not describe the sight of Miss Henrietta Barrett in a dress. Never before had he seen a woman—and he had seen many women—who looked quite so . . . well, wrong.

Her gown was an irritating shade of lavender with far too many bows and fripperies. In addition to its general ugliness, it was also obviously uncomfortable because she kept tugging awkwardly at the material. Either that or the dress simply didn't fit her, which, Dunford noted upon closer inspection, it didn't. The hem was a bit too short, the bodice slightly too tight, and if he didn't know better, he'd swear there was a small tear in the right sleeve.

Hell, he *did* know better, and he *would* swear the dress was torn. Put plainly, Miss Henrietta Barrett looked a fright.

But, on the brighter side, she smelled quite pleasant. Almost like—he sniffed discreetly—lemons.

"Good evening, my lord," she said when she met him before dinner in the parlor. "I trust you settled in nicely."

He bowed graciously to her. "Perfectly, Miss Barrett. May I commend you again on this smoothly running household."

"Call me Henry," she said automatically.

"Everybody does," he finished for her.

Despite herself, Henry felt a laugh welling up in her throat. Good God, she'd never even considered that she might come to *like* the man. That would be a disaster.

"May I escort you in to dinner?" Dunford inquired politely, offering her his arm.

Henry placed her hand on his elbow as he led her into the dining room, deciding there was no harm in spending an enjoyable evening in the company of the man who was—and she had to remind herself of this fact—the enemy. After all, she wanted to lull him into thinking she had befriended him, didn't she? This Mr. Dunford didn't strike her as a numskull, and she was fairly certain that if he even suspected she was trying to get rid of him it would take half of His Majesty's army to eject him from Cornwall. No, better just to let him reach his own conclusion that life at Stannage Park was not quite his cup of tea.

Besides, no man had ever offered her his arm before. Breeches and all, Henry was still too much of a female to resist his courtly gesture.

"Are you enjoying yourself here, my lord?" she asked once they were seated.

"Very much so, although it has only been a few hours." Dunford dipped his spoon into his beef consommé and took a sip. "Delicious."

"Mmm, yes. Mrs. Simpson is a treasure. I don't know what we'd do without her."

"I thought Mrs. Simpson was the housekeeper."

Henry, sensing an opportunity, schooled her face into a mask of earnest innocence. "Oh, she is, but she often cooks as well. We haven't an extensive staff here, in case you hadn't noticed." She smiled, fairly certain he *had* noticed. "More than half of the servants you met this afternoon actually work outside the house, in the stables and the garden and such."

"Is that so?"

"I suppose we ought to try to hire a few more servants, but they can be terribly dear, you know."

"No," he said softly, "I didn't know."

"You didn't?" Henry replied, her brain working very, very quickly. "That must be because you have never had to manage a household before."

"Not one as large as this, no."

"That must be it, then," she said, a trifle too enthusiastically. "If we were to hire more servants, we'd have to cut back in other areas."

"Would we?" One corner of Dunford's mouth tilted up in a lazy smile as he took a sip of his wine.

"Yes. We would. As it is, we really don't have the food budget we ought to have."

"Really? I find this meal delicious."

"Well, of course," Henry said loudly. She cleared her throat, forcing her voice into a softer tone. "We wanted your first night here to be special."

"How thoughtful of you."

Henry swallowed. He had an air about him, as if all the secrets of the universe were locked up in his head. "Starting tomorrow," she said, amazed that her voice sounded perfectly normal, "we'll have to go back to our regular menu."

"Which is?" he prodded.

"Oh, this and that," she said, waving her hand to stall for time. "Quite a bit of mutton. We eat the sheep once their wool is no longer good."

"I wasn't aware wool went bad."

"Oh, but it does." Henry smiled tightly, wondering if he could tell she was lying through her teeth. "When the sheep get old, their wool gets . . . stringy.

We can't get a good price for it. So we use the animals for food."

"Mutton."

"Yes. Boiled."

"It's a wonder you aren't thinner."

Reflexively, Henry looked down at herself. Did he think she was scrawny? She felt a strange sort of ache—almost like sorrow—and then brushed it aside. "We don't scrimp on the morning meal," she blurted out, unwilling to give up her favorite sausage and eggs. "After all, one needs proper nourishment when one breaks one's fast. And we need our strength here at Stannage Park, what with all the chores."

"Of course."

"So it's a good breakfast," Henry said, cocking her head, "followed by porridge for lunch."

"Porridge?" Dunford very nearly choked on the word.

"Yes. You'll develop a taste for it. Never fear. And then dinner is usually soup, bread, and mutton, if we have any."

"If you have any?"

"Well, it's not every day that we slaughter one of our sheep. We have to wait until they're old. We do get a nice price for the wool."

"I'm sure the good people of Cornwall are ever grateful to you for clothing them."

Henry schooled her face into a perfect mask of blank innocence. "I'm sure most of them don't know where the wool for their garments comes from."

He stared at her, obviously trying to discern if she could possibly be that obtuse.

Henry, uncomfortable with the sudden silence, said, "Right. So that is why we eat mutton. Sometimes."

"I see."

Henry tried to assess his rather noncommittal tone but found she couldn't read his thoughts. She was walking a fine line with him and she knew it. On the one hand she wanted to show him he wasn't suited for country life. On the other hand, if she made Stannage Park out to be an understaffed, mismanaged nightmare, he could fire the lot of them and start from scratch, which would be a disaster.

She frowned. He couldn't fire *her,* could he? Could someone get rid of a ward?

"Why the long face, Henry?"

"Oh, nothing," she replied quickly. "I was just doing a bit of mathematics in my head. I always frown when I do mathematics."

She's lying, Dunford thought. "And what, pray tell, were your equations concerning?"

"Oh, rents and crops, that sort of thing. Stannage Park is a *working* farm, you know. We all work very hard."

Suddenly the long explanation about food took on new meaning. Was she trying to scare him off? "No, I didn't know."

"Oh, yes. We've quite a number of tenants, but we also have people who work directly for us, harvesting crops and raising livestock and such. It's quite a bit of work."

Dunford smiled wryly. She *was* trying to scare him off. But why? He was going to have to find out a bit more about this odd woman. If she wanted a war, he'd be happy to oblige, no matter how sweetly and innocently she disguised her attacks. Leaning forward, he set out to conquer Miss Henrietta Barrett the same way he'd conquered women across Britain.

Simply by being himself.

He started out with another one of those devastating smiles.

Henry didn't stand a chance.

She thought she was made of stern stuff. She even managed to say to herself, "I am made of stern stuff," as the force of his charm washed over her. But her stuff obviously wasn't that stern because her stomach somersaulted, landed somewhere in the vicinity of her heart, and to her utter horror, she heard herself sigh.

"Tell me about yourself, Henry," Dunford said.

She blinked, as if suddenly waking up from a rather languorous dream. "Me? There isn't very much to tell, I'm afraid."

"I rather doubt that, Henry. You are rather an uncommon female."

"Uncommon? Me?" The last word came out as a squeak.

"Well, let's see. You obviously wear breeches more than you do dresses because I've never seen a woman look less comfortable in a gown than you do tonight . . ."

She knew it was the truth, but it was unbelievable how much it hurt to hear him say it.

"Of course, it could just be that the gown does not fit you properly, or that the material is itchy . . ."

She brightened a bit. The dress was four years old, and she had grown considerably during that period.

Dunford held out his right hand as if he were counting off her eccentricities. His middle finger stretched out to join his index finger as he said, "*You* run a small but, from the looks of it, profitable estate and apparently have done so for the past six years."

Henry gulped and silently ate her soup as another one of his fingers shot out.

"You weren't frightened or even the least bit put off by what I can only describe as the most immense animal of the porcine variety I have ever seen, a sight that would send most of the women of my acquaintance into vapors, and I can only deduce that you are on a first-name basis with said animal."

Henry frowned, not quite certain how to interpret that.

"You have an air of command one usually sees only in men, and yet you are feminine enough not to cut your hair, which, incidentally, is quite beautiful." Another finger.

Henry blushed at his compliment but not before she wondered if he were actually going to start in on his other hand.

"And finally . . ." He stretched out his thumb. ". . . you answer to the unlikely name of Henry."

She smiled weakly.

He looked down at his hand, now splayed out like a starfish. "If that doesn't qualify you as an uncommon female, I really don't know what would."

"Well," she began hesitantly, "perhaps I am a little odd."

"Oh, don't call yourself odd, Henry. Let others do that, if they insist. Call yourself original. It has a much nicer ring to it."

Original. Henry quite liked that. "His name is Porkus."

"Excuse me?"

"The pig. I *am* on a first-name basis with him." She smiled sheepishly. "His name is Porkus."

Dunford threw back his head and laughed. "Oh, Henry," he gasped. "You are a treasure."

"I will take that as a compliment, I think."

"Please do."

She took a sip of her wine, not realizing she had already drunk more than usual. The footman had been assiduously refilling her glass after nearly every sip. "I suppose I did have an unusual upbringing," she said recklessly. "That is probably why I am so different."

"Oh?"

"There weren't many children nearby, so I didn't get much of a chance to see what other little girls were like. Most of the time I played with the stablemaster's son."

"And is he still at Stannage Park?" Dunford wondered if perhaps she had a lover tucked away somewhere. It seemed likely enough. She was, as they had decided, an unusual young woman. She had flouted convention enough already; how much difference would a lover make?

"Oh, no. Billy married a girl from Devon and moved away. I say, you're not asking me all these questions just to be polite, are you?"

"Absolutely not." He grinned devilishly. "Of course I do hope I'm being polite nonetheless, but I really am quite interested in you." And he was. Dunford had always been interested in people, had always wondered what made the human race tick. At his home in London, he often stared out the window for hours, just watching the people go by. And at parties he was a brilliant conversationalist, not because he tried to be, but because he was usually genuinely interested in what people had to say. It was part of the reason why so many women had fallen for him.

It was, after all, somewhat uncommon for a man to actually listen to what a woman had to say.

And Henry certainly wasn't immune to his charms. It was true that men did listen to her every day, but they were people who worked for Stannage Park, in effect worked for her. No one besides Mrs. Simpson ever took the time to ask after her. Slightly flustered by Dunford's interest, she hid her unease by adopting her usual cheeky attitude. "And what about you, my lord? Did you have an unusual upbringing?"

"As normal as could be, I'm afraid. Although my mother and father were actually somewhat fond of each other, which is rather unusual among the *ton,* but other than that, I was a typical British child."

"Oh, I doubt that."

"Really?" He leaned forward. "And why is that, Miss Henrietta?"

She took another healthy sip of her wine. "Please do not call me Henrietta. I detest the name."

"But I'm afraid that every time I call you Henry, it brings to mind a rather unpleasant school chum at Eton."

She shot him a jaunty grin. "*I'm* afraid that you'll just have to adjust."

"You have been giving orders for too long."

"Perhaps, but you obviously have not been accepting them for long enough."

"Touché, Henry. And don't think I haven't noticed that you managed to sidestep explaining why you doubt I had a typical upbringing."

Henry pursed her lips and looked down at her wineglass which, paradoxically, was still quite full. She could have sworn she'd drunk at least two glasses. She took another sip. "Well, you're not exactly a typical man."

"Is that so?"

"Indeed." She waved her fork in the air for emphasis before drinking a bit more wine.

"And how am I atypical?"

Henry chewed on her lower lip, dimly aware that she had just been cornered. "Well, you're quite friendly."

"And most Englishmen aren't?"

"Not to me."

His lips curved wryly. "They obviously don't know what they are missing."

"I say," she said, narrowing her eyes, "you aren't being sarcastic, are you?"

"Believe me. Henry, I have never been less sarcastic. You are quite the most interesting person I've met in months."

She scanned his face for signs of duplicity but found none. "I believe you mean it."

He bit back another smile, silently regarding the woman sitting across from him. Her expression was a delightful combination of arrogance and concern, slightly clouded by tipsiness. She was waving her fork in the air as she spoke, seemingly oblivious to the morsel of pheasant dangling perilously off the end. "Why aren't men friendly to you?" he asked softly.

Henry wondered why it was so easy to talk to this man, whether it was the wine or just him. Either way, she decided, the wine couldn't hurt. She took another sip. "I think they think I'm a freak," she finally said.

Dunford paused at her bald honesty. "You're certainly not that. You just need someone to teach you how to be a woman."

"Oh, I know how to be a woman. I'm just not the kind of woman men want."

Her speech was risqué enough to make him cough on his food. Reminding himself that she had no idea what she was saying, he swallowed and murmured, "I'm sure you're exaggerating."

"I'm sure you're lying. You yourself just said I was odd."

"I said you were uncommon. And that doesn't mean that no one would want, er, be interested in you." Then, to his horror, he realized he could be interested in her.

Quite, if he let himself think about it too much. With a mental groan, he pushed the thought away. He had no time in his life for a country-bred miss. Despite her rather odd behavior, Henry wasn't the sort of woman with whom one did anything other than marry, and he certainly didn't want to marry her.

Still, there was something rather intriguing about her . . .

"Shut up, Dunford," he muttered.

"Did you say something, my lord?"

"Not at all, Henry, and please don't bother with the 'my lord.' I'm not used to it, and furthermore, it seems rather out of place if I'm calling you Henry."

"Then what should I call you?"

"Dunford. Everyone does," he said, unconsciously echoing her earlier words.

"Don't you have a first name?" she asked, surprising herself with the flirtatious tone of her voice.

"Not really."

"What does that mean, 'not really'?"

"I suppose that officially, yes, I do have one, but no one ever uses it."

"But what is it?"

He leaned forward, slaying her with another one of his lethal smiles. "Does it matter?"

"Yes," she retorted.

"Not to me," he said blithely, chewing on some pheasant.

"You can be rather irritating, Mr. Dunford."

"Just Dunford, if you please."

"Very well. You can be rather irritating, Dunford."

"So I've been told from time to time."

"Of that I have no doubt."

"I suspect that people have occasionally commented on your abilities to irritate as well, Miss Henry."

Henry had to smile sheepishly. He was absolutely right. "I suppose that's why we get on so famously."

"So we do." Dunford wondered why he was so surprised to realize it, then decided there was no use wondering. "A toast, then," he said, raising his glass. "To the most irritating twosome in Cornwall."

"In Britain!"

"Very well, in Britain. Long may we irritate."

Later that night, as Henry was brushing out her hair for bed, she started to wonder. If Dunford was so much fun, why was she so eager to boot him off the estate?

Chapter 3

Henry woke the next morning with a most vexing headache. She staggered out of bed and splashed some water on her face, all the while wondering why her tongue felt so strange. Positively woolly.

It must have been the wine, she thought, smacking her tongue against the roof of her mouth. She wasn't used to having it with dinner, and then Dunford coerced her into making that toast with him. She tried rubbing her tongue against her teeth. Still woolly.

She pulled on her shirt and breeches, secured her hair back with a green ribbon, and made it into the upstairs hall just in time to intercept a maid who appeared to be on her way to Dunford's room.

"Oh, hello, Polly," Henry said, planting herself firmly in the maid's path. "What are you about this morning?"

"His Lordship rang, Miss Henry. I was just going to see what he wants."

"I'll take care of it." Henry gave the maid a big, close-lipped smile.

Polly blinked. "All right," she said slowly. "If you think—"

"Oh, I definitely do think," Henry interrupted, placing her hands on Polly's shoulders and turning her around. "I think all the time, as a matter of fact. Now, why don't you go find Mrs. Simpson? I'm certain she'll have something pressing that needs doing." She gave Polly a little push and watched as she disappeared down the stairs.

Henry sucked in her breath as she tried to figure out what to do next. She had half a mind to turn around and ignore Dunford's summons, but the blasted man would only pull the bellpull again, and when he asked why no one had answered his previous summons—of course Polly was going to say Henry had intercepted her.

Taking very slow steps to allow herself time to compose a plan, she walked down the hall to his room. She lifted up her hand to knock on the door and then paused. The servants never knocked before entering rooms. Should she just enter? She was, after all, performing a servant's task.

But she was not a servant.

And for all she knew, he could be naked as the day he was born.

She knocked.

There was a slight pause, then she heard his voice. "Enter."

Henry opened the door just a touch and slid her head around the corner. "Hello, Mr. Dunford."

"Just Dunford," he said automatically before doing a double take, tightening his robe around his body, and saying, "Is there any particular reason you are in my chamber?"

Henry summoned up her courage and entered the

room fully, her eyes briefly flickering over his valet, who was preparing a shaving lather in the corner. She returned her gaze to Dunford, who, she noted, looked awfully good in his robe. He had very nice ankles. She'd seen ankles before; she'd even seen legs. This was a farm, after all. But his were very, very nice.

"Henry," he barked.

"Oh, yes." She straightened. "You rang."

He cocked an eyebrow. "When did you start answering the bell? I rather thought you were in a position to pull it yourself."

"Oh, I am. Of course I am. I just wanted to make certain you are comfortable. It has been ever so long since we've had a guest here at Stannage Park."

"Especially one who owns the place," he said dryly.

"Well, yes. Of course. I shouldn't want you to think we're lacking in any way. So I thought I'd see to your needs myself."

He smiled. "How intriguing. It has been quite some time since I have been bathed by a woman."

Henry gulped and took a reflexive step back. "I beg your pardon."

His face was all innocence. "I rang to ask the maid to draw me a bath."

"But I thought you bathed yesterday," she said, trying very hard not to smile. Oh, the man was not as clever as he thought. He couldn't have given her a better opportunity if he'd tried.

"This time I'm afraid it will have to be *I* who begs *your* pardon."

"Water is at a premium, you know," she said earnestly. "We need it for the animals. They need some to drink, and now that the weather is growing warmer, we have to make certain we have enough to cool them down."

He didn't say anything.

"We certainly do not have enough to bathe every day," Henry continued blithely, getting into the spirit of her ruse.

Dunford's mouth tightened. "As evidenced by your lovely fragrance yesterday."

Henry swallowed down the urge to ball her hand into a fist and pop him one. "Exactly." She looked over at Dunford's valet, who appeared to be having palpitations at the thought of his employer so disheveled.

"I can assure you," Dunford was saying, humor not at all evident in his voice, "that I have no intention of allowing my person to smell like a pigsty during my visit to Cornwall."

"I'm sure it won't come to that," Henry replied.

"Yesterday was a bit of an exceptional case. I was, after all, constructing a pigpen. I assure you that we allow extra baths after work in the pigpen."

"How positively hygienic of you."

Henry did not miss the sarcasm in his voice. Indeed, the veriest dullard would have found it difficult to miss. "Right. So tomorrow, of course, you will be able to bathe."

"Tomorrow?"

"When we get back to work on the pigpen. Today is Sunday. Even we don't perform such demanding chores on Sunday."

Dunford had to work very hard not to let another acidic comment pass through his lips. It looked as if the chit were enjoying herself. Enjoying his distress, to be precise. He narrowed his eyes and regarded her a little more closely. She blinked and looked at him with an expression of pure earnestness.

Maybe she *wasn't* enjoying his distress. Maybe they *didn't* have enough water to bathe every day. He had never before heard of such a problem in a well-run household, but maybe Cornwall received less rain than the rest of England.

Hold on just a second, his brain screamed. This was England. It always rained. Everywhere. He leveled a suspicious look in her direction.

She smiled.

He chose his words slowly and carefully. "How often may I expect to bathe while in residence, Henry?"

"Certainly once a week."

"Once a week will not be adequate," he replied, his voice deliberately even. He saw her falter. Good.

"I see." She chewed on her lower lip for a moment. "I suppose this is your house, so I suppose if you want to bathe with greater frequency, it is your right to do so."

He suppressed the urge to say, "It damn well is."

She sighed. It was a great, big heartfelt sigh. The annoying chit sounded as if the weight of three worlds were on her shoulders. "I shouldn't want to take water away from the animals," she said. "It is growing warmer, you know, and—"

"Yes, I know. The animals need to stay cool."

"Right. They do. A sow died last year from heat exhaustion. I shouldn't like that to happen again, so I suppose if *you* want to bathe more frequently . . ."

She paused, quite dramatically, and Dunford wasn't certain he wanted to know what was coming next.

". . . well, I suppose I could cut down on *my* baths."

Dunford recollected her rather distinct scent when they met. "No, Henry," he said quickly, "I certainly shouldn't want you to do that. A lady should . . . that is to say—"

"I know, I know. You're a gentleman down to your very toes. You don't want to deprive a lady. But I can assure you, I am no ordinary lady."

"That much was never in doubt. But all the same—"

"No, no," she said with an expansive wave of her hand. "There is nothing else to be done. I cannot take water from the animals. I take my position here at Stannage Park very seriously, and I could not be so remiss in my duties. I shall see to it that you are able to bathe twice a week, and I—"

Dunford heard himself groan.

"—I will bathe every other week. 'Twill be no great hardship."

"For you, perhaps," he muttered.

"It's a good thing I bathed yesterday."

"Henry," he began, wondering how to approach this issue without being unforgivably rude. "I really don't want to deprive you of bathwater."

"Oh, but this is your home. If you want to bathe twice a week—"

"I want to bathe every day," he ground out, "but I will content myself with twice a week, provided you do the same." He gave up all hope of approaching the discussion politely. This was quite the most bizarre conversation he'd ever had with a female—not that Henry seemed to qualify as a female in any sense of the word with which he'd been previously acquainted. There was that beautiful hair of hers, of course, and one could not easily dismiss her silvery-gray eyes . . .

But females simply did not engage in lengthy discussions about bathing. *Especially* in a gentleman's bedroom. Especially *especially* when the gentleman in question was wearing nothing but a robe. Dunford liked to think of himself as rather open-minded, but really, this was too much.

She exhaled. "I shall consider it. If it would please you, I could check on the water stores. If it is in ample supply, I might be able to accommodate you."

"I would appreciate that. Very much."

"Right." She put her hand on the doorknob. "Now that we have that settled, I'll let you return to your morning ablutions."

"Or lack thereof," he said, unable to summon enough enthusiasm even to twist his mouth into a wry smile.

"It is not as bad as that. We certainly have enough water to provide you with a small basinful every morning. You'd be surprised how far that will go."

"I probably would not be at all surprised."

"Oh, but one really can achieve a measure of cleanliness with just a bit of water. I'd be happy to give you detailed instructions."

Dunford felt the first stirrings of humor. He leaned forward, a rakish gleam in his eye. "That could prove most interesting."

Henry immediately blushed. "Detailed *written* instructions, that is. I—I—"

"That won't be necessary," Dunford said, taking pity on her. Maybe she was more of a female than he thought.

"Good," she said gratefully. "I appreciate that. I don't know why I brought it up. I—I'll just go down to breakfast. You should come soon. It is our most filling meal, and you'll need your strength—"

"Yes, I know. You explained it in great detail last night. I had better eat well in the morning, because it's porridge at noon."

"Yes. I think we have a bit of leftover pheasant, so it won't be as austere as usual, but—"

He held up his hand, not wanting to hear anything more about the slow starvation she had planned for him. "Say no more, Henry. Why don't you go down to breakfast? I shall join you shortly. My ablutions, as you so gently called them, shan't take very long this morning."

"Yes, of course." She hurried out of the room.

Henry managed to make it halfway down the hall before she had to stop and lean against the wall. Her entire body was shaking with mirth, and she could barely stand. The expression on his face when she told him he could bathe only once a week—priceless! Topped only by his expression when she told him she would bathe only every two weeks.

Ridding herself of Dunford, Henry reflected, was not going to take as long as she had originally anticipated.

Going without a bath was not going to be fun, Henry had always been quite fastidious. But it was not too great a sacrifice for Stannage Park, and besides, she had a feeling that her lack of cleanliness was going to be harder on Dunford than on her.

She made her way down to the small dining room. Breakfast had not yet been laid on the table, so she headed into the kitchen. Mrs. Simpson was standing in front of the stove, sliding sausages around on a skillet so as not to burn them.

"Hello, Simpy."

The housekeeper turned around. "Henry! What are you doing here? I would have thought you'd be busy with our new guest."

Henry rolled her eyes. "He isn't our guest, Simpy. We're *his* guests. Or at least I am. You have an official position."

"I know this has been difficult for you."

Henry just smiled, judging it imprudent to let Mrs. Simpson know she had actually been enjoying herself this morning. After a long pause she said, "Breakfast smells lovely, Simpy."

The housekeeper shot her an odd look. "Same food as every day."

"Perhaps I am hungrier than usual. And I shall have to eat my fill, because the new Lord Stannage is somewhat—shall we say—austere."

Mrs. Simpson slowly turned around. "Henry, what on earth are you trying to tell me?"

Henry shrugged helplessly. "He wants porridge for lunch."

"Porridge! Henry, if this is one of your crazy schemes—"

"Really, Simpy, do you think I'd go that far? You know how much I detest porridge."

"I suppose we could have porridge. I shall have to make something special for dinner, though."

"Mutton."

"Mutton?" Mrs. Simpson's eyes widened in disbelief.

Henry let her shoulders rise and fall in another expressive shrug. "He likes mutton."

"I do not believe you for one second, Miss Henrietta Barrett."

"Oh, all right. The mutton was my idea. No need for him to know how well he can eat here."

"Your little plans are going to be the death of you."

Henry leaned closer to the housekeeper. "Do you want to be turned out on your ear?"

"I don't see—"

"He can do that, you know. He can turn every last one of us out. Better to be rid of him before he can be rid of us."

There was a long pause before Mrs. Simpson said, "Mutton it is, then."

Henry paused before she opened the door leading out to the rest of the house. "And don't cook it too well. A little dry perhaps. Or make the sauce just a touch too salty."

"I draw the line at—"

"All right, all right," Henry said quickly. Getting Mrs. Simpson to prepare mutton when she had beef, lamb, and ham at her disposal had been enough of a battle. She was never going to succeed in getting her to prepare it badly.

Dunford was waiting for her in the small dining room. He was standing in front of a window, staring out over the fields. He obviously didn't hear her come in, for he started when Henry cleared her throat.

He turned around, smiled, motioned to the window with a tilt of his head, and said, "The land is lovely. You have done an excellent job in your management."

Henry flushed at the unexpected compliment. "Thank you. Stannage Park means a great deal to me." She allowed him to pull a chair out for her and sat down just as a footman brought in breakfast.

They ate in near silence. Henry was aware that she needed to eat as much as possible—the noonday meal was sure to be a dismal affair. She glanced over at Dunford, who was eating with similar desperation. Good. He wasn't looking forward to porridge either.

Henry speared her last sausage with her fork and forced herself to pause in her virtual inhalation of food. "I thought I might show you 'round Stannage Park this morning."

Dunford could not give an immediate reply, as his mouth was full of eggs. After a moment he said, "An excellent idea."

"I thought you'd want to become better acquainted with your new estate. There is much to learn if you want to manage it properly."

"Is that so?"

This time Henry was the one who had to pause as she finished chewing the last of her sausage. "Oh, yes. I'm sure you realize that one has to keep abreast of rents and crops and tenants' needs, but if one wants real success, one really must go the extra mile."

"I'm not certain I want to know what this 'extra mile' entails."

"Oh, this and that." Henry smiled. She looked down at Dunford's empty plate. "Shall we be off?"

"By all means." He stood as soon as she did and let her lead the way out of the house.

"I thought we might begin with the animals," Henry said.

"I suppose you know them all by name," he said, only half-joking.

She turned around, her face lit up with a brilliant smile. "But of course!" Really, this man was making it easy. He kept handing her the loveliest opportunities. "A happy animal is a productive animal."

"I'm not familiar with that particular axiom," Dunford muttered.

Henry pushed open a wooden gate that led into a large, hedgerow-lined field. "You've obviously spent too much time in London. It is a commonly expressed sentiment around here."

"Does it also apply to humans?"

She turned around to face him. "Excuse me?"

He smiled innocently. "Oh, nothing." He rocked back on his heels, trying to figure out this oddest of females. Was it possible she had names for all the animals? There had to be at least thirty sheep in this field alone. He smiled again and pointed off to the left. "What is that one called?"

Henry looked a little startled by his question. "Her? Oh, Margaret."

"Margaret?" He raised his brows. "What a delightfully English name."

"She's an English ewe," Henry said peevishly.

"And that one?" He pointed to the right.

"Thomasina."

"And that one? And that one? And that one?"

"Sally, uh, Esther, uh, uh . . ."

Dunford cocked his head to the side, enjoying watching her trip over her tongue.

"Isosceles!" she finished triumphantly.

He blinked. "I suppose that one over there is called Equilateral."

"No," she said smugly, pointing across the field. "*That* one is." She crossed her arms. "I have always enjoyed the study of geometry."

Dunford was silent for a moment, a fact for which Henry was extremely grateful. It hadn't been easy coming up with names at the drop of a hat. He'd been trying to trip her up, asking for the names of all those sheep. Was he on to her?

"You didn't believe I knew all of the names," she said, hoping her direct confrontation of the issue would diffuse any suspicious thoughts he was harboring.

"No," he admitted.

She smiled loftily. "Have you been listening?"

"I beg your pardon?"

"Which one is Margaret?"

His mouth fell open.

"If you're to run Stannage Park, you must know which is which." She tried very hard to keep any trace of snideness from her voice. She rather thought she succeeded. To her ear she sounded just like someone whose only concern was the success of the farm.

After a moment's concentration Dunford pointed to a sheep and said, "That one."

Drat! He was right. "And Thomasina?"

He was obviously warming to the exercise because he looked rather jovial as he pointed his finger and said, "That one."

Henry was just about to say, "Wrong," when she realized that she had no idea if he was wrong or not. Which one had she called Thomasina? She'd thought it was the one by the tree, but they were all moving about, and—

"Was I correct?"

"Excuse me?"

"Is that sheep or is that sheep not Thomasina?"

"No, it isn't," Henry said decisively. If she couldn't recall which one was Thomasina, she doubted very much that he could.

"I really think that's Thomasina." He leaned back against the gate, looking very confident and very male.

"That one is Thomasina," she snapped, pointing at random.

He broke out into a very wide grin. "No, that one is Isosceles. I'm sure of it."

Henry swallowed convulsively. "No, no. It's Thomasina. I'm certain of it," she said. "But don't worry, I'm sure you'll learn all of the names soon. You need only put your mind to it. Now, why don't we continue our tour?"

Dunford pushed off against the gate. "I cannot wait."

He was whistling to himself as he followed her out of the field. This was going to be a most interesting morning.

Interesting, he later reflected, was perhaps not the correct word.

By the time he and Henry arrived back at the house for their midday meal—a scrumptious bowl of hot, sticky porridge—he had mucked out the stable stalls, milked a cow, been pecked by three separate hens, weeded a vegetable garden, and fallen into a trough.

And if the trough accident just happened to be the result of Henry's tripping over a tree root and bumping into him—well, there was no way to prove it, was there? Considering that the dunking was the closest thing he was going to get to a bath anytime soon, he decided not to get angry about it just yet.

Henry was up to something, and it was damned intriguing watching her, even if he didn't yet know what she was trying to achieve.

As they sat down to eat, Mrs. Simpson brought in two steaming bowls of porridge. She set the larger one down in front of Dunford, saying, "I filled it right to the top, this being your favorite and all."

Dunford tilted his head slowly and looked at Henry, one eyebrow raised in a most questioning manner.

Henry looked pointedly at Mrs. Simpson, waited for the housekeeper to leave, and then whispered, "She felt dreadful that we have to serve you porridge. I'm afraid I fibbed just a bit and told her you adore it. It made her feel so much better. Surely a little white lie is justified if it is for the greater good of mankind."

He dipped his spoon into the unappetizing cereal. "Somehow, Henry, I have a feeling you've taken that sentiment to heart."

The day, Henry reflected as she brushed out her hair later that evening before going to bed, had been an unqualified success. Almost.

She didn't think he realized she had tripped over that tree root and pushed him into the trough on purpose, and the entire porridge episode had been, in her opinion, nothing short of brilliant.

But Dunford was shrewd. One couldn't spend an entire day with the man without realizing that fact. And as if that weren't enough, he'd been acting so bloody *nice* to her. At their evening meal he'd been a lovely companion, asking so attentively about her childhood and laughing at her anecdotes of growing up on a farm.

If he didn't have so many redeeming qualities, it would be ever so much easier to scheme to get rid of him.

But, Henry reminded herself sternly, the fact that he seemed to be a nice person in no way detracted from the even more pressing fact that he had the power to remove her from Stannage Park. She shuddered. What would she do away from her beloved home? She knew nothing else, had no idea how to go about in the world at large.

No, she had to find a way to make him leave Cornwall. She *had* to.

Her resolve once again firm, she set down the hairbrush and stood up. She started to make her way over to the bed but was stopped mid-stride by the pathetic grumblings of her stomach.

Lord, she was hungry.

It had seemed an inspired plan that morning to starve him out of residence, but she'd neglected the quite pertinent fact that she'd be starving herself as well.

Ignore it, Henry, she told herself.

Her stomach roared.

She glanced at the clock. Midnight. The house would be quiet. She could creep down to the kitchen, grab some food, and consume it back here in her room. She could be in and out within minutes.

Not bothering to don a wrapper, she tiptoed out of her room and down the stairs.

* * *

Damn, he was hungry! Dunford lay in bed, unable to sleep. His stomach was making the most hideous noises. Henry had dragged him all over the countryside that day in a route tailor-made to exhaust him, and then she'd had the gall to smile as she fed him porridge and cold mutton.

Cold mutton? *Blech!* And if it didn't taste bad enough, there hadn't been enough of it.

Surely there had to be something in the house he could eat that wouldn't jeopardize her precious animals. A biscuit. A radish. Even a spoonful of sugar.

He hopped out of bed, pulled on a robe to cover his naked form, and slipped out of the room. He tiptoed as he passed Henry's room—it wouldn't do to wake the little tyrant. A rather nice and endearing tyrant she was, but nonetheless, he rather thought it behooved him not to alert her to his little sojourn to the kitchens.

He made his way down the stairs, slipped around the corner, and crept through the small dining room to the—wait! Was that a light in the kitchen?

Henry.

The blasted girl was eating.

She was wearing a long, white, cotton nightgown which floated angelically around her.

Henry? An angel?

Ha!

He scooted himself against the wall and peeked around the corner, careful to keep himself in shadows.

"God," she was muttering, "I hate porridge." She shoved a biscuit into her mouth, washed it down with a glass of milk, and then picked up a slice of—was that ham?

Dunford's eyes narrowed. It certainly wasn't mutton.

Henry took another long and—from the sound of

her sigh—satisfying swig of milk before she started to clean up.

Dunford's first urge was to stomp into the kitchen and demand an explanation, but then his stomach let out another loud rumbling. With a sigh he secreted himself behind an armoire as Henry tiptoed through the small dining room. He waited until he heard her footsteps on the stairs, then he ran into the kitchen and finished off the ham.

Chapter 4

"Wake up, Henry." Maryanne, the upstairs maid, gently shook her shoulders. "Henry, wake up."

Henry rolled over and mumbled something that sounded vaguely like "go away."

"But you insisted, Henry. You made me swear I'd get you out of bed at half past five."

"Mmmph, grmmph . . . didn't mean it."

"You said you'd say that, and that I should ignore you." Maryanne gave Henry a shove. "Wake up!"

Henry, who'd been more than halfway asleep, suddenly bolted wide awake and sat up so quickly she started to shake. "What? Who? What's going on?"

"It's just me, Henry. Maryanne."

Henry blinked. "What the devil are you doing here? It's still dark out. What time is it?"

"Half past five," Maryanne explained patiently. "You asked me to wake you up extra early this morning."

"I did?" Oh, yes . . . Dunford. "I did. Right. Well, thank you, Maryanne. That will be enough."

"You made me swear I'd stay in the room until you got out of bed."

She was far too smart for her own good, Henry decided as she realized she had been about to curl back up under the covers. "Right. I see. Well, nothing to it, I guess." She swung her legs over the side of the bed. "Lots of people get up this—" Yawn.

She stumbled over to her dressing table, where a clean pair of breeches and white shirt were laid out.

"You might want a jacket, too," Maryanne said. "It's chilly outside."

"It would be," Henry muttered as she pulled on her clothing. As devoted as she was to country life, she never, ever got out of bed before seven, and even that was an hour to be avoided. But if she was going to convince Dunford that he was not suited to life at Stannage Park, she was going to have to stretch the truth a bit.

She paused as she was buttoning her shirt. She did still want him to go, didn't she?

Of course she did. She strode over to a basin and splashed cold water on her face, hoping it would make her look more awake. That man had deliberately set out to charm her. It didn't matter that he'd succeeded, she thought perversely. It only mattered that he had done it deliberately, probably because he wanted something from her.

But then again, what could he possibly want from her? She had absolutely nothing he needed.

Unless of course he had realized she was trying to get rid of him and he was trying to stop her.

Henry pondered this as she pulled her hair back and fastened it like a pony's tail. He had seemed sincere when he told her he was interested in her upbringing. He was her guardian, after all, if only for a few more months. There was certainly nothing odd about a little guardianlike concern.

But was he concerned about his ward? Or about how he could suck his newfound estate dry?

She groaned. Funny how a little candlelight could make the world seem so innocent and rosy. In the harsh light of morning, she could see things more clearly.

She made a little annoyed sound in the back of her throat. Harsh light of morning, her foot. It was still dark out.

But that didn't mean she didn't realize he was up to something—even if she wasn't quite certain what exactly that was. What if he had a secret agenda of his own? Henry shuddered at the thought.

With fresh determination, she pulled on her boots, grabbed a candle, and strode out into the hall.

Dunford was staying in the master suite, only a few doors down from her own room. She took a deep breath for courage and knocked loudly on his door.

No response.

She knocked again.

Still nothing.

Did she dare?

She did.

She grasped the doorknob and turned, letting herself into his room. He was sleeping soundly. Very soundly.

Henry almost felt guilty for what she was about to do. "Good morning!" she said in what she hoped was an ingratiatingly cheerful voice.

He didn't move.

"Dunford?"

He mumbled something, but other than that there was no indication he was the least bit awake.

She stepped closer and tried again. "Good morning!"

He made another sleepy noise and rolled over to face her.

Henry caught her breath. Lord, but he was handsome. Just the sort of man who had never paid any attention to her at county dances. Without thinking, she reached out to touch his finely molded lips, then caught herself when she was but an inch away. She jerked back as if she'd been burned, an odd reaction as she hadn't even touched him.

Don't lose your courage now, Henry. She gulped and reached out again, this time toward his shoulder. She poked him gingerly. "Dunford? Dunford?"

"Mmm," he said sleepily. "Lovely hair."

Henry's hand flew to her hair. Had he been talking about her? Or to her? Impossible. The man was still asleep.

"Dunford?" Another poke.

"Smell good," he mumbled.

Now she knew he wasn't talking about her.

"Dunford, it's time to wake up."

"Be quiet, sweetie, and get back into bed."

Sweetie? Who was sweetie?

"Dunford . . ."

Before she realized what was happening, his hand landed heavily on the back of her neck and she tumbled into the bed. "Dunford!"

"Shhh, sweetie, kiss me."

Kiss him? Henry thought frantically. Was he crazy? Or was she crazy because for a split second she was tempted to oblige him?

"Mmm, so sweet." He nuzzled her neck, his lips trailing upward to the underside of her chin.

"Dunford," she said shakily, "I think you're still asleep."

"Mmm-hmm, whatever you say, sweetie." His hand stole around to her backside, pulling her more tightly against him.

Henry gasped. They were separated by her clothing and the blankets, but she could still feel his hardness burning against her. She had grown up on a farm; she knew what it meant. "Dunford, I think you've made a mistake . . ."

He seemed not to hear. His lips had moved to her earlobe, and he was nibbling sweetly, so sweetly that Henry could feel herself melting. Dear God, she was melting right here in the arms of a man who had obviously mistaken her for someone else. Not to mention the small fact that he was sort of her enemy.

But the tingles traveling up and down her spine proved far stronger than common sense. What would it feel like to be kissed? To be kissed, truly and deeply, right on the mouth? No man had ever so much as given her a peck before, and it didn't seem likely that one would anytime soon. And if she had to take advantage of Dunford's sleepy state . . . well, so be it. Arching her neck ever so slightly, she turned her face to his, offering him her lips.

He took them greedily, his lips and tongue moving expertly against her mouth. Henry felt the breath leave her body, felt herself straining for something more. Hesitantly, she touched her hand to his shoulder. His muscle leaped at the contact, and he groaned and pulled her closer.

So this was passion. Surely this wasn't so sinful. Surely she could allow herself to enjoy this, at least until he woke up.

Until he woke up? Henry froze. How on earth would she be able to explain this to him? Frantically, she began to struggle in his arms. "Dunford! Dunford, stop!" Summoning all her strength, she shoved against him so hard she landed on the floor with a loud thump.

"What on earth?"

Henry swallowed nervously. He sounded awake.

His face appeared over the side of the bed. "Curse it, woman! What the devil are you doing here?"

"Waking you up?" Her words came out more like a question than she would have liked.

"What the—" He uttered a word Henry had never heard, then exploded with, "For Chrissakes, it's still dark out!"

"That's when we get up around here," she said loftily, lying through her teeth.

"Well, good for you. Now get out!"

"I thought you wanted me to show you the estate."

"In the morning," he ground out.

"It *is* morning."

"It is still night, you miserable little hellion." He clenched his teeth, fighting the urge to get up, stride across the room, and pull open the curtains to prove to her that the sun had not yet come up. In all truth the only thing stopping him was his nakedness. His nakedness and his . . . arousal.

What the hell?

He looked back over at her. She was still sitting on the floor, her eyes wide with an expression that hovered somewhere between nervousness and desire.

Desire?

He looked at her a little more closely. Wisps of hair floated around her face; he couldn't imagine that someone as efficient as Henry would have arranged them that way on purpose if she were planning to spend the day outside. Her lips looked unbearably pink and slightly swollen, as if she'd just been kissed.

"What are you doing on the floor?" he asked in a very low voice.

"Well, as I said, I came in to wake you up—"

"Save it, Henry. What are you doing on the *floor?*"

She had the grace at least to blush. "Oh. That's a long story, actually."

"Obviously," he drawled out, "I have all day."

"Hmmm, yes, so you do." Her mind spun frantically until she realized there was nothing she could say that would be remotely plausible, even the truth. He certainly wouldn't believe he had initiated a kiss with her.

"Henry . . ." There was no mistaking the threat in his voice.

"Well," she stalled, deciding with a sense of dread she'd have to tell him the truth and face his horrified reaction. "I, um, I came in to wake you up, and you, um, you seem to be a rather sound sleeper." She looked up hopefully at him, praying that he might possibly decide that that was explanation enough.

He crossed his arms, obviously waiting for more.

"You . . . I think you mistook me for someone else," she continued, painfully aware of the blush creeping across her face.

"And who, pray tell, was that?"

"Someone you call sweetie, I'm afraid."

Sweetie? That was what he called Christine, his mistress, who was tucked away in London. An uncomfortable feeling began to form in the pit of his stomach. "And then what happened?"

"Well, you grabbed my neck, and I fell on the bed."

"And?"

"And that's all," Henry said quickly, suddenly realizing she could avoid telling the entire truth. "I shoved against you and woke you up, and in the process I fell on the floor."

His eyes narrowed. Was she leaving something out? He had always been very active in his sleep. He couldn't count the number of times he had woken up in the middle of making love to Christine. He didn't even want to think about what he might have initiated with Henry. "I see," he said in clipped tones. "I apologize for any untoward behavior committed against your person while I was asleep."

"Oh, it was nothing, I assure you," Henry said gratefully.

He looked down at her expectantly.

She looked back, an innocent smile on her face.

"Henry," he finally said. "What time is it?"

"What time is it?" she echoed. "Why, I think it must be almost six by now."

"Precisely."

"Excuse me?"

"Get out of my room."

"Oh." She scrambled to her feet. "You'll be wanting to get dressed, of course."

"I'll be *wanting* to go back to sleep."

"Hmm, yes, of course you will, but if you don't mind my saying so, it's highly unlikely you'll be able to fall asleep again. You might as well just get dressed."

"Henry?"

"Yes?"

"Get *out!*"

She flew from the room.

Twenty minutes later Dunford joined Henry at the breakfast table. He was dressed casually, but Henry could tell with one glance that his clothes were far too fine for building a pigpen. She thought briefly about telling him this, then thought better of it. If he ruined his clothing, all the more reason for him to want to leave.

Besides, she rather doubted he owned anything suitable for building a pigpen.

He sat down across from her and grabbed a piece of toast with a movement so vicious she knew he was fuming.

"Couldn't get back to sleep?" Henry murmured.

He glared at her.

Henry pretended not to notice. "Would you like to look at the *Times?* I'm nearly done with it." Without waiting for him to reply, she pushed the paper across the table.

Dunford glanced down and scowled. "I read that two days ago."

"Oh. So sorry," she replied, unable to keep a trace of mischief out of her voice. "It takes a few days for the paper to get all the way out here. We're the end of the world, you know."

"So I'm coming to realize."

She suppressed a smile, pleased with how well her plans were progressing. After the bizarre scene earlier that morning, her determination to see him back in London had quadrupled. She was horribly aware of what one of his smiles did to her insides—she didn't particularly want to know what one of his kisses would do if she let it go to completion.

Well, that was not entirely true. She was dying to know what one of his kisses would do—she was just painfully certain he would never care to let her find out. The only way he was going to kiss her again was if he mistook her for another woman, and the chances of that happening twice were small indeed. Besides, Henry did have a measure of pride, even if she had conveniently forgotten about it that morning. Much as she'd enjoyed his kiss, she didn't particularly relish knowing he really wanted someone else.

Men like him didn't want women like her, and the sooner he left, the sooner she could go back to feeling good about herself.

"Oh, look!" she exclaimed, her face a miracle of cheerfulness. "The sun is coming up."

"I can hardly contain my excitement."

Henry choked on her toast. At least getting rid of him was going to be interesting. She decided not to provoke him further until he finished his breakfast. Men could be nasty on empty stomachs. At least that's what Viola had always told her. Downing a forkful of eggs, she turned her attention to the brilliant sunrise unfolding through the window. First the sky tinted lavender, then striped itself in orange and pink. Henry was certain there was no place on earth as beautiful as Stannage Park that very minute. Unable to contain herself, she sighed.

Dunford heard the noise and regarded her curiously. She was gazing, enraptured, out the window. The look of awe on her face was humbling. He had always enjoyed outdoor pursuits, but never before had he seen a human being so obviously filled with respect and wonder for the forces of nature. She was a complex woman, his Henry.

His Henry? When had he started thinking of her in possessive terms?

Since she tumbled into your bed this morning, his mind replied wryly. *And stop pretending you don't remember you kissed her.*

It had all come back to him while he'd been getting dressed. He hadn't meant to kiss her, hadn't even realized at the time that it was Henry in his arms. But that didn't mean he didn't remember every little detail now:

the curve of her lips, the silky feel of her hair against his bare chest, the now familiar scent of her. Lemons. For some reason she smelled like lemons. He couldn't quite stop his lips from twitching as he hoped the lemony fragrance was more de rigueur than her piggy scent of the day they met.

"What's so funny?"

He looked up. Henry was regarding him curiously. He quickly schooled his features back into a scowl. "Do I look as if something is funny?"

"You *did,*" she muttered, turning back to her breakfast.

He watched her eat. She took a bite and then returned her gaze to the window, where the sun was still painting the sky. She sighed again. She obviously loved Stannage Park very much, he reflected. More than he'd ever seen one person love a piece of land.

That was it! He couldn't believe what a fool he'd been not to have realized it before. Of course she wanted to get rid of him. She'd been running Stannage Park for six years. She'd poured her entire adult life and a good portion of her childhood into this estate. She couldn't possibly welcome interference from a total stranger. Hell, he could probably boot her off the premises if he wanted. She was no relation to him.

He'd have to obtain a copy of Carlyle's will to see the exact terms as pertained to Miss Henrietta Barrett, if there were any. The solicitor who'd come by to tell him about his inheritance . . . what was his name . . . ? Leverett . . . yes, Leverett had said he'd forward a copy of the will, but it hadn't reached him by the time he left for Cornwall.

The poor girl was probably terrified. And furious. He glanced up at her impossibly cheerful facade. He'd wager she was more furious than terrified. "You like it here a great deal, don't you?" he asked abruptly.

Startled by his sudden willingness to actually converse with her, Henry coughed a bit before finally answering, "Yes. Yes, of course. Why do you ask?"

"No reason. Just wondering. One can see it in your face, you know."

"See what?" she asked hesitantly.

"Your love for Stannage Park. I was watching you while you were watching the sunrise."

"Y-you were?"

"Mmm-hmm." And that, apparently, was all he was going to say on the matter. He turned back to his breakfast and ignored her completely.

Henry worriedly chewed on her lower lip. This was a bad sign. Why would he care about how she felt unless he were somehow planning to use it against her? If he wanted revenge, nothing could be so excruciatingly painful as being banished from her beloved home.

But then again, why would he want revenge against her? He might not like her, he might even find her rather annoying, but she'd given him no reason to hate her, had she? Of course not. She was letting her imagination get the better of her.

Dunford watched her surreptitiously over his eggs. She was worried. Good. She deserved it after hauling him out of bed this morning at a most uncivilized hour. Not to mention her clever little scheme to starve him out of Cornwall. And the bathing situation—he'd have admired her for her ingenuity if her manipulations had been directed at anyone but himself.

If she thought she could push him around and eventually off of his own property, she was mad.

He smiled. Cornwall was going to be good fun indeed.

He continued to eat his breakfast with slow, deliberate bites, fully enjoying her distress. Three times she started to say something then thought the better of it. Twice she nibbled on her lower lip. And once he even heard her mutter something to herself. He thought it sounded rather like "damned fool," but he couldn't be certain.

Finally, after deciding he'd made her wait long enough, he set his napkin down and stood up. "Shall we?"

"By all means, my lord." She wasn't able to keep a trace of sarcasm out of her voice. She'd been finished with her meal for over ten minutes.

Dunford wasn't above feeling some perverse satisfaction at her irritation. "Tell me, Henry. What is first on our agenda?"

"Don't you remember? We're constructing a new pigpen."

A singularly unpleasant feeling rolled around in his stomach. "I suppose that is what you were doing when I arrived." He didn't have to add, "When you smelled so atrociously bad."

She smiled knowingly at him over her shoulder and preceded him out the door.

Dunford wasn't sure whether he was furious or amused. She was planning to lead him on a merry chase, he was sure of it. Either that or work him to the bone. Still, he figured he could outsmart her. After all, he knew what she was up to, and she didn't know he had figured it out.

Or did she?

And if she did, did that mean she now had the edge?

It being barely seven in the morning, his brain refused to compute the ramifications of this.

He followed Henry out past the stables to a structure he guessed was a barn. His experience with country life had been limited to the aristocracy's ancestral seats, most of which were quite removed from anything resembling a working farm. Farming was left to tenants, and the *ton* usually didn't want to see their tenants unless rents were due. Hence his confusion.

"This is a barn?" he queried.

She looked stunned that he would even ask. "Of course. What did you think it was?"

"A barn," he snapped.

"Then why ask?"

"I was merely wondering why your dear friend Porkus was being kept in the stables rather than here."

"Too crowded here," she replied. "Just look inside. We have lots of cows."

Dunford decided to take her word for it.

"There is plenty of room in the stables," she continued. "We don't have very many horses. Good mounts are very expensive, you know." She smiled innocently at him, hoping he'd had his heart set on inheriting a stable full of Arabians.

He shot her an irritated look. "I know how much horses cost."

"Of course. The team on your carriage was beautiful. They are yours, aren't they?"

He ignored her and walked ahead until his foot connected with soft mushy ground. "Shit," he muttered.

"Exactly."

He glared at her, thinking himself a saint for not going for her throat.

She bit back a smile and looked away. "This is where the pigpen will be."

"So I gathered."

"Mmm, yes." She glanced down at his now not-so-elegantly clad foot and smiled. "That is probably cow."

"Thank you so much for informing me. I'm sure the distinction will prove most edifying."

"Hazards of life on a farm," she said breezily. "I'm actually surprised it wasn't cleaned up. We do try to keep clean around here."

He wanted desperately to remind her of her appearance and smell two days earlier, but even in his supreme irritation he was too much of a gentleman to do so. He contented himself to saying doubtfully, "In a pigpen?"

"Pigs are actually not as slovenly as most people think. Oh, they like mud and all that, but not . . ." She looked down at his foot. ". . . you know."

He smiled tightly. "All too well."

She put her hands on her hips and looked around. They had started the stone wall that would enclose the pigs, but it was not high enough yet. It was taking a long time because she had insisted the foundation be particularly strong. A weak foundation was the reason the earlier pen had crumbled. "I wonder where everyone is," she muttered.

"Sleeping, if they have any idea what's good for them," Dunford replied acerbically.

"I suppose we could get started on our own," she said doubtfully.

For the first time all morning he smiled broadly and meant it. "I know less than nothing about stonemasonry, so I vote we wait." He sat down on a half-finished wall, looking quite satisfied.

Henry, refusing to let him think she thought he might be right about anything, stomped across the construction area to a pile of stones. She leaned down and picked one up.

Dunford raised his brows, well aware that he ought to help her but completely unwilling to do so. She was quite strong, surprisingly so.

He rolled his eyes. Why was he surprised about anything having to do with her? Of course she'd be able to lift a large stone. She was Henry. She could probably lift *him.*

He watched her as she carried the stone over to one of the walls and set it down. She exhaled and wiped her brow. Then she glared at him.

He smiled—one of his best, he thought. "You ought to bend your legs when you lift the stones," he called out. "It's better for your back."

"It's better for your back," she mimicked under her breath. "Lazy, good-for-nothing, stupid little—"

"Excuse me?"

"Thank you for your advice." Her voice was sweetness personified.

He smiled again, this time to himself. He was getting to her.

She must have repeated this task twenty times before her workers finally arrived. "Where have you been?" she snapped. "We've been here ten minutes already."

One of the men blinked. "But we're early, Miss Henry."

The skin around her mouth tightened. "We start at six forty-five."

"We didn't get here until seven," Dunford called out helpfully.

She turned around and leveled a deadly stare in his direction. He smiled and shrugged his shoulders.

"We didn't start until half past seven on Saturday," one of the workers said.

"I'm sure you're mistaken," Henry lied. "We started much earlier than that."

Another builder scratched his head. "I don't think so, Miss Henry. I think we started at half past seven."

Dunford smirked. "I guess country life doesn't begin

that early after all." He neglected to mention that he tried to avoid getting up much before noon when in London.

She glared at him again.

"Why so testy?" he asked, schooling his features into a mask of boyish innocence. "I thought you liked me."

"I *did,*" she ground out.

"And now? I'm crushed."

"Next time you might think about helping instead of watching me lug stones across a pigpen."

He shrugged. "I told you I have no experience in stonemasonry. I wouldn't want to ruin the entire project."

"I suppose you're right," Henry said.

Her voice came out a little too smoothly. Dunford grew worried. He raised his brows in question.

"After all," she continued, "if the previous pigpen had been constructed properly, we wouldn't have to be building a new one today."

Dunford suddenly felt a little queasy. She looked altogether too pleased with herself.

"Therefore, it would probably be wise not to let one as inexperienced as yourself near the structural aspects of the pen."

"As opposed to the un-structural aspects?" he asked dryly.

She beamed. "Exactly!"

"Meaning?"

"Meaning . . ." She walked across the pen and picked up a shovel. "Congratulations, Lord Stannage, you are now commander of the shovel, lord of the slop."

He didn't think her smile could grow any wider, but it did. And she wasn't faking the expression one bit. She jerked her head toward a foul-smelling pile of something Dunford had never seen before and then walked back over to the other workers.

It took all of his restraint not to run after her and slap the shovel against her backside.

Chapter 5

Two hours later he was ready to kill her.

Even his outraged mind, however, recognized that murder was not a viable option, and so he contented himself with devising various plans to make her suffer.

Torture was probably too trite, he decided, and he didn't have the stomach to use it on a female. Although . . . He looked over at the person in the baggy breeches. She appeared to be smiling as she lugged the stones. She was no ordinary female.

He shook his head. There were other ways to make her miserable. A snake in her bed perhaps? No, the blasted woman probably liked snakes. A spider? Didn't everyone hate spiders?

He leaned on his shovel, well aware he was acting childishly and not caring in the least.

He had tried everything to get out of this disgusting job, and not just because the work was difficult and the smell was . . . well, the smell was revolting, there was no way around that. Mostly he just didn't want her to feel she had bested him.

And she *had* bested him, the hellish little chit. She had him, a lord of the realm (albeit a rather new one), shoveling slop and manure and God himself probably didn't want to know what else. And he was neatly cornered, because to get out of it meant to admit he was a sissified London dandy.

He had pointed out that all of the slop would get in her way as she built the wall. She had merely instructed him to put it in the center. "You can smooth it out later," she had said.

"But some might get on your shoes."

She had laughed. "Oh, I'm used to that." Her tone had implied she was far tougher than he.

He ground his teeth and slapped some slop down into a pile. The stench was beyond overwhelming. "I thought you said pigs are clean."

"Cleaner than people usually think, but not as clean as you and I." She looked at his messy boots, amusement dancing in her gray eyes. "Well, usually."

He muttered something rather unsavory before shooting back, "I thought they didn't like . . . you know."

"They don't."

"Well?" he demanded, planting his shovel into the ground and putting his other hand on his hip.

Henry walked over and sniffed the air above the pile he was making. "Oh, dear. Well, I guess some got mixed in by accident. Happens often, actually. So sorry." She smiled at him and went back to work.

He let out a discreet growl, mostly just to make himself feel better, and marched over to the slop pile. He thought he could control his temper. He usually thought of himself as an easygoing man. But when he heard one of the men say, "Work's going so much faster now that *you're* helping, Henry," it was all he could do not to strangle her. He didn't know why she had been so smelly the day he arrived, but it was now apparent it wasn't because she'd been knee-deep in muck, helping to build the pigpen. A red haze of fury blinded him as he wondered what other disgusting tasks she was planning to take on just to convince him they were daily chores for the lord of the manor.

His teeth clenched together as he stuck his shovel into the smelly mush, scooped some up, and made to carry it to the center of the pigpen. On the way over, however, it slid off the shovel and onto Henry's shoes.

Pity, that.

She whirled around. He waited for her to burst out with, "You did that on purpose!" but she kept silent, motionless except for a slight narrowing of her eyes. Then, with a flick of her ankle, the slop spattered onto his trousers.

She smirked, waiting for *him* to say, "You did that on purpose!" but he also remained silent. Then he smiled at her, and she knew she was in trouble. Before she had time to react, he'd lifted his leg and planted the sole of his boot against her breeches, leaving a muddy footprint on the front of her thigh.

He cocked his head, waiting for her to retaliate.

She briefly considered picking up some of the slop and smearing it on his face but decided he'd have too much time to react; besides, she wasn't wearing gloves. She glanced quickly to the left to confuse him, then slammed her foot down on his.

Dunford let out a howl of pain. "That is *enough!*"

"You started it!"

"You started it before I even arrived, you conniving, unruly . . ."

She waited for him to call her a bitch, but he couldn't do it. Instead, he grabbed her around the middle, heaved her over his shoulder, and stalked off with her.

"You can't do this!" she shrieked, pounding his back with surprisingly effective fists. "Tommy! Harry! Someone! Don't let him do this!"

But the men who had been working on the wall didn't move. Openmouthed, they stared at the unbelievable sight of Miss Henrietta Barrett, who hadn't let anyone get the better of her in years, being forcibly removed from the pigpen.

"Maybe we shoulda helped her," Harry said.

Tommy shook his head, watching her writhing form disappear over the hillside. "I don't know. He is the new baron, you know. If he wants to carry Henry off, he's got a right to do it, I guess."

Henry obviously didn't agree because she was still screaming, "You have no right to do this!" Dunford finally dumped her down next to a small shed where they kept farming tools. Luckily no one was in sight.

"Oh?" His tone was utterly imperious.

"Do you know how long it has taken to win the respect of the people here? Do you? A long time, I'll tell you. A bloody long time. And you ruined it. Ruined it!"

"I doubt the collective population of Stannage Park is going to decide you are unworthy of respect because of my actions," he spit out, "although your *own* may cause you trouble."

"What do you mean by my 'own'? You're the one who dumped the slop on my feet, in case you don't recall."

"And you're the one who had me shoveling that shit in the first place!" It occurred to Dunford that that was the first time he'd ever spoken quite so crudely to a female. It was amazing how furious she could make him.

"If you're not up to the task of running a farm, you can go right on home to London. We will survive just fine without you."

"That's what this is about, isn't it? Little Henry is terrified I'm going to take her toy away from her and is trying to get rid of me. Well, let me tell you something, it'll take a lot more than a twenty-year-old girl to scare me off."

"Don't patronize me," she warned.

"Or what? What will you do to me? What could you possibly do to me that will cause me any harm?"

To Henry's utter horror, her lower lip began to quiver. "I could . . . I could . . ." She had to think of something; she had to. She couldn't let him win. He'd boot her off the estate, and the only thing worse than having no place to go was never seeing Stannage Park again. Finally, out of desperation, she blurted out, "I could do anything! I know this place better than you! Better than anyone! You wouldn't even—"

Quick as lightning, he had her pinned up against the shed and was jabbing his index finger into her shoulder. Henry couldn't breathe—she'd entirely forgotten how, and the murderous look in his eyes made her legs turn to jelly.

"Don't," he spat out, "make the mistake of getting me angry."

"You're not angry now?" she croaked in disbelief.

He let her go abruptly and smiled, cocking a brow as she slid down into a crouch. "Not at all," he said smoothly. "I merely wanted to set some ground rules."

Henry's mouth fell open. The man was *insane*.

"First of all, no more devious little plots to try to get rid of me."

Her throat worked convulsively.

"And no lies!"

She gasped for breath.

"And—" He paused to look down at her. "Oh, Christ. Don't cry."

She bawled.

"No, please, don't cry." He reached for his handkerchief, realized it was stained with slop, then shoved it back in his pocket. "Don't cry, Henry."

"I never cry," she gasped, barely able to get the words out between sobs.

"I know," he said soothingly, crouching down to her level. "I know."

"I haven't cried in years."

He believed her. It was impossible to imagine her crying—it was impossible to believe it even though she was doing so right in front of him. She was so capable, so self-possessed, not at all the sort to give way to tears. And the fact that he had been the one to drive her to this—it wrenched his heart. "There you go," he murmured, awkwardly patting her shoulder. "Now, now. It's all right."

She took great gulps of air, trying to still her sobs, but they had no effect.

Dunford looked around frantically, as if the green hills would somehow tell him how to get her to stop crying. "Don't do that." This was awful.

"I have no place to go," she wailed. "No place. And no one. I have no family."

"Shhh. It's all right."

"I just wanted to stay." She gasped and sniffled. "I just wanted to stay. Is that so bad?"

"Of course not, dear."

"It's just that this is my home." She looked up at him, her gray eyes made silver by her watery tears. "Or it was, at least. And now it's yours, and you can do whatever you want with it. And with me. And— Oh, God, I'm such a fool. You must hate me."

"I don't hate you," he replied automatically. It was the truth, of course. She'd irritated and annoyed the hell out of him, but he didn't hate her. In fact, she'd somehow managed to earn his respect, something he never gave unless deserved. Her methods may have been skewed, but she had been fighting for the one thing in the world she truly loved. Few men could claim such purity of purpose.

He patted her hand again, trying to calm her down. What had she said about his being able to do whatever he wanted with her? That certainly made no sense. He supposed he could force her to leave Stannage Park if he so desired, but that didn't quite constitute *anything*. Although he supposed that was the worst fate Henry could imagine; it was understandable she'd be a bit melodramatic about it. Still, something struck him as odd. He made a mental note to discuss it with her later, when she wasn't so distraught.

"Now, Henry," he said, thinking that the time had come to lay her fears to rest. "I'm not going to send you away. Why on earth would I do that? And furthermore, have I given you any indication that was my intention?"

She gulped. She had just assumed she would have to take the offensive in this battle of wills. She glanced up at him. His brown eyes looked very concerned. Perhaps there had never been need for a battle. Maybe she should have waited to assess the new Lord Stannage before deciding she had to send him back to London.

"Have I?" he asked softly.

She shook her head.

"Think about it, Henry. I'd be a fool to send you

away. I'm the first to admit I don't know a thing about farming. Either I run the estate into the ground or I hire someone to oversee it. And why should I bring in a stranger when I've someone who already knows everything there is to know?"

Henry looked down, unable to face him. Why did he have to be so reasonable and so just plain nice? She felt wretchedly guilty about all her schemes to oust him from the district, including those she hadn't yet carried out. "I'm sorry, Dunford. I'm really sorry."

He brushed aside her apology, not wanting her to feel any worse than she already did. "No harm done." He looked down at himself wryly. "Well, except to my clothing perhaps."

"Oh! I'm so sorry!" She burst into tears again, this time horrified. His clothing must have been terribly expensive. She'd never seen anything so fine in her life. She didn't think they made garments like his in Cornwall.

"*Please* don't trouble yourself over it, Henry," he said, surprised to hear he sounded almost as if he were begging her not to feel badly. When had her feelings grown quite so important to him? "If this morning wasn't enjoyable, at least it was . . . shall we say . . . interesting, and my clothing was worth the sacrifice if it means we've reached a truce of sorts. I have no wish to be awakened before dawn next week only to be informed I have to single-handedly slaughter a cow."

Her eyes widened. How did he *know?*

Dunford caught the change in her expression, interpreted it correctly, and winced. "You, dear girl, could probably teach Napoleon a thing or two."

Henry's lips twitched. It was watery, but it was definitely a smile.

"Now," he continued, standing up. "Shall we head back to the house? I'm starving."

"Oh!" she said, swallowing uncomfortably. "I'm sorry."

He rolled his eyes. "Now what are you sorry for?"

"For making you eat that awful mutton. And the porridge. I hate porridge."

He smiled gently. "It is a testament to your love of Stannage Park that you were able to eat an entire bowl of that slop yesterday."

"I didn't," she admitted. "I ate only a few spoonfuls. I dumped the rest of it into an urn when you weren't looking. I had to go back and clean it out later."

He chuckled, unable to help himself. "Henry, you are like no one I have ever met."

"I'm not certain that's such a good thing."

"Nonsense. Of course it is. Now, then, shall we be off?"

She reached out and grabbed the hand he was holding out to her. Slowly she rose to her feet. "Simpy makes very good biscuits," she said softly, the very tone of her voice implying a peace offering. "With butter and ginger and sugar. They're delicious."

"Splendid. If she doesn't have some on hand, we shall have to coerce her into making a batch. I say, we don't have to finish the pigpen, do we?"

She shook her head. "I *was* working on it Saturday, but mostly just supervising. I think the men were a bit surprised by my help this morning."

"I know they were surprised. Tommy's jaw dropped halfway to his knees. And please tell me you don't usually get up this early."

"No. I'm dreadful in the morning. I can't get anything done before nine o'clock unless I absolutely have to."

Dunford smiled wryly as he realized the extent of her previous determination to be rid of him. She really must have wanted him gone to get up at half past five in the morning. "If you detest morning people as much as I do, then I think we shall get on famously."

"I expect so." She smiled tremulously as they walked to the house. A friend. That was what he was going to be to her. It was a thrilling thought. She really hadn't had any friends since she'd reached adulthood. Oh, she got on very well with all the servants, but there was always that air of employer and employee that kept them from getting too close. With Dunford, however, she had found friendship, even if they had gotten off to a rocky start. Still, there was one thing she wanted to know. Softly she said his name.

"Yes?"

"When you said you weren't angry . . ."

"Yes?"

"Were you?"

"I was rather annoyed," he admitted.

"But not angry?" She sounded as if she didn't believe him.

"Believe me, Henry, when I get angry, you'll know."

"What happens?"

His eyes clouded over slightly before he answered. "You don't want to know."

She believed him.

An hour or so later, after they had both bathed, Henry and Dunford met in the kitchen over a plate of Mrs. Simpson's ginger biscuits. While they were busy fighting over the last one, Yates arrived.

"A letter arrived for you earlier this morning, my lord," he intoned. "From your solicitor. I left it in the study."

"Excellent," Dunford replied, pushing out his chair and rising to his feet. "That must be the rest of the papers concerning Stannage Park. A copy of Carlyle's will, I think. Would you care to read it, Henry?" He didn't know if she felt slighted by the fact that the property had gone to him. It was entailed, that was true, and Henry couldn't have inherited in any case, but that did not mean she wasn't hurt by it. By asking her if she wanted to read Carlyle's will, he was trying to assure her that she was still an important figure at Stannage Park.

Henry shrugged as she followed him into the hall. "If you wish. It is rather straightforward, I think. Everything to you."

"Carlyle didn't leave you anything?" Dunford raised his brows in shock. It was unconscionable to leave a young woman penniless and adrift.

"I suppose he thought you would take care of me."

"I will certainly make sure you are comfortably situated, and you will always have a home here, but Carlyle should have provided for you. I never even met the man. He couldn't have had any idea if I had any sort of principles whatsoever."

"I imagine he thought you couldn't be *that* bad if you were related to him," she teased.

"Still . . ." Dunford opened the door to the study and walked in. But when he reached the desk there was no letter waiting for him, just a pile of shredded paper. "What on earth?"

The blood drained from Henry's face. "Oh, no."

"Who would do such a thing?" He planted his hands on his hips and turned to face her. "Henry, do you know all the servants personally? Who do you think—"

"It's not the servants." She sighed. "Rufus? Rufus?"

"Who the hell is Rufus?"

"My rmbblet," she mumbled, getting down on her hands and knees.

"Your *what?*"

"My rabbit. Rufus? Rufus? Where are you?"

"Do you mean to tell me you have a pet rabbit?" Dear God, did this woman do anything normal?

"He's usually very sweet," she said weakly. "Rufus!"

A small bundle of black-and-white fur darted across the room.

"Rufus! Come back here! Bad bunny! Bad bunny!"

Dunford started to shake with mirth. Henry was chasing the rabbit around the room, stooped down with her arms outstretched. Every time she tried to grab it, however, it wriggled out of her grasp.

"Rufus!" she said warningly.

"I don't suppose you could have acted like the rest of humanity and gotten a cat or dog."

Henry, recognizing a reply wasn't necessary, didn't say anything. She stood straight, planted her hands on her hips, and sighed. Where had he gone off to?

"I think he darted behind the bookcase," Dunford said helpfully.

Henry tiptoed over and peered behind the large wooden piece. "Shhh. Go stand on the other side."

He followed her orders.

"Do something to scare him."

He looked over at her with a doubtful expression. Finally he got down on his hands and knees and said in a gruesome voice, "Hello, little bunny. Rabbit stew for supper tonight."

Rufus scrambled to his feet and ran straight into Henry's waiting arms. Realizing he had been trapped, he started to squirm, but Henry kept a firm hand on him, calming him down by saying, "Shhhh."

"What are you going to do with him?"

"Put him back in the kitchen where he belongs."

"I should think he belongs outside. Or in the stew pot."

"Dunford, he's my pet!" She looked stricken.

"Loves pigs and rabbits," he muttered. "A kind-hearted lass."

They marched back to the kitchen in silence, the only sound being Rufus's growl when Dunford tried to pet him.

"Can a rabbit growl?" he asked, unable to believe his ears.

"Obviously he can."

When they reached the kitchen, Henry deposited her furry bundle on the floor. "Simpy, would you give me a carrot for Rufus?"

"Did that little imp escape again? He must have slipped out when the door was open." The housekeeper picked up a carrot from a pile of root vegetables and dangled it in front of the rabbit. He sank his teeth into it and pulled it out of her hand. Dunford watched with interest as Rufus gnawed the carrot into nothingness.

"I'm really very sorry about your papers," Henry said, aware she had apologized more that day than she had in the past year.

"So am I," he said absentmindedly, "but I can always write a note to Leverett and have him send out another copy. Another week or so won't hurt."

"Are you certain? I shouldn't want to ruin any of your plans."

He sighed, wondering how his life had been turned upside down by this woman in less than forty-eight hours. Correction: by this woman, a pig, and a rabbit.

He assured Henry that the destroyed papers were not a permanent setback and then took his leave of her, returning to his rooms to read over some documents he'd brought with him and to sneak some much needed rest. Even though he and Henry had reached a truce, he was still somehow loath to admit to her that she had exhausted him. It somehow made him feel like less of a man.

He would have felt much better had he known that Henry had retired to her room for the exact same reason.

Later that night Dunford was reading in bed when it suddenly occurred to him that it was going to be another week before he found out exactly how Carlyle had provided for Henry in his will. That was really the only reason he'd been eager to read the document. Although Henry had insisted that Carlyle had not bothered with her, Dunford found that hard to believe. At the very least Carlyle would have had to appoint a guardian for her, wouldn't he? After all, Henry was only twenty.

She was an amazing woman, his Henry. One had to admire her single-minded determination. Yet for all her capability, he still felt an odd sort of responsibility for her. Perhaps it had been the wobble in her voice when she had apologized for her schemes to oust him from Stannage Park. Or the sheer agony in her eyes when she had admitted she had no place else to go.

Whatever the case, he wanted to make certain she had a secure place in the world.

But before he could do that, he had to see how Carlyle had provided for her in his will, if at all. Another week wouldn't make much of a difference, would it? He shrugged and turned his attention back to his book. He read for several minutes until his concentration was interrupted by a noise on the carpet.

He looked up but saw nothing. Dismissing it as the creaking of an old house, he started reading again.

Patter, patter, patter. There it was again.

This time when Dunford looked up, he saw a pair of long, black ears poke up over the edge of the bed. "Oh, for God's sake," he groaned. "Rufus."

As if on cue, the rabbit vaulted up onto the bed, landing squarely on top of the book. He looked up at Dunford, his little pink nose twitching up and down.

"What do you want, bunny?"

Rufus quirked an ear and leaned forward as if to say, "Pet me."

Dunford placed his hand between the rabbit's ears and began to scratch. With a sigh, he said, "This certainly isn't London."

Then, as the rabbit rested its head against his chest, he realized with surprise that he didn't want to be in London.

In fact, he didn't want to be anywhere but here.

Chapter 6

Henry spent the next few days introducing Dunford to Stannage Park. He wanted to learn every last detail about his new property, and she liked nothing better than to expound upon the many excellent qualities of the estate. While they toured the house and surrounding lands, they chatted about this and that, sometimes about nothing in particular, sometimes about the great mysteries of life. For Henry, Dunford was the first person who ever had wanted to spend this kind of time with her. He was interested in what she had to say, not only about estate matters, but also about philosophy, religion, and just plain life in general. Even more flattering was the fact that he seemed to care about her opinion of him. He tried to look offended when she didn't laugh at his jokes, rolled his eyes when he didn't laugh at hers, and elbowed her in the ribs when neither of them could summon up the mirth to laugh at someone else's.

In short, he became her friend. And if her stomach

did strange things every time he smiled . . . Well, she could learn to live with that. She supposed he had that effect on all women.

It didn't occur to Henry that these were the happiest few days of her life, although if she had taken the time to think about it, she would have realized that was exactly what they were.

Dunford was equally taken with his companion. Henry's love for Stannage Park was infectious, and he found himself not just interested in but actually caring about the details of the estate and its people. When one of the tenants safely gave birth to her first child, it had been his idea to bring by a basket of food so she wouldn't have to tax herself with cooking for the next week. And he surprised even himself when he stopped by the newly constructed pigpen to slip a raspberry tart to Porkus. The pig did seem to have a sweet tooth, he rationalized, and for all his size he was actually kind of cute.

But he would have enjoyed himself even if Stannage Park hadn't been his. Henry was delightful company. She possessed a freshness and an honesty he hadn't seen in years. Dunford had been blessed with wonderful friends, but after so long in London, he had begun to think that no one's soul was free of at least a little cynicism. Henry, on the other hand, was marvelously open and direct. Not once had he seen the familiar mask of world-weary boredom cloud her features. Henry seemed to care too much about everything and everyone to allow herself to be bored.

This was not to say she was a wide-eyed innocent willing to believe the best of everyone. She had a wicked wit and was not above employing it from time to time when pointing out a villager she found exceedingly foolish. Dunford was inclined to forgive her this weakness; he usually agreed with her assessment of foolish people.

And if every now and then he found himself looking at her oddly, wondering how her brown hair turned gold in the sun or why she always smelled vaguely of lemons . . . Well, that was only to be expected. It had been a long time since he'd been with a woman. His mistress had been in Birmingham for a fortnight, visiting her mother, when he left. And Henry could be rather fetching in her own unconventional way.

Not that what he felt for her was anything remotely resembling desire. But she was a woman, and he was a man, and so naturally he'd be aware of her. And of course he had kissed her once, even if that had been an accident. It was to be expected that he'd remember that kiss every now and then when she was near.

Such thoughts, however, were far from his mind as he poured himself a drink in the drawing room one evening a week after his arrival. It was nearly time for them to partake of the evening meal, and Henry would arrive any minute now.

He winced. It would be a ghastly sight. As unconventional as Henry was, she still dressed for dinner, and that meant putting on one of those hideous garments—he shuddered to call them gowns. To give her credit, she seemed to be aware they were awful. To give her even greater credit, however, she managed to act as if it didn't matter. If he hadn't grown to know her so well during the past few days, he never would have dreamed she didn't think her clothing was, if not the height of fashion, at least passably attractive.

But he had noticed how carefully she avoided looking in the mirrors that adorned the walls of the drawing room where they met before dinner. And when she found herself trapped by her reflection, she couldn't hide the pained grimace that flickered across her features.

He wanted to help her, he realized. He wanted to buy her gowns and teach her to dance and— It was stunning, this. How much he wanted to help her.

"Stealing the liquor again?" Her teasing voice brought him out of his reverie.

"It's my liquor if you recall, minx." He turned his head to look at her. She was wearing that abominable lavender creation again. He couldn't decide if it was the worst or best of the lot.

"So it is." She shrugged. "Might I have a little then?"

Wordlessly, he poured her a glass of sherry.

Henry sipped at it thoughtfully. It had become her habit to have a glass of wine with him before dinner, but no more than that. She had discovered what a lightweight she was the night he arrived. She had a sinking suspicion she would end up making calf eyes at him all through dinner if she allowed herself more than this one small sherry.

"Was your afternoon pleasant?" Dunford asked suddenly. He had spent the previous few hours by himself, poring over estate documents. Henry had gladly left him alone with the musty papers; she'd already examined them, and he certainly didn't need her to help him read.

"Yes, it was quite. I checked in on some of the tenants. Mrs. Dalrymple asked me to thank you for the food."

"I'm glad she enjoyed it."

"Oh, yes. I cannot think why we have not thought to do it before. Of course, we always send a congratulatory gift, but food for a week is much better, I think."

They sounded like an old married couple, Dunford thought with surprise. How odd.

Henry sat down on an elegant but faded sofa, tugging awkwardly at her dress as she did so. "Did you finish with those papers?"

"Almost," he said distractedly. "You know, Henry, I've been thinking."

"Have you?" She smiled impishly. "How very taxing."

"Minx. Be quiet and listen to what I have to say."

She tilted her head in a movement that seemed to say, "Well?"

"Why don't the two of us make a sojourn into town?"

She answered him with a puzzled expression. "We went to the village two days ago. Don't you recall? You wanted to meet the local merchants."

"Of course I recall. My mind is not given to forgetfulness, Henry. I'm not that old."

"Oh, I don't know," she said, her face a perfect deadpan. "You must be at least thirty."

"Nine-and-twenty," he bit out before he realized she was teasing.

She smiled. "Sometimes you're such an easy mark."

"My gullibility aside, Henry, I'd like to take a trip into town. And I don't mean the village. I think we should take ourselves to Truro."

"Truro?" It was one of Cornwall's larger towns, and Henry avoided it like the plague.

"You sound less than enthusiastic."

"I, um, I just . . . Well, to be frank, I just went." That wasn't entirely a lie. She'd gone two months ago, but it felt like yesterday. She always felt so awkward among strangers. At least the local people had gotten used to her eccentricities and accepted them. Most even held her in some measure of respect. But strangers were another thing altogether. And Truro was the worst. Although it was not as popular as it had been during the previous century, members of the *ton* still vacationed there. She could just hear them whispering unkind things about her. Fashionable ladies would laugh at her dress. Men would snicker at her lack of ladylike manners. And then, inevitably, a local would discreetly inform them that she was Miss Henrietta Barrett, but she went by the boy's name Henry, and don't you know but she parades around in breeches all the time.

No, she definitely didn't want to go to Truro.

Dunford, unaware of her distress, said, "But I've never been. Be a good sport and show me 'round."

"I-I'd really rather not, Dunford."

His eyes narrowed as he finally noticed she looked uncomfortable. To be honest, she always looked uncomfortable in those ridiculous dresses, but she looked particularly so just now. "Really, Henry, it won't be so bad as that. Will you come along as a favor for me?" He smiled at her.

She was lost. "All right."

"Tomorrow, then?"

"Whatever you wish."

Henry felt her stomach roil as their coach neared Truro the next day. Good God, this was going to be awful. She always hated it when she had to go to town, but this was the first time it actually had made her feel physically ill.

She didn't even try to delude herself that her dread had nothing to do with the man sitting cheerfully next to her. Dunford had become her friend, damn it, and she didn't want to lose him. What would he think when he heard people whispering about her? When a lady made a sotto voce comment about her dress that she knew she was intended to hear? Would he be ashamed of her? Would he be humiliated to be with her? Henry didn't particularly want to find out.

Dunford was aware of Henry's nervous fidgeting but pretended not to notice. She would be embarrassed if he commented on it, and he had no wish to hurt her. Instead, he kept up a cheerful facade, commenting on the scenery as it rolled by their window and making idle comments about the affairs of Stannage Park.

Finally they arrived in Truro. Henry thought she could not feel any sicker than she did, but she soon found she was wrong.

"Come along, Henry," Dunford said briskly. "It isn't like you to dally."

She caught her lower lip between her teeth as she allowed him to help her down. There was a chance, she supposed, he wouldn't realize what other people thought of her. Perhaps all the ladies would have sheathed their claws for the day, and he wouldn't hear any vicious whispers. Henry lifted her chin a notch. On the off chance that none of her nightmares came true, she might as well act as if she hadn't a worry in the world.

"I'm sorry, Dunford." She shot him a cheeky grin. *Her* cheeky grin. He had often commented he'd never seen another like it. She hoped it would assure him she was no longer distraught. "My mind has been wandering, I'm afraid."

"And where has it up and wandered to?" His eyes flashed devilishly.

Dear God, why was he always so nice? It would make it that much more painful when he dropped her. *Don't think about that,* she yelled at herself. *It might not happen.* She willed the pain out of her eyes and shrugged carelessly. "Stannage Park, where else?"

"And what has you so worried, minx? Afraid Porkus isn't going to deliver her piglets safely?"

"Porkus is a *male,* silly."

He clutched his heart in mock terror. "Then there is all the more reason to worry. This could be a most difficult birth."

Despite herself, Henry smiled. "You are incorrigible."

"Being incorrigible yourself, you must have intended that as a compliment."

"I suspect you will take it as a compliment no matter what I say." She tried to make her tone a grumble, but her lips twitched.

He took her arm and began to walk. "You do know how to slay a man, Henry."

She looked over at him dubiously. Never had she counted among her achievements the ability to skillfully manipulate the opposite sex. Until Dunford, she had never been able to get one of them to think of her as a normal woman.

If he noticed her expression, he did not comment on it. They walked on, Dunford asking questions about every storefront they passed. He paused in front of a small eatery. "Are you hungry, Henry? Is this a good tea shop?"

"I've never been."

"No?" He looked surprised. In the twelve years she'd lived in Cornwall, she'd never stopped for tea and cakes? "What about when Viola was alive?"

"Viola didn't like Truro. She always said there was too much of the *ton* here."

"There is some truth in that," he agreed, suddenly turning to face a shop window to avoid being recognized by an acquaintance across the street. Nothing was less appealing at the moment than having to make polite conversation. He had no wish to get sidetracked from his goal. After all, he had dragged Henry out here for a *reason.*

Henry looked at the window display in surprise. "I had no idea you were interested in lace."

He focused his eyes and realized that he appeared to be avidly examining the wares of a shop that seemed to deal in nothing but lace. "Yes, well, there are a number of things you don't know about me," he murmured, hoping that would be the end of that.

Henry wasn't terribly encouraged by the fact that he was a connoisseur of lace. He probably draped it on all his mistresses. And she had no doubt that he'd had a few. Who was "sweetie," after all? She could understand it, she supposed. The man was twenty-nine years old. One couldn't expect he'd lived the life of a monk. And he was mind-numbingly handsome. He would certainly have had his pick of women.

She sighed dejectedly, suddenly eager to be away from the lace shop.

They passed by a milliner, a bookshop, and a greengrocer, then Dunford suddenly exclaimed, "Ah, look, Henry. A dress shop. Just what I need."

She crinkled her brow in confusion. "I think they make only ladies' clothing here, Dunford."

"Excellent." He yanked on her arm and dragged her to the doorway. "I need to buy a gift for my sister."

"I didn't know you had a sister."

He shrugged. "I believe I said there were a great many things you do not know about me?"

She shot him a waspish look. "I'll wait outside, then. I detest dress shops."

He had no doubt about that. "But I'll need your help, Henry. You're just about her size."

"If I'm not *exactly* her size, nothing will fit properly." She took a step backward.

He took her arm, opened the door, and propelled her through it. "It's a risk I'm willing to take," he said cheerily. "Ah, hello," he said, calling out to the modiste across the room. "We need to buy a dress or two for my sister here." He motioned to Henry.

"But I'm not—"

"Hush, minx. It will be easier all around this way."

Henry had to agree he was probably correct. "Oh, all right," she grumbled. "I suppose this is what one does for a friend."

"Yes," Dunford agreed, looking down at her with an odd expression. "I suppose this is."

The dressmaker, quickly assessing the obvious quality and expert tailoring of Dunford's clothing, hurried to their sides. "How may I help you?" she inquired.

"I would like to purchase a few dresses for my sister."

"Of course." She looked over at Henry, who had never in her life been more ashamed of her appearance. The mauve day dress she was wearing was truly appalling, and she didn't know why she even owned it. Carlyle had picked it up for her, she recalled. She remembered the occasion. He was going to Truro on a bit of business, and Henry, realizing she was outgrowing her clothing, had asked him to purchase a dress for her. Carlyle had probably just grabbed the first thing he saw.

But it looked wretched on her, and from the modiste's expression, Henry could see the woman agreed. She had known the dress wasn't right the minute she'd seen it, but returning it would have necessitated her coming to town. She so hated traveling to Truro—especially for this sort of embarrassing thing—that she had forced herself to believe a dress was a dress and all it really needed to do was cover a body up.

"Why don't you go over there and look at some

bolts of fabric?" Dunford said, giving her arm a little squeeze.

"But—"

"Shush." He could see in her eyes that she'd been about to point out that she didn't know what his sister would like. "Just humor me and take a look."

"As you wish." She ambled over and inspected the silks and muslins. Oh, how soft they were. Hastily she put them down. It was silly to moon over pretty fabrics when all she needed were shirts and breeches.

Dunford watched her lovingly finger the bolts of cloth and knew he had done the right thing. Taking the dressmaker aside, he whispered, "I fear my sister's wardrobe has been sadly neglected. She has been staying with my aunt who, it is apparent, possesses little fashion sense."

The dressmaker nodded.

"Have you anything that is ready to wear today? I'd like nothing better than to be rid of that thing she has on now. You can use her measurements to fashion a few more."

"I have one or two I could quickly alter to her size. In fact there is one right there." She pointed to a pale yellow day dress draped over a dressmaker's model. Dunford was just about to say that it would do when he saw Henry's face.

She was staring at the dress like a starving woman.

"That dress will be perfect," he whispered emphatically. Then, in a louder voice: "Henrietta, my dear, why don't you try on the yellow dress? We'll have Mrs. . . ." He paused, waiting for the dressmaker to fill in the gap.

"Trimble," she supplied.

". . . Mrs. Trimble make the necessary alterations."

"Are you certain?" Henry asked.

"Very."

She needed no further urging. Mrs. Trimble quickly took the dress off the model and motioned for Henry to follow her into a back room. While they were gone, Dunford idly examined the fabrics on display. The pale yellow might look good on Henry, he decided. He picked up a bolt of sapphire-blue lawn. That might be nice, too. He wasn't certain. He'd never done this sort of thing before and had no idea how to go about it. He'd always assumed women somehow *knew* what to wear. Lord knew his good friends Belle and Emma were always perfectly turned out.

But now he realized they always looked so fashionable because they had been taught how by Belle's mother, who had always been the epitome of elegance. Poor Henry had had no one to guide her in such matters. No one to teach her simply how to be a girl. And certainly no one to teach her what to do as a woman.

He sat down as he waited for her to return. It seemed to be taking an interminably long time. Finally, giving in to impatience, he called out, "Henry?"

"Just one moment!" Mrs. Trimble replied. "I just need to take in the waist a bit more. Your sister is very slender."

Dunford shrugged. He wouldn't know. Most of the time she wore baggy men's clothing, and her dresses were so ill-fitting it was hard to tell what was under them. He frowned, vaguely remembering the feel of her that time he'd kissed her. He couldn't remember much—he'd been half asleep at the time—but he did recall she'd seemed quite well-formed, rather fresh and feminine.

Just then Mrs. Trimble stepped back into the room. "Here she is, sir."

"Dunford?" Henry poked her head around the corner.

"Don't be shy, minx."

"Promise not to laugh?"

"Why on earth would I laugh? Now get out here."

Henry stepped forward, her eyes hopeful, fearful, and quizzical, all at the same time.

Dunford caught his breath. She was transformed. The yellow color of the dress suited her perfectly, bringing out the gold highlights in her hair. And the cut of the dress, while certainly not revealing in any way, somehow managed to hint at the promise of innocent womanhood. Mrs. Trimble had even changed her hairstyle, taking it out of its braid and pinning some locks atop her head. Henry was nibbling nervously on her lower lip as he examined her, and she exuded a shy loveliness that was as enticing as it was puzzling, considering he'd never dreamed she had a shy bone in her body.

"Henry," he said softly, "you look . . . you look . . ." He searched for the right word but couldn't find it. Finally he burst out with, "You look so *nice!*"

It was the most perfect thing anyone had ever said to her.

"Do you think so?" she breathed, reverently touching the dress. "Do you really think so?"

"I know so," he said firmly. He looked up at Mrs. Trimble. "We'll take it."

"Excellent. I can bring you some fashion plates to look at, if you'd like."

"Please."

"But Dunford," Henry whispered urgently, "this is for your sister."

"How could I give that dress to my sister when it looks so utterly charming on you?" he asked in what he hoped was a practical tone. "Besides, now that I think of it, you probably could use a new dress or two."

"I *have* outgrown the ones I have," she said, sounding a bit wistful.

"Then you shall have it."

"But I haven't any money."

"It's my present."

"Oh, but I couldn't let you do that," she said quickly.

"Why ever not? It's my money."

She looked torn. "I don't think it's proper."

He *knew* it wasn't proper but wasn't about to tell her so. "Look at it this way, Henry. If I didn't have you, I'd have to hire someone to manage Stannage Park."

"You could probably do it on your own now," she said brightly, giving him a reassuring pat on the arm.

He almost groaned. Trust Henry to disarm him with kindness. "I probably wouldn't have the time to do it. I have obligations in London, you know. So the way I see it, you save me a man's wages. Probably three men's wages. A dress or two is the least I can do, considering."

Put that way, it didn't sound quite so improper, Henry decided. And she did love the dress. She'd never felt so womanly before. In this dress she might even learn to glide when she walked, like those fashionable women-on-rollers she had always envied. "All right," she said slowly. "If you think it's the right thing."

"I know it's the right thing. Oh, and Henry?"

"Yes?"

"You don't mind if we let Mrs. Trimble dispose of the frock you wore here, do you?"

She shook her head gratefully.

"Good. Now come over here, if you please, and look at some of these fashion plates. A woman needs more than one dress, don't you think?"

"Probably—but probably not more than three," she said haltingly.

He understood. Three was all her pride would allow. "You're probably right."

They spent the next hour choosing two more dresses for Henry, one in the deep sapphire lawn Dunford had picked out earlier, and one in a seafoam green Mrs. Trimble insisted made Henry's gray eyes glow. They would be delivered to Stannage Park in a week's time. Henry almost blurted out that she would be happy to return herself if necessary. She'd never dreamed she'd hear herself think it, but she didn't mind the thought of having to make another trip into Truro. She didn't like to think she was so shallow that a mere dress could make her happy, but she had to concede that it gave her a new sense of self-confidence.

As for Dunford, he now realized one thing: whoever had picked out her hideous dresses, it hadn't been Henry. He knew a thing or two about women's fashion, and he could tell from her selections that her taste ran to a quiet elegance with which no one could find fault.

And he realized one other thing: it made him unbelievably happy to see Henry this happy. It was an amazing thing, really.

When they reached the carriage, she didn't say anything until they were well on their way home. Finally she looked over at him with knowing eyes and said, "You don't have a sister, do you?"

"No," he said quietly, quite unable to lie to her.

She was silent for a moment. Then she placed her hand shyly on top of his. "Thank you."

Chapter 7

Dunford found he was oddly disappointed when Henry came down to breakfast the next day wearing her usual men's shirt and breeches. She caught his expression, grinned cheekily, and said, "Well, you wouldn't expect me to get my only good dress dirty, would you? Haven't we made plans to hike the perimeter of the estate today?"

"You are right, of course. I have been looking forward to it all week."

She sat down and served herself some eggs from the platter in the middle of the table. "Just like a man to want to know exactly what he owns," she said loftily.

He leaned forward, his eyes gleaming. "I am the king of my domain, and don't you forget it, minx."

She burst out laughing. "I say, Dunford, you would have made a superb medieval lord. I think there is quite an autocratic streak buried somewhere within you."

"And it's so very much fun when it surfaces."

"For you perhaps," she retorted, still grinning.

He smiled along with her, completely unaware of how that particular facial expression of his affected her. Henry felt her stomach do a little flip-flop and quickly swallowed a bite of breakfast, hoping it would settle her down.

"Hurry up, Hen," he said impatiently. "I want to get an early start."

Mrs. Simpson emitted a loud "harumph" at that, since it was, after all, already half past ten.

"I just sat down," Henry protested. "I'll probably swoon at your feet this afternoon if I don't have proper nourishment."

Dunford snorted. "I find the image of you swooning a difficult picture to accept." He drummed his fingers on the table, tapped his foot, whistled a jaunty tune, slapped his hand against his thigh, drummed his fingers on the table again . . .

"Oh, stop!" Henry threw her napkin at him. "Sometimes you are nothing but a big baby." She stood up. "Give me a moment to put on a jacket. It's a bit chilly out."

He stood. "Ah, what bliss it is to have you at my beck and call."

The look she gave him was mutinous, to say the least.

"Do smile, Henry. I cannot bear it when you're grumpy." He cocked his head and tried to look boyishly contrite. "Say you'll forgive me. Please. Please. Pleeeeease."

"For goodness sake, stop!" she laughed. "You must know I was never angry."

"I know." He grabbed her hand and started pulling her toward the door. "But you're so much fun to provoke. Come along now, we have a great deal of territory to cover today."

"Why does it suddenly sound as if I've joined the army?"

Dunford made a little hop as he avoided stepping on Rufus. "I was a soldier once."

"Were you?" She looked up in surprise.

"Mmm-hmm. On the peninsula."

"Was it dreadful?"

"Very." He opened the door, and they walked out into the crisp sunshine. "Don't believe the stories you hear about the glory of war. Most of it is appalling."

She shuddered. "I would think so."

"It's far, far nicer to be here in Cornwall, as you say at the end of the world, in the company of quite the most charming young woman I've ever had the pleasure to meet."

Henry flushed and turned away, unable to hide her embarrassment. He couldn't possibly mean it. Oh, she didn't think he was lying—he wasn't the sort to do that. He was merely saying in his own way that they were friends, that she was the first female with whom he'd become quite so chummy. Then again, she'd heard him mention two married ladies with whom he was friends, so that couldn't be it.

Still, he couldn't possibly be forming a *tendre* for her. As she'd said before, she wasn't the sort of woman men wanted, at least not when they had all of London from which to choose. With a sigh, she pushed the thought from her mind and resolved simply to enjoy the day.

"I always assumed a Cornish estate would have cliffs and crashing waves and all that," Dunford said.

"Most of them do. We happen to be squarely in the middle of the county, however." Henry kicked a pebble in her path, aiming it straight, then kicked it again when she caught up with it. “You don’t need to go very far to get to the ocean, though.”

“I would imagine not. We should take a jaunt there soon.”

Henry was so excited by the prospect that she started to blush. To hide her reaction, she fixed her gaze downward and concentrated on kicking her pebble.

They walked amiably to the estate’s eastern border. “We have a fence up on this side,” Henry explained as they neared the stone wall. “It’s not ours, actually, but Squire Stinson’s. He got it into his head that we were encroaching upon his land a few years back and put up this wall to keep us out.”

“And were you?”

“Encroaching upon his land? Of course not. It’s far inferior to Stannage Park. The wall does have one excellent use, however.”

“Keeping the odious Squire Stinson away?”

She cocked her head. “That’s a boon, certainly, but I was thinking of this.” She scrambled to the top of the wall. “It’s great fun to walk upon.”

“I can see that.” He vaulted up behind her, and they walked single file to the north. “How far does the wall stretch?”

“Oh, not far. About a mile or so. Where Squire Stinson’s property ends.”

To his surprise, Dunford found himself looking at *her* end—her rear end, to be precise. To his even greater surprise, he found he was enjoying the view immensely. Her breeches were baggy, but each time she took a step, they tightened around her, outlining her shapely form.

He shook his head in dismay. What on earth was wrong with him? Henry wasn’t the sort for a dalliance, and the last thing he wanted to do was muck up their fledgling friendship with romance.

"Is something wrong?" Henry called out. "You're awfully silent."

"Just enjoying the view." He bit his lip.

"It is lovely, isn't it? I could gaze at it all day."

"As could I." If he hadn't been balanced atop a stone wall, he would have kicked himself.

They skipped along the wall for nearly ten minutes until Henry suddenly stopped and whirled around. "*This* is my favorite part."

"What is?"

"This tree." She motioned to an immense tree which grew from their side of the property but whose limbs ventured over the wall. "Stand back," she said, her voice hushed. She took a step toward the tree, stopped, and turned around. "Farther."

Dunford was curious but took a step back.

She approached the tree cautiously, reaching her arm slowly out, as if afraid the tree might bite her.

"Henry," Dunford called out. "What are you—"

She yanked her hand back. "Hush!" Once again her face was set in deep concentration, and she stretched out her arm toward the knothole.

Suddenly Dunford was aware of a low buzzing sound, almost like—

Bees.

In utter horror, Dunford watched as she inserted her hand into the swarming hive. A pulse beat furiously in his temple; his heart pounded in his ears. The damned chit was going to get herself stung a thousand times, and there was nothing he could do about it because an attempt to stop her would only infuriate the insects.

"Henry," he said in a low but commanding voice. "Come back here this instant."

She used her free hand to wave him away. "I've done it before."

"Henry," he repeated. He could feel a thin veil of sweat breaking out upon his brow. Any minute now the bees were going to realize their hive had been invaded. They were going to sting—and sting and sting. He could try to pull her back, but what if she jostled the hive? His face paled. "Henry!"

She slowly withdrew her arm, a large chunk of honeycomb in her hand. "I'm coming, I'm coming." She ambled back toward him, smiling as she skipped along the length of the wall.

Dunford's paralyzing fear drained away once he saw she was safely away from the hive, but it was quickly replaced by pure primitive rage. Rage that she had dared to take such stupid, useless risks, rage that she had done it in front of him. He leaped off the wall, pulling her down with him. The sticky piece of honeycomb fell to the ground.

"Don't you ever, *ever* do that again! Do you hear me?" He shook her violently, his fingers pressing cruelly into her skin.

"I told you—I've done that before. I was never in any danger—"

"Henry, I have seen grown men *die* from a bee sting." His voice caught on the words.

She swallowed. "I have heard of that. I think only a very few people react to stings that way, and certainly not I. I—"

"Tell me you won't do it again." He shook her harder. "Give me your vow."

"Ow! Dunford, please," she pleaded. "You're hurting me."

He relaxed his grip slightly but the urgency never left his voice. "Your vow."

Her eyes searched his face, trying to make sense of this. A muscle was twitching spasmodically along the side of his throat. He was furious, far beyond what she'd seen when they'd had that argument about the pigpen. And even more foreboding, she sensed he was fighting to contain an even greater rage. She tried to speak, but her words came out in a whisper. "You once told me that when you were really angry, I'd know."

"Your vow."

"You're angry now."

"Your vow, Henry."

"If it means that much to you . . ."

"Your vow."

"I-I swear," she said, her gray eyes wide with confusion. "I swear I won't go into the beehive again."

It took a few moments, but eventually his breathing returned to normal, and he felt able to loosen his grip on her shoulders.

"Dunford?"

He didn't know why he did it. Lord knows he hadn't intended to do it, hadn't even thought he'd wanted to do it until she said his name in that soft quavering voice, and something inside of him snapped. He crushed her to him, murmuring her name over and over into her hair. "Oh, God, Henry," he said hoarsely. "Don't ever frighten me like that again, do you understand?"

She didn't understand anything except that he was holding her so very close. It was something she hadn't even dared to dream about. She nodded against his chest—anything to keep him holding her like this. The strength of his arms was stunning, the smell of him intoxicating, and the simple feeling that for this brief moment she might possibly be loved was enough to carry her through the rest of her days.

Dunford fought to understand why he had reacted so violently. His brain tried to argue that she had never been in any real danger, that she had obviously known what she was doing. But the rest of him—his heart, his soul, his body—screamed otherwise. He had been gripped by a shattering fear, far worse than anything he had ever felt on the battlefields of the peninsula. Then he suddenly realized he was holding her—holding her far closer than was proper. And the damning thing about it was that he didn't want to let go.

He wanted her.

That was a chilling enough thought to make him suddenly release her. Henry deserved better than a dalliance, and he hoped he was man enough to keep his desires under control. It wasn't the first time he had wanted a proper young lady, and it probably wouldn't be the last. The difference between him and the blackguards of society, however, was that he did not see young virgins as sport. He wasn't going to start with Henry. "Don't do that again," he said abruptly, not knowing whether the gruffness in his voice was directed at himself or her.

"I-I won't. I gave you my promise."

He nodded curtly. "Let's be on our way."

Henry looked down at the forgotten honeycomb. "Do you— Never mind." She doubted he'd want a taste of it now. She looked at her fingers, still sticky. There was nothing to do but lick them clean, she supposed.

The silence was overwhelming as they traveled the length of Stannage Park's eastern border. Henry thought of a thousand things to say, saw a thousand things she wanted to point out to him, but in the end lacked the courage to open her mouth. She didn't like this new tenseness. For the past few days she had felt so utterly comfortable with him. She could say anything, and he wouldn't laugh, unless of course she'd meant him to. She could be herself.

She could be herself, and he would still like her.

But now he seemed a stranger, dark and forbidding, and she felt as awkward and tongue-tied as she had all those times she had had to go into Truro—except for that last time, when he'd bought her the yellow dress.

She stole a look at him. He was so kind. He must care for her a bit. He wouldn't have gotten so upset about the beehive if he didn't.

They reached the north end of the eastern border, and Henry finally broke the silence. "We turn west here," she said, motioning to a large oak tree.

"I suppose there is a hive in that one, too," he said, hoping he'd managed to inject a sufficient note of teasing into his voice. He turned around. Henry was licking her fingers. Desire uncurled in his chest, quickly spreading to the rest of his body.

"What? Oh, no. No, there isn't." She smiled hesitantly in his direction, praying their friendship was returning to normal. Or if not, that he would hold her again because she'd never felt as safe and warm as she had in his arms.

They turned left and began walking the northern border. "This ridge marks the edge of the property," Henry explained. "It runs the entire length. The northern border is actually fairly short, less than a half mile, I think."

Dunford looked out on the land—his land, he thought proudly. It was beautiful, rolling and green. "Where do the tenants live?"

"On the other side of the house. They're all to the southwest. We'll see their houses toward the end of our hike."

"Then what is that?" He pointed toward a small thatched cottage.

"Oh, it's abandoned. Has been as long as I've lived here."

"Shall we explore?" He smiled at her, and Henry was almost able to convince herself that the scene by the tree had never happened.

"I'm game," she said brightly. "I've never been inside."

"I find it hard to believe there is an inch of Stannage Park you haven't explored, inspected, appraised, and mended."

She smiled sheepishly. "I never went inside as a child because Simpy told me it was haunted."

"And you believed her?"

"I was very small. And then . . . I don't know. It's difficult to break old habits, I suppose. There was never any reason to go in."

"You mean you're still afraid," he said, his eyes twinkling.

"Of course not. I said I'd go in, didn't I?"

"Lead on, then, my lady."

"I will!" She marched across the open field and stopped when she reached the cottage door.

"Aren't you going to go in?"

"Aren't you?" she shot back.

"I thought you were leading the way."

"Perhaps you're afraid," she challenged.

"Terrified," he said, his smile so lopsided there was no way she could believe he was serious.

She turned to face him, her hands on her hips. "We all must learn to face our fears."

"Exactly," he said softly. "Open the door, Henry."

She took a deep breath, wondering why this was so difficult. She supposed that childhood fears stayed with a person long into adulthood. Finally she pushed open the door and looked inside. "Why, look!" she exclaimed in wonder. "Someone must have loved this cottage very much."

Dunford followed her in and looked around. The interior was musty, a testament to long years of disuse, but the cottage still managed to retain a certain homey quality. On the bed was a brightly colored quilt, faded a bit with age but still cheerful. Sentimental knickknacks adorned a set of shelves, and tacked to a wall was a drawing that only a child could have made.

"I wonder what happened to them," Henry whispered. "There was obviously a family here."

"Illness perhaps," Dunford suggested. "It isn't uncommon for a single disease to take away an entire village, much less a family."

She kneeled in front of a wooden chest at the foot of the bed. "I wonder what is in here." She lifted the lid.

"What did you find?"

"Baby clothes." She picked up a tiny smock, tears unaccountably pricking her eyes. "It's full of baby clothes. Nothing but."

Dunford got down on his hands and knees next to her and peered under the bed. "There is a cradle down here, too."

Henry felt crushed by an overwhelming melancholy. "Their baby must have died," she whispered. "It's so sad."

"There now, Hen," Dunford said, obviously touched by her grief. "It happened years ago."

"I know." She tried to smile at her foolishness, but it came out wobbly. "It's just . . . Well, I know what it is like to lose one's parents. It must be a hundred times worse to lose one's child."

He stood up, took her hand, and led her to the bed. "Sit down."

She perched on the edge of the bed and then, unable to get comfortable, scrambled on top and leaned her back against the pillows resting against the headboard. She wiped a tear from the corner of her eye. "You must think I'm very foolish."

What Dunford was thinking was that she was very, very special. He'd seen her brisk, efficient side and he'd seen her joking, teasing side. But he'd never guessed she had such a sentimental streak. It was buried deep within her, to be sure, underneath layers of men's clothes and cheeky attitude, but it was there nonetheless. And there was something so utterly feminine about it. He'd seen a glimpse of it the day before in the dress shop, when she had gazed at the yellow dress with such a deep and unconcealed longing. But now . . . It quite unmanned him.

He sat on the edge of the bed and touched the side of her cheek with his hand. "You will make a superb mother someday."

She smiled gratefully at him. "You're so kind, Dunford, but I probably will never have children."

"Why not?"

She giggled even beneath her tears. "Oh, Dunford, one's got to have a husband to have children, and who is going to want me?"

In any other woman he would have thought that statement an obvious lure for compliments, but he knew Henry didn't have a devious, conniving bone in her body. He could see in her clear, gray eyes that she truly didn't believe any man would ever want to marry her. He wanted to wipe away the resigned pain he saw on her face. He wanted to shake her and say that she was foolish, utterly foolish. But most of all he wanted to make her feel better.

And he told himself that that was the only reason he swayed toward her, his face drawing ever nearer to hers. "Don't be silly, Henry," he whispered. "A man would have to be a fool not to want you."

She stared at him, unblinking. Her tongue darted out to moisten her lips, which had suddenly gone dry. Unfamiliar with the highly charged tension that now surrounded her, she tried to resort to levity, but her voice came out shaky and sad. "Then there are many, many fools in Cornwall, for no one has ever looked twice at me."

He leaned in closer. "Provincial idiots."

Her lips parted in surprise.

Dunford lost the ability to reason, lost all sense of what was right and good and proper. He knew only what was necessary, and it was suddenly very necessary that he kiss her. How was it that he had never noticed how pink her mouth was? And had he ever before seen lips that trembled so deliriously? Would she taste like lemons, like that faint maddening scent that seemed to follow her everywhere?

He didn't just want to find out. He had to.

He brushed his lips gently against hers, shocked by the electric tingle that traveled through him at this barest of touches. He drew back slightly, just far enough for him to see her face. Her eyes were open very wide, their gray depths filled with wonder and longing. A question seemed to be forming on her lips, but he could see that she had no idea how to put it into words.

"Ah, Lord, Henry," he murmured. "Who would have guessed?"

As his mouth descended once again, Henry gave in

to her wildest desire and reached up to touch his hair. It was unbelievably soft, and she couldn't bear to let go, even when his tongue darted out to [illegible] the outline of her lips and every other muscle in her body went limp with longing. His lips moved sideways, traveling lightly along her jawline to her ear. Her hand still retained its hold on his hair.

"It's so soft," she said, wonder making her voice husky. "Almost as soft as Rufus."

A deep chuckle rumbled in Dunford's chest. "Oh, Henry," he laughed. "That is certainly the first time I have been compared to a rabbit. Was I found wanting?"

Henry, suddenly shy, only shook her head.

"Rabbit got your tongue?" he teased.

She shook her head again. "No, you do."

Dunford groaned and leaned down to capture her mouth again. He'd been holding back during the last two kisses, he realized, out of concern for her innocence. But now he found his restraint was gone, and he plunged his tongue into the warm recesses of her mouth, exploring her intimately. God, she was sweet, and he wanted her . . . he wanted every inch of her. He took a ragged breath and slid his hand under her jacket to cup her breast. It was far fuller than he'd expected, and so very womanly. It was sinful how thin the fabric of her shirt was. He could feel the heat of her, feel her heartbeat speeding up, feel her nipple puckering beneath his touch. He moaned again. He was lost.

Henry gasped at this new intimacy. No man had ever touched her there. *She* didn't even touch her breasts unless she was bathing. It felt . . . good, but it also felt wrong, and panic began to rise within her. "No!" she cried out, wrenching away from him. "I can't."

Dunford groaned her name, his voice painfully hoarse.

Henry only shook her head as she scrambled to her feet, unable to say anything else. Words just couldn't manage to get by this choking feeling in her throat. She couldn't do this, she just couldn't, even if part of her wanted so desperately for him to touch his lips to hers again. The kisses she could justify. They made her feel so warm and tingly and so very *loved* that she could just manage to convince herself they weren't so very sinful, and she wasn't a fallen woman, and he really did care for her . . .

She stole a peek at him. He had risen from the bed and was cursing violently under his breath. She didn't understand why he wanted her. No man had ever wanted her before, and certainly no man had ever, even for an instant, come close to loving her. She looked at him again. His face was haggard. "Dunford?" Her voice was hesitant.

"It won't happen again," he said roughly.

Henry's heart sank, and she realized suddenly that she did want it to happen again, only . . . only she wanted him to love her, and that, she supposed, was why she'd pulled away from him.

"It's—it's all right," she said softly, wondering why on earth she was trying to comfort him.

"No, it isn't," he bit out, intending to say that she deserved better, but so filled with self-loathing he couldn't bear the sound of his own voice.

Henry heard only his harshness, and she gulped convulsively. He didn't want her, after all. Or at least he didn't want to want her. She was a freak—a boyish, plain-speaking, unattractive freak. No wonder he was so horrified by his actions. If there had been another eligible woman anywhere near Stannage Park, he surely wouldn't have paid Henry the least bit of mind. No, Henry thought, that wasn't true. They still would have been friends, Dunford hadn't been faking that. But he certainly never would have kissed her.

Henry wondered if she could possibly hold back her tears until they got back home.

Chapter 8

Supper that night was a silent affair. Henry wore her new yellow dress, and Dunford complimented her on it, but beyond that they seemed unable to converse.

As he finished the last few bites of his dessert, Dunford thought he'd like nothing better than to retire to his room with a bottle of whiskey, but after having to watch Henry's stricken expression all through the meal, he realized that he was going to have to do something to mend this rift. Setting down his napkin, he cleared his throat and said, "I thought I might have a glass of port. Since there are no ladies here with whom you may retire, I would be honored if you would join me."

Henry's eyes flew to his face. Surely he wasn't trying to tell her he thought of her as a *man?* "I've never had port before. I don't know if we have any."

Dunford stood. "You must. Every household does."

Henry followed him with her eyes as he walked around the table to pull out her chair. He was so handsome, so very handsome, and for a moment she had actually thought he wanted her. Or at least he had acted as if he had. And now . . . Now she didn't know what to think. She stood up and noticed he was looking at her expectantly. "I've never seen any here," she said, deciding that he was merely waiting for a reply about the port.

"Didn't Carlyle ever entertain?"

"Not very often, actually, although I fail to see what that has to do with port—or with gentlemen."

He eyed her curiously. "After a dinner party it is customary for the ladies to retire to the drawing room while the gentlemen indulge in a bit of port."

"Oh."

"Surely you were not ignorant of the custom?"

Henry flushed, painfully aware of her lack of social polish. "I did not know. How ill-bred you must have thought me this past week—lingering over supper. I'll leave you now." She took a few steps toward the door, but Dunford caught her arm.

"Henry," he said, "if I hadn't been interested in your conversation, believe me, I would have made you aware of it. I mentioned the port because I thought we might enjoy a drink together, not because I wanted to rid myself of your company."

"What do the ladies drink?"

"I beg your pardon?" He blinked, completely at a loss.

"When they retire to the drawing room," Henry explained. "What do the ladies drink?"

He shrugged his shoulders helplessly. "I haven't the faintest idea. I don't think they drink anything."

"That seems horribly unfair."

He smiled to himself. She was beginning to sound more like the Henry for whom he had come to care so much. "You may disagree once you get your first taste of port."

"If it is so very dreadful, why do you drink it?"

"It isn't dreadful. It is merely an acquired taste."

"Hmmm." Henry seemed lost in thought for a moment. "I still think it is a horribly unfair practice, even if port tastes as bad as pig swill."

"Henry!" Dunford was appalled at the tone of his voice. He sounded like his mother.

She shrugged. "Excuse my language, if you will. I'm afraid I've been trained to put on my good manners only for company, and you really don't qualify as that any longer."

The conversation had swung so far into the improbable that Dunford felt tears of mirth welling up in his eyes.

"But as for the port," she continued, "it seems to me you gentlemen probably have a merry old time of it in the dining room with the ladies gone, talking about wine and women and all sorts of interesting things."

"More interesting than wine or women?" he teased.

"I can think of a hundred things more interesting than wine or women . . ."

He realized with surprise that he couldn't think of anything more interesting than the woman standing before him.

"Politics, for example. I try to read about it in the *Times,* but I am not such a lackwit that I don't realize quite a bit goes on that does not get reported in the paper."

"Henry?"

She cocked her head.

"What has any of this to do with port?"

"Oh. Well, what I was endeavoring to explain is that you gentlemen have a grand time while the ladies have to sit in a stuffy, old drawing room, conversing about embroidery."

"I have no idea what the ladies talk about when they retire," he murmured with just the barest hint of a smile. "But somehow I doubt it is embroidery."

She shot him a look that said she didn't believe him in the slightest.

He sighed and held up his hands in mock surrender. "As you can see, I am trying to rectify this injustice by inviting you to join me in a glass of port this evening." He looked around. "That is, if we can find some."

"There is nothing here in the dining room," Henry said. "Of that I am certain."

"In the drawing room then. With the other spirits."

"It's worth a try."

He let her lead the way to the drawing room, noting with satisfaction how well her new dress seemed to fit. Too well. He frowned. She really had quite a nice shape, and he didn't like the idea of someone else discovering that fact.

They reached the drawing room, and Henry crouched down to look in a cabinet. "I don't see any," she said. "Although, never having seen a bottle of port, I really haven't the faintest idea what I'm looking for."

"Why don't you let me have a peek?"

She stood and changed places with him, her breast accidentally brushing against his arm as she did so. Dunford suppressed a groan. This had to be some sort of cruel joke. Henry was the most unlikely temptress imaginable, yet here he was, hard and straining and wanting nothing more than to throw her over his shoulder again, this time to haul her up to his room.

Coughing slightly to mask his discomfort, he bent to look in the cabinet. No port. "Well, I suppose a glass of brandy will do just as well."

"I hope you're not disappointed."

He threw her a sharp look. "I am not so enamored of my spirits that I am crushed at the loss of a glass of port."

"Of course not," she said quickly. "I never meant to imply you were. Although . . ."

"Although what?" he snapped. This constant state of arousal was shortening his temper.

"Well," she said thoughtfully, "I should think that someone overly enamored of spirits would be just the sort who wouldn't care which type of spirit he imbibed."

He sighed.

Henry moved to a nearby sofa and sat, feeling much more like herself than she had at dinner. It was the silence that had been so difficult. Once he started talking to her, she found it was easy to respond. They were back on familiar territory now—laughing and teasing one another mercilessly—and she could practically feel her misplaced self-confidence flowing back through her veins.

He poured a glass of brandy and held it out to her. "Henry," he said. He cleared his throat before continuing with, "About this afternoon . . ."

Her hand closed so tightly around the glass she was surprised it didn't shatter. She opened her mouth to speak, but nothing came out. She swallowed, trying to moisten her throat. So much for feeling like herself again. Finally she managed to say, "Yes?"

He coughed again. "I should never have behaved as I did, I . . . ah . . . I behaved badly, and I apologize."

"Think nothing of it," she replied, trying very hard to sound carefree. "I won't."

He frowned. It certainly had been his intention to put the kiss behind him—he was eight different kinds of a cad for even *thinking* of taking advantage of her—but he was oddly disappointed that she intended to forget about it completely. "That is probably for the best." He cleared his throat yet again. "I suppose."

"I say, is something wrong with your throat? Simpy makes an excellent home remedy. I'm sure she could—"

"There is nothing wrong with my throat. I'm just a trifle . . ." He searched for a word. ". . . uncomfortable. That is all."

"Oh." She smiled weakly. It was so much easier to try to be helpful than to deal with the fact that he was so disappointed with their kiss. Or maybe he had been disappointed because she had broken it off. She frowned. Surely he didn't think she was the sort of woman who would . . . She couldn't even complete the thought. Glancing up at him nervously, she opened her mouth and her words came out in a violent tumble.

"I'm sure you're right. It's for the best, I suppose, to forget about everything, because the thing is, I wouldn't want you to think that I . . . well, that I'm the kind of woman who—"

"I don't think that of you," he cut in, his voice oddly curt.

She heaved a great sigh of relief. "Oh, good. I don't know really what came over me, I'm afraid."

Dunford knew exactly what had come over her, and he knew it had been entirely his fault. "Henry, don't worry—"

"But I do worry! You see, I don't want this to spoil our friendship, and— We are friends, aren't we?"

"Of course." He looked affronted that she had even asked.

"I know I'm being forward, but I don't want to lose you. I really like having you as my friend, and the truth is—" She let out a choked laugh. "The truth is, you're just about the only friend I've got, besides Simpy, but that really isn't the same thing, and—"

"Enough!" He couldn't bear to hear her broken voice, to hear the loneliness in her every word. Henry had always thought she led a perfect existence here at Stannage Park—she had told him as much on numerous occasions. She didn't even realize there was an entire world past the Cornwall border, a world of parties and dances and . . . friends.

He set his brandy snifter down on a table and crossed the room, driven simply by a need to comfort her. "Don't talk like that," he said, surprised by the sternness of his voice. He pulled her into a benign hug, resting his chin on the top of her head. "I'll always be your friend, Henry. No matter what happens."

"Truly?"

"Truly. Why wouldn't I be?"

"I don't know." She pulled away just far enough so she could see his face. "Lots of people seem to find reasons."

"Hush up, minx. You're a funny one, but you're certainly more likable than unlikable."

She grimaced. "What a lovely way of phrasing it."

He laughed out loud as he let her go. "And that, my dear Henry, is exactly why I like you so damned much."

Dunford was preparing for bed later that night when Yates rapped on his door. It was customary for servants to enter rooms without knocking, but Dunford had always found that practice to be singularly unappealing when the room in question was one's bedroom, and he had instructed the Stannage Park servants accordingly.

At Dunford's answer, Yates entered the room, carrying a rather large envelope. "This arrived from London today, my lord. I placed it on the desk in your study, but—"

"But I didn't go into my study today," Dunford finished for him. He took the envelope from Yates's hand. "Thank you for bringing it up. I think it's the former Lord Stannage's will. I've been eager to read it."

Yates nodded and left the room.

Too lazy to get up to find a letter opener, Dunford slipped his index finger under the envelope flap and pulled the sealing wax apart. Carlyle's will, just as he had expected. He skimmed the document for Henry's name; he could read the rest of it at length the next day. For now, his main concern was how Carlyle had provided for his ward.

He reached the third page before the words "Miss Henrietta Barrett" jumped out at him. Then, to his utter surprise, he saw his own name.

Dunford's jaw dropped. He was Henry's guardian.

Henry was his ward.

That made him a—good God, he was one of those appalling men who took advantage of their wards. The gossip mill was rife with tales of lecherous old men who either seduced their wards or sold them off to the highest bidder. If he had felt shame over his behavior that afternoon, the emotion had now tripled. "Oh, my God," he whispered. "Oh, my *God*."

Why hadn't she told him?

"Henry!" he bellowed.

Why hadn't she told him?

He sprang to his feet and grabbed his robe. "Henry!"

Why hadn't she told him?

By the time he made it into the hall, Henry was already there, her slender form wrapped in a faded green dressing gown. "Dunford," she said anxiously. "What is wrong?"

"This!" He practically shoved the papers in her face. "This!"

"What? What is this? Dunford, I can't tell what these papers are when you've got them plastered against my face."

"It's Carlyle's will, Miss Barrett," he bit out. "The one naming me your guardian."

She blinked. "And?"

"That makes you my ward."

Henry stared at him as if a portion of his brain had just flown out his ear. "Yes," she said placatingly, "that's usually how it works."

"Why didn't you tell me?"

"Tell you what?" Henry looked from side to side. "I say, Dunford, do we need to carry on this conversation in the middle of the hall?"

He spun on his heel and stalked into her room. She hurried after him, not at all sure that it was an advisable idea for the two of them to be alone in her bedroom. But the alternative was to have him rail at her in the hall, and that was decidedly unappealing.

He shut the door firmly, then turned on her again. "Why," he asked, his voice laced with barely controlled fury, "didn't you tell me that you were my ward?"

"I thought you knew."

"You thought I *knew?*"

"Well, why wouldn't you?"

He opened his mouth, then shut it. Hell, the chit had a point. Why *didn't* he know? "You still should have told me," he muttered.

"I would have if I'd even dreamed you didn't know."

"Oh, God, Henry," he groaned. "Oh, God. This is a disaster."

"Well," she bristled, "I'm not *that* dreadful."

He shot her an irritated look. "Henry, I *kissed* you this afternoon. Kissed you. Do you understand what that means?"

She looked at him dubiously. "It means you kissed me?"

He grabbed her by the shoulders and shook. "It means—Christ, Henry, it's practically incestuous."

She caught a lock of her hair between her fingers and began to twirl. The movement was meant to calm her nerves, but her hand was jerky and cold. "I don't know if I would call it *incestuous.* It certainly isn't that much of a sin. Or at least I don't think so. And since we've both agreed it isn't going to happen again—"

"Curse it, Henry, will you be quiet? I'm trying to think." He raked his hand through his hair.

She drew back, affronted, and clamped her mouth shut.

"Don't you see, Henry? You're now my *responsibility.*" The word fell distastefully from his lips.

"You're too kind," she muttered. "I'm not so bad, you know, as far as responsibilities go."

"That's not the point, Hen. This means . . . Hell, it means . . ." He let out a short bark of ironic laughter. Only a few hours earlier he'd been thinking he'd like to take her to London, to introduce her to his friends and show her that there was more to life than Stannage Park. Now it seemed he *had* to. He was going to have to give her a season and find her a husband. He was going to have to find someone to teach her how to be a lady. He glanced down at her face. She still looked rather irritated with him. Hell, he hoped whoever ladyfied her didn't change her too much. He rather liked her the way she was.

Which brought him to another point. Now, more than ever, it was imperative that he keep his hands off her. She'd be ruined as it was if the *ton* found out they'd been living unchaperoned here in Cornwall. Dunford took a ragged breath. "What the hell are we going to do?"

The question had obviously been directed at himself, but Henry decided to answer it anyway. "I don't know what *you're* going to do," she said, hugging her arms to her chest, "but *I'm* not going to do anything. Anything other, that is, than what I've already been doing. You've already admitted I'm uniquely qualified to oversee Stannage Park."

His expression said that he regarded her as hopelessly naive. "Henry, we both can't stay here."

"Why ever not?"

"It isn't proper." He winced as he said it. Since when had he become such a stickler for propriety?

"Oh, pish and bother propriety. I don't give a whit for it, in case you hadn't—"

"I noticed."

"—noticed. It makes no sense in our case. You own the place, so you shouldn't have to leave, and I run it, so I *cannot* leave."

"Henry, your reputation . . ."

That seemed to strike her as uproariously funny. "Oh, Dunford," she gasped, wiping tears from her eyes, "that's rich. That is *rich.* My reputation."

"What the devil is wrong with your reputation?"

"Oh, Dunford, I haven't got a reputation. Good or bad. I'm so odd, people have enough to talk about without worrying about how I act with men."

"Well, Henry, perhaps it is time you started thinking

about your reputation. Or at the very least, acquiring one."

If Henry hadn't been so puzzled by his odd choice of words, she might have noticed the steely undertone to his voice. "Well, the point is moot anyway," she said breezily. "You have been living here for over a week already. If I had been worried about a reputa—that is to say, *my* reputation, it would be well past destroyed."

"Nonetheless, I will procure rooms at the local inn on the morrow."

"Oh, don't be silly! You didn't give two figs about the impropriety of our living arrangements this past week. Why should you now?"

"Because," he bit out, his temper badly strained, "you are now my responsibility."

"That is quite the most asinine reasoning I have ever encountered. In my opinion—"

"You have too many opinions," he snapped.

Henry's mouth fell open. "Well!" she declared.

Dunford began to pace the room. "Our situation cannot remain as such. You cannot continue to carry on like a complete hoyden. Someone is going to have to teach you some manners. We'll have to—"

"I cannot believe your hypocrisy!" she burst out. "It was all very well for me to be the village freak when I was just an acquaintance, but now that I'm your *responsibility*—"

Her words died a swift death, for Dunford had grabbed her by the shoulders and pinned her against the wall. "If you call yourself a freak one more time," he said in a dangerous tone, "for the love of God I will not be held responsible for my actions."

Even in the candlelight she could see the barely leashed fury in his eyes, and she gulped with a healthy dose of fear. Still, she had never been terribly prudent, and so she continued, albeit in a much lower voice. "It does not reflect well upon your character that you did not care about my reputation up to this point. Or does your concern extend only to your wards, not your friends?"

"Henry," he said, a muscle twitching in his neck, "I think the time has come for you to stop talking."

"Is that an order, oh, dear guardian?"

He took a very deep breath before replying. "There is a difference between guardian and friend, although I hope I may be both to you."

"I think I liked you better when you were just my friend," she muttered belligerently.

"I expect that will be so."

"I expect that will be so," she mimicked, not in the least trying to hide her ire.

Dunford's eyes began to search the room for a gag. His gaze fell upon her bed, and he blinked, suddenly realizing what an idiot he must have sounded, preaching on about propriety when he was standing here in her bedroom, of all places. He looked over at Henry and finally noticed she was wearing her dressing gown—her dressing gown! And it was frayed and torn in places and showed altogether too much leg.

Suppressing a groan, he moved his gaze to her face. Her mouth was clamped shut in a mutinous line, and he suddenly thought that he'd really like to kiss her again, harder and faster this time. His heart was pounding for her, and he realized for the first time what a thin line there was between fury and desire. He wanted to *dominate* her.

Thoroughly disgusted with himself, he turned on his heel, strode across the room, and gripped the doorknob. He was going to have to get out of this house fast. Yanking the door open, he turned to her and said, "We will discuss this further in the morning."

"I expect we shall."

Later Henry reflected that it was probably for the best that he'd left the room before hearing her retort. She didn't think he'd been desirous of a reply.

Chapter 9

The rest of Henry's new dresses arrived the next morning, but she donned her white shirt and breeches just to be contrary.

"Silly man," she muttered as she yanked on her clothing. Did he think he would be able to change her? To turn her into a delicate vision of femininity? Did he think she would simper and bat her eyelashes and spend her days painting watercolors?

"Ha!" she barked out. He wasn't going to have any easy time of it. She wouldn't be able to learn to do all those things even if she wanted to. With her unwilling, it was past impossible.

Her stomach growled impatiently, so Henry pulled on her boots and made her way down to the breakfast room. She was surprised to see that Dunford was already there; she had gotten up exceptionally early, and he was one of the only people she knew who was less of a morning person than she.

His eyes raked over her costume as she sat down,

but she couldn't discern even a flicker of emotion in their chocolatey depths. "Toast?" he said blandly, holding out a platter.

She plucked a piece off the plate and set it down in front of her.

"Jam?" He held out a pot of something red. Raspberry, Henry thought absently, or maybe currant. She didn't really care which, just started spreading it on her toast.

"Eggs?"

Henry set down her knife and spooned some scrambled eggs onto her plate.

"Tea?"

"Will you stop!" she burst out.

"Just trying to be solicitous," he murmured, dabbing discreetly at the corner of his mouth with a napkin. "I can feed myself, my lord," she bit out, reaching inelegantly across the table for a plate of bacon.

He smiled and took another bite of his food, aware of the fact that he was goading her and enjoying it immensely. She was miffed at him. She didn't like his proprietary attitude. Dunford rather doubted anyone had ever told her what to do in her entire life. From what he'd heard of Carlyle, the man had given her an indecent amount of freedom. And although he was certain she'd never admit it, Dunford had a feeling Henry was a little upset that he hadn't given a thought to her reputation until now.

On that score, Dunford reflected resignedly, he was guilty. He'd been having so much fun learning about his new estate that he hadn't given a thought to his companion's unmarried status. Henry comported herself so, well, *oddly*—there was really no other word for it—that it just hadn't occurred to him that she was (or should be) bound by the same rules and conventions as the other young ladies of his acquaintance.

As these thoughts passed through his mind, he began to tap his fork absently against the table. The monotonous sound went on until Henry looked up, her expression telling him she was absolutely *convinced* his sole purpose in life was to vex her.

"Henry," he said in what he hoped was his most affable tone. "I've been thinking."

"Have you? How very prodigious of you."

"Henry . . ." His voice held an unmistakable air of warning.

Which she ignored. "I have always admired a man who attempts to broaden his mind. Thinking is a good starting point, although it might tax you—"

"Henry."

This time she shut up.

"I was thinking . . ." He paused, as if daring her to make a comment. When she wisely did not, he continued. "I should like to leave for London. This afternoon, I think."

Henry felt an inexplicable knot of sadness ball up in her throat. He was leaving? It was true that she was annoyed with him, angry even, but she didn't want him to *go.* She was becoming accustomed to having him around.

"You're coming with me."

For the rest of his life Dunford wished he had had some way of preserving the expression on her face. Shock did not describe it. Neither did horror. Neither did dismay nor fury nor exasperation. Finally she spluttered, "Are you insane?"

"That is a distinct possibility."

"I am not going to London."

"I say you are."

"What would I do in London?" She threw up her arms. "And even more importantly, who will take my place here?"

"I'm sure we can come up with someone. There is no end of good servants at Stannage Park. After all, you trained them."

Henry chose to ignore the fact that he had just paid her a compliment. "I'm not going to London."

"You don't have a choice." His voice was deceptively mild.

"Since when?"

"Since I became your guardian."

She glared furiously at him.

He took a sip of his coffee and assessed her over the rim of his cup. "I suggest you don one of your new gowns before we depart."

"I told you, I'm not leaving."

"Don't push me, Henry."

"Don't push *me!*" she burst out. "Why are you dragging me off to London? I don't want to go! Don't my feelings count for anything?"

"Henry, you've never been to London."

"There are millions of people in this world, my lord, who live perfectly happy lives without ever setting one foot in our nation's capital. I assure you I am one of them."

"If you don't like it, you can leave."

She rather doubted that. She certainly wouldn't put it past him to tell a few white lies to get her to bend to his will. She decided to try a different tactic. "Taking me to London isn't going to solve my chaperonage dilemma," she said, trying to sound levelheaded. "In fact, leaving me here is a much better solution. Everything will go back to the way it was before you arrived."

Dunford sighed wearily. "Henry, tell me why you don't want to go to London."

"I'm too busy here."

"The real reason, Henry."

She caught her lower lip between her teeth. "I just—I just don't think I would enjoy it. Parties and balls and all that. It's not for me."

"How do you know? You've never been."

"Look at me!" she exclaimed in humiliated fury. "Just look at me." She stood and motioned to her attire. "I would be laughed out of even the most undiscriminating of drawing rooms."

"Nothing that a dress wouldn't fix. Didn't two of them arrive just this morning, by the way?"

"Don't mock me! It is much deeper than that. It's not just my clothing, Dunford, it's me!" She gave her chair a frustrated kick and moved to the window. She took a few deep breaths, trying to calm her racing heart, but it didn't seem to work. Finally she said in a very low voice, "Do you think I would amuse your London friends? Is that it? I have no desire to become some sort of freak-show entertainment. Are you going to—"

He moved so swiftly and silently she didn't even realize he'd changed places until his hands were on her, whirling her around to face him. "I believe I told you last night not to refer to yourself as a freak."

"But that's what I am!" Henry was mortified by the catch in her voice and the tears trailing down her cheeks, and she tried to wriggle out of his grasp. If she had to act the weak fool, couldn't he let her do it in private?

But Dunford held firm. "Don't you see, Henry?" he said, his voice achingly tender. "That is why I'm taking you to London. To prove to you that you're not a freak, that you're a lovely and desirable woman, and any man would be proud to call you his own."

She stared at him, unblinking, barely able to digest his words.

"And any woman," he continued softly, "would be proud to call you her friend."

"I can't do it," she whispered.

"Of course you can. If you put your mind to it." He let out a rich chuckle. "Sometimes, Henry, I think you can do anything."

She shook her head. "No," she said softly.

Dunford let his hands drop to his sides and walked over to the adjacent window. He was stunned by the depth of his concern for her, amazed at how badly he wanted to repair her self-confidence. "I can hardly believe this is you speaking, Henry. Is this the same girl who runs what is possibly the best-tended estate I have ever seen? The same girl who boasted to me she could ride any horse in Cornwall? The same girl who took a decade off my life when she stuck her hand in an active beehive? After all that, it is difficult to imagine that London will present much of a challenge to you."

"It's different," she said, her voice barely a whisper.

"Not really."

She didn't answer.

"Did I ever tell you, Henry, that when I met you I thought you were the most remarkably self-possessed young woman I had ever met?"

"Obviously I'm not," she said, choking on the words.

"Tell me this, Hen. If you can supervise two dozen servants, take charge of a working farm, and build a pigpen, for God's sake, why do you think you won't be up to the task of a London season?"

"Because I can do all that!" she burst out. "I know how to ride a horse, and I know how to build a pigpen, and I know how to run a farm. *But I don't know how to be a girl!*"

Dunford was shocked into silence by the vehemence of her reply.

"I don't like doing anything if I don't do it well," she bit out.

"It seems to me," he began slowly, "that all you need is a little practice."

She shot him a scathing look. "Don't patronize me."

"I'm not. I'll be the first to admit I thought you didn't know how to wear a dress, but look how well you did with the yellow frock. And you obviously have very good taste when you choose to exert it. I do know a thing or two about ladies' fashion, you know, and the dresses you chose are lovely."

"I don't know how to dance." She crossed her arms defiantly. "And I don't know how to flirt, and I don't know who should sit next to whom at a dinner party, and—and I didn't even know about port!"

"But Henry—"

"And I won't go to London to make a fool of myself. I won't!"

He could only watch as she raced from the room.

Dunford set the date of their departure back by a day, recognizing that there was no way he could push Henry any further while she was in such a state and still live with his conscience. He walked quietly by her room several times, his ears straining for signs that she was crying, but all he heard was silence. He never even once heard her moving about.

She didn't come down for the noonday meal, which surprised him. Henry did not have a delicate appetite, and he rather thought she would be famished by now. She had not, after all, had the chance to eat very much of her breakfast. He wandered down to the kitchen to ask if she'd requested a tray to be sent up to her room. When he was informed she had not, he cursed under his breath and shook his head. If she did not appear for supper, he'd go up to her room and drag her down himself.

As it happened, such drastic measures were not necessary, for Henry appeared in the drawing room at teatime, her eyes slightly red-rimmed but nonetheless dry. Dunford stood immediately and motioned to the chair next to him. She flashed him a grateful smile, probably because he'd resisted the temptation to make a crack about her behavior that morning.

"I-I am sorry for making such a cake of myself at breakfast," she said. "I assure you I am ready to discuss the matter like a civilized adult. I hope we can do so."

Dunford thought wryly that part of the reason he liked her so well was that she was so unlike any of the civilized adults he knew. And he hated this overly correct speech of hers. Maybe taking her to London would be a mistake. Maybe society would beat the freshness and spontaneity out of her. He sighed. No, no, he'd keep an eye on her. She wouldn't lose her sparkle; in fact, he'd make sure she shone even more brightly. He glanced over at her. She looked nervous. And expectant.

"Yes?" he said, inclining his head slightly.

She cleared her throat. "I thought—I thought perhaps you could tell me why you want me to come to London."

"So you may come up with logical reasons why you should not go?" he guessed.

"Something like that," she admitted, with just the barest hint of her signature cheeky smile.

Her honesty—and the sparkle in her eyes—quite disarmed him. He smiled back at her, another one of those devastating grins, and was gratified to see her lips part slightly in reaction. "Please sit," he said, motioning again to the chair. She sat down, and he followed suit. "Tell me what you want to know," he said with an expansive motion of his arm.

"Well, to start with, I think—" She stopped, her expression one of utmost consternation. "Don't look at me that way."

"What way?"

"Like . . . like . . ." Dear Lord, had she been about to say *like you're going to devour me?* "Oh, never mind."

He smiled again, hiding this one beneath a cough and his hand. "Do go on."

"Right." She looked at his face, then decided that that was a mistake as he was far too handsome and his eyes were glinting and—

"You were saying?" he was saying.

Henry blinked herself back into reality. "Right. I was saying, um, what I was saying is that I'd like to know what exactly you hope to accomplish by taking me to London."

"I see."

He didn't say anything more, which so irritated her that she was finally compelled to retort, "Well?"

Dunford had clearly been using the delay to frame a response. "I suppose I hope to accomplish many things," he replied. "First and foremost, I'd like you to have a bit of fun."

"I can have—"

"No, please," He held up a hand. "Let me finish, and then you shall have your turn."

She nodded rather imperiously and waited for him to continue.

"As I was saying, I'd like for you to have some fun. I think you might enjoy a bit of the season if you would only let yourself. You are also badly in need of a new wardrobe, and please do not argue with me on that score because I know you know you're sadly lacking in that area." He paused.

"Is that all?"

He couldn't help but chuckle. She was so eager to argue her case. "No," he said. "I was merely pausing for breath." When she did not smile at his teasing, he added, "You do breathe from time to time, don't you?"

This earned him a scowl.

"Oh, all right," he capitulated. "Tell me your objections thus far. I'll finish when you're done."

"Right. Well, first of all, I have lots of fun here in Cornwall, and I see no reason why I need to travel across the country to look for more fun. It seems deuced paganish to me."

"Deuced paganish?" he echoed in disbelief.

"Don't laugh," she warned.

"I won't," he assured her. "But deuced paganish? Where the devil did you come up with that?"

"I was merely trying to point out that I have responsibilities here and have no wish for a frivolous lifestyle. Some of us have more important things to do than fritter our time away, looking for activities with which to amuse ourselves."

"Of course."

She narrowed her eyes, trying to detect any sarcasm in his voice. Either he was serious or else he was a master at deception, because he looked utterly earnest.

"Did you have any other objections?" he asked politely.

"Yes. I will not quibble with you over the fact that I need a new wardrobe, but you have forgotten a pertinent fact. I have no money. If I couldn't afford new gowns here in Cornwall, I don't see how I could afford any in London, where everything is surely more expensive."

"I'll pay for them."

"Even I know that isn't proper, Dunford."

"It probably wasn't proper last week when we went to Truro," he acquiesced with a shrug. "But now I'm your guardian. It couldn't be more proper."

"But I cannot allow you to spend your money on me."

"Perhaps I want to."

"But you cannot."

"I believe I know my own mind," he said dryly. "Probably a bit better than you do, I imagine."

"If you want to spend your money, I'd much rather you put it into Stannage Park. We could use a bit of work on the stables, and there is a piece of land adjoining the southern border I've had my eye on—"

"That wasn't what I had in mind."

Henry crossed her arms and clamped her mouth shut, fresh out of objections to his scheme.

Dunford regarded her petulant expression and correctly guessed that she was ceding the floor to him. "If I may continue . . . Let me see, where was I? Fun, wardrobe, oh, yes. It might do you a bit of good to get a little town polish. *Even,*" he said loudly as he saw her mouth open in consternation, "if you have no intention of ever returning to London again. It is always good to be able to hold one's own with the best in the land—and the snobbiest, I suppose—and there is no way you'll be able to do that if you do not know what's what. The port was a good example."

A flush stained her neck.

"Any objections there?"

She shook her head mutely. She hadn't felt the need for social polish up to now; she ignored and was ignored by most of Cornwall society and was fairly content with the arrangement, but she had to admit he had a point. Knowledge was always a good thing, and it certainly couldn't hurt to learn how to comport herself a little more properly.

"Good," he said. "I always knew you had exceptional common sense. I'm glad you're showing it now."

Henry rather thought he was being somewhat condescending but decided not to comment on it.

"Also," Dunford continued, "I think it would do you a great deal of good to meet some people your age and make some friends."

"Why do you sound as if you're lecturing to an errant child?" she muttered.

"Forgive me. *Our* age, I should say. I'm not so very much older than you, I suppose, and my two closest female friends can't be more than a year older than you, if that."

"Dunford," Henry said, trying to stave off the embarrassed flush that was staining her cheeks, "the very reason I most object to going to London is that I don't think people will like me. I don't mind being alone here at Stannage Park, where I truly am alone. I quite like it, as a matter of fact. But I do not think I will enjoy being alone in a ballroom full of hundreds of people."

"Nonsense," he said dismissively. "You'll make friends. You just haven't been in the right situation before. Or the right clothing," he added dryly. "Not, of course, that one ought to judge a person on his or her wardrobe, but I can see where people would be slightly, er, suspicious of a female who doesn't seem to own a dress."

"And you, of course, are going to buy me a closetful of dresses."

"Just so," he replied, pointedly ignoring her sarcasm. "And don't worry about making friends. My friends will adore you; I'm sure of it. And they will introduce you to other nice people, and so on and so forth."

She didn't have any other cogent arguments on that particular point, so she had to settle for a loud grumble to express her ire.

"Finally," Dunford said, "I know you adore Stannage Park and would like to spend the rest of your life here, but perhaps, just perhaps, Henry, you might someday like to have a family of your own. It is exceedingly selfish for me to keep you here for myself, although Lord knows I would like to have you around because I'll never find an estate manager who will do a better job—"

"I'm more than happy to stay," she interjected quickly.

"Have you never given any thought to marrying?" he asked softly. "Or children? Neither is a distinct possibility if you remain here at Stannage Park. As you have pointed out, there is nobody worth his salt right here in the village, and I think you have effectively scared off most of the gentry around Truro. If you go to London, you might meet a man who captures your fancy. Maybe," he said in a teasing voice, "he will even turn out to be from Cornwall."

I fancy *you!* she wanted to scream. Then she was horrified because she hadn't realized until that moment just how much she did fancy him. But beyond this infatuation—and she was loath to call it anything deeper than that—he had struck a chord. She did want children, although she had refused to let herself think about it much up to now. The possibility of her actually finding someone to marry—someone who'd be willing to marry *her,* she thought dryly—had always been so remote that thinking about children brought only pain. But now—oh, Lord, why was she suddenly picturing children who looked exactly like Dunford? Right down to his warm brown eyes and devastating smile. It was more painful than anything she could imagine because she knew that the adorable imps never would be hers.

"Henry? Henry?"

"What? Oh, I'm sorry. I was just thinking about what you said."

"Don't you agree then? Come to London, if only for just a little while. If you don't like any of the men there, you may return to Cornwall, but at least then you can say you explored all your options."

"I could always marry *you,*" she blurted out. She clapped her hand to her mouth, horrified. Where had that come from?

"Me?" he croaked.

"Well, I mean . . ." Oh dear, oh dear, how to patch this up? "What I mean is, if I married you, then, um, I wouldn't have to go to London to look for a husband so I would be happy, and you wouldn't have to pay me to oversee Stannage Park so you would be happy, and . . . um . . ."

"Me?"

"I can see you're surprised. I'm surprised too. I'm not even sure why I suggested it."

"Henry," he said gently, "I know exactly why you suggested it."

He did? She suddenly felt very warm.

"You don't know very many men," he continued. "You are comfortable with me. I'm a much safer option than going out and meeting gentlemen in London."

That's not it at all! she wanted to yell. But of course she didn't. And of course she didn't tell him the real reason those words had burst forth from her mouth. Better just to let him think she was too scared to leave Stannage Park.

"Marriage is a very big step," he said.

"Not so big," she said, wildly thinking that she'd already half-dug herself into a ditch—why not broaden the hole? "What I mean to say is, there is the marriage bed and all that, and I must admit I have no experience in that direction beyond, well, *you know.* But I was raised on a farm, after all, and am not entirely ignorant. There are sheep here, and we breed those, and I can't see how it would be so very different and—"

He arched one arrogant brow. "Are you likening me to a *sheep?*"

"No! Of course not, I . . ." She paused, swallowed convulsively, then swallowed again. "I . . ."

"You what, Henry?"

She couldn't tell if his voice was icy cold, shocked into disbelief, or merely heartily amused.

"I . . . uh . . ." Oh, Lord, this would have to go down in history as the worst day, no, the worst *minute* of her life. She was an idiot. A bacon-brain. A fool, fool, fool, fool, *fool!* "I . . . uh . . . I guess maybe I should go to London." *But I'm coming back to Cornwall as soon as I can,* she silently swore. He wasn't going to tear her from her home.

"Splendid!" He rose, looking supremely pleased with himself. "I'll tell my valet to begin packing immediately. I'll have him take care of your things as well. I don't see any reason to bring anything other than the three dresses we bought last week in Truro, do you?"

She shook her head weakly.

"Right." He crossed to the door. "So just pack up any personal items and knickknacks you might want to bring, and Henry?"

She looked up at him in question.

"We'll just forget about this little conversation, shall we? The last bit that is."

She managed to stretch her lips into a smile, but what she really wanted to do was hurl the brandy decanter at him.

Chapter 10

At ten the following morning Henry was dressed, ready, and waiting on the front steps. She wasn't particularly pleased that she had agreed to go to London with Dunford, but she was damned if she wasn't going to behave with a bit of dignity. If Dunford thought he would have to drag her kicking and screaming from the house, he was mistaken. She had donned her new green dress and matching bonnet, and had even managed to locate an old pair of Viola's gloves. They were a bit worn, but they did the trick, and Henry found that she actually liked the feel of the soft, fine wool on her hands.

The bonnet, however, was another story altogether. It itched her ears, blocked her peripheral vision, and was a general nuisance. It took all of her patience—which, admittedly, wasn't much—not to rip the blasted thing from her head.

Dunford arrived a few minutes later and gave her an approving nod. "You look lovely, Henry."

She smiled her thanks but decided not to put too much stock in his compliment. It sounded like the sort of thing he said automatically to any woman in his vicinity.

"Is that all you have?" he asked.

Henry looked down at her meager valise and nodded. She hadn't even enough to fill a proper trunk. Just her new dresses and some of her well-worn men's clothing. Not that she was likely to need breeches and a jacket in London, but one never could be sure.

"No matter. We'll rectify that soon."

They climbed up into the carriage and were on their way. Henry caught her bonnet on the door frame as she was getting in, a circumstance which caused her to mutter most ungraciously under her breath. Dunford thought he heard her say, "Bloody bleeding blooming bonnet," but he couldn't be certain. Either way, he was going to have to warn her to curb her tongue once they reached London.

Still, he couldn't resist teasing her about it, and with an astonishingly straight face he said, "Bee in your bonnet?"

Henry turned on him with a murderous glare. "It's a dreadful contraption," she said vehemently, yanking the offending piece off of her head. "Serves no purpose whatsoever that I can deduce."

"I believe it is meant to keep the sun off your face."

She shot him a look that said quite clearly, "Tell me something I don't already know."

Dunford had no idea how he managed not to laugh. "You may come to like them eventually," he said mildly. "Most ladies don't seem to like the sun on their faces."

"I'm not most ladies," she retorted. "And I've done very well without a bonnet for years, thank you."

"And you have freckles."

"I do not!"

"You do. Right here." He touched her nose and then moved to a spot along her cheekbone. "And here."

"You must be mistaken."

"Ah, Hen, I cannot tell you how much it pleases me to find that you have a bit of feminine vanity within you after all. Of course you never did cut your hair, so that must count for something."

"I am not vain," she protested.

"No, you're not," he said solemnly. "It's one of the loveliest things about you."

Was it any wonder, Henry thought with a sigh, that she was becoming so infatuated with him?

"Still," he continued, "it's rather gratifying to see you have a few of the failings the rest of us humans share, if only in short measure."

"Men," Henry declared firmly, "are every bit as vain as women. I'm sure of it."

"You are most probably right," he said agreeably. "Now, do you want to give me that bonnet? I'll put it over here where it won't be crumpled."

She handed him the headpiece. He turned it over in his hand before setting it down. "Deuced flimsy little thing."

"It was obviously invented by men," Henry announced, "for the sole purpose of making women more dependent upon them. It completely blocks my peripheral vision. How is a lady meant to get anything done if she cannot see anything that isn't directly in front of her?"

Dunford only laughed and shook his head. They sat in companionable silence for about ten minutes, until he sighed and said, "It's good to be on our way. I was afraid I was going to have to do physical battle with you over Rufus."

"Whatever do you mean?"

"I was half expecting you to insist we bring him along."

"Don't be silly," she scoffed.

He smiled at her briskly sensible attitude. "That rabbit would probably chew up my entire house."

"I couldn't care less if he chewed up the Prince Regent's unmentionables. I didn't bring Rufus because I thought it would be dangerous for him. Some bacon-brained French chef would probably have him in the stew pot within days."

Dunford rocked with silent laughter. "Henry," he said, wiping his eyes, "please don't lose your distinctive brand of humor when you get to London. Although," he added, "you might find it prudent to refrain from speculating about Prinny's intimate apparel."

Henry couldn't help but smile in return. It was just like him to make certain she had a good time, the wretched man. She was trying to go along with his plans with some modicum of dignity, but that didn't mean she had to enjoy herself. He was making it quite difficult for her to succeed in her attempts to picture herself as a beleaguered martyr.

And, indeed, he made it quite difficult all day long, keeping up an endless stream of friendly chatter. He pointed out sights along the way, and Henry listened and watched avidly. She hadn't been out of the southwest of England in years, not since she'd been orphaned and moved to Stannage Park, actually. Viola had taken her on a short holiday in Devon once, but beyond that Henry hadn't set foot out of Cornwall.

They stopped briefly for lunch, but that was their only break, for Dunford explained he wanted to make good time. They could get more than halfway to London that day if they didn't dally. The hurried pace took its toll, however, and by the time they pulled into a roadside inn for the night, Henry was extremely weary. Dunford's carriage was exceptionally well sprung, but nothing could disguise some of the deeper ruts in the road. She was jolted out of her tired state, however, by her companion's surprising announcement.

"I'm going to tell the innkeeper you are my sister."

"Why?"

"It seems prudent. It really isn't quite proper for us to be traveling in this fashion without a chaperone, even if you are my ward. I'd rather not raise any ill-bred speculation about you."

Henry nodded, conceding his point. She had no wish for some drunken lout to paw at her simply because he thought her a loose woman.

"We can get away with it, I think," Dunford mused, "as we've both got brown hair."

"Along with half the population of Britain," she said pertly.

"Hush up, minx." He resisted the urge to tousle her hair. "It'll be dark. No one will notice. And put your bonnet back on."

"But then no one will see my hair," she teased. "All that work will be for nothing."

He smiled boyishly. "All that work, eh? You must be dreadfully tired, expending all that energy to grow your hair brown."

She batted the offending bonnet at him.

Dunford alighted, whistling to himself as he did so. So far the journey had been a complete success. Henry had, if not forgotten, at least suppressed her pique at being bullied into coming to London. Furthermore, she mercifully had not mentioned the kiss they had shared in the abandoned cottage. In fact, all signs pointed to the conclusion that she had completely forgotten about it.

Which bothered him.

Damn, but it bothered him.

But it didn't bother him half as much, however, as the fact that he had been bothered by it in the first place.

This was getting far too confusing. He gave up thinking about it and helped her down from the carriage.

They walked into the inn, one of the grooms trailing behind with their valises. Henry was relieved to see that it appeared to be satisfactorily clean. She hadn't slept on any sheets save for the ones at Stannage Park for years, and she always knew exactly when those had last been washed. It finally occurred to her just how much she had controlled her own existence up to now. London would be quite an adventure. If only she could get over this paralyzing fear of polite society . . .

The innkeeper, recognizing Quality when he saw it, quickly rushed over to their sides.

"We require two rooms," Dunford said briskly. "One for myself and one for my sister."

The innkeeper's face fell. "Oh, dear. I was hoping you were married because I've only one room left and—"

"Are you quite certain?" Dunford's voice was like ice.

"Oh, milord, if I could boot someone out for you, I would, I swear, but the entire place is full of Quality tonight. The Dowager Duchess of Beresford is passing through, and she's got quite a collection with her. Needed six rooms altogether, what with all her grandchildren."

Dunford groaned. The Beresford clan was notorious for its fertility. At last count the dowager duchess—a nasty, old woman who certainly would not look kindly upon being asked to give up one of her rooms—had twenty grandchildren. Lord only knew how many of them were here tonight.

Henry, however, had no such knowledge of the Beresfords and their amazing fecundity, and presently was having trouble breathing due to the panic rushing through her body. "Oh, but you must have another room," she blurted out. "You must."

The innkeeper shook his head. "Only one. I'll be sleeping in the stables as it is. But surely the two of you won't mind sharing so much, since you're brother and sister and all. It's not very private, I know, but—"

"I'm a very private person," Henry said desperately, grabbing hold of his arm. "Extraordinarily so."

"Henrietta, dear," Dunford said, gently uncurling her fingers from their death grip on the innkeeper's elbow, "if he hasn't another room, he hasn't another room. We'll have to make do."

She eyed him warily, then immediately calmed down. Of course, Dunford must have a plan. That was why he sounded so collected and self-assured. "Of course, Du . . . er, Daniel," she improvised, realizing belatedly that she didn't know his given name. "Of course. How silly of me."

The innkeeper relaxed visibly and handed Dunford the key. "There is room in the stables for your grooms, milord. It'll be a tight squeeze, but I think there'll be a spot for everyone."

Dunford thanked him and then saw to the task of showing Henry to their room. The poor girl had gone white as a sheet. True, the blasted bonnet hid most of her face, but it was not difficult to deduce that she was not happy with the sleeping arrangements.

Well, curse it, neither was he. He was not in the least pleased by the thought of sleeping in the same room with her all night. His damned body was getting aroused just thinking about it. More than a dozen times that day he had wanted to grab her and kiss her senseless right there in the carriage. The deuced chit would never know the level of self-control he had exerted.

It wasn't when they were talking. Then, at least, he could keep his mind off her body and on the conversation. It happened when they lapsed into silence, and he'd look up and see Henry staring out the window, her eyes aglow. Then he'd look at her mouth, which was *always* a mistake, and she'd go and do something like lick her lips, and the next thing he knew he was clutching the seat cushions just to keep from reaching for her.

And those delectable, very pink lips were pursed just then as Henry planted her hands on her hips and looked around the room. Dunford followed her gaze to the large bed that dominated the chamber and gave up any hope that he wasn't going to spend the night uncomfortably hard. "Who's Daniel?" he tried to joke.

"You, I'm afraid, since you never told me your given name. Don't say anything that will give yourself away."

"My lips are sealed," he said, bowing grandly, all the while wishing they were sealed on hers.

"What *is* your real name?"

He smiled devilishly. "Secret."

"Oh, please," she scoffed.

"I'm serious." He actually managed to school his features into an expression of such earnest honesty, that for a moment she believed him. He moved stealthily to her side and clapped his hand over her mouth. "A state secret," he whispered, looking furtively toward the window. "The very livelihood of the monarchy depends upon it. If revealed, it could topple our interests in India, not to mention—"

Henry yanked off her bonnet and batted him with it. "You're incorrigible," she sputtered.

"I have been told," he said with an unabashed grin, "that I frequently act with a decided lack of gravity."

"I'll say." She planted her hands on her hips again and resumed her perusal of the room. "Well, Dunford, this is a bind. What is your plan?"

"My plan?"

"You have one, don't you?"

"I haven't the faintest idea what you're talking about."

"For our sleeping arrangements," she ground out.

"I hadn't really thought about it," he admitted.

"What?" she screeched. Then, realizing she sounded decidedly shrewish, she modified her tone and added, "We can't both sleep . . . there." She motioned to the bed.

"No," he sighed, thinking that he was bone tired, and if he couldn't make love to her that night—which he knew he couldn't do no matter how many times he had unwillingly fantasized about it during the past few days—then at least he'd like to get a good night's sleep on a soft mattress. His eyes traveled to a wing chair in the corner of the room. It looked dreadfully upright, just the sort of chair that was meant to encourage good posture. Not very comfortable for sitting, much less sleeping. He sighed again, this time loudly. "I suppose I can sleep in the chair."

"The chair?" she echoed.

He pointed at the piece of furniture in question. "Four legs, a seat. All in all, a rather useful item for one's home."

"But it's—it's *here*."

"Yes."

"*I'll* be here."

"That is also true."

She stared at him as if he did not speak English. "We cannot both sleep here."

"The alternative is that I sleep in the stables, which, I assure you, I have no wish to do. Although . . ." He cast an eye at the chair. ". . . at least I would be able to lie down. However, the innkeeper said the stables were even more crowded than the inn, and quite frankly, after my experience with your pigpen, the delicate smell of animals has been engraved permanently on my mind. Or in my nose, as the case may be. The thought of spending the night wedged in between horse droppings is decidedly unpalatable."

"Maybe they just mucked the stalls?" she said hopefully.

"There is nothing to stop them from doing their business in the middle of the night." He closed his eyes and shook his head. Never in a million years would he have dreamed he'd one day be discussing horse manure with a lady.

"All—all right," she said, looking dubiously at the chair. "I—um, I need to change, though."

"I'll just wait in the hall." He straightened his spine and walked from the room, deciding he was the noblest, most chivalrous, and possibly the most stupid man in all Britain. As he leaned against the wall just outside the door, he could hear her moving around. He tried desperately not to think about what those sounds meant, but it was impossible. Now she was unbuttoning her frock . . . Now she was letting it slip from her shoulders . . . Now she was . . .

He bit his lip hard, hoping the pain would steer his thoughts in a more appropriate direction. It didn't work.

The devil of it all was that he knew she wanted him

too. Oh, not in quite the same way and certainly not with the same intensity. But it was there. Despite her sarcastic mouth, Henry was a complete innocent and did not know how to hide the dreamy feeling in her eyes whenever they accidentally brushed up against each other. And the kiss . . .

Dunford groaned. She had been perfect, so completely responsive until he'd lost control and scared her. In retrospect, he thanked God she had become frightened, because he wasn't certain he would have been able to stop.

But despite the hungry cravings of his body, it was definitely not his intention to seduce Henry. He wanted her to have a season, as was her due. He wanted her to meet some women her age and make some friends for the first time in her life. He wanted her to meet some men and . . . He frowned. No, he decided with the resigned expression of a young child who has been told he absolutely, positively must eat his brussels sprouts, he *did* want her to meet some men. She deserved to have her choice of England's best.

And then perhaps his life could find its way back to normal. He'd visit his mistress, which he *badly* needed to do, he'd game with his friends, make the endless round of parties, and continue his much envied bachelor life.

He'd been one of the few people he knew who'd been truly content with his existence. Why the devil would he want to change anything?

The door opened, and Henry's face poked around the corner. "Dunford?" she said quietly. "I'm done. You can come in now."

He groaned, not certain whether the sound was born of stifled desire or plain tiredness, and pushed himself away from the wall. He walked back into the room.

Henry was standing near the window, clutching her faded wrapper tightly around her.

"I've seen you in your dressing gown before," he said, quirking what he hoped was a friendly and decidedly *platonic* smile.

"I-I know, but . . ." She shrugged helplessly. "Do you want me to wait in the hall while you change?"

"In your dressing gown? I think not. I may have seen you so attired, but I certainly don't want to share the privilege with the rest of the inn's occupants."

"Oh. Of course."

"Especially with that old Beresford dragon and her brood about. They're probably on their way to London for the season and won't hesitate to tell the entire *ton* they saw you wandering half naked around a public inn." He raked his hand wearily through his hair. "We should take pains to avoid them in the morning."

She nodded nervously. "I suppose I could close my eyes. Or turn my back."

He thought that this was probably not the best time to inform her that he preferred to sleep in the nude. Still, it would be damned uncomfortable to sleep in his clothing. Perhaps his dressing gown . . .

"Or I could hide under the covers," Henry was saying. "Then you would be assured of your modesty."

Dunford blinked in disbelief and amusement as she dove into the bed and crawled under the blankets until she resembled a very large molehill.

"How is that?" she queried, her voice considerably muffled.

He tried to disrobe but found that his shoulders were shaking with mirth. "Perfect, Henry. It's perfect."

"Just tell me when you're done!" she called.

Dunford quickly shed his clothing and pulled out his dressing gown. For one brief moment he was entirely and quite splendidly naked, and a shiver of thrill ran through him at the sight of the big lump in the bed. He took a ragged breath and pulled on his dressing gown. *Not now,* he told himself sternly. *Not now and not with this girl. She deserves better. She deserves to make her own choices.*

He tied the sash of his robe tightly around his waist. He probably should have left on his undergarments, but damn it, the chair was going to be uncomfortable enough. He'd just have to make certain his robe did not open during the night. The poor girl would probably faint at the sight of a naked man as it was. Lord knows what would happen if she saw one who was quite aroused, as he undoubtedly would be, all through the night.

"I'm all done, minx," he said. "You can come out now."

Henry poked her head out from under the covers. Dunford had dimmed the candles, but the moonlight was filtering in through the gauzy curtains, and she could see his very large, very male form standing by the chair. She sucked in her breath. She'd be all right as long as he didn't smile at her. If he did that, she would be lost. Dimly it occurred to her she probably couldn't see him smile in the dark, but those grins of his were so devastatingly effective, she was convinced she could probably feel the force of one through a brick wall.

She settled against the pillows and closed her eyes, trying *very* hard not to think about him.

"Goodnight, Hen."

"Goodnight, Dun."

She heard him chuckle at her shortening of his name. *Just don't smile,* she prayed. She didn't think he did; she was certain she would have heard it in his laugh if his lips had stretched out to their full, rakish grin. Just to be sure, however, she opened one eye and peered over at him.

Of course she couldn't see his expression, but it was a marvelous excuse to look at him. He was settling into that wing chair—well, trying to settle into it at least. She hadn't noticed how . . . how very *vertical* it was. He moved, and then moved again, and then again. He must have shifted positions two dozen times before he finally stilled. Henry bit her lip. "Are you comfortable?" she called out.

"Oh, quite."

It was that very particular tone of voice which held no trace of sarcasm but rather suggested that the speaker was trying quite hard to convince someone of something that was obviously not true.

"Oh," Henry said. What was she supposed to do? Accuse him of lying? She stared at the ceiling for thirty seconds and then decided—why not?

"You're lying," she said.

He sighed. "Yes."

She sat up. "Maybe we could . . . Well, that is to say . . . There must be *something* we can do."

"Do you have any suggestions?" His tone was quite dry.

"Well," she stalled, "I don't need all of these blankets."

"Warmth is not my problem."

"But perhaps you could lay one on the floor and make a makeshift mattress out of it."

"Don't worry about it, Henry. I'll be fine."

Another patently false statement.

"I can't just lie here and watch you be uncomfortable," she said worriedly.

"Close your eyes and go to sleep, then. You won't see a thing."

Henry lay back down and managed to stay in that position for a full minute. "I can't do it," she burst out, bolting upright again. "I just can't do it."

"Can't do what, Henry?" He sighed—a very long-suffering sort of sigh.

"I can't lie here when you're so uncomfortable."

"The only place I'm going to be more comfortable is in the bed."

There was a very long pause. Finally—"I can do it if you can do it."

Dunford decided that they had vastly different interpretations of the word "it."

"I'll scoot very, very far over to the side." She started to scoot. "Very far."

Against all better judgment, he actually considered the idea. He lifted his head to watch her. She was so far to the edge of the bed that one of her legs was falling over the side.

"You can sleep on the other side," she was saying. "Just stay at the edge."

"Henry . . ."

"If-you're-going-to-do-it-do-it-now," she said, the entire sentence coming out as one long word. "For in a moment I will surely regain my senses and rescind the offer."

Dunford looked at the empty spot on the bed and then down at his body, which was sporting an enormous erection. Then he looked at Henry. *No, don't do that!* His gaze quickly shifted back to the empty spot on the bed. It looked very, very comfortable—so comfortable, in fact, that it might just be possible for him to relax enough for his body to calm down.

He looked back at Henry. He hadn't meant to do it, hadn't wanted to do it, but his eyes were inclined to follow the dictates of a body part other than his mind.

She was sitting up and staring at him. Her thick, straight, brown hair had been pulled back into a plait which was surprisingly erotic. Her eyes—well, by all rights it should have been too dark to see them, but he could swear he could see them glow silver in the moonlight.

"No," he said hoarsely, "the chair will do just fine, thank you."

"If I know you are uncomfortable, I shan't be able to sleep." She sounded remarkably like a damsel in distress.

Dunford shuddered. He had never been able to resist playing hero. Slowly he got to his feet and walked to the empty side of the bed.

How bad could it be?

Chapter 11

Very, very bad.

Very, very, *very* bad.

An hour later Dunford was still wide awake, his entire body stiff as a board for fear that he might accidentally brush up against her. Furthermore, he couldn't risk lying in any position other than on his back because when he'd first crawled in and lay on his side, he could smell her on the pillow.

Curse it, why couldn't she have stayed in just one place? Was there any reason why she should have lain on one side of the bed and then moved to the other to make room for him? Now all of the pillows smelled like her, like that vague lemony scent that always wafted around her face. And the blasted chit moved so much in her sleep that even staying on his back didn't protect him completely.

Don't breathe through your nose, he chanted internally. *Don't breathe through your nose.*

She rolled over, emitting a soft sigh.

Close your ears.

She made some funny little snapping sound with her lips, then rolled over again.

It's not her, a little piece of his mind screamed. This would happen with any woman.

Oh, give it up, the rest of his brain replied. *You want Henry, and you want her bad.*

Dunford gritted his teeth and prayed for sleep.

He prayed *hard.*

And he was not a religious man.

Henry felt warm. Warm and soft and . . . content. She was having the most beautiful dream. She wasn't entirely certain what was happening in the dream, but whatever it was, it was leaving her feeling utterly indulged and languid. She shifted in her sleep, sighing contentedly as the smell of warm wood and brandy drifted under her nose. It was a lovely smell. Rather like Dunford. He always smelled like warm wood and brandy, even when he hadn't had a drop of drink. Funny how he managed that. Funny how his smell was in her bed.

Henry's eyelids fluttered open.

Funny how *he* was in her bed.

She let out an involuntary gasp before she remembered she was at an inn on the way to London and had done what no gently bred lady would ever ever do. She had offered to share her bed with a gentleman.

Henry bit her lip and sat up. He had looked so uncomfortable. Surely it wasn't such a sin to spare him a night of tossing and turning followed by several days of an aching back. And it wasn't as if he'd touched her. Hell, she thought indelicately, he didn't need to. The man was a human furnace. She probably would have felt the warmth of his body clear across the room.

The sun was beginning to come up, and the entire room was bathed in a rosy glow. Henry looked down at the man lying next to her. She rather hoped this entire escapade did not ruin her reputation before she even managed to acquire one, but if it did, she thought wryly, it would be rather ironic, considering she'd done nothing of which to be ashamed—besides wanting him, of course.

She admitted that to herself now. These strange sensations he elicited in her—they were desire, plain and simple. Even if she knew she couldn't act on these feelings, there was no use lying to herself about them.

This honesty was becoming painful, however. She knew she couldn't have him. He didn't love her, and he wasn't going to. He was bringing her to London to marry her off. He'd said as much.

If only he weren't so darned nice.

If she could hate him, everything would be so much easier. She could be mean and vicious and convince him to release her from his life. If he were insulting to her, her desire for him would certainly wither and fade.

Henry was discovering that love and desire were, for her at least, irrevocably entwined. And part of the reason she was so crazy about him was that he was such a good person. If he were a lesser man, he wouldn't own up to his responsibility as her guardian, and he wouldn't insist on taking her to London and giving her a season.

And he certainly wouldn't be doing all this because he wanted her to be *happy.*

Clearly, he was not an easy man to hate.

Hesitantly, she reached out her hand and brushed a lock of dark brown hair away from his eyes. Dunford mumbled sleepily and then yawned. Henry jerked her arm back, fearful that she had woken him.

He yawned again, this time very loudly, and lazily opened his eyes.

"I'm sorry I woke you up," she said quickly.

"Was I sleeping?"

She nodded.

"So there really is a God," he muttered.

"Excuse me?"

"Just a little morning prayer of thanks," he said dryly.

"Oh." Henry blinked in surprise. "I had no idea you were so religious."

"I'm not. That is—" He paused and exhaled. "It's remarkable what can prompt a man to discover religion."

"I'm sure," she murmured, having not a clue what he was talking about.

Dunford turned his head on the pillow so that he was facing her. Henry looked damned good first thing in the morning. Wispy tendrils of hair had escaped from her braid and were curling gently around her face. The soft light of morning seemed to turn these errant strands to spun gold. He took a deep breath and shuddered, willing his body not to react.

It did not, of course, obey.

Henry, meanwhile, had suddenly realized her clothing was on a chair clear across the room. "I say," she said nervously, "this certainly is awkward."

"You have no idea."

"I . . . um . . . I'll be wanting to get my clothes, and I'll need to get up to get them."

"Yes?"

"Well, I don't think you ought to be seeing me in my nightgown, even if you did sleep with me last night. Oh, dear," she said in a choked voice, "that didn't come out quite the way I intended. What I meant to say was that we slept in the same bed, which I suppose is almost as bad."

Dunford reflected—rather painfully—that almost didn't really count.

"At any rate," she prattled on, awkwardness making her words run together, "I really can't get up to get my clothing, and my dressing gown appears to be just out of reach. I'm not exactly certain how this is so, but it is, so perhaps you ought to get up first, as I've already seen you—"

"Henry?"

"Yes?"

"Shut *up*."

"Oh."

He closed his eyes in agony. He wanted nothing other than to stay motionless under the covers all day. Well, that wasn't entirely true. What he really wanted to do involved the young woman sitting next to him, but that wasn't going to happen, so he was opting for staying hidden. Unfortunately, part of his body *really* didn't want to stay hidden, and he had no idea how he was meant to get up first without scaring ten years off of her life.

Henry sat stock still until she couldn't stand it any longer. "Dunford?"

"Yes?" It was amazing how a single word could convey such feeling. And not good feelings, either.

"What are we going to do?"

He took a deep breath—possibly his twentieth of the morning. "You are going to bury yourself under the covers as you did last night, and I am going to get dressed."

She obeyed his order with alacrity.

He rose with an unabashed groan and crossed the room to where he'd left his clothing. "My valet will have a fit," he muttered.

"What?" she yelled from beneath the covers.

"I said," he said more loudly, "that my valet will have a fit."

"Oh, *no,*" she moaned, sounding considerably distressed.

He sighed. "What is it now, Hen?"

"You really should have your valet," came the muffled reply. "I feel dreadful."

"Don't," he ordered sharply.

"Don't what?"

"Don't feel dreadful," he practically snapped.

"But I can't help it. We're going to be arriving in London today, and you'll want to look nice for your friends and . . . and for whomever else you want to look nice and . . ."

How was it, he wondered, that she managed to sound as if she would be irrevocably hurt if he did not avail himself of his valet?

"It's not as if I have a maid, so I'm sure to look rumpled anyway, but there is no need for *you* to do so."

He sighed.

"Therefore you must get back into bed."

That, he thought, was a very bad idea.

"Hurry up now," she said briskly.

He voiced his feelings. "This is a very bad idea, Hen."

"Trust me."

He couldn't help the short bark of ragged laughter that flew from his mouth.

"Just get back into bed and hide under the covers," she explained patiently. "I'll get up and get dressed. Then I'll go downstairs and summon your valet. You'll look beautiful."

Dunford turned to face the large, extremely vocal lump in the bed. "Beautiful?" he echoed.

"Beautiful, handsome, whatever it is you want to be called."

He had been called handsome many times, by many different women, but never had he felt as pleased as he did that very moment. "Oh, all right," he sighed. "If you insist." A few seconds later he was back in the bed, and she was scurrying out and across the room.

"Don't peek," she called out as she pulled her dress over her head. It was the same one she'd worn the previous day, but she had laid it carefully on a chair the night before, and she supposed it was less wrinkled than those in her valise.

"I wouldn't dream of it," he lied blandly.

A few moments later she said, "I'll summon your valet." Then he heard the click of the door.

After sending Hastings up to his employer, she wandered into the dining room, hopeful that she could order some breakfast. She had a feeling she wasn't supposed to be there unescorted, but she didn't know what else to do. The innkeeper spied her and hurried to her side. She had just finished ordering when she saw a little old lady with blue hair out of the corner of her eye. She looked unbelievably regal and haughty. The Dowager Duchess of Beresford. It had to be. Dunford had warned her not to let the lady see her at all costs.

"In our room," Henry blurted out in a strangled voice. "We'd like breakfast in our room." Then she took off like a shot, praying the duchess hadn't seen her.

Henry ran up the stairs and burst into the room, not giving a thought to its inhabitants. With slowly dawning horror, she realized Dunford was only half dressed. "Oh, my," she breathed, staring at his naked chest, "I'm so sorry."

"Henry, what happened?" he asked urgently, oblivious to the shaving lather on his face.

"Oh, dear. I'm sorry. I–I'll just stand in the corner with my back turned."

"Henry, for God's sake, what is wrong?"

She stared at him with wide silver eyes. He was going to come to her, she thought. He was going to touch her, and he wasn't wearing a shirt. Then she belatedly noticed the presence of the valet. "I must have entered the wrong room," she hastily fabricated. "Mine is right next door. It was just . . . I saw the duchess . . . and . . ."

"Henry," Dunford said in an unbelievably patient voice. "Why don't you wait in the hall? We're almost done here."

She nodded jerkily and nearly flew back into the hall. A few minutes later the door opened to reveal Dunford, looking marvelously debonair. Her stomach did a somersault. "I ordered breakfast," she blurted out. "It should be here any minute now."

"Thank you." Noting her discomfort, he added, "I apologize if our rather unconventional stay here has disturbed you in any way."

"Oh, no," she said quickly, "it hasn't *disturbed* me. It's just . . . I just . . . Well, you've got me thinking about reputations and such."

"As well you should. London, I'm afraid, will not afford you the same measure of freedom you enjoyed in Cornwall."

"I know that. It's just . . ." She paused thankfully as she watched Hastings slip out of the room. Dunford shut the door a discreet halfway. When she continued, it was in a loud whisper. "It's just that I *know* I shouldn't be seeing you without your shirt on, no matter how nice you may look, because it makes me feel quite odd, and I shouldn't encourage you after—"

"Enough," he said in a strangled voice, holding up a

hand as if to ward off the innocently erotic words tumbling from her mouth.

"But—"

"I said *enough.*"

Henry nodded and then stepped aside to allow the innkeeper to enter with breakfast. She and Dunford watched in silence as he laid the table and left the room. Once she was seated, she looked up at him and said, "I say, Dunford, did you realize—"

"Henry?" he interrupted, terrified she was going to say something delightfully improper and convinced he would not be able to control his reaction to it.

"Yes?"

"Eat your eggs."

Many hours later they reached the outskirts of London. Henry practically had her face plastered up against the glass windows of the coach, she was so excited. Dunford pointed out a few of the sights, assuring her there would be plenty of time for her to see the rest of the city. He would take her sightseeing just as soon as they had hired a maid to act as her escort. Until then he would have one of his female friends show her around.

Henry swallowed nervously. Dunford's friends were undoubtedly sophisticated and dressed in the first stare of fashion. She was nothing more than a country bumpkin. She had a sinking feeling she would not know what to do when she met them. And Lord knew she had no idea what to say.

This was particularly distressing to a woman who had prided herself on always having a ready retort.

As their carriage rolled toward Mayfair, the houses grew progressively grander. Henry could barely keep her mouth shut as she stared. Finally she turned to her companion and said, "Please tell me you don't live in one of these mansions."

"I don't." He gave her a lopsided smile.

Henry breathed a sigh of relief.

"But you will."

"Excuse me?"

"You didn't think you could live in the same house as I, did you?"

"I hadn't really thought about it."

"I'm sure you'll be able to stay with one or another of my friends. I'm just going to drop you off at my house to wait until I make arrangements for you."

Henry felt rather like a piece of baggage. "Won't I be an imposition?"

"In one of these houses?" He quirked a brow and waved his hand at one of the opulent mansions. "You could go for weeks without anyone even noticing your presence."

"How very encouraging," she muttered.

Dunford chuckled. "Don't worry, Hen. I have no intention of settling you with a miserable harridan or a doddering old fool. I promise you'll be happy with your living arrangements."

His voice was so rich and reassuring that Henry couldn't help but believe him.

The carriage turned into Half Moon Street and came to a stop in front of a neat little town house. Dunford alighted, then turned to help Henry down. "This," he said with a smile, "is where I live."

"Oh, but it's lovely!" Henry exclaimed, feeling overwhelmingly relieved that his home wasn't too grand.

"It's not mine. I only lease it. It seems silly to purchase a house when we've a family home right here in London."

"Why don't you live there?"

He shrugged. "I'm too lazy to move, I suppose. I probably should. The house has rarely been occupied since my father's death."

Henry let him lead her into a bright and airy drawing room. "But in all seriousness, Dunford," she said, "if no one is using the house here in London, wouldn't it make sense for you to use it? This is a lovely house. I'm sure it costs a pretty penny to lease it. You could invest those funds . . ." She broke off when she realized Dunford was laughing.

"Oh, Hen," he gasped. "Don't ever change."

"You may be sure that I won't," she said pertly.

He clucked her under the chin. "Was ever a female so practical as you, I wonder?"

"Most males are not, either," she retorted, "and I happen to think practicality is a good trait."

"And so it is. But as for my house—" He bestowed his most devilish grin upon her, sending her heart and mind into a whirl of giddy confusion. "—at nine and twenty I'd rather not be living under a watchful parental eye. Oh, and by the way, you'll want not to talk about such matters among *ton* ladies. It's considered crass."

"Well, what *can* I talk about, then?"

He paused. "I don't know."

"Just as you didn't know what ladies talk about when they retire after supper. It's probably dreadfully dull."

He shrugged. "Not being a lady, I have never been invited to listen to their conversations. But if you're interested, you can ask Belle. You'll probably meet her this afternoon."

"Who is Belle?"

"Belle? Oh, she is a great friend of mine."

Henry began to sense an emotion that felt uncannily like jealousy.

"She's recently married. Used to be Belle Blydon, but now she's Belle Blackwood. Lady Blackwood, I suppose I should call her."

Trying to ignore the fact that she felt rather relieved at this Belle person's married state, Henry said, "And she was Lady Belle Blydon before that, I imagine?"

"She was, actually."

She swallowed. All these lords and ladies were a trifle unsettling.

"Don't let Belle's blue blood send you into palpitations," Dunford said briskly, walking across the room to a closed door. He put his hand on the knob and pushed it open. "Belle is extremely unpretentious, and besides, I'm sure that with a little training, you'll be able to hold your head high with the best of us."

"Or the worst," Henry muttered, "as the case may be."

If Dunford heard her, he pretended not to. Henry's eyes followed him as he walked into what appeared to be his study. He bent over a desk and quickly shuffled through some papers. Curious, she followed him in, perching impishly on the side of the desk. "What are you looking at?"

"Nosy brat."

She shrugged.

"Just some correspondence that accumulated while I was gone. And some invitations. I want to be careful about what you attend at first."

"Afraid I might embarrass you?"

He looked up sharply, relief evident on his face when he saw she was only teasing. "Some of the *ton* events are mind-numbingly dull. I wouldn't want to make a bad impression on you the first week out. This, for example." He held up a snowy white invitation. "A musicale."

"But I think I would enjoy a musicale," Henry said. Not to mention the fact that she probably would not have to make conversation for the bulk of the evening.

"Not," he said emphatically, "when it's being given by my Smythe-Smith cousins. I went to two of them last year, and only because I love my mother. I believe it was said that after hearing dear Philippa, Mary, Charlotte, and Eleanor play Mozart, one would know exactly how it would sound if performed by a herd of sheep." Shuddering with distaste, he crumpled up the invitation and dropped it carelessly on the desk.

Henry, spying a small basket that she guessed was used for discarded paper, picked up the crumpled invitation and lobbed it in. When it hit its mark, she let out a soft whoop of triumph, clasping her hands together and raising her arms in the air in a victory salute.

Dunford just closed his eyes and shook his head.

"Well, goodness," she said pertly. "You can't expect me to abandon all of my hoydenish habits, can you?"

"No, I suppose not." And, he thought with a tinge of pride, he didn't really want her to.

An hour later Dunford was seated in Belle Blackwood's parlor, telling her about his unexpected ward.

"And you had no idea you were her guardian until Carlyle's will arrived a week and a half later?" Belle asked disbelievingly.

"Not even an inkling."

"I can't help but chuckle, Dunford, to think of you as a young lady's guardian. You, as a defender of maidenly virtue? It's a most improbable scenario."

"I'm not such a profligate that I cannot steer a young lady through society," he said, stiffening his spine. "And that brings me to two other points. First, as pertains to the phrase 'young lady.' Well, I have to say that Henry is a trifle unusual. And second, I will need your help, and not only a show of support. I need to find someplace for her to live. She can't stay at my bachelor's lodgings."

"Fine, fine," Belle said, waving her hand dismissively. "Of course I'll help her, but I want to know why she's so unusual. And did you just call her *Henry?*"

"It's short for Henrietta, but I don't think anyone's called her by her full name since she learned how to speak."

"It has some style," Belle mused. "If she can carry it off."

"I have no doubt she can, but she'll need a bit of guidance. She's never been to London before. And her female guardian died when she was only fourteen. No one has taught Henry how to be a lady. She is completely ignorant of most of the customs of polite society."

"Well, if she's bright, it shouldn't be too much of a challenge. And if you like her so much, I'm sure I won't mind her company."

"No, I'm sure you'll get on famously. Perhaps too famously," he said with a sinking feeling. He had a sudden vision of Belle and Henry and God knows what other females aligning themselves into a coalition. There was no telling what they could accomplish—or destroy—if they worked together. No man would be safe.

"Oh, do not try to wound me with your beleaguered male expression," Belle said. "Tell me a little about this Henry."

"What do you want to know?"

"I don't know. What does she look like?"

Dunford pondered this, wondering why it was so

difficult to describe her. "Well, her hair is brown," he began. "Mostly brown, that is. There are streaks of gold in it. Well, not really streaks, but when the sun hits it just so, it looks quite blond. Not like yours, but . . . I don't know, not quite brown anymore."

Belle fought the urge to jump on the table and dance with glee, but ever the strategist, she schooled her features into a polite but interested mask and asked, "And her eyes?"

"Her eyes? They're gray. Well, actually more silvery than gray. I suppose most people would just call them gray, however." He paused. "Silver. They're silver."

"Are you certain?"

Dunford opened his mouth, about to say that they must be silvery-gray, when he noted the teasing tone in Belle's voice and clamped his mouth shut.

Belle's lips twitched as she suppressed a smile. "I'd be happy to have her stay here. Or better yet, we'll install her at my parents' house. No one would dare cut her if my mother gave her support."

Dunford stood. "Good. When may I bring her?"

"The sooner the better, I think. We don't want her over at your lodgings for a minute longer than is necessary. I'll call on my mother immediately and meet you there."

"Excellent," he said curtly, giving her a slight bow.

Belle watched him as he strode from the room, then finally allowed her jaw to drop in shock over the way he had described Henry. The thousand pounds were hers. She could practically feel the money in her hand.

Chapter 12

Belle's mother, as expected, took Henry firmly under her wing. She couldn't quite manage to call her by her nickname, however, preferring to use the more formal "Henrietta." "Not," Caroline had said, "that I disapprove of your moniker. It is simply that my husband's name is also Henry, and it's rather disconcerting for me to use it on a girl of your tender years."

Henry had only smiled and told her that that was just fine. It had been so long since she had had a maternal figure that she would have been inclined to let Caroline call her Esmerelda if she so desired.

Henry hadn't wanted to enjoy her time in London, but Belle and her mother were making it exceedingly difficult for her to keep her spirits low. They conquered her fears with kindness, slayed her uncertainties with jokes and good humor. Henry missed her life at Stannage Park, but she had to allow that Dunford's friends had brought a certain measure of happiness into her life that she hadn't even realized was missing.

She had forgotten what it meant to have a family.

Caroline had grand plans for her new charge, and within the first week, Henry had visited the modiste, the milliner, the modiste, the bookshop, the modiste, the glove shop, and, of course, the modiste. More than once, Caroline had shaken her head and declared that *she* had never seen a young lady who needed quite so many articles of clothing at one time.

Which was why, Henry thought in agony, they were at the dressmaker's shop for the seventh time in one week. The first couple of visits had been exciting, but now it was exhausting.

"Most of us," Caroline said with a pat on the hand, "try to do this a bit at a time. With you, however, that wasn't an option."

Henry smiled tightly in response as Madame Lambert jabbed another pin in her side.

"Oh, Henry," Belle laughed. "Do try not to look quite so pained."

Henry shook her head. "I think she drew blood that time."

The dressmaker choked back her indignation, but Caroline, the much-esteemed Countess of Worth, hid her smile behind her hand. When Henry went into the back room to change, she turned to her daughter and whispered, "I think I like this girl."

"I know I do," Belle replied firmly. "And I think Dunford does too."

"You don't mean to say he is interested in her?"

Belle nodded. "I don't know if he knows it yet. If he does, he certainly does not want to admit it."

Caroline pursed her lips. "It's high time that young man settled down."

"I have a thousand pounds riding on it."

"You don't!"

"I do. I wagered him several months ago that he would be married within a year."

"Well, we'll certainly have to make sure that our dear Henrietta blossoms into a veritable goddess." Caroline's blue eyes sparkled with matchmaking mischief. "I shouldn't want my only daughter to lose such a large sum of money."

The next day Henry was eating breakfast with the earl and countess when Belle stopped by with her husband, Lord Blackwood. John was a handsome man with warm brown eyes and thick, dark hair. He also, Henry noticed with surprise, limped.

"So this is the lady who has had my wife so busy for the past week," he said graciously, leaning over and kissing her hand.

Henry blushed, unused to the courtly gesture. "I promise you may have her back soon. I'm almost done with my pre-society studies."

John stifled a laugh. "Oh, and what have you learned?"

"*Very* important things, my lord. For example, if I am going up a flight of stairs, I must follow a gentleman, but if I am going down, he must follow me."

"I assure you," he said with an amazingly straight face, "that that is a useful thing to know."

"Of course. And the horror of it is, I have been doing it wrong all these years and did not even know it."

John managed to hold on to his deadpan expression for one more exchange. "And were you incorrect going up or going down?"

"Oh, going up, to be sure. You see," she said, leaning forward conspiratorially, "I am vastly impatient, and I cannot imagine having to wait for a gentleman if I want to go upstairs."

John burst out laughing. "Belle, Caroline, I think you have a success on your hands."

Henry turned and nudged Belle with her elbow. "Did you notice I managed to use 'vastly'? It wasn't easy, you know. And how was that for flirting? So sorry I had to use your husband, but he was the only gentleman about."

There was a loud "ahem" from the head of the table.

Henry smiled innocently as her eyes flew to the face of Belle's father. "Oh, I beg your pardon, Lord Worth, but I cannot flirt with you. Lady Worth would *kill* me."

"And I wouldn't?" Belle asked, laughter dancing in her bright blue eyes.

"Oh, no, you're much too kind."

"And I'm not?" Caroline teased.

Henry opened her mouth, shut it, then opened it again to say, "I believe I have gotten myself into a bit of a bind."

"And what bind is that?"

Henry's heart lurched at the achingly familiar voice. Dunford was standing in the doorway, looking breathtakingly handsome in buff-colored breeches and a bottle-green coat. "I thought I'd drop in and check on Henry's progress," he said.

"She's doing superbly," Caroline replied. "And we are delighted to have her. I haven't laughed so much in years."

Henry smiled cheekily. "I'm very entertaining."

John and the earl both coughed, presumably to cover their smiles.

Dunford, however, didn't bother to hide his. "I was also wondering if you'd like to go for a walk this afternoon."

Henry's eyes lit up. "Oh, I would like that above all else." Then she spoiled the effect by nudging Belle again and saying, "Did you hear that? I managed to use 'above all else.' It's a silly phrase, to be sure, but I think I am finally beginning to sound like a debutante."

No one was able to hide his smile that time.

"Excellent," Dunford replied. "I shall come for you at two." He nodded to the earl and countess, saying that he would see himself out.

"I'll take my leave now as well," John said. "I've much to do this morning." He dropped a kiss on the top of his wife's head and followed Dunford through the door.

Belle and Henry excused themselves and retired to the drawing room, where they planned to go over titles and rules of precedence until the midday meal. Henry was not in the least excited about the prospect.

"How did you like my husband?" Belle asked once they were seated.

"He was lovely, Belle. He is obviously a man of great kindness and integrity. I could see it in his eyes. You are very lucky to have him."

Belle smiled and even blushed just a little. "I know."

Henry tossed her a sideways smile. "And he is quite handsome, too. The limp is very dashing."

"I have always thought so. He used to be frightfully self-conscious about it, but now I think he barely notices it."

"Was he injured in the war?"

Belle nodded, her expression growing dark. "Yes. He's very lucky to have the leg at all."

They were both silent for a moment, and then Henry suddenly said, "He reminds me a bit of Dunford."

"Dunford?" Belle blinked in surprise. "Really? Do you think so?"

"Absolutely. Same brown hair and eyes, although perhaps Dunford's hair is a bit thicker. And I think his shoulders might be a trifle broader."

"Really?" Belle leaned forward interestedly.

"Mmmm. And he's very handsome, of course."

"Dunford? Or my husband?"

"Both," Henry said quickly. "But . . ." Her words trailed off, as she realized it would be unforgivably rude to point out that Dunford was obviously the more handsome of the two.

Belle, of course, *knew* her husband was obviously better looking, but nothing in the world would have pleased her more than to hear that Henry disagreed. She smiled and made a soft murmuring sound, subtly encouraging Henry to continue speaking.

"And," Henry added, obliging Belle fully, "it was just lovely of your husband to kiss you good-bye. Even I know enough of the *ton* to know that is not considered de rigueur."

Belle didn't even have to look at Henry to know she was wishing that Dunford would do the same to her.

When the clock struck two, Henry had to be dissuaded from waiting on the doorstep. Belle managed to get her to sit in the drawing room and tried to explain that most ladies chose to remain upstairs and keep their callers waiting for several minutes. Henry didn't listen.

Part of the reason she was so excited to see Dunford was that she had discovered a newfound appreciation for herself and her qualities as a woman. Belle and her family seemed to like her tremendously, and it was her understanding that they were very well respected among the *ton*. And although Caroline's constant fussing with her hair and wardrobe could be most vexing, it was beginning to give Henry hope that she just might be pretty after all. Not ravishingly beautiful like Belle, whose wavy, blond hair and bright blue eyes had inspired sonnets among the more poetically minded of the *ton,* but she was certainly not wholly unattractive.

As Henry's self-esteem inched upward, she began to think that she just might have a tiny chance of inducing Dunford to love her. He already liked her; surely that was half the battle. Maybe she could compete with the sophisticated ladies of the *ton,* after all. She wasn't really certain how to make this miracle occur, but she did know that she was going to have to spend as much time as possible in his presence if she was going to make any progress.

And that was why, when she looked up at the clock and noticed it was two o'clock, her heart began to race.

Dunford arrived at two minutes past the hour and discovered Belle and Henry studying a copy of *Debrett's Peerage.* Or rather, Belle was trying very hard to force Henry to study it, and Henry was trying very hard to toss the book out the window.

"I see you're enjoying your time together," Dunford drawled.

"Oh, very much," Belle returned, snatching the book before Henry managed to drop it into an antique spittoon.

"Very much, my lord," Henry echoed. "I'm supposed to call you 'my lord,' I've discovered."

"I would that you meant it," he muttered under his breath. Such obedience from Henry would be a boon, indeed.

"Not Baron or Baron Stannage," she continued. "Apparently no one uses the word 'baron' except when talking *about* someone. Bloody useless title, I think, if no one knows you've got it."

"Er, Henry, you might want to curb your use of the word 'bloody,' " Belle felt obliged to point out. "And everyone does know he's got the title. That's what *this* is all about." She motioned to the book in her hand.

"I know." Henry made a face. "And do not worry, I won't say 'bloody' in public unless someone has severed one of my arteries and I'm in danger of bleeding to death."

"Er, and that's another thing," Belle said.

"I know, I know, no mention of anatomy in public, either. I'm afraid I was raised on a farm, and we are not quite so squeamish."

Dunford took her arm and said to Belle, "I'd better get her out of the house before she burns it down from boredom."

Belle bid them both a good time, and they were on their way, a housemaid trailing a respectable few feet behind them.

"This is most odd," Henry whispered after they had reached the edge of Grosvenor Square. "I feel as if I am being stalked."

"You'll get used to it." He paused. "Are you truly enjoying yourself here in London?"

Henry thought about that before answering. "You were right about making friends. I adore Belle. And Lord and Lady Worth have been most kind. I suppose I didn't know what I was missing by remaining so isolated at Stannage Park."

"Good," he replied, patting her gloved hand.

"But I do miss Cornwall," she said wistfully. "Especially the clean air and the green fields."

"And Rufus," he teased.

"And Rufus."

"But are you glad you came?" Dunford stopped walking. He didn't realize it, but he was holding his breath, so important was it to him that she reply in the affirmative.

"Yes," she said slowly. "Yes, I think so."

He smiled gently. "You only *think* so?"

"I'm afraid, Dunford."

"Of what, Hen?" He stared at her, his eyes intent.

"What if I make a cake of myself? What if I do something beyond the pale without even knowing it?"

"You won't, Hen."

"Oh, but I *could.* It would be so easy."

"Hen, Caroline and Belle say you're making great strides. They know a great deal about society. If they say you are ready to make your debut, I assure you, you're ready."

"They have taught me so much, Dunford. I know that. But I also know they can't possibly teach me everything in a fortnight. And if I do something wrong . . ." Her words trailed off, and her silvery eyes glowed large and luminous with apprehension.

He wanted so badly to pull her into his arms, to rest his chin upon her head and assure her that everything would be all right. But they were standing in a public garden, and so he had to content himself with saying, "What will happen if you do something wrong, minx? Will the world fall apart? Will the heavens crash down upon us? I think not."

"Please don't make light of this," she said, her lower lip trembling.

"I'm not. Hen, I only meant—"

"I know," she interrupted, her voice wobbly. "It's just that—well, you know already I'm not very good at being a girl, and if I do something wrong, it reflects badly upon *you.* And Lady Worth and Belle and their whole family, and they have been so kind to me and—"

"Henry, *stop,*" he implored. "Just be yourself. Everything will be fine, I promise you."

She looked up at him. After what seemed like an

eternity, she finally nodded. "If you say so. I trust you."

Dunford felt something inside of him lurch and then fall into place as he stared into the silvery depths of her eyes. His body was swaying closer to hers, and he wanted nothing more than to rub his thumb against her pink lips, warming them for a kiss.

"Dunford?"

The soft sound of her voice brought him out of his reverie. He quickly resumed walking, his pace suddenly so fast that Henry practically had to run to keep up with him. Damn it, he swore at himself. He had not brought her to London just so he might continue seducing her. "How is your new wardrobe coming along?" he asked abruptly. "I see you're wearing one of the dresses we purchased in Cornwall."

It took Henry a moment to reply, so confused was she by the sudden change of pace. "Very well," she replied. "Madame Lambert is finishing up the last-minute alterations. Most should be ready by early next week."

"And your studies?"

"I'm not certain that one could call them studies. It certainly doesn't seem a terribly noble endeavor to memorize ranks and orders of preference. I suppose *someone* ought to know that younger sons of marquesses rank below eldest sons of earls, but I do not see why it has to be me." She forced her lips into a smile, hoping to restore his good humor. "Although *you* might be interested in the fact that barons rank above the speaker of the House of Commons, but not, I'm afraid, above sons of marquesses, elder or younger."

"As I ranked below them when I was a mere mister," he replied, thankful that conversation had been steered back to the mundane, "I won't torture myself over the fact that they are still above me, so to speak."

"But you must adopt an air of lordly imperiousness

the next time you encounter the speaker of the House of Commons," Henry instructed with a smile.

"Silly chit."

"I know. I probably should learn to behave with more gravity."

"Not with me, I hope. I like you the way you are."

That familiar giddy feeling returned. "I still do have a number of things to learn, however," she said, glancing at him sideways.

"Such as?"

"Belle tells me I need to learn how to flirt."

"Belle would," he muttered.

"I practiced a bit on her husband this morning."

"You did what?"

"Well, I didn't mean it," Henry said quickly. "And I certainly wouldn't have done so if it weren't completely obvious that he is madly in love with Belle. He seemed a safe choice to try out my skills."

"Stay away from married men," he said sternly.

"*You* aren't married," she pointed out.

"What the hell does that mean?"

Henry glanced idly in the window of a shop they were passing before replying. "Oh, I don't know. I suppose it means I should practice on you."

"Are you serious?"

"Oh, come now, Dunford. Be a good sport. Will you teach me how to flirt?"

"I'd say you're doing just fine on your own," he muttered.

"Do you think so?" she asked, her face a perfect picture of delight.

His body reacted instantly to the radiant joy in her expression, and he told himself not to look at her again. Ever.

But she was tugging on his arm, not to be denied, and pleading, "Won't you please teach me? Please?"

"Oh, all right," he sighed, knowing that this was a most inadvisable idea.

"Oh, splendid. Where shall we start?"

"It's a lovely day today," he said, not quite able to put any feeling into the words.

"Yes, it is, but I thought we were going to concentrate on flirting."

He looked at her and then wished he hadn't. His eyes always managed to somehow slide down to her lips. "Most flirtations," he said, taking a ragged breath, "begin with the inanities of polite conversation."

"Oh, I see. All right. Begin again, then, if you will."

He took a deep breath and said flatly, "It's a lovely day today."

"It certainly is. It makes one long to spend time out of doors, don't you think?"

"We *are* out of doors, Henry."

"I'm pretending we're at a ball," she explained. "And may we turn into the park? Perhaps we can find a bench upon which to sit."

Dunford steered them silently into Green Park.

"May we begin again?" she asked.

"We haven't progressed much thus far."

"Nonsense. I'm certain we'll succeed once we get started. Now, I just said that the day makes one long to spend time out of doors."

"Certainly," he replied laconically.

"Dunford, you are not making this easy." She spotted a bench and sat down, making space for him next to her. Her maid stood quietly under a tree ten or so yards away.

"I don't want to make it easy. I don't want to do this at all."

"Surely you see the necessity of my knowing how to converse with gentlemen. Now please help me and try to get into the spirit of the endeavor."

Dunford's jaw clenched. She was going to have to learn she couldn't push him too far. He curved his lips into a wicked half-smile. If it was flirting she wanted, it was flirting she was going to get. "All right. Let me begin anew."

Henry smiled happily.

"You're beautiful when you smile."

Her heart dropped down to her feet. She couldn't say a word.

"Flirting takes two, you know," he drawled. "You'll be thought a lackwit if you don't have anything to say."

"I-I thank you, my lord," she said, working up her boldness. "That is indeed a compliment, coming from you."

"And just what does that mean, pray tell?"

"It is certainly no secret that you are a connoisseur of women, my lord."

"You have been gossiping about me."

"Not at all. I cannot help it if your behavior makes you a frequent topic of conversation."

"Excuse me?" he said icily.

"The women throw themselves at you, I hear. Why have you not married one of them, I wonder?"

"That is not for you to wonder, sweetheart."

"Ah, but I cannot help where my mind wanders."

"*Never* let a man call you sweetheart," he ordered.

It took her a second to realize that he had broken character. "But it was only *you,* Dunford," she said in an excruciatingly placating tone.

Somehow that managed to make him feel as if he were a feeble, gout-ridden old man. "I am just as dangerous as the rest of them," he said in a hard voice.

"To me? But you're my guardian."

If they hadn't been in the middle of a public park, he would have grabbed her and shown her just how dangerous he could be. It was amazing how she could provoke him. One moment he was trying to be the wise but stern guardian, and the next he was desperately trying to restrain himself from taking her for a tumble.

"All right," Henry said, warily assessing his thunderous expression. "How about this. La, sir, but you should not call me sweetheart."

"It's a start, but if you happen to be holding a fan, I strongly urge you to poke it into the bounder's eye as well."

Henry was a bit heartened by the note of possessiveness she sensed in his voice. "But as it happens, I am not currently in possession of a fan, and what would I do if a gentleman does not heed my verbal warning?"

"Then you should run in the opposite direction. Quickly."

"But just for the sake of argument, let's say I am cornered. Or perhaps I am in the middle of a crowded ballroom and do not want to make a scene. If you were flirting with a young lady who had just told you not to call her sweetheart, what would you do?"

"I would accede to her wishes and bid her good night," he said starchily.

"You would not!" Henry accused with a playful smile. "You're a terrible rake, Dunford. Belle told me."

"Belle talks too much," he muttered.

"She was merely warning me of the gentlemen with whom I must be on my guard. And," she said, shrugging delicately, "when she named the rakes, you were near the top of the list."

"How kind of her."

"Of course, you are my guardian," she said thoughtfully. "And so merely being seen with you will not ruin my reputation. That is certainly fortunate, as I do so enjoy your company."

"I would say, Henry," Dunford said with deliberate slowness and evenness, "that you do not need very much more practice on how to flirt."

She smiled brightly. "I will take that as a compliment, coming from *you.* I understand you are a master of the art of seduction."

Her words made him extremely irritated, indeed.

"However, I think you're being overly optimistic. I probably do need just a bit more practice. To give me the self-confidence to face the *ton* at my first ball," she explained, her face looking marvelously earnest. "Perhaps I might be able to enlist Belle's brother. He is finishing up at Oxford soon, I understand, and will be returning to London for the season."

It was Dunford's opinion that Belle's brother Ned was still a trifle green, but he was nonetheless well on his way to becoming a rake. And then there was the annoying point that he was extremely good-looking, having been blessed with the same stunning blue eyes and marvelous bone structure as Belle. Not to mention the even more vexing fact that he would be residing under the same roof as Henry.

"No, Henry," Dunford said in a very low, very dangerous voice. "I do not think you should practice your feminine wiles on Ned."

"Do you think not?" she asked blithely. "He seems a perfect choice."

"It would be extremely dangerous to your health."

"Whatever does that mean? I cannot imagine that Belle's brother would ever hurt me."

"But *I* would."

"You would?" she breathed. "What would you do?"

"If you think," he bit out, "that I'm going to answer that question, you are feeble-minded, if not insane."

Henry's eyes widened. "Oh, my."

"Oh, my, indeed. I want you to listen to me," he said, his eyes boring dangerously into hers. "You are to stay away from Ned Blydon, you are to stay away from married men, and you are to stay away from *all* of the rakes on Belle's list."

"Including you?"

"Of course not including me," he snapped. "I'm your goddamned guardian." He clamped his mouth shut, barely able to believe he'd lost his temper to the extent that he'd sworn at her.

Henry, however, seemed not to notice his foul language. "*All* of the rakes?"

"All of them."

"Then whom may I set my cap for?"

Dunford opened his mouth, fully intending to rattle off a list of names. To his surprise, he couldn't come up with even one.

"There must be someone," she prodded.

He glared at her, thinking that he'd like to take his hand and wipe that impossibly cheerful expression off her face. Or better yet, he'd do it with his mouth.

"Don't tell me I'm going to have to spend the entire season with just *you* for a companion." It was difficult, but Henry just managed to keep the hopefulness out of her voice.

Dunford abruptly stood, practically hauling her up along with him. "We'll find someone. In the meantime let's go home."

They hadn't taken three steps when they heard someone call out Dunford's name. Henry looked up and saw an extremely elegant, extremely well-dressed, and extremely beautiful woman heading their way. "A friend of yours?" she asked.

"Lady Sarah-Jane Wolcott."

"Another of your conquests?"

"No," he said testily.

Henry quickly assessed the predatory gleam in the woman's eye. "She'd like to be."

He turned on her. "*What* did you just say?"

She was saved from having to reply by the arrival of Lady Wolcott. Dunford greeted her and then introduced the two ladies.

"A ward?" Lady Wolcott trilled. "How charming."

Charming? Henry wanted to echo. But she kept her mouth shut.

"How utterly domestic of you," Lady Wolcott continued, touching Dunford's arm—rather suggestively, in Henry's opinion.

"I don't know if I would call it 'domestic,' " Dunford replied politely, "but it certainly has been a new experience."

"Oh, I'm sure." Lady Wolcott wet her lips. "It's not at all in your usual style. You are usually given to more athletic—and masculine—pursuits."

Henry was so livid she thought it a wonder she didn't start hissing. Her hand quite involuntarily clenched, forming claws she *really* wanted to rake across the elder lady's face.

"Rest assured, Lady Wolcott," Dunford replied, "I am finding my role as guardian to be most informative and character-building."

"Character-building? Pish. How dull. You'll soon grow bored. Come and call when you do. I'm sure we can find ways to entertain ourselves."

Dunford sighed. Normally he'd have been tempted to take Sarah-Jane up on her rather blatant offer, but with Henry in tow he suddenly felt the need to take the moral high road. "Tell me," he said sharply. "How is Lord Wolcott faring these days?"

"Doddering away in Dorset. As usual. He's really of no concern here in London." She gave Dunford one last seductive smile, nodded sleekly at Henry, and was on her way.

"Is *that* how I am meant to behave?" Henry asked disbelievingly.

"Absolutely not."

"Then—"

"Just be yourself," he said curtly. "Just be yourself, and stay away from—"

"I know. I know. Stay away from married men, Ned Blydon, and rakes of every variety. Just be so good as to let me know if you think of someone else I must add to the list."

Dunford scowled.

Henry smiled all the way home.

Chapter 13

One week later Henry was ready to be presented to society. Caroline had decided that her charge would make her bow at the annual Lindworthy bash. It was always a huge affair, Caroline had explained, so if Henry was a smashing success, everyone would know about it.

"But what if I am a miserable failure?" Henry had asked.

Caroline had given her a smile that said she did not think that was much of a worry and said, "Then you shall be able to lose yourself in the crowd."

Fairly reasonable logic, Henry had thought.

Belle came over on the night of the ball to help her dress. They had chosen a gown of white silk shot through with silver thread. "You are very lucky, you know," she said as she and a maid helped Henry into it. "Young ladies just out are supposed to wear white, but many look hideous in the color."

"Do I?" Henry asked quickly, panic rising in her

eyes. She wanted to look perfect. As perfect as she could, at least, with what graces God had bestowed upon her. She desperately wanted to show Dunford she could be the kind of woman he'd want by his side here in London. She had to prove to him—and to herself—that she could be more than a farm girl.

"Of course not," Belle said reassuringly. "Mama and I never would have let you buy this gown had it not looked perfectly enchanting on you. My cousin Emma wore violet at her debut. It shocked some, but, as Mama said, white makes Emma look yellow. Better to defy tradition than to look like a pot of custard."

Henry nodded as Belle did up the buttons at the back of her gown. She tried to turn around to look in the mirror, but Belle put a gently restraining hand on her shoulder, saying, "Not yet. Wait until you can see the full effect."

Belle's maid Mary spent the next hour carefully arranging her hair, curling it here and teasing it there. Henry waited in agonized suspense. Finally Belle popped a pair of diamond earbobs on her ears and draped a matching necklace around her throat.

"But whose are these?" Henry asked in a surprised voice.

"Mine."

Henry immediately reached up to her ears to remove the jewelry. "Oh, but I couldn't."

Belle pulled her hand back down. "Of course you can."

"But what if I lose them?"

"You won't."

"But what if I do?" Henry persisted.

"Then it will by my fault for having lent them to you. Now be quiet and take a look at our handiwork." Belle smiled and turned her around to face the mirror.

Henry was stunned into silence. Finally she whispered, "Is that me?" Her eyes seemed to sparkle in time with the diamonds, and her face glowed with innocent promise. Mary had swept her thick hair into an elegant French twist and then pulled feathery tendrils out to curl mischievously around her face. These wisps glowed gold in the candlelight, lending her an almost ethereal air.

"You look magical," Belle said with a smile.

Henry stood slowly, still unable to believe the reflection in the glass was really hers. The silver threads in her dress caught the light when she moved, and as she walked across the room, she shimmered and sparkled, looking not quite of this world, almost too precious to touch. She took a deep breath, trying to control some of the heady feelings rushing through her. She had never known, never dreamed she could feel beautiful. And she did. She felt like a princess—like a fairy princess with the world at her feet. She could conquer London. She could glide across the floor even more gracefully than the women with rollers for feet. She could laugh and sing and dance until dawn. She smiled and hugged herself. She could do anything.

She even thought she could make Dunford fall in love with her. And that was the headiest feeling of all.

The man who occupied her thoughts was presently waiting downstairs with Belle's husband John and their good friend Alexander Ridgely, the Duke of Ashbourne.

"So tell me," Alex was saying as he swirled some whiskey around in a glass. "Who exactly is this young woman I'm supposed to champion this evening? And how did you manage to get yourself a ward, Dunford?"

"Came with the title. It was even more of a shock than the barony, to tell the truth. Thank you, by the way, for coming by to lend your support. Henry hasn't been out of Cornwall since she was ten or so, and she's terrified at the prospect of a London season."

Alex immediately pictured a meek, retiring miss and sighed. "I'll do my best."

John caught his expression, grinned, and said, "You'll like this girl, Alex. I guarantee it."

Alex arched a brow.

"I'm serious." John decided to pay Henry the highest of compliments by saying she reminded him of Belle, but then he remembered he was speaking to a man who was as besotted with his wife as John was with his own. "She's rather like Emma," John said instead. "I'm certain the two of them will get along quite famously."

"Oh, please," Dunford scoffed. "She's nothing like Emma."

"Pity for her, then," Alex said.

Dunford shot him an annoyed look.

"Why don't you think she's like Emma?" John asked mildly.

"If you had seen her in Cornwall, you'd know. She wore breeches all the time and managed a farm, for God's sake."

"I find your tone hard to discern," Alex said. "Was that supposed to make me admire the girl or scorn her?"

Another scowl from Dunford. "Just beam approvingly in her general direction and dance with her once or twice. As much as I loathe the way society panders to you, I'm not above using your position to ensure her success."

"Anything you wish," Alex said affably, ignoring his friend's caustic comments. "Although don't think I'm doing this for you. Emma said she'd have my head if I didn't help Belle out with her new protégé."

"As well you should," Belle said pertly, entering the room in a cloud of blue silk.

"Where is Henry?" Dunford asked.

"Right here." Belle stepped aside to let Henry enter.

All three men looked at the woman in the doorway, but they all saw different things.

Alex saw a rather attractive young lady with a remarkable air of vitality in her silver eyes.

John saw the woman he'd come to like and admire tremendously this past week, looking rather fetching and grown-up in her new gown and coiffure.

Dunford saw an angel.

"My God, Henry," he breathed, taking an involuntary step toward her. "What happened to you?"

Henry's face crumpled. "Don't you like it? Belle said—"

"No!" he burst out, his voice oddly raw. He rushed forward and clasped her hands. "I mean yes. I mean you look marvelous."

"Are you certain? Because I could change—"

"Don't change a *thing*," he said sternly.

She stared up at him, knowing her heart was in her eyes but quite unable to do a thing about it. Finally Belle broke in, saying in an amused voice, "Henry, I really must introduce you to my cousin."

Henry blinked and turned to the black-haired, green-eyed man standing next to John. He was magnetically handsome, she thought rather objectively, but she hadn't even noticed him when she'd walked into the room. She hadn't been able to see anyone except Dunford.

"Miss Henrietta Barrett," Belle said, "may I present the Duke of Ashbourne?"

Alex took her hand and dropped a light kiss on her knuckles. "I'm delighted to meet you, Miss Barrett," he said smoothly, casting a wicked glance at Dunford, who had clearly just realized he'd made a cake of himself over his ward. "Not as delighted as our friend Dunford, perhaps, but delighted nonetheless."

Henry's eyes danced, and a wide smile broke out over her face. "Please call me Henry, your grace—"

"Everybody does," Dunford finished for her.

She shrugged helplessly. "It's true. Except for Lady Worth."

"Henry," Alex said, testing the sound of it out. "It suits you, I think. Certainly more than does Henrietta."

"I don't think *Henrietta* suits anyone," she replied. Then she offered him her cheeky smile, and Alex saw in an instant why Dunford was falling like a rock for this girl. She had spirit, and although she didn't realize it yet, she had beauty, and Dunford didn't have a chance.

"I expect not," Alex said. "My wife is expecting our first child in two months. I shall have to make certain we don't name her Henrietta."

"Oh, yes," Henry said suddenly, as if she'd just remembered something important. "You're married to Belle's cousin. She must be lovely."

Alex's eyes softened. "Yes, she is. I hope you get a chance to meet her. She would like you very much."

"Not half as much as I will like her, I'm sure, as she had the good sense to marry *you*." Henry shot a daring glance over at Dunford. "Oh, but please forget I said that, your grace. Dunford has insisted I not speak to married men." As if to illustrate her point, she took a step back.

Alex burst out laughing.

"Ashbourne is permissible," Dunford said with a half-suppressed groan.

"I hope I'm not off limits too," John added.

Henry looked askance at her beleaguered guardian.

"John is fine as well," he said, his voice growing slightly irritable.

"My congratulations, Dunford," Alex said, wiping the tears of laughter from his eyes. "I predict you'll have a resounding success on your hands. The suitors will be breaking down your door."

If Dunford was pleased by his friend's pronouncement, it didn't show on his face.

Henry beamed. "Do you really think so? I must confess I know very little about going about in society. Caroline has told me I am oftentimes a touch too candid."

"That," Alex said in a self-assured voice, "is why you are going to be a success."

"We should be on our way," Belle cut in. "Mama and Papa have already left for the ball, and I told them we would be along shortly. Shall we all go in one carriage? I think we'll be able to squeeze in."

"Henry and I will go alone," Dunford said smoothly, taking her arm. "There are a few things I would like to discuss with her before she is presented." He steered her toward the doorway, and together they swept from the room.

It was probably just as well that he couldn't see the three identical smiles of amusement directed at their backs.

"What was it you wanted to talk to me about?" Henry asked once their carriage had started out.

"Nothing," he admitted. "I thought you might like a few moments of peace before we arrive at the party."

"That is very thoughtful of you, my lord."

"Oh, for God's sake," he scowled. "Whatever you do, do *not* call me 'my lord.' "

"I was just practicing," she murmured.

There was a moment of silence, then he asked, "Are you nervous?"

"A bit," she admitted. "Your friends are lovely, though, and they put me quite at ease."

"Good." He patted her hand in a paternal manner.

Henry could feel the heat of his hand through both of their gloves, and she ached to prolong the touch. But she didn't know how to do this, so she did what she always did when her emotions bubbled too close to the surface: she grinned impishly. Then she patted *his* hand.

Dunford leaned back, thinking that Henry must be marvelously self-contained to tease him in such a manner on the eve of her debut. She turned abruptly away from him to stare out the window as London rolled by. He studied her profile, noting curiously that the jaunty look that had been in her eye had disappeared. He was about to ask her about this when she wet her lips.

Dunford's heart slammed in his chest.

He had never dreamed Henry would be so transformed by a fortnight in London, never thought the cheeky country girl could grow into this alluring—although equally cheeky—woman. He longed to touch the line of her throat, to run his hand along the embroidered edge of her neckline, to delve his fingers into the magnificent warmth that lay below it . . .

He shuddered, well aware that his thoughts were leading his body in a rather uncomfortable direction. And he was becoming painfully cognizant of the fact that he was beginning to care for her too damned much, and certainly not in the way a guardian was meant to care for his ward.

It would be so easy to seduce her. He knew he had the power to do so, and even though Henry had grown frightened at their last encounter, he didn't think she would try to stop him again. He could wash her over with pleasure. She'd never even know what had hit her.

He shuddered, as if the physical motion could restrain him from leaning across the seat and taking the first step toward his goal. He hadn't brought Henry to London to seduce her. Good Lord, he thought wryly, how many times had he had to repeat that refrain during the past few weeks? But it was true, and she had a right to meet all of London's eligible bachelors. He was going to have to back off and let her see for herself who else was out there.

It was that damned chivalrous instinct. Life would be a lot simpler if his honor didn't always intrude when it came to this girl.

Henry turned back to face him, and her lips parted slightly, startled by the harsh expression etched in his face. "Is something wrong?" she quietly asked.

"No," he replied, a little more gruffly than he'd intended.

"You're upset with me."

"Why on earth would I be upset with you?" he all but snapped.

"You certainly *sound* as if you're upset with me."

He sighed. "I'm upset with myself."

"But why is that?" Henry asked, her face showing her concern.

Dunford cursed himself under his breath. Now what was he to say? *I'm upset because I want to seduce you? I'm upset because you smell like lemons and I'm dying to know why? I'm upset because—*

"You don't have to say anything," Henry said, clearly sensing he did not want to share his feelings with her. "Just let me cheer you up."

His groin tightened at the thought.

"Shall I tell you what happened to Belle and me yesterday? It was most amusing. It was . . . No, I can see that you do not want to hear."

"That's not true," he forced himself to say.

"Well, we went to Hardiman's Tea Shoppe, and . . . You're not listening."

"I am," he assured her, working his face back into a more pleasant expression.

"All right," she said slowly, giving him an assessing glance. "This lady came in, and her hair was quite green . . ."

Dunford made no remark.

"You're *not* listening," she accused.

"I was," he started to protest. Then he saw her dubious expression and admitted with a boyish grin, "I wasn't."

She smiled at him then, not the familiar cheeky smile to which he'd grown so accustomed, but one born of sheer mirth, artless in its beauty.

Dunford was entranced. He leaned forward, not realizing what he was doing.

"You want to kiss me," she whispered with wonder.

He shook his head.

"You do," she persisted. "I can see it in your eyes. You're looking at me the way I always want to look at you, but I don't know how, and—"

"Shhh." He pressed his finger to her lips.

"I wouldn't mind," she whispered against him.

Dunford's blood pounded. She was an inch away from him, a vision in white silk, and she was giving him *permission* to kiss her. Permission to do what he'd been aching to do . . .

His finger slid from her mouth, catching on her full lower lip in its descent.

"Please," she whispered.

"This doesn't mean anything," he murmured.

She shook her head. "Nothing."

He leaned forward and cupped her face in his hands. "You're going to go to the ball, meet some nice gentleman . . ."

She nodded. "Anything you say."

"He'll court you . . . Maybe you'll fall in love."

She said nothing.

He was just a hair's breadth away. "And you'll live happily ever after."

She said, "I hope so," but the words were lost against his mouth as he kissed her with such longing and tenderness that she thought she would surely burst with love. He kissed her again, and then again, his lips soft and gentle, his hands warm on her cheeks. Henry moaned his name, and he dipped his tongue between her lips, unable to resist the soft temptation of her mouth.

The new intimacy shattered whatever control he'd been exerting over himself, and his last rational thought was that he mustn't muss her hair . . . His hands slid down to her back, and he pressed her against him, reveling in the heat of her body. "Oh, God, Henry," he groaned. "Oh, Hen."

Dunford could feel her acquiescing and *knew* he was a blackguard. If he had been anywhere other than in a moving carriage on the way to Henry's first ball, he probably would not have had the fortitude to stop, but as it was . . . Oh, Christ, he couldn't ruin her. He wanted her to have a perfect time.

It didn't occur to him that this might be her idea of a perfect time.

He took a ragged breath and tried to tear his lips from hers, but he made it only to her jawline. Her skin was so soft, so warm, he couldn't resist trailing a kiss all the way up to her ear. Finally he managed to pull away, loathing himself for taking such advantage of her. He placed his hands on her shoulders, needing to keep her at arm's length, then realized that any touch between them was potentially explosive, so he pulled back his hands and moved across the seat cushion. Then he moved to the opposite seat.

Henry touched her tingling lips, too innocent to understand his desire was being held in check by a very thin thread. Why had he moved so far away? She knew he was right to stop the kiss. She knew she ought to thank him for it, but couldn't he have remained by her side and at least held her hand? "That certainly didn't mean anything," she tried to joke, her voice breaking on the words.

"For your sake, it had better not."

What did that mean? Henry cursed herself for not having the courage to ask. "I–I must look a mess," she said instead, her voice sounding very hollow to her ears.

"Your hair is fine," he said flatly. "I was careful not to muss it."

That he could have approached their kiss with such cold, clinical detachment was like a bucket of icy water washing over her. "No, of course not. You wouldn't want to ruin me on my first night out."

On the contrary, he thought wryly, he wanted very much to ruin her. To ruin her over and over and over. He wanted to laugh at the poetic justice of it all. After a couple of years of chasing after women and then a decade of having *them* chase after *him,* he'd finally been brought down by a slip of a girl, fresh out of Cornwall, whom he was honor-bound to protect. Good Lord, as her guardian it was practically his sacred duty to keep her pure and chaste for her future husband, whom, incidentally, he was supposed to help her find and choose. He shook his head, as if trying to give himself a stern reminder that this incident was not to be repeated.

Henry saw him shake his head and thought he was replying to her desperate remark about not wanting to ruin her, and cold humiliation prompted her to say, "No, I mustn't do anything to damage my reputation. I might not catch a husband then, and that is the objective here, isn't it?" She glanced over at Dunford. He was pointedly not looking at her, and his jaw was clenched so tightly, she thought his teeth would surely shatter. So he was upset—good! Upset didn't even come close to what she was feeling. She gave a frantic laugh and then added, "I know you say I may return to Cornwall if I wish, but we both know that is a sham now, don't we?'

Dunford turned, but she didn't give him the chance to speak.

"A season," she was saying, her voice rising in pitch, "has only one purpose, and that is to get the lady in question married off and thus off of one's hands. In this case, I suppose, the hands in question would appear to be yours, although you don't seem to be doing such a very good job of getting me off of them."

"Henry, be quiet," he ordered.

"Oh, certainly, my lord. I'll be quiet. A perfectly prim and proper young miss. I wouldn't want to be anything other than the ideal debutante. Heaven forbid I ruin my chances for a good match. Why, I might even catch a viscount."

"If you are lucky," he bit out.

Henry felt as if she'd been slapped. Oh, she knew his primary goal was to marry her off, but it still hurt so much to hear him say it. "Per-perhaps I won't marry," she said, trying for a defiant tone but not quite succeeding. "I don't have to, you know."

"I would hope that you do not purposefully sabotage your chances for finding a husband just to spite me."

She stiffened. "Don't hold yourself in such high esteem, Dunford. I have more important things to think about than spiting you."

"How fortunate for me," he drawled.

"You are hateful," she spat out. "Hateful and . . . and . . . and hateful!"

"Such a vocabulary."

Henry's cheeks flushed red with shame and fury. "You're a cruel man, Dunford. A monster! I don't even know why you kissed me. Did I do something to make you hate me? Did you want to punish me?"

No, his tortured mind responded, *he wanted to punish himself.*

He let out a ragged sigh and said, "I don't hate you, Henry."

But you don't love me either, she wanted to cry out. *You don't love me, and it hurts so much.* Was she so awful? Was there something *wrong* with her? Something that compelled him to degrade her by kissing her so thoroughly yet for no reason other than—God, she couldn't think of any reason. It certainly wasn't the same kind of passion she'd been feeling. He'd been so cold and detached when he was talking about her hair.

She gasped, suddenly realizing to her complete mortification that tears were welling up in her eyes. She hastily turned her face and wiped them away, not caring that the salty drops were probably staining the fine kid of her gloves.

"Oh, God, Hen," Dunford said, compassion in his voice. "Don't—"

"Don't what?" she burst out. "Don't cry? You're a fine one to ask that of me!" She crossed her arms mutinously and used every ounce of her iron will to dry up every tear in her body. After a minute or so she actually felt she was returning to at least some semblance of normality.

And just in time, too, because the carriage rolled to a halt, and Dunford said flatly, "We're here."

Henry wanted nothing more than to just go home.

All the way back to Cornwall.

Chapter 14

Henry held her head high as Dunford helped her down from the carriage. It nearly broke her heart when his hand touched hers, but she was learning how to keep her emotions off her face. If Dunford happened to glance her way, all he would see was a perfectly composed visage, with no sign of grief or anger—but with no sign of happiness either.

They had just alighted when the Blackwoods' carriage arrived behind them. Henry watched as John helped Belle down. Belle immediately rushed to her side, not bothering to wait while Alex disembarked. "What's wrong?" she exclaimed, noting Henry's uncharacteristically tense face.

"Nothing," Henry lied.

But Belle heard the hollowness in her voice. "Obviously *something* is wrong."

"It's nothing, really. I'm just nervous, that's all."

Belle rather doubted Henry could have grown quite that nervous during the short carriage ride. She shot a withering glare in Dunford's direction. He immediately turned away and struck up a conversation with John and Alex.

"What did he do to you?" Belle whispered angrily.

"Nothing!"

"If that is true," Belle said as she gave her a look indicating she didn't for a second believe it was, "then you still had best compose yourself immediately before we go in."

"I am composed," Henry protested. "I don't think I have ever been quite this composed in my life."

"Then un-compose yourself." Belle took Henry's hands in an urgent embrace. "Henry, I've never seen your eyes look so dead. I'm sorry to have to say it that way, but it's the truth. There is nothing to fear. Everyone will love you. Just go in there and be yourself." She paused. "Except for the cursing."

A reluctant smile quivered on Henry's lips.

"And leave off talk of farming," Belle added quickly. "Especially that bit about the pig."

Henry could feel the sparkle returning to her eyes. "Oh, Belle, I do love you. You have been such a good friend."

"You make it very easy," Belle returned, giving her hands an affectionate squeeze. "Are you ready? Good. Dunford and Alex are going to escort you in together. That should ensure you make a big splash. Before Alex married, they were the two most eligible gentlemen in the country."

"But Dunford didn't even have a title."

"It didn't matter. The ladies wanted him anyway."

Henry understood all too well why. But he didn't want her. At least not in any permanent way. A fresh wave of humiliation washed over her as she glanced at him. She suddenly felt an overwhelming need to prove to herself that she was worthy of love, even if Dunford did not agree. Her chin moved up a notch, and a dazzling smile crossed her face. "I'm ready, Belle. I am going to have a *lovely* time."

Belle looked slightly taken aback by Henry's sudden vehemence. "Let's be on our way then. Dunford! Alex! John! We're ready to go in."

The three gentlemen reluctantly broke off their conversation, and Henry found herself flanked by Dunford and Alex. She felt terribly small; both men were a good inch over six feet and rather broad through the shoulders. She knew she was going to be the envy of every lady in the ballroom; she hadn't met too many men of the *ton,* but surely most of them lacked the sheer virility of the three men in her party.

They made their way inside and waited in line for the butler to announce them. Without even realizing it, Henry began to move closer and closer to Alex's side, pulling away from Dunford. Finally Alex leaned down and whispered, "Are you all right, Henry? It's almost our turn."

Henry turned and flashed him the same stunning smile she'd just used on Belle. "I am perfect, your grace. Perfect. I am going to *slay* London. I shall have the *ton* at my feet."

Dunford heard her words and stiffened, pulling her back toward him. "Watch what you do, Henry," he whispered cuttingly. "It wouldn't do for you to make your entrance draped over Ashbourne. It's common knowledge he's devoted to his wife."

"Don't worry," she returned with an insincere grin. "I won't embarrass you. And I promise to be off your hands as soon as possible. I shall endeavor to have *dozens* of marriage proposals. By next week if I can."

Alex had an idea what was going on, and his lips

twitched. He was not so honorable that he was not enjoying Dunford's distress.

"Lord and Lady Blackwood!" the butler boomed.

Henry's breath caught in her throat. They were next.

Alex nudged her playfully and whispered, "Smile."

"His grace, the Duke of Ashbourne! Lord Stannage! Miss Henrietta Barrett!"

A hush fell over the crowd. Henry was not so vain and deluded as to think the *ton* had lost their voices over her incomparable beauty, but she did know that they were all dying to get a look at the lady who'd somehow managed to make her debut on the arms of two of the most desirable men in Britain.

The five friends then made their way over to Caroline, further ensuring Henry's success by proclaiming to the world that the influential Countess of Worth was sponsoring her.

Within minutes Henry was surrounded by young men and women, all eager to make her acquaintance. The men were curious—who was this unknown female and how had she managed to snare the attention of both Dunford and Ashbourne? (The *on-dit* that she was Dunford's legal ward had yet to circulate.) The women were even more curious—for exactly the same reason.

Henry laughed and flirted, teased and sparkled. By sheer force of will she managed to push Dunford from her mind. She pretended each man she met was Alex or John, and each woman was Belle or Caroline. This mental ruse allowed her to relax and be herself—and once she did that, people warmed to her instantly.

"She is a breath of fresh air," Lady Jersey declared, not caring in the least that she was being terribly trite.

Dunford overheard this comment and tried to be proud of his ward, but he couldn't manage it over the irritating possessiveness he felt every time some young fop kissed her hand. And that was nothing compared to the searing spurts of jealousy that rocked through him every time she smiled at one of the many older, more experienced men who also flocked to her side.

Caroline was just now introducing her to the Earl of Billington, a man he usually liked and respected. Damn it, that was the same cheeky smile she usually gave *him.* Dunford made a mental note not to sell Billington the prized Arabian he'd been nosing after all spring.

"I see your ward has made quite a killing."

Dunford turned his head to see Lady Sarah-Jane Wolcott. "Lady Wolcott," he said, lazily inclining his head.

"She's quite a success."

"Yes, she is."

"You must be proud."

He managed a curt nod.

"I must say, I wouldn't have predicted it. Not that she isn't attractive," Lady Wolcott hastened to add. "But she is not in the usual style."

Dunford fixed a deadly stare upon her. "In looks or in personality?"

Sarah-Jane was either exceedingly foolish or she just didn't notice the furious gleam in his eyes. "Both, I suppose. She is rather forward, don't you think?"

"No," he bit off, "I don't."

"Oh." The corners of her lips turned up ever-so-slightly. "Well, I'm sure everyone will realize that soon." She offered him a pouty smile and then moved on.

Dunford swiveled his head to regard Henry once more. *Was* she being too forward? She did have a rather vibrant laugh. He'd always taken it as a sign of a happy and delightful person, but a different sort of man might see it as an invitation. He moved over to Alex's side, where he could keep a better eye on her.

Henry, meanwhile, had managed to convince herself that she was having a splendid time. Everyone seemed to think she was terribly attractive and witty, and to a woman who had spent most of her life without friends, this was a heady combination, indeed. The Earl of Billington was paying her particular attention, and she could tell from the stares she was receiving that he was not usually given to paying court to young debutantes. Henry found him rather attractive and personable and began to think that if there were more men like him, she just might be able to find someone with whom she could be happy. Perhaps even the earl. He seemed intelligent, and although his hair was reddish brown, his warm brown eyes reminded her of Dunford's.

No, Henry thought, that should not be a point in the earl's favor.

Then again, she decided in the spirit of fairness, it shouldn't necessarily be a point against him either.

"And do you ride, Miss Barrett?" the earl was saying.

"Of course," Henry replied. "I grew up on a farm, after all."

Belle coughed.

"Really? I had no idea."

"In Cornwall." Henry decided to spare Belle the agony. "But you do not want to hear about my farm. There must be thousands just like it. Do *you* ride?" She asked that last question with a teasing look in her eye; it was a given that all gentlemen rode.

Billington chuckled. "May I have the pleasure of escorting you for a ride in Hyde Park sometime soon?"

"Oh, but I couldn't do that."

"I'm crushed, Miss Barrett."

"I don't even know your name," Henry continued, her smile lighting up her face. "I couldn't possibly make an appointment to ride with a man I know only as 'the earl.' It's terribly daunting, you know, being merely a 'miss' myself. I'll be quaking the entire time for fear I'll offend you."

This time Billington laughed loudly. He gave her a smart bow. "Charles Wycombe, madam, at your service."

"I should love to go for a ride with you, Lord Billington."

"Do you mean to tell me I went to the trouble of introducing myself to you, and you still mean to call me 'Lord Billington'?"

Henry cocked her head to the side. "I really don't know you very well, Lord Billington. It would be dreadfully improper of me to call you Charles, don't you think?"

"No," he said with a lazy smile, "I don't."

A warm feeling flushed through her, almost, but not quite, identical to what she felt when Dunford smiled at her. Henry decided she liked this feeling even better. There was still that lovely sensation of being wanted, cared for, possibly loved, but with Billington she managed to retain some measure of control. When Dunford chose to bestow one of his grins on her, it was like going over a waterfall.

She could sense him near her, and she glanced to her left. He was there, just as she had known he would be, and he gave her a mocking nod. For one moment Henry's entire body reacted, and she forgot how to breathe. Then her mind retook control, and she turned resolutely back to Lord Billington. "It is good to know your given name, even if I do not intend to use it," she said with a secret smile. "For it is difficult to *think* of you as 'the earl.' "

"Does that mean you will think of me as Charles?"

She shrugged delicately.

It was at that point that Dunford decided he had better intercede. Billington looked as if he wanted nothing more than to take Henry's hand, lead her out to the garden, and kiss her senseless. Dunford found that feeling unpleasantly easy to understand. He took three swift steps and was at her side, putting his arm through hers in a most proprietary manner.

"Billington," he said with as much warmth as he could muster, which, admittedly, wasn't much.

"Dunford. I understand you are responsible for bringing this delightful creature to the attention of the *ton.*"

Dunford nodded. "I am her guardian, yes."

The orchestra struck up the first chords of a waltz. Dunford's hand stole down Henry's arm and settled around her wrist.

Billington executed another bow in Henry's direction. "May I have the pleasure of this dance, Miss Barrett?"

Henry opened her mouth to reply, but Dunford was faster. "Miss Barrett has already promised this dance to me."

"Ah, yes, as her guardian, of course."

The earl's words made Dunford want to rip his lungs out. And Billington was a friend. Dunford clenched his jaw and resisted the urge to growl. What the hell was he going to do when men with whom he *wasn't* friends began to court her?

Henry frowned in irritation. "But—"

Dunford's hand tightened considerably around her wrist. Her protest died a quick death. "It was very nice to meet you, Lord Billington," she said with unfeigned enthusiasm.

He nodded urbanely. "Very nice, indeed."

Dunford scowled. "If you'll excuse us." He started to lead Henry out toward the dance floor.

"Perhaps I don't want to dance with you," Henry ground out.

He arched a brow. "You don't have any choice."

"For a man who is intensely eager to have me married off, you're doing quite a good job of scaring away my suitors."

"I didn't scare Billington away. Trust me, he'll show up on your doorstep tomorrow morning, flowers in one hand, chocolates in the other."

Henry smiled dreamily, mostly just to irritate him. When they reached the dance floor, however, she noticed that the orchestra had begun a waltz. It was still a relatively new dance, and debutantes were not allowed to waltz without the approval of society's leading matrons. She ground to a stubborn halt. "I can't," she said. "I don't have permission."

"Caroline took care of it," he said brusquely.

"Are you certain?"

"If you do not start dancing with me in one second, I will yank you forcibly into my arms, creating such a scene that—"

Henry put her hand on his shoulder with alacrity. "I don't understand you, Dunford," she said as he began to twirl her across the floor.

"Don't you?" he said darkly.

Her eyes flew to his. What did that mean? "No," she said with quiet dignity. "I don't."

He tightened his hold on her waist, unable to resist the temptation of her soft body under his hand. Hell, he didn't even understand himself these days.

"Why is everyone staring at us?" Henry whispered.

"Because, my dear, you are the latest craze. This season's Incomparable. Surely you realize that."

His tone and expression made her flush angrily. "You might try to be a little happy for me. I thought the purpose of this trip was to give me some social polish. Now that I've got it, you can't stand the sight of me."

"That," he said, "is about as far from the truth as anything I've heard."

"Then why . . ." Her words trailed off. She didn't know how to ask what was in her heart.

Dunford could feel the conversation veering toward dangerous waters and sought to bail out quickly. "Billington," he said curtly, "is reputed to be quite a catch."

"Almost as good as you?" she sneered.

"Better, I imagine. But I would advise you to watch your step around him. He's not some young dandy you can wrap around your finger."

"That is precisely why I like him so much."

His hand tightened yet again around her waist. "If you tease him, you may find yourself getting what you ask for."

Her silvery eyes turned hard. "I was not teasing him, and you know it."

He shrugged disdainfully. "People are already talking."

"They are not! I know they aren't. Belle would have said something to me."

"When would she have had the chance? Before or after you teased him into trying to get you on a first-name basis?"

"You're horrid, Dunford. I don't know what has happened to you, but I don't like you very much anymore."

Funny, he didn't like himself much, either. And he liked himself even less when he said, "I saw the way you looked at him, Henry. Having been the recipient of that expression myself, I know exactly what it meant. He thinks you want him, and not just as a matrimonial prize."

"You bastard," she hissed, trying to pull away from him.

His grip turned to steel. "Don't even think about leaving me in the middle of the dance floor."

"I'd leave you in hell if I could."

"I'm sure you would," he said coolly, "and I have no doubt I'll meet the devil in time. But as long as I'm here on this earth, you will dance with me, and you will do so with a smile on your face."

"Smiling," she said hotly, "is not part of the deal."

"And what deal would that be, dear Hen?"

She narrowed her eyes. "One of these days, Dunford, you're going to have to decide whether you like me or you don't, because quite honestly, I cannot be expected to anticipate your moods. One moment you're quite the nicest man I know, and the next you're the devil himself."

" 'Nice' is such a bland word."

"I wouldn't trouble myself over it if I were you, because that is not the adjective I would use to describe you right now."

"I assure you, I was not having palpitations over it."

"Tell me, Dunford, what is it that makes you so horrid every now and then? Earlier this evening you were so lovely." Her eyes grew wistful. "So kind to assure me I looked all right."

He thought wryly that she looked far better than "all right." And *that* was at the root of the problem.

"You made me feel like a princess, an angel. And now . . ."

"And now what?" he asked in a low voice.

She looked him straight in the eye. "Now you're trying to make me feel like a whore."

Dunford felt as if he'd been punched, but he welcomed the pain. He deserved no less. "That, Hen," he finally said, "is the agony of unfulfilled desire."

She missed a step. "*Whaaaat?*"

"You heard me. You cannot have failed to realize I want you."

She blushed and swallowed nervously, wondering if it were at all possible that the other five hundred partygoers did not notice her distress. "There is a difference between wanting and loving, my lord, and I will not accept one without the other."

"As you wish." The music ended, and Dunford executed a smart bow.

Before Henry had a chance to react, he disappeared into the crowd. Guided by instinct, she made her way to the perimeter of the ballroom, intending to find a washroom where she might have a few moments of privacy to regain her composure. She was waylaid, however, by Belle, who said that there were a few people she wanted Henry to meet.

"Could it wait for a few minutes? I really need to go to the retiring room. I think—I think I have a small tear in my dress."

Belle knew precisely with whom Henry had been dancing and guessed something was amiss. "I'll go with you," she declared, much to the consternation of her husband, who was prompted to ask Alex why it was that ladies always seemed to need to go to the retiring room in pairs.

Alex shrugged. "It's destined to be one of the great mysteries of life, I think. I for one am deathly afraid of finding out what exactly goes on in these retiring rooms."

"It's where they keep all the good liquor," Belle said pertly.

"That explains it, then. Oh, by the by, have any of you seen Dunford? I wanted to ask him something." He turned to Henry. "Weren't you just dancing with him?"

"I'm sure I haven't the slightest idea where he is."

Belle smiled stiffly. "We'll see you later, Alex. John." She turned to Henry. "Follow me. I know the way." She navigated her way around the edge of the ballroom with remarkable speed, stopping only to pluck two glasses of champagne off a tray. "Here," she said, handing one to Henry. "We might need these."

"In the washroom?"

"With no men about? It's the perfect place for a toast."

"I don't much feel like celebrating right now, I must say."

"I thought not, but a drink might be just the thing."

They turned into a hallway, and Henry followed Belle into a small chamber which was lit with half a dozen candles. A large mirror covered one wall. Belle shut the door and turned the key. "Now," she said briskly, "what is wrong?"

"Noth—"

"And don't say 'nothing,' for I won't believe it."

"Belle . . ."

"You might as well tell me, for I'm dreadfully nosy and always find out everything sooner or later. If you don't believe me, just ask my family. They'll be first to confirm it."

"It is only the excitement of the evening, I tell you."

"It's Dunford."

Henry looked away.

"It's quite obvious to me you're more than halfway

in love with him," Belle said bluntly, "so you might as well be honest."

Henry's head whipped back to face her. "Does everyone else know?" she asked in a whisper that hovered somewhere between terror and humiliation.

"No, I don't think so," Belle lied. "And if they do, I'm sure they are all cheering you on."

"It's no use. He doesn't want me."

Belle raised her brows. She had seen the way Dunford looked at Henry when he thought no one was looking. "Oh, I think he *wants* you."

"What I meant was, he doesn't—he doesn't love me," Henry stammered.

"That question is also open to debate," Belle said with a thoughtful expression. "Has he kissed you?"

Henry's blush was answer enough.

"So he has! I thought as much. That is a very good sign."

"I don't think so." Henry's eyes slid to the floor. She and Belle had become very good friends this past fortnight, but they had never spoken quite so frankly. "He, um, he, um . . ."

"He what?" Belle prodded.

"He seemed so utterly in control afterward, and he moved all the way across the carriage as if he wanted nothing to do with me. He didn't even hold my hand."

Belle was more experienced than Henry, and she immediately recognized that Dunford was terrified he would lose control. She wasn't entirely certain why he was trying to behave so honorably. Any fool could see they were a perfect couple. A small indiscretion before marriage could easily be overlooked. "Men," Belle finally declared, taking a swig of champagne, "can be idiots."

"Excuse me?"

"I don't know why people persist in believing women are inferior, when it is quite clear that men are the more feeble-minded of the two."

Henry stared at her blankly.

"Consider this: Alex tried to convince himself he wasn't in love with my cousin only because he thought he didn't want to get married. And John—now this one is even more asinine—he tried to push me away because he had it in his head that something that happened in his past made him unworthy of me. Dunford obviously has some equally featherbrained reason for trying to keep you at arm's length."

"But why?"

Belle shrugged. "If I knew that, I'd probably be prime minister. The woman who finally understands men will rule the world, mark my words. Unless . . ."

"Unless what?"

"It *cannot* be that wager."

"What wager?"

"A few months ago I wagered Dunford he would be married within a year." She looked over at Henry apologetically.

"You did?"

Belle swallowed uncomfortably. "I believe I said he would be 'tied up, leg-shackled, and loving it.' "

"He is making me miserable because of a *bet?*" Henry's voice rose considerably on the last word.

"It might not be the wager," Belle said quickly, realizing she had not improved the situation.

"I would like to wring . . . his . . . neck." Henry punctuated the sentence by tossing back the contents of her champagne glass.

"Try not to do it here at the ball."

Henry stood up and planted her hands on her hips.

"Don't worry. I wouldn't want to give him the satisfaction of knowing I care."

Belle chewed nervously on her lip as she watched Henry stalk from the room. Henry did care. Very much.

Chapter 15

Dunford had slipped away to the card room, where he proceeded to win a staggering amount of money through no ability of his own. Lord knew he was finding it difficult to keep his mind on the game.

After a few rounds Alex wandered over. "Mind if I join you?"

Dunford shrugged. "Not at all."

The other men at the vingt-et-un table shifted their chairs to make room for the duke.

"Who is winning?" Alex inquired.

"Dunford," Lord Tarryton replied. "Quite handily."

Dunford shrugged again, a disinterested expression affixed to his face.

Alex took a sip of whiskey as his hand was dealt and then took a look at the face-down card. Glancing sideways at Dunford, he said, "Your Henry turned out to be quite a success."

"She isn't 'my' Henry," Dunford all but snapped.

"Isn't Miss Barrett your ward?" Lord Tarryton asked.

Dunford looked at him, nodded curtly, and said, "Deal me another card."

Tarryton did so, but not before saying, "I wouldn't be surprised if Billington came up to scratch on this gel."

"Billington, Farnsworth, and a few others," Alex said with his most affable smile.

"Ashbourne?" Dunford's voice was colder than ice.

"Dunford?"

"Shut *up*."

Alex suppressed a smile and asked for another card.

"What I don't understand," Lord Symington, a graying man in his mid-fifties, was saying, "is why no one ever heard of her before. Who are her people?"

"I believe Dunford is 'her people' now," Alex said.

"She comes from Cornwall," Dunford replied tersely, regarding his pair of fives with a bored expression. "Before that, Manchester."

"Has she a dowry?" Symington persisted.

Dunford paused. He hadn't even thought of that. He could see Alex looking at him with a quizzical expression, one eyebrow arrogantly raised. It would be so easy to say that no, Henry didn't have a dowry. It was the truth, after all. Carlyle had left the chit penniless.

Her chances at an advantageous marriage would be greatly reduced.

She could end up dependent on him forever.

It was damned appealing . . .

Dunford sighed, cursing himself once again for this revolting impulse of his to play the hero. "Yes," he sighed. "Yes, she does."

"Well, that's good news for the chit," Symington replied. " 'Course she probably wouldn't have had too much trouble without it. Lucky for you, Dunford.

Wards can be deuced annoying business. I have one I've been trying to unload for three years. Why God invented Poor Relations I'll never know."

Dunford studiously ignored him, then flipped over his card, an ace. "Twenty-one," he said, not sounding the least bit excited at the fact that he had just won nearly a thousand pounds.

Alex leaned back and smiled broadly. "This must be your lucky night."

Dunford shoved his chair back and stood up, pushing the other cardplayers' vouchers carelessly into his pocket. "Indeed," he drawled as he made his way back to the door leading to the ballroom. "The luckiest bloody night of my life."

Henry decided that she would capture at least three more hearts before she had to leave, and she succeeded handily. It seemed so easy—she wondered why she had never before realized that men could be managed so effortlessly.

Most men, that is. The men she didn't want.

She was letting Viscount Haverly twirl her around the dance floor when she spied Dunford. Her heart missed a beat and her feet missed a step before she could remind herself that she was furious with him.

But every time Haverly turned her around, there was Dunford, leaning lazily against a pillar with his arms folded. The expression on his face did not invite the other partygoers to come over and try to engage him in conversation. He looked terribly sophisticated in his black evening clothes, unbearably arrogant, and very, very male.

And his eyes were following her, a lazy, hooded gaze—one that sent shivers up and down her spine.

The dance came to an end, and Henry sank into a respectful curtsy. Haverly bowed and said, "Shall I return you to your guardian? I see him just over there."

Henry thought of a thousand things to say—she had another partner for the next dance and he was on the other side of the room; she was thirsty and wanted a glass of lemonade; she needed to talk to Belle—but in the end she only nodded, seemingly having lost the power to speak.

"Here you are, Dunford," Haverly said with a good-natured grin as he deposited Henry by his side. "Or perhaps I should say Stannage now. I understand you've come into a title."

"Dunford is still fine," he replied with such urbane blandness that Haverly quickly stammered his good-byes and was off.

Henry frowned. "You didn't have to scare him like that."

"Didn't I? You seem to be acquiring an unseemly number of beaux."

"I have not behaved in an untoward manner and you know it," she retorted, hot anger staining her cheeks.

"Hush, minx, you are attracting attention."

Henry thought she might cry upon hearing him use her friendly nickname in such derisive tones. "I don't care! I don't. I just want . . ."

"What *do* you want?" he asked, his voice low and intense.

She shook her head. "I don't know."

"I should think you *don't* want to attract attention. That might endanger your quest to become the reigning belle of the season."

"*You* are the one who is endangering it, scaring off my suitors like that."

"Hmmm. I shall have to rectify my damage then, won't I?"

Henry regarded him suspiciously, unable to discern his motives. "What do you want, Dunford?"

"Why, just to dance with you." He took her arm and prepared to lead her back onto the dance floor. "If only to put to rest any nasty gossip that we do not deal well with one another."

"We *don't* deal well with one another. Not anymore, at least."

"Yes," he said dryly, "but no one else needs to know that, do they?" He pulled her into his arms, wondering what on earth had prompted him to dance with her again. It was a mistake, of course, just as any prolonged contact with her these days was a mistake, certain only to lead to a hard and intense longing.

And this longing was moving inexorably from his body to his soul.

But the feel of her was too much to resist. The waltz allowed him to get just close enough to her to detect that maddening scent of lemons, and he inhaled it as if it would save his life.

He was coming to care for her. He recognized that now. He wanted her on *his* arm at these social events, not prancing around with every eligible fop, dandy, and Corinthian in London. He wanted to muck through the fields of Stannage Park, holding her hand. He wanted to lean down—right now—and kiss her until she was senseless with desire.

But she no longer desired only him. He should have snatched her up before introducing her to the *ton,* for now she'd had a taste of social success and was savoring the triumph. The men were flocking to her side, and she was beginning to realize that she could have her pick of husbands. And, Dunford thought grimly, he had all but promised her she could have that pick. He had to let her have the fun of being courted by dozens of beaux before making any serious attempt for her hand himself.

He closed his eyes, almost in pain. He wasn't used to denying himself anything—at least nothing he *really* wanted. And he really wanted Henry.

She was watching the emotions filter across his face, growing more apprehensive by the second. He looked angry, as if having to hold her was a dreadful chore. Her pride stung, she summoned up what was left of her courage and said, "I know what this is about, you know."

His eyes snapped open. "What what is about?"

"This. The way you're treating me."

The music drew to a close, and Dunford escorted her to an empty alcove where they could continue the conversation in relative privacy. "How am I treating you?" he finally asked, dreading the answer.

"Horribly. Worse than horribly. And I know why."

He chuckled, unable to help himself. "Really?" he drawled.

"Yes," Henry said, cursing herself for the slight stammer in her voice. "Yes, I do. It's that damned wager."

"What wager?"

"You know which wager. The one with Belle."

He looked at her blankly.

"That you won't get married!" she burst out, mortified that their friendship had come to this. "You bet her a thousand pounds you wouldn't get married."

"Yes," he said hesitantly, not following her logic.

"You don't want to lose a thousand pounds by marrying me."

"Good God, Henry, is *that* what you think this is about?" Disbelief registered on his face, in his voice, in the stance of his body. He wanted to tell her he'd gladly pay the thousand pounds to have her. He'd pay a hundred thousand pounds if he had to. He hadn't even thought of the damned bet in over a month. Not since he'd met her, and she'd turned his life upside down, and . . . He fought for words, not at all certain of what to say to salvage this disaster of an evening.

She was about to cry—not tears of sadness, but of hot shame and humiliated fury. When she heard the supreme disbelief in his voice, she knew—positively *knew*—he cared not a whit for her. Even their friendship seemed to have disintegrated in the space of an evening. It wasn't the thousand pounds that was holding him back. She was a fool for even dreaming that he was pushing her away for something as silly as a bet.

No, he hadn't been thinking about the bet. No man could have faked the surprise she'd seen and heard. He was pushing her away simply because he wanted to push her away, simply because he didn't want *her.* All he wanted was to get her safely married, off his hands, and out of his life.

"If you'll excuse me," she choked out, pulling desperately away from him, "I have a few more hearts to capture this evening. I'd like an even dozen."

Dunford watched as she disappeared into the crowd, never dreaming she would make her way straight to one of the ladies' retiring rooms, lock the door, and spend the next half hour in miserable solitude.

The bouquets began to arrive early the next morning: roses of every shade, irises, tulips imported from Holland. They filled the Blydons' drawing room and spilled out into the foyer. The scent was so overwhelming and pervasive that the cook even grumbled she couldn't smell the food she was preparing.

Henry was most definitely a success.

She woke relatively early the next morning. Relatively compared to the other members of the household, that was. By the time she made her way downstairs, it was nearly noon. When she reached the breakfast room, she was surprised to see a mahogany-haired stranger sitting at the table. She stopped short, startled by his presence until he looked up at her with eyes of such a bright blue that she knew he had to be Belle's brother.

"You must be Ned," she said, curving her lips into a welcoming smile.

Ned raised a brow as he stood. "I'm afraid you have the advantage over me."

"I'm sorry. I am Miss Henrietta Barrett." She held out her hand. Ned took it and regarded it for a moment, as if trying to decide whether he ought to kiss or shake it. Finally, he kissed it.

"I'm very pleased to make your acquaintance, Miss Barrett," he said, "although I must confess I am at a bit of a loss as to your presence here at such an early hour."

"I am a houseguest," she explained. "Your mother is sponsoring me for the season."

He pulled out a chair for her. "Is she? I daresay you'll be a smashing success, then."

She shot him a jaunty smile as she sat. "Smashing."

"Ah, yes. You must be the reason for the bouquets in the front hall."

She shrugged. "I'm surprised your mother didn't inform you of my presence. Or Belle. She has spoken about you a great deal."

His eyes narrowed as his heart sank. "You've become friendly with Belle?" He saw all his hopes for a flirtation with this girl going up in smoke.

"Oh, yes. She is quite the best friend I have ever

had." She spooned some eggs on her plate and scrunched her nose. "I do hope these are not too cold."

"They'll warm them," he replied with a wave of his hand.

Henry took a hesitant bite. "They're just fine."

"What precisely has Belle told you about me?"

"That you're quite nice, of course, most of the time, that is, and that you are trying very hard to acquire a rake's reputation."

Ned choked on his toast.

"Are you all right? Would you like some more tea?"

"I'm fine," he gasped. "She told you *that?*"

"I thought it was exactly the sort of thing a sister might say about her brother."

"Indeed."

"I hope I have not dashed any of your plans to make a conquest of *me,*" Henry said blithely. "Not that I think so highly of my beauty or countenance that I imagine everyone wants to make a conquest of me. I merely thought you might be thinking about it simply for reasons of convenience."

"Convenience?" he echoed blankly.

"Seeing as how I'm living right under your roof."

"I say, Miss Barrett—"

"Henry," she interjected. "Please call me Henry. Everybody does."

"Henry," he muttered. "Of course you would be called Henry."

"It suits me better than Henrietta, don't you think?"

"I rather think I do," he said with great feeling.

She took another bite of egg. "Your mother insists upon calling me Henrietta, but that is only because your father's name is Henry. But you were saying?"

He blinked. "I was?"

"Yes, you were. I believe you said, 'I say, Miss Barrett,' and then I interrupted you and told you to call me Henry."

He blinked again, trying to recover his train of thought. "Oh, yes. I believe I was about to ask you if anyone had ever told you that you are quite frank."

She laughed. "Oh, *everyone.*"

"Somehow that does not surprise me."

"It never surprises me either. Dunford keeps telling me there are advantages to subtlety, but I've never been able to discern them." She immediately cursed herself for bringing *him* into the conversation. There was no one she wanted to talk about—or even think about—less.

"You know Dunford?"

She swallowed a piece of ham. "He's my guardian."

Ned had to cover his mouth with his napkin to keep from spitting out the tea he'd been sipping. "He's your *what?*" he asked disbelievingly.

"I seem to be getting similar reactions across London," she said with a puzzled shake of her head. "I gather he is not what most people would deem suitable guardian material."

"That is certainly one way to describe the matter."

"He's a terrible rake, I hear."

"That is another way to describe it."

She leaned forward, her eyes sparkling devilishly silver. "Belle tells me that *you* are trying to establish the exact sort of reputation he has."

"Belle talks too much."

"Funny, he said the exact same thing."

"That doesn't surprise me in the least."

"Do you know what I think, Ned? I may call you Ned, mayn't I?"

His lips twitched. "Of course."

She shook her head. "I don't think you're going to be able to carry off the rake act."

"Really?" he drawled.

"Yes. You're trying very hard, I can see. And you did say 'really' with just the right note of condescension and bored civility one would expect from a rake."

"I'm glad to see I'm living up to your standards."

"Oh, but you're not!"

Ned started to wonder where he got the fortitude not to laugh. "Really?" he drawled again, in exactly the same awful tone.

Henry let out a chuckle. "Very good, my lord, but do you want to know why I do not think you could ever be a proper rake?"

He plunked his elbows down on the table and leaned forward. "You can see I'm waiting in desperate anticipation."

"You're too nice!" She said this with a flourish of her arm.

He sat back. "Is that a compliment?"

"To be sure, it is."

Ned's eyes twinkled. "I cannot express the depth of my relief."

"Frankly—and I believe we have already established the fact that I am usually frank—"

"Oh, indeed."

She shot him a vaguely annoyed look. "Frankly, I am beginning to find the dark and brooding type to be vastly overrated. I met several last night, and I think I shall contrive not to receive them today should they call."

"They'll be crushed, I'm sure."

Henry ignored him. "I'm going to endeavor to look for a *nice* man."

"Then I should be at the top of your list, shouldn't I?" Ned was surprised to discover he didn't half mind the idea.

She sipped nonchalantly at her tea. "We should never suit."

"Why is that?"

"Because, my lord, you don't *want* to be nice. You need time to get over your delusions of rakehood."

This time Ned did laugh. Quite heartily. When he finally settled down, he said, "Your Dunford is quite a rake, and he is a rather nice chap. A bit domineering at times, but nice nonetheless."

Henry's face turned to stone. "First of all, he is not 'my' Dunford. And more importantly, he isn't nice at all."

Ned immediately sat up a little straighter. He didn't think he had ever met anyone who didn't like Dunford. It was exactly why he was so successful at being a rake. He was utterly charming unless one managed to get him really angry, and then he was deadly.

Ned gave Henry a sideways glance and wondered if she'd gotten Dunford really angry. He'd wager she had.

"Say, Henry, are you busy this afternoon?"

"I suppose I ought to be home to receive callers."

"Nonsense. They'll want you more if they think you're not available."

She rolled her eyes. "If I could find a *nice* man, I wouldn't have to play these games."

"Maybe. Maybe not. We'll probably never know, as I don't think there exists a man as nice as you want."

Except Dunford, Henry thought sadly. Before he'd turned so cruel. She remembered him at the dress shop in Truro. *Don't be shy, minx . . . Why on earth would I laugh? How could I give that dress to my sister when it looks so utterly charming on you?* But he didn't have a sister. He'd brought her to the dress shop just to make her feel better. All he had wanted to do was help her build her self-confidence.

She shook her head. She would never understand him.

"Henry?"

She blinked. "What? Oh, I'm sorry, Ned. I was wool-gathering, I suppose."

"Would you like to go for an excursion? I thought we might make a round of the shops, pick up a trinket or two."

Her eyes focused on his face. He was grinning boyishly, his bright eyes expectant. Ned liked her. Ned wanted to be with her. Why didn't Dunford? *No, don't think of that man.* Just because one person rejected her didn't mean she was wholly unlovable. Ned liked her. She had sat here at breakfast just being herself and Ned had liked her just fine. And Billington had liked her the night before. And Belle certainly did—and so did her parents.

"Henry?"

"Ned," she said decisively, "I would love to spend the day with you. Shall we be off now?"

"Why not? Why don't you collect your maid and meet me in the foyer in fifteen minutes?"

"Let's try for ten."

He gave her a jaunty salute.

Henry hurried up the stairs. Maybe this trip to London wouldn't turn out to be a complete disaster after all.

A half mile away, Dunford was lying on his bed, nursing a hellish hangover. He was still dressed in his evening clothes, much to his valet's profound consternation. He'd barely drunk anything at the ball, he'd come home nauseatingly sober. Then he'd proceeded to down almost an entire bottle of whiskey, as if the drink could expunge the evening from his memory.

It didn't work.

Instead, he stank like a tavern, his head felt as if it had been run over by the entire British cavalry, and his bedclothes were a mess from the boots he hadn't managed to take off the night before.

All because of a woman.

He shuddered. He'd never thought he'd get it this bad. Oh, he'd seen his friends topple, one by one, bitten by that bug they call marriage, all nauseatingly in love with their spouses. It was insane, really—no one married for love, no one.

Except his friends.

Which had led him to wondering. Why not him? Why couldn't he settle down with someone about whom he actually cared? And then Henry had virtually been dropped in his lap. One look in those silver eyes, and he should have known not even to try to fight it.

Well, maybe not, he amended. He wasn't so hung over that he couldn't admit it hadn't quite been love at first sight. Certainly these feelings had not begun until sometime *after* the pigpen incident. Perhaps it had been in Truro, when he'd bought her the yellow dress. Maybe that was when it had started.

He sighed. Hell, did it really matter?

He stood up, moved to a chair by the window, and stared aimlessly at the people walking up and down Half Moon Street. What the bloody hell was he supposed to do now? She hated him. If he hadn't been so damned set on playing a bloody hero, he could have married her twice by now. But no, he had to bring her to London, had to insist she be allowed to meet all of the *ton*'s eligible gentlemen before she made any decisions. He had to push her away and push her away and push her away, all because he was afraid he couldn't keep his hands off her.

He should have just ravished her and hauled her off to the altar before she had a chance to think straight. That's what a *real* hero would have done.

He stood abruptly. He could win her back. He just had to stop acting like such a jealous bastard and start being nice to her again. He could do that.

Couldn't he?

Chapter 16

Apparently he couldn't.

Dunford was walking up Bond Street, intending to purchase a bouquet at a florist before heading to Grosvenor Square to call on Henry.

Then he saw them. Henry and Ned, to be precise. Damn it, he had told her very specifically to stay away from the young Viscount Burwick. Henry was just the sort of young lady Ned would find fascinating and probably utterly necessary to his establishment of a rake's reputation.

Dunford hung back, watching them as they peered into the window of a bookshop. They appeared on excellent terms. Ned was laughing at something Henry was saying, and she was poking him playfully in the arm. They looked quite disgustingly happy together.

Suddenly it seemed quite logical that Henry would set her cap for Ned. He was young, handsome, personable, and rich. Most importantly, he was the brother of Henry's newfound best friend. Dunford knew the Earl and Countess of Worth would just love to welcome Henry into the family.

Dunford had been irritated by all the attention paid to Henry the previous night, but nothing in his life had ever prepared him for the violent surge of jealousy that ripped through him when she leaned up and whispered something in Ned's ear.

He acted without thinking—he must have, he later reflected, because he never would have behaved like such an idiotic boor if his mind had been working properly. Within seconds he managed to plant himself firmly between them. "Hello, Henry," he said, flashing her an even, white smile which did not even pretend to reach his eyes.

She gnashed her teeth, presumably as a prelude to a stinging rebuke.

"Good to see you're back from university, Ned." He said this without even glancing at the younger man.

"Just keeping Henry company," Ned said with a knowing tilt of his head.

"I cannot thank you enough for your services," Dunford replied tightly, "but they are no longer necessary."

"I think they are," Henry cut in.

Dunford fixed a deadly stare on Ned. "I find myself in need of a discussion with my ward."

"In the middle of the street?" Ned asked, his eyes wide with mock innocence. "Surely you'd rather I returned her home. Then you could speak with her in the comfort of our sitting room, with tea and—"

"Edward." Dunford's voice was like velvet-covered steel.

"Yes?"

"Do you remember the last time we crossed purposes?"

"Ah, but I'm much older and wiser now."

"Not nearly as old and wise as I am."

"Ah, but whereas you are nearing the realm of old and feeble, I am still young and strong."

"Is this a *game?*" Henry asked.

"Be quiet," Dunford snapped. "This is none of your concern."

"Isn't it?" Unable to believe his nerve and Ned's sudden defection to the camp of stupid, mindless, arrogant males, she threw up her arms and walked away. The two of them probably wouldn't even notice her absence until she was halfway down the street, so obsessed were they with their rooster-like strutting.

She was wrong.

She'd taken only three steps when a firm hand closed around the sash at her waist and reeled her back in.

"You," Dunford said icily, "aren't going anywhere." He turned his gaze to Ned. "And you are. Make yourself scarce, Edward."

Ned looked at Henry, his expression telling her that if she just said the word, he'd take her back home that instant. She doubted he could best Dunford in an out-and-out fight, although a draw was possible. But surely Dunford wouldn't want to cause such a scene in the middle of Bond Street. Chin up, she told him so.

"Do you really believe that, Henry?" he asked, his voice low.

She nodded jerkily.

He leaned forward. "I'm angry, Henry."

Her eyes widened as she remembered his words back at Stannage Park.

Don't make the mistake of making me angry, Henry.

You're not angry now?

Believe me, when I get angry you'll know.

"Uhh, Ned," she said quickly, "perhaps you had better leave."

"Are you certain?"

"There is no need to play the knight in bloody shining armor," Dunford snapped.

"You'd better go," Henry said. "I'll be fine."

Ned didn't look convinced, but he acceded to her wishes and walked stiffly away.

"What was the meaning of that?" Henry demanded, turning on Dunford. "You were deplorably rude, and—"

"Hush," he said, looking disgustingly composed. "We'll cause a scene, if we haven't done so already."

"You just said you didn't care if we caused a scene."

"I didn't say I didn't care. I merely implied that I would be willing to cause one to get what I want." He took her arm. "Come along, Hen. We need to talk."

"But my maid . . ."

"Where is she?"

"Right there." She motioned to a woman standing a few paces away. Dunford went over to speak with her, and she scurried off with alacrity.

"What did you say to her?" Henry asked.

"Nothing other than that I am your guardian, and you will be safe with me."

"Somehow I doubt that," she muttered.

Dunford was inclined to agree with her, considering how badly he wanted to drag her back to his town house, haul her up the stairs, and have his wicked way with her. But he remained silent, partly because he didn't care to frighten her, and partly because he realized his thoughts were sounding like a bad novel and he didn't want his words to do the same.

"Where are we going?" she asked.

"For a carriage ride."

"A carriage ride?" she echoed doubtfully, glancing about for a carriage.

He began to walk, skillfully moving her along so

she didn't realize she was being pulled. "We are going to my house, and then we are getting into one of my carriages and riding around London, because that is just about the only place I can get you alone without utterly destroying your reputation."

For a moment Henry forgot he had humiliated her the previous night. She even forgot that she was thoroughly furious with him, so heartened was she by his desire to be alone with her. But then she remembered. *Good God, Henry, is* that *what you think this is about?* It hadn't been his words that were so damning; it had been the tone of his voice and the expression on his face.

She chewed nervously on her lower lip as she quickened her pace to keep up with his long strides. No, he certainly was not enamored of her, and that meant she should not be the least bit excited by the fact that he wanted to be alone with her. He most likely was planning to deliver a blistering set-down about her supposedly scandalous behavior the night before. In all truth Henry did not think she had behaved in any improper fashion, but Dunford certainly seemed to think that she had done something wrong, and no doubt he wanted to tell her precisely why.

It was with dread that she mounted the steps to his town house, and it was with even greater dread that she descended them a few minutes later on her way to the carriage. Dunford helped her up, and as she settled onto the soft cushion, she heard him tell the driver, "Go wherever you like. I'll rap when we're ready to be taken back to Grosvenor Square to return the lady."

Henry scooted further back into the corner, cursing herself for her uncustomary cowardice. It wasn't so much that she was scared of a scolding; rather, she feared the impending loss of a friendship. The bond they had forged at Stannage Park was now held together by only a few fragile threads, and she had a feeling that it would be severed altogether that afternoon.

Dunford entered the carriage and sat opposite her. He spoke sharply and without preamble. "I very specifically told you to stay away from Ned Blydon."

"I chose not to follow your advice. Ned is a very nice person. Handsome, personable—a perfect escort."

"That is precisely why I wanted you to keep him at arm's length."

"Are you telling me," she asked, her eyes turning to steel, "that I may not make friends?"

"I am telling you," he ground out, "that you may not consort with young men who have spent the last year going out of their way to become the worst sort of rake."

"In other words, I may not be friends with a man who is almost, but not quite, as bad as you are."

The tips of his ears reddened. "What I am, or rather what you perceive me to be, is irrelevant. I am not the one courting you."

"No," she said, unable to keep a twinge of sadness from her voice, "you are not."

Perhaps it was the hollowness in her voice, perhaps it was simply the fact that there was not the slightest gleam of happiness in her eyes, but Dunford suddenly wanted more than anything to lean over and pull her into his arms. Not to kiss, merely to comfort. He didn't think, however, that she would welcome such an overture. Finally he took a ragged breath and said, "I did not intend to act like such a complete bastard this afternoon."

She blinked. "I . . . ah . . ."

"I know. There isn't much you can say that would constitute a suitable reply."

"No," she said dazedly. "There isn't."

"It was only that I had told you very specifically to stay away from Ned, and it appeared you'd made as much of a conquest of him as you had Billington and Haverly. And Tarryton, of course," he added acidly. "I should have realized what he was about once he started grilling me about you at the card table."

She stared at him in amazement. "I don't even know who Tarryton is."

"Then we may truly count you as a success," he said with a caustic laugh. "Only the Incomparables don't know who their suitors are."

She leaned forward a fraction of an inch, her brow furrowed and her eyes perplexed.

He had no idea what her action meant, so he leaned forward, too, and said, "Yes?"

"You're jealous," she said, disbelief rendering her words barely audible.

He knew it was true, but some little piece of his soul—some very arrogant and very male piece of his soul—balked at her accusation, and he said, "Don't flatter yourself, Henry, I—"

"No," she said, her voice growing louder. "You are." Her lips parted with amazement, and the corners began to curve upward in an openmouthed smile.

"Well, Christ, Henry, what do you expect? You flirt with every man under the age of thirty and at least half of those older than that. You poke *darling* Ned in the chest, whisper in his ear—"

"You're jealous." She didn't seem able to say anything else.

"Isn't that what you intended?" he spat out, furious with himself, furious with her, furious even with the damned horses pulling his carriage.

"No!" she burst out. "No. I . . . I just wanted . . ."

"What, Henry?" he said urgently, placing his hands on her knees. "What did you want?"

"I just wanted to feel somebody wanted me," she said in a very small voice. "You didn't anymore and—"

"Oh, Christ!" He was across the carriage and next to her in less than a second, pulling her into his arms and crushing her against him. "You thought I didn't *want* you anymore?" he said with a crazy laugh. "My God, Hen, I haven't been able to sleep at night for wanting you. I haven't read a book. I haven't been to a horse race. I just lie on my bed, staring at the ceiling, trying in vain not to imagine you're with me."

Henry pushed against his chest, desperately needing to put some space between them. Her mind was reeling from his incredible statement, and she just couldn't reconcile his words with his actions of late. "Why did you keep insulting me?" she asked. "Why did you keep pushing me away?"

He shook his head in self-derision. "I'd promised you the world, Henry. I'd promised you the opportunity to meet every eligible bachelor in London, and suddenly all I wanted to do was hide you away and keep you for myself. Don't you understand? I wanted to ruin you," he said, his words deliberately blunt. "I wanted to ruin you so that no other man would have you."

"Oh, Dunford," she said softly, placing her hand on his.

He grasped it like a starving man. "You weren't safe with me," he said hoarsely. "You're not safe with me now."

"I think I am," she whispered, placing her other hand in his. "I know I am."

"Hen, I promised you . . . God damn it, I promised you."

She wet her lips. "I don't want to meet all those other men. I don't want to dance with them, and I don't want their flowers."

"Hen, you don't know what you're saying. I'm not being fair. You should have the chance—"

"Dunford," she interjected, giving his hands an urgent squeeze. "You don't always have to kiss a lot of frogs to recognize a prince when you find one."

He stared at her as if she were a priceless treasure, unable to believe the emotion shining from her eyes. It enveloped him, warmed him, made him feel he could conquer the world. He placed two fingers on the underside of her chin, tipping her face up toward his. "Oh, Hen," he said, his voice catching oddly on the words. "I'm such an idiot."

"No, you're not," she said quickly, out of reflexive loyalty. "Well, maybe a little," she amended. "But just a little."

He could feel his body begin to shake with silent laughter. "Is it any wonder I need you so much? You always know when I need to be brought down a peg." He brushed a fleeting kiss against her lips. "And when I need flattery and praise." His mouth touched hers again. "And when I need to be touched . . ."

"Like right now?" she asked, her voice quavering.

"Especially right now." He kissed her again, this time with a gentle urgency meant to wipe any last doubts from her mind. She wrapped her arms around his neck and tilted her body toward his, giving him silent permission to deepen the kiss.

And he did. He'd been fighting this need for her for weeks, and there was no denying the temptation of her willing body in his arms. His tongue dipped into her mouth, probing and tasting, running along the edge of her teeth—anything to bring her closer to him. His hands slid around to her back, desperately trying to feel the heat and shape of her body through the material of her dress. "Henry," he rasped, trailing his lips across her cheek to her ear. "God, how I want you. You." He caught her earlobe between his teeth. "Only you."

Henry moaned, flooded with sensation, unable to speak. The last time he had kissed her, she had sensed that his heart had not been as deeply moved by the intimacy as his body. But now she could feel his love. It was in his hands, his lips; it poured forth from his eyes. He may not have said the words, but the emotion was there, almost palpable in the air. She suddenly felt as if she had permission to love him. It was all right to try to show him her feelings because he felt the same way.

She moved in his arms so she could kiss his ear the way he had hers. He flinched when she ran her tongue along the edge, and she pulled quickly away. "I'm sorry," she said, her words rushing out in a nervous jumble. "Did I displease you? I thought that since I liked it, you might too. I only—"

He placed his hand over her mouth. "Hush, minx. It was beautiful. I just wasn't expecting it."

"Oh. I'm sorry," she said as soon as he moved his hand.

"*Don't* apologize." He smiled lazily. "Just do it again."

She looked up at him, her eyes saying, *Really?*

He nodded and then, just to tease her, turned his head until his ear was only a few inches away. She smiled, mostly to herself, then leaned forward again, tentatively running her tongue along the lobe. Somehow it seemed too wicked to use her teeth as he had done.

He withstood the torture of her delightfully inexperienced caresses for as long as he could, but less than a minute later his desire was so hot he couldn't stop himself from grasping her face with his hands and drawing her in for another searing kiss.

His hands plunged into her hair, pulling it wantonly free of its pins. He buried his face in it, breathing in that intoxicating scent of lemons that had been teasing him for weeks. "Why does it smell like that?" he murmured, trailing kisses along her hairline.

"Why does . . . What?"

He chuckled at the passionate fog clouding her eyes. She was such a treasure—without artifice of any kind. When he kissed her, she held nothing back. She might realize the kind of power she held over him, but he was certain she would never use it. He pinched a lock of her hair with his fingers and used it to tickle her nose. "Why does your hair smell like lemons?"

To his surprise, she blushed. "I use lemon juice when I wash my hair," she admitted. "Viola always told me it would make it lighter."

He looked at her indulgently. "Another piece of evidence that you possess the same failings as the rest of us, minx. Using lemons to lighten your hair. Tsk, tsk."

"It has always been my best feature," she said sheepishly. "That's why I never cut it. It would have made much more sense to wear it short at Stannage Park, but I just could not bring myself to do it. I thought I might as well make the best of it, considering that the rest of me was rather ordinary."

"Ordinary?" he said softly. "I think not."

"You don't have to flatter me, Dunford. I know I'm passably attractive, and I'll admit I did look rather nice in my white gown last night, but— Oh, dear, you must think I'm dangling after compliments."

"No." He shook his head. "I don't."

"Then you must think I'm a goose, prattling on about my hair."

He touched her face, smoothing her eyebrows with his thumbs. "I think your eyes are pools of liquid silver, and your brows are angel wings—soft and delicate." He leaned down and brushed a feathery kiss on her lips. "Your mouth is soft and pink and perfectly shaped, with an enchantingly full lower lip and corners that always look as if they are about to turn up into a smile. And your nose—well, it's a nose, but I must confess I have never seen one that pleased me more."

She stared at him, mesmerized by the husky timbre of his voice.

"But do you know what is best of all?" he continued. "Underneath this delightful package are a beautiful heart, a beautiful mind, and a beautiful soul."

Henry didn't know what to say, didn't know what she *could* say that would even approach the emotion of his words. "I . . . I . . . thank you."

He responded by kissing her gently on the forehead.

"Do you like the smell of lemons?" she blurted out nervously. "I could stop."

"I love the smell of lemons. Do whatever pleases you."

"I don't know if it works," she said with a lopsided smile. "I've been doing it for so long I don't know what it would look like if I stopped. It might look just the same."

"Just the same would be perfect," he said solemnly.

"But what if I stopped and my hair turned quite dark?"

"That would be perfect, too."

"Silly man. They cannot both be perfect."

He seized her face in his hands. "Silly woman. *You* are perfect, Hen. It doesn't matter how you look."

"I think you are quite perfect, too," she said softly, covering his hands with her own. "I remember the first time I saw you. I thought you were the most handsome man I'd ever seen."

He pulled her onto his lap, willing himself to be content just to cuddle her this way. He knew he couldn't let himself kiss her even one more time. His body was aching for more, but it would have to wait. Henry was an innocent. Even more importantly, she was *his* innocent, and she deserved to be treated with respect. "If I recall," he said, lazily tracing circles on her cheek, "the first time you saw me you paid considerably more attention to the pig than to me."

"That wasn't the first time I saw you. I had been watching you from my window." Her expression suddenly grew sheepish. "Actually, I remember thinking that you had an especially fine pair of boots."

He let out a howl of laughter. "Are you telling me you love me for my *boots?*"

"Well . . not anymore," she said with a slight stammer. Was he trying to tease her into admitting to him that she loved him? She was suddenly afraid—afraid she might declare her love for him and he would have nothing to say in return. Oh, this was so difficult. *She* knew he loved her—she could see it in everything he did—but she wasn't sure he realized it yet, and she didn't think she could bear the pain of his murmuring an inanity like, "I care for you, too, sweetheart."

She decided he had no ulterior motive because he appeared oblivious to her internal distress. Trying to look very grave, he bent down and lifted her skirts up a couple of inches. "Your boots are very nice, too," he said, admirably managing a straight face.

"Oh, Dunford, you do make me happy."

She was looking away from him when she said that,

but he could hear the smile in her voice. "You make me happy, too, minx. Unfortunately, I fear I had better get you home before they begin to panic at your absence."

"You did practically abduct me."

"Ah, but the end most definitely justified the means."

"You are probably correct, but I do agree with you that I need to return. Ned will be wildly curious."

"Ah, yes, our dear friend Ned." With a resigned expression, Dunford rapped on the wall, signaling the coachman to drive to the Blydon mansion in Grosvenor Square.

"You must be kinder to Ned," Henry said. "He is a lovely person, and I am sure he will be a good friend."

"I'll be kind to Ned once he's found a woman of his own," Dunford grumbled.

Henry said nothing, too delighted with his obvious jealousy to scold him.

They sat in contented silence for several minutes while the carriage made its way to Grosvenor Square. Finally it rolled to a halt. "I wish I didn't have to leave," Henry said wistfully. "I wish I could stay in this carriage forever."

Dunford hopped down, then put his hands around her waist to help her alight. He held on slightly longer than was necessary once her feet touched the ground. "I know, Hen," he said, "but we've the rest of our lives ahead of us." He bent over her hand, kissed it gallantly, then watched while she walked up the stairs and into the house.

Henry stood in the foyer for a few seconds, trying to comprehend the events of the last hour. How was it that her life could be so perfectly turned around in so short a time?

We've the rest of our lives ahead of us. Had he

meant that truly? Did he want to marry her? Her hand flew to her mouth.

"Good God, Henry! Where have you been?"

She looked up. Ned was striding purposefully down the hall. She didn't reply, merely stood there staring at him, her hand still over her mouth.

Ned immediately grew alarmed. Her hair was a mess, and she didn't seem able to speak. "What is going on?" he demanded. "What the devil did he do to you?"

We've the rest of our lives ahead of us.

Her hand fell away from her mouth. "I think . . ." Her brow furrowed slightly and she tilted her head to the side. Her eyes looked utterly bewildered, and if asked, she wouldn't have been able to describe a single item in the hall. She probably couldn't even have identified the person in front of her without taking a second look. "I think . . ."

"What, Henry? What?"

"I think I just got engaged."

"You *think* you got engaged?"

We've the rest of our lives ahead of us.

"Yes. I think I rather did."

Chapter 17

"What did you do?" Belle asked, her voice containing more than a twinge of sarcasm. "Ask yourself for permission to marry her?"

Dunford grinned. "Something like that."

"This is something straight out of a very bad novel, you know. The guardian marrying his ward. I can't believe you're doing it."

Dunford didn't believe for a moment that Belle had not been working actively toward this very end for several weeks. "Can't you?"

"Well, I can, actually. She suits you perfectly."

"I know."

"How did you propose? Something terribly romantic, I hope."

"Actually I haven't asked her yet."

"Don't you think you're being a trifle premature, then?"

"Asking Ashbourne to invite us out to Westonbirt? Not at all. How else am I supposed to arrange some time alone with her?"

"You're not engaged yet. Technically you don't deserve any time alone with her."

Dunford's smile was one of pure male arrogance. "She'll say yes."

Belle's expression grew irritated. "It would serve you right if she refused."

"She won't."

Belle sighed. "You're probably right."

"At any rate, much as I'd like to get a special license and marry her next week, I'm going to have to accept a more conventional engagement period. The *ton* will be titillated enough by the fact that she's my ward, I want no undue speculation about her character. If we marry too hastily, someone is bound to do a spot of sleuthing and find out we were unchaperoned for over a week in Cornwall."

"You've never cared overly much about *ton* whispers before," Belle mused.

"I still don't," he said sharply. "Not for myself at least, but I will not expose Henry to any scurrilous gossip."

Belle bit back a smile. "I'll be expecting that thousand pounds posthaste."

"And you shall have it—gladly. Just so long as you and Blackwood head out to Westonbirt along with us. It will seem more of a house party if three couples are there."

"Dunford, I'm not going to stay with Alex and Emma when John and I have a home not fifteen minutes away."

"But you will come out to the country next week? It would mean a great deal to Henry."

And anything that meant a great deal to Henry obviously meant a great deal to Dunford. Belle smiled. He'd fallen hard for this girl, and she couldn't have been happier for him. "Anything for Henry," she said with a magnanimous wave of her arm. "Anything for Henry."

A few days later Dunford and Henry left—with Caroline's blessing—for Westonbirt, the Ashbourne estate in Oxfordshire. At Dunford's rather vocal urging, Alex and Emma had hastily arranged a house party for their closest friends—Dunford, Henry, and the Blackwoods, who promised to come by each day although they insisted on spending their nights at their nearby home, Persephone Park.

The carriage's occupants numbered four, Lady Caroline steadfastly refusing to let Henry go unless her maid and Dunford's valet acted as chaperones during the three-hour trip to the country. Dunford had the good sense to keep his grumblings to himself; he didn't want to do anything that might jeopardize this precious week he'd been given. Alex and Emma, as a married couple, were proper chaperones, but they also had a soft spot for romance. Belle, after all, had met and fallen in love with her husband under their not-always-so-watchful eyes.

Henry remained silent during most of the trip, unable to think of anything she wanted to say to Dunford in front of the servants. Her mind was brimming with things she wanted to tell him, but it all seemed so *personal* now, even down to the sway of the carriage and the color of the grass outside. She contented herself with frequent glances and secret smiles, all of which Dunford noticed, for he was quite unable to take his eyes off her the entire trip.

It was mid-afternoon when they turned onto the long, tree-lined drive that led to Westonbirt. "Oh, it's lovely," Henry said, finding her voice at last. The immense structure had been built in the shape of an E, to honor the then-reigning Queen Elizabeth. Henry had always preferred more modest structures, like Stannage Park, but Westonbirt somehow managed to possess a homey air despite its size. Perhaps it was the windows, which glinted like cheerful smiles, or the flower beds, which grew in wild abandon all along the drive. Whatever it was, Henry fell in love on the spot.

She and Dunford disembarked and made their way up the steps to the front door, which had already been swung open by Norwood, Westonbirt's elderly butler. "Do I look presentable?" Henry whispered as they were shown into an airy parlor.

"You look fine," he replied, looking rather amused at her anxiety.

"I am not too rumpled from the trip?"

"Of course not. And even if you were, it would not matter. Alex and Emma are friends." He gave her hand a reassuring pat.

"Do you think she will like me?"

"I know she will like you." He suppressed the urge to roll his eyes. "What has gotten into you? I thought you were excited to make this trip to the country."

"I am. I'm just nervous, that is all. I want the duchess to like me. I know that she is a special friend of yours, and—"

"Yes, she is, but *you* are even more special."

Henry flushed with pleasure. "Thank you, Dunford. It's just that she is a duchess, you know, and—"

"And what? Alex is a duke, and that didn't seem to stop you from practically charming the breeches off him. If he had met you before Emma, I'd have had quite a fight on my hands."

Henry blushed again. "Don't be silly."

He sighed. "Think whatever you like, Hen, but if I

hear one more worried comment come out of your mouth, I shall have to kiss you into silence."

Her eyes lit up. "Really?"

He exhaled and rested his forehead against his hand. "What am I going to do with you, minx?"

"Kiss me?" she said hopefully.

"I suppose I'll have to do just that." He leaned forward and brushed his lips gently against hers, carefully avoiding any deeper contact. He knew that if his body touched hers in any way, even just his hand on her cheek, he would be unable to stop himself from hauling her roughly into his arms. There was nothing he'd rather do, of course, but the Duke and Duchess of Ashbourne were expected at any moment, and Dunford had no particular desire to be caught *flagrante delicto*.

A discreet cough sounded from the doorway.

Too late.

Dunford pulled away, catching a glimpse of Henry's pinkening cheeks as he swerved his gaze to the doorway. Emma was trying very hard not to smile. Alex wasn't trying at all.

"Oh, *God*," Henry groaned.

"No, just me," Alex said affably, trying to put her at ease, "although my wife has, on more than one occasion, accused me of confusing myself with the one of whom you speak."

Henry smiled, very weakly.

"Good to see you, Ashbourne," Dunford muttered, getting to his feet.

Alex led his heavily pregnant wife to a comfortable chair. "I expect it would have been much better to see me five minutes hence," he murmured in Dunford's ear as he crossed the room to Henry. "Delightful to see you again, Henry. I'm glad to see you've conquered our dear friend here. Between you and me, he didn't stand a chance."

"I . . . uh . . ."

"For goodness sake, Alex," Emma said, "if you say one more thing to embarrass her, I shall have your head."

Only Henry could see Alex's face as he tried very hard to appear contrite, and she had to put her hand over her mouth to stop herself from laughing out loud.

"Perhaps you would like to be introduced to the virago in the yellow chair?" he said with a quirky half-smile.

"I see no virago," Henry said archly, catching Emma's smile from across the room.

"Dunford," Alex said, taking Henry's hand as she rose to her feet, "this woman is as blind as a bat."

Dunford shrugged, sharing an amused look with Emma.

"My darling wife," Alex said. "May I present—"

"That's 'darling virago wife' to you," Emma said pertly, her eyes twinkling mischievously at Henry.

"Of course. How remiss of me. My darling virago wife, may I present Miss Henrietta Barrett of Cornwall, lately of your Aunt Caroline's guest room."

"I am *very* pleased to meet you, Miss Barrett," the duchess said, and Henry rather thought she meant it.

"Please call me Henry. Everybody does."

"And you must call me Emma. I wish everybody would."

Henry decided instantly that she liked the young, flame-haired duchess and wondered why on earth she had been so apprehensive about meeting her. She was, after all, Belle and Ned's first cousin, and if that wasn't superb recommendation, she didn't know what was.

Emma stood up, ignoring the protests of her concerned husband, took Henry's arm, and said, "Let's be off. I am so eager to talk with you, and we can be much more frank without *them.*" She flicked her head in the direction of the gentlemen.

Henry smiled helplessly. "All right."

"I cannot tell you how happy I am to finally meet you," Emma said as soon as they reached the hall. "Belle has written all about you, and I am so excited that Dunford has finally met his match. Not that I don't think you are lovely in your own right, but I have to admit, mostly I'm just pleased that Dunford has met his match."

"You *are* frank."

"Not half as much as you, if Belle's letters are any indication. And I couldn't be more pleased." Emma grinned at Henry as she steered them down a wide hallway. "Why don't I show you 'round Westonbirt while we chat? It's really a lovely home, for all its size."

"I think it's magnificent. Not at all forbidding."

"No," Emma mused, "it's not. Funny, that. It was meant to be, I think. But anyway, I *am* glad you are also frank. I have never had very much patience for the doublespeak of the *ton*"

"Nor I, your grace."

"Oh, please call me Emma. I hadn't a title of any sort until last year, and I still haven't gotten used to all the servants bobbing curtseys every time I walk by. If my friends don't use my given name, I shall probably die of too much formality."

"I should be very pleased to be counted among your friends, Emma."

"And I among yours. Now, you must tell me. How did Dunford propose? Something original, I hope."

Henry felt her face grow hot. "I'm not certain. That is to say, he hasn't exactly asked . . ."

"He hasn't asked you yet?" Emma blurted out. "That conniving little wretch."

"Now see here," Henry began, feeling the need to defend him even though she wasn't certain of the charge.

"No offense meant," Emma said quickly. "At least no major offense. I expect he did it so that we would turn a blind eye if the two of you happened to wander off on your own. He told us you were engaged, you know."

"He did?" Henry said uncertainly. "That's good, isn't it?"

"Men," Emma muttered. "Always going around thinking that a woman will marry them without even bothering to ask. I might have known he'd do something like this."

"It means that he is *going* to ask me, I should think," Henry said dreamily. "And I can't help but be happy about that because I do want to marry him."

"Of course you do. Everybody wants to marry Dunford."

"What?"

Emma blinked, as if just suddenly returning in full to the conversation. "Except me, of course."

"Well, you couldn't, anyway," Henry felt obliged to point out, unable to pinpoint when exactly the conversation had veered into the bizarre. "As you are already married, that is."

"I meant before I married." Emma laughed. "What a widgeon you must think me. I don't usually have so much difficulty remaining on one topic. It's the babe, I think." She patted her stomach. "Well, probably not, but it's deuced convenient to be able to let it shoulder the blame for all my idiosyncrasies."

"Of course," Henry murmured.

"I only meant to say that Dunford is very popular. *And* he is a very good man. Rather like Alex. A woman would have to be a fool to turn down a proposal from a man like that."

"Except there is the little problem that he hasn't exactly proposed yet."

"What do you mean 'exactly'?"

Henry turned and glanced through a window which looked out onto a cheery courtyard. "He has implied that we will be married, but he hasn't asked me directly."

"I see." Emma caught her lower lip between her teeth as she thought. "I expect he wants to propose here at Westonbirt. More of a chance to get you alone. He'll probably want to, er, kiss you when he asks, and he'll not want to have to worry about Aunt Caroline swooping down to rescue you at any moment."

Henry didn't particularly want to be rescued from Dunford, so she made an inarticulate sound that was meant to convey agreement.

Emma cast a sideways glance at her new friend. "I can see from your expression that he has kissed you already. No, don't blush, I'm quite used to such goings-on. I had as much trouble when I had to chaperone Belle."

"You chaperoned Belle?"

"And did a dreadful job of it, too. But no matter. You will be delighted to learn I will probably be just as lax with you."

"Er, yes," Henry stammered. "That is to say, I think so." She spied a bench covered in rose damask. "Do you mind if we sit down for a moment? I'm suddenly very weary."

Emma sighed. "I tired you out, didn't I?"

"No, of course not . . . Well," Henry admitted as she sat down, "yes."

"I have a tendency to do that to people," Emma said, lowering herself down onto the bench. "I don't know why."

Four hours later Henry had a feeling she knew exactly why. Emma Ridgely, Duchess of Ashbourne, had quite the most energy she'd ever seen a person possess, herself included. And Henry had never thought of herself as a particularly languid person.

It wasn't that Emma bustled about with nervous energy. Quite the opposite; the petite woman was the epitome of grace and sophistication. It was simply that everything Emma did or said was infused with such vitality that her companions were left breathless just watching her.

It was easy to see why her husband so adored her. Henry only hoped Dunford would one day come to love her with such single-minded devotion.

The evening meal was a delightful affair. Belle and John had not yet arrived from London, so it was just Dunford, Henry, and the Ashbournes. Henry, still slightly unaccustomed to taking her meals with anyone other than the Stannage Park servants, reveled in the company, shaking with mirth at the stories her companions told of their childhoods and adding a few of her own.

"Did you really try to move the beehive closer to the house?" Emma laughed, patting her breastbone as she tried to regain her breath.

"I have a dreadful passion for sweets," Henry explained, "and when the cook told me I couldn't have more than one a day because we didn't have enough sugar, I decided to rectify the problem."

"That will teach Mrs. Simpson to make up excuses," Dunford said.

Henry shrugged. "She's never minced words with me since."

"But weren't your guardians terribly upset with you?" Emma persisted.

"Oh, yes," Henry replied with an animated wave of her fork. "I thought Viola was going to faint. *After* she had me drawn and quartered. Luckily she was in no shape to punish me, what with twelve bee stings on her arms."

"Oh, dear," Emma said. "Were you stung as well?"

"No, it's amazing, but I wasn't stung at all."

"Henry seems to have a way with bees," Dunford said, trying very hard not to remember his own reaction to Henry's beehive exploits. He felt an incredible surge of pride as he watched her turn back to Emma, apparently to answer another question about the beehive. His friends loved Henry. He had known they would, of course, but it still filled him with joy to see her so happy. For what must have been the hundredth time that day alone, he marveled at his blind good luck in finding the one woman in the world who so obviously suited him in every way.

She was marvelously direct and efficient, yet her capacity for pure, sentimental love knew no bounds; his heart still ached whenever he remembered that day at the abandoned cottage when she cried over the death of an unknown baby. She had a wit to match his own; one didn't even need to hear her speak to know she was uncommonly intelligent—it was right there in the silvery sparkle of her eyes. She was terribly brave and damn near fearless; she'd have to be to try to—and succeed at—running a modest-sized estate and farm for six years. And, Dunford thought, a half-smile creeping onto his lips, she melted in his arms every time they touched, turning his blood to fire. He ached for her every minute of the day and wanted nothing more than to show her with his hands and lips the depth of his love for her.

So this was love. He almost chuckled out loud right there at the dining table. No wonder the poets spoke so highly of it.

"Dunford?"

He blinked and looked up. Alex was apparently trying to ask him a question. "Yes?"

"I asked," Alex repeated, "if Henry has given you similar cause for alarm in recent weeks."

"If you don't count her continued adventures with the beehives of Stannage Park, then she has been the soul of dignity and decorum."

"Really?" Emma asked. "What did you do?"

"Oh, it was nothing," Henry replied, not daring to glance at Dunford. "All I did was reach in and pull out a bit of honeycomb."

"What you did," he said sternly, "was nearly get yourself stung by a hundred angry insects."

"Did you really put your hand into a beehive?" Emma leaned forward interestedly. "I should love to know how to do it."

"*I* should be forever in your debt," Alex interjected, directing his words at Henry, "if you would endeavor never to teach my wife how."

"I wasn't in any danger," Henry said quickly. "Dunford likes to exaggerate."

"He does?" Alex asked, raising his brows.

"He was very anxious," she told him, then turned to Emma as if she had to explain. "He gets very anxious."

"Anxious?" Emma echoed.

"Dunford?" Alex asked at the very same time.

"You must be joking," Emma added, in a tone that suggested there could be no other possible alternative.

"Suffice it to say," Dunford cut in, eager to make short work of this line of conversation, "that she managed to take ten years off my life, and that is the end of the subject."

"I suppose it will have to be," Henry said, looking at Emma with a little shrug, "as he has made me promise never to eat honey again."

"He did? Dunford, how could you? Even Alex hasn't been that beastly."

If her husband objected to the implication that he might be *a little* beastly, he made no comment.

"Just so that I do not go down in history as the most overbearing man in Britain, Emma, I did not forbid her to eat honey." Dunford turned back to Henry. "I merely made you promise not to procure it yourself, and frankly, this conversation has grown tedious."

Emma leaned toward Henry and whispered in a voice that could be heard clearly on the other side of the table, "I have never seen him this way."

"Is that good?"

"Very."

"Emma?" Dunford said, his voice frighteningly casual.

"Yes, Dunford?"

"It is only my extreme good manners and the fact that you are a lady that prevent me from telling you to shut up."

Henry looked frantically at Alex, positive that he was about to call Dunford out for insulting his wife. But the duke merely covered his mouth and started to choke on something that must have been a laugh, for he hadn't taken a bite in several minutes.

"Extreme good manners, indeed," Emma replied tartly.

"It certainly cannot be the fact that you are a lady,"

Henry said, thinking that Dunford must be very good friends with the Ashbournes if Alex was laughing at what might have been perceived as an insult to Emma. "Because he once told me to shut up, and I have it on the best authority that I am a lady as well."

This time Alex started to cough so violently that Dunford felt compelled to whack him on the back. Of course, he just may have been looking for an excuse to do so.

"And whose authority is that?" Dunford asked.

"Why, yours of course." Henry leaned forward, her eyes glinting devilishly. "And you should know."

Emma joined her husband in a duet of coughing spasms.

Dunford sat back in his seat, a reluctant smile of admiration creeping across his face. "Well, Hen," he said, waving his arm at the duke and duchess, "we seem to have made short work of these two."

Henry tilted her head to the side. "It wasn't very difficult, was it?"

"Not at all. Presented no challenge whatsoever."

"Emma, my dear," Alex said, regaining his breath, "I think our honor has just been impugned."

"I'll say. I haven't laughed so hard for ages." Emma stood and motioned for Henry to follow her into the drawing room. "Let's be off, Henry, and leave these gentlemen to their stuffy cigars and port."

"There you have it, minx," Dunford said as he rose to his feet. "You'll finally be able to find out what goes on when the ladies retire after supper."

"Did he call you 'minx'?" Emma asked as she and Henry exited the room.

"Er, yes, he calls me that sometimes."

Emma rubbed her hands together. "This is better than I thought."

"Henry! Wait just a moment!"

Henry turned around to see Dunford striding quickly toward her. "If I might have a quick word with you," he said.

"Yes, yes, of course."

He drew her aside and spoke in a low whisper that Emma, no matter how hard she pricked her ears, could not hear. "I need to see you tonight."

Henry thrilled at the urgency in his voice. "You do?"

He nodded. "I need to speak with you privately."

"I'm not certain . . ."

"*I've* never been more certain. I'll rap on your door at midnight."

"But Alex and Emma—"

"Always retire at eleven." He smiled rakishly. "They enjoy their privacy."

"All right, but—"

"Good. I'll see you then." He dropped a quick kiss on her forehead. "Not a word of this to anyone."

Henry blinked and watched him return to the dining room.

Emma was at her side with remarkable speed for one who was seven months pregnant. "What was that all about?"

"Nothing, really," Henry mumbled, knowing she I was a bad liar and yet trying to attempt to brazen it out nonetheless.

Emma snorted her disbelief.

"No, really. He just, ummm—he told me to behave myself."

"To behave yourself?" Emma said doubtfully.

"You know, not to make a spectacle of myself or anything like that."

"Now that is a clanker if ever I heard one," Emma retorted. "Even Dunford must realize it would be impossible for you to create any kind of scene in my drawing room with only me for company."

Henry smiled weakly.

"It is apparent, however," Emma continued, "that I'm not going to get the truth out of you, so I won't waste my valuable energy trying."

"Thank you," Henry murmured as they resumed their walk toward the drawing room. As she strode alongside Emma, she clenched her fist into an excited little ball. Tonight he would tell her he loved her. She could feel it.

Chapter 18

11:57.

Henry clutched at the folds of her dressing gown as she glanced at the clock on her bedside table. She was a fool for going along with this, an idiot for being so in love with him that she had agreed to this scheme even though she knew her behavior was beyond indecent. She chuckled wryly to herself when she remembered how unconcerned with etiquette she'd been back at Stannage Park. Unconcerned and unknowing. A fortnight in London had made clear to her that if there was one thing a young lady was not to do, it was let a man into her bedroom, especially when the rest of the house was dark and asleep.

But she couldn't seem to manage to summon enough maidenly fear to refuse him. What she wanted and what she knew was right were two distinctly different things, and desire was winning out over propriety by a vast margin.

11:58.

She sat down on the bed and then, realizing where she was, jumped up as if burned. "Calm yourself, Henry," she muttered, crossing her arms, uncrossing them, then crossing them again. As she paced across the room, she wandered by a mirror, caught sight of her stern countenance, and then uncrossed her arms again. She didn't want to receive him lounging on her bed, but there was no need to look quite so forbidding.

11:59.

A light rap sounded on the door. Henry flew across the room and opened it. "You're early," she whispered frantically.

"I am?" Dunford reached into his pocket for his watch.

"Will you come inside?" she hissed, yanking him in. "Anyone could see you out there."

Dunford dropped his watch back into his pocket, smiling broadly all the while.

"And stop smiling!" she added rather fiercely.

"Why?"

"Because it—it *does* things to me!"

Dunford shifted his gaze up to the ceiling in an attempt to keep from laughing out loud. If she thought that statement would get him to stop smiling, she was addled in the brain.

"What did you need to talk with me about?" she whispered.

He moved to her side in two easy paces. "In a minute," he murmured. "First I have to . . ."

He let his lips complete the sentence as they captured hers in a searing kiss. He hadn't meant to kiss her right away, but she'd looked so damned adorable in her dressing gown with her hair floating around her face. She made a soft mewling sound, and her body shifted slightly, settling into his large frame.

Reluctantly, he drew himself away. "We're not going to get anything done if we continue on like . . ." His words trailed off as he caught the dazed expression on Henry's face. Her lips looked unbearably pink, even in the candlelight, and they were slightly parted and damp. "Well, perhaps one more . . ."

He pulled her against him again, his lips searching hers in another remarkably thorough kiss. She was kissing him back with just as much feeling, and he dimly realized that her arms had wound themselves around his neck. A tiny spark of reason, however, somehow managed to remain active in his brain, and once again he disentangled himself. "That's *enough,*" he muttered, the scolding intended solely for himself. Taking a shuddering breath, he looked up.

Big mistake. Another fiery bolt of need rocked through him at the sight of her. "Why don't you just sit over there?" he said hoarsely, waving his hand in no particular direction.

Henry had no idea that the kiss had left him as shaken as it had her, and she took his direction literally. Her eyes followed his arm's motion, and she said, "On the bed?"

"No! I mean—" He cleared his throat. "Please do *not* sit on the bed."

"All right," she said slowly, moving to a straight-backed, blue-and-white-striped chair.

Dunford walked over to the window and looked out, trying to give his body time to cool down. Now that he was actually here, in Henry's room at midnight, he wasn't at all certain that he was following the wisest course of action. In fact, he was convinced he was not. He had originally planned to take Henry out for a picnic the next day and propose to her then. But that night at dinner, it had suddenly hit him that his feelings went beyond affection and desire. He loved her.

No, he didn't just love her. He *needed* her. He needed her like he needed food and water, like the flowers at Stannage Park needed the sun. He smiled wryly. He needed her like she needed Stannage Park. He remembered how, one morning at breakfast back in Cornwall, she'd been gazing out the window with an expression of pure rapture. He imagined that must be how his face looked every time he saw her.

And so while he was sitting there in Westonbirt's informal dining room, a piece of asparagus dangling off his fork, it suddenly had become imperative that he tell her all this that night. These feelings were so powerful they were painful to keep inside. Making a secret assignation had seemed the only option.

He had to tell her how much he loved her, and as God was his witness, he wasn't going to leave this room until she told him the very same thing.

"Henry." He turned around. She was sitting up very straight in her chair. He cleared his throat and said again, "Henry."

"Yes?"

"I probably should not have come tonight."

"No," she said, not sounding as if she meant it.

"But I needed to see you alone, and tomorrow seemed an eternity away."

Her eyes widened. It was not like Dunford to speak in such dramatic terms. He looked quite agitated, almost nervous, and it definitely was not like him to be nervous about anything. Abruptly he closed the distance between them, then knelt on the floor at her feet.

"Dunford," she said in a strangled voice, not at all sure what she was meant to do.

"Shhh, my love," he said. And then he realized that was it exactly. She was his love.

"I love you, Henry," he said, his voice like rough

velvet. "I love you like I never dreamed I could love a woman. I love you like everything in this world that is beautiful and good. Like the stars in the sky, and like each and every blade of grass at Stannage Park. I love you like the facets of a diamond, and Rufus's pointy ears, and—"

"Oh, Dunford," she burst out, "I love you too. I do. So much." She slid to the floor next to him and grasped his hands with hers. She kissed each one, then both together. "I love you so much," she murmured again. "So very much, and for so very long."

"I've been an idiot," he said. "I should have realized what a treasure you are the moment I saw you. I've wasted so much time."

"Only a month," she said tremulously.

"It seems like forever."

She moved to sit down on the carpet, pulling him down with her. "It has been the most precious month of my life."

"I hope to make the rest of your life just as precious, my love." He reached into his pocket and pulled something out. "Will you marry me?"

Henry had known he would propose, had expected it on that trip to the country even, but still she was overcome. Tears welled up in her eyes, and she could only nod, having apparently lost the power of speech.

Dunford uncurled the fingers of his fist to reveal a stunning diamond ring, an oval-cut stone set very simply in a plain gold band. "I couldn't find anything to rival the sparkle in your eyes," he said softly. "This was the best I could do."

"It's beautiful," she breathed. "I have never owned anything like this before." She looked up anxiously. "Are you certain we can afford it?"

Dunford let out a short burst of laughter, amused by

her concern for their finances; obviously she didn't realize that, although previously untitled, his was one of the wealthiest families in England. He was also absurdly pleased with the way she had said, "Are you certain *we* can afford it?" He lifted her hand to his lips, gallantly kissed it, and then said, "I assure you, minx, we still have enough left over to buy an entire new flock of sheep for Stannage Park."

"But several of the wells need fixing, and—"

"Shush." He pinched her lips shut. "You don't have to worry about money anymore."

"I neber exacdly worried aboud id," she tried to say while he was still holding her mouth closed. He sighed and let go, and she continued, "I'm just thrifty, that's all."

"That's fine." He tilted her chin up with his index finger and placed a sweet kiss on her lips. "But if I want to be a little extravagant once in a while and buy my wife a present, I expect no complaints from you about it."

Henry admired the ring he'd slipped on her finger, a shiver of excitement rushing through her at his use of the word "wife." "None," she murmured, feeling quite frivolous and utterly feminine. After regarding the ring from the left, the right, and two inches away from the flickering candle, she looked back up and asked plainly, "When can we be married?"

He took her face in his hands and kissed her again. "I think this is what I love best about you."

"What?" she asked, not caring in the least that she was fishing for compliments.

"You are utterly frank, disarmingly forthright, and refreshingly direct."

"All good qualities, I hope?"

"But of course, minx, although I suppose you could

have been slightly more forthright with me when I first arrived at Stannage Park. We might have been able to clear up that whole mess without venturing into the pigpen."

Henry smiled. "But when can we be married?"

"In two months time, I think," he said, the words sending an agonizing wave of frustration through his body.

"Two *months?*"

"I'm afraid so, my love."

"Are you insane?"

"Apparently, for I will most probably perish for wanting you during that time."

"Then why don't you simply get a special license and be done with it next week? It cannot be that difficult to obtain one. Emma said she and Alex were married by special license." She paused and frowned. "Now that I think of it, I think Belle and John were, too."

"I don't want you hurt by any gossip regarding a hasty marriage," he said gently.

"I'll be more hurt if I can't have you!" she said, not gently at all.

Another wave of desire pulsed through his body. He didn't think she'd meant the word "have" in the carnal sense, but it inflamed him nonetheless. Forcing his voice into even tones, he said, "There will be talk because I am your guardian. I don't want to make it any worse, especially since it would not be very difficult for anyone to discover that we were alone for more than a week in Cornwall."

"I didn't think you cared about *ton* gossip."

"I care for you, minx. I don't want to see you hurt."

"I won't be. I promise. One month?"

There was nothing he wanted more than to have the

wedding in one *week,* but he was trying to be mature about the matter. "Six weeks."

"Five."

"All right," he said, giving in easily because his heart was on her side even if his mind was not.

"Five weeks," she said, not sounding terribly pleased with her victory. "It's so long."

"Not so long, minx. You'll have many things to keep you busy."

"I will?"

"Caroline will want to help you shop for your trousseau, and I expect that Belle and Emma will want to take part as well. I'm certain my mother would also want to assist, but she is vacationing on the Continent."

"You have a mother?"

He quirked a brow. "Did you think mine was some sort of divine birth? My father was a remarkable man, but even he was not *that* talented."

Henry screwed up her face to show him that his teasing would not be taken seriously. "You never mention her. You rarely mention your parents at all."

"I don't see much of my mother now that my father has passed on. She prefers the warmer climes of the Mediterranean."

An awkward silence fell between them as Henry suddenly realized she was sitting on the floor of her bedroom in her dressing gown in the company of a rakishly virile man who was exhibiting no intentions of leaving anytime soon.

And the most appalling thing was that she was not the least bit uncomfortable about it. She sighed, thinking she must have the soul of a fallen woman.

"What's that about, darling?" Dunford murmured, touching her cheek.

"I was just thinking I ought to ask you to leave," she whispered.

"You *ought* to?"

She nodded. "But I don't want to."

He took a ragged breath. "Sometimes I think you don't know what you say."

She placed her hand in his. "I do know."

He felt like a man being willingly led to torture. He leaned forward, knowing that this could only end in a solitary frigid bath but unable to resist the temptation of a few stolen kisses. He traced the outline of her lips with his tongue, savoring the sweet taste of her. "You're so lovely," he murmured. "Exactly what I wanted."

"Exactly?" she echoed with a quavering laugh.

"Mmm-hmm." He slipped his hand inside her dressing gown and let it rest on her chemise-covered breast. "Not that I knew it at the time."

Henry let her head fall back as his lips trailed down the line of her throat. The heat of him seemed to be everywhere, and she was helpless against this onslaught of her senses. Her breath came in irregular pants and then stopped altogether when his hand on her breast gently squeezed. "Oh, God, Dunford," she gasped, fighting for air, "oh, my God."

His other hand slid down the length of her back until it cupped the round firmness of her derrière. "It's not enough," he said fiercely. "Lord help me, it's not enough." Holding her tightly against his frame, he lowered her down until her back laid against the carpet. In the flickering candlelight her brown hair seemed to sparkle with tiny sunbursts of gold. Her eyes were like molten silver, languid and drugged with desire. They were beckoning him . . .

With shaking hands he parted the silky folds of her robe. Her nightgown was white cotton, sleeveless yet almost virginal. The thought raced through his mind that he was the first man ever to see her like this—and the only man who ever would. He'd never dreamed he could feel this possessive, but the sight—and the feel and the smell—of her untouched body created a firestorm of primitive instinct that made him want to brand her as his.

He wanted to own her, to devour her. God help him, he wanted to lock her away where no other man could see her.

Henry stared at his face, watching it turn into a mask of fierce emotion. "Dunford?" she said hesitatingly. "What's wrong?"

He gazed at her for a moment, as if trying to memorize her features, right down to the tiny birthmark next to her right ear. "Nothing," he finally said. "It's just . . ."

"Just what?"

He let out a hoarse, self-deprecating laugh. "It's just—the things you make me feel—" He lifted her hand and placed it over his racing heart. "It's so strong—it frightens me."

Henry's breath caught in her throat. She'd never dreamed he could be frightened by anything. His eyes were blazing with an unfamiliar intensity, and she wildly wondered if her own looked the same. His grip on her hand loosened, and she moved her fingers up to his face, gently running one over his lips.

He growled with pleasure, then caught her hand once more, imprisoning it at his mouth. He kissed her fingertips, lingering over each one as if it were a delectable sweet. Then he moved back to her index finger, tracing lazy circles around its tip with his tongue.

"Dunford," she gasped, barely able to think with the bolts of pleasure shooting up her arm.

He took her finger further into his mouth, sucking gently as he ran his tongue over her fingernail. "You've been washing your hair," he said softly.

"H–how did you know?"

He sucked again gently before replying. "You taste like lemons."

"They have an orangery here," she said, barely recognizing her voice. "There is a lemon tree, and Emma said I might—"

"Hen?"

"What?"

He smiled, slowly and lazily. "I don't want to hear about Emma's lemon tree."

"I didn't think you did," she said dumbly.

He leaned down a few inches. "What I do want to do is kiss you."

She didn't move, couldn't move, so mesmerized was she by the blazing light in his eyes.

"And I think you want me to kiss you, too."

Tremulously, she nodded.

He closed the distance between them until his lips were resting gently against hers. He explored her slowly and teasingly, demanding nothing of her that she wasn't prepared to give. Henry could feel her entire body tingle. Every inch of her was alive with the heat of his body. Her lips parted slightly, and a soft moan escaped.

The change in Dunford was instantaneous. That tiny, whimpering sound of desire triggered something deep and desperate within him, and he became a fierce aggressor, branding her body with his own. His hands were everywhere—exploring the gentle curve of her waist, running up and down the smooth length of her legs, sinking into the heavy mass of her hair. He groaned her name over and over, almost like a litany of desire. It was as if he were drowning; clinging to her was his only means of staying afloat.

And then, once again, it wasn't enough.

His fingers, surprisingly nimble, slipped the buttons of her nightgown loose, and he spread the thin, white cotton open.

He sucked in his breath. "My God, Henry," he whispered reverently. "You're beautiful."

Her hands moved reflexively to cover herself, but he held them away, saying, "Don't. They're perfect."

Henry laid perfectly still, uncomfortable under his unwavering gaze. She felt too bare and exposed. "I–I can't," she finally said, trying to push her nightgown back up.

"Yes," he murmured, realizing that her discomfort stemmed more from her feelings of vulnerability than from fear of their intimacy. "You can." He covered one of her breasts with his large hand, deriving an inordinate amount of pleasure from the way her nipple puckered under his touch.

He leaned down, just barely catching the disbelieving expression on her face as he took one peak into his mouth. She gasped and bucked beneath him. Her hands clutched at his head, and he got the feeling she wasn't certain whether she was trying to pull him closer or push him away. He teased her puckered skin, running his tongue around its perimeter as his hands squeezed the gentle roundness of her breasts.

Henry wasn't sure if she was dead or alive. She didn't particularly feel as if she were dead, but she'd never been dead before, so how would she know? And she had certainly never experienced such intense feelings while alive.

Dunford dragged his head up and peered into her face. "What are you thinking about?" he asked huskily, amused and curious about the odd expression on her face.

"You wouldn't believe it," she said with a shaky laugh.

He quirked a smile, deciding he'd rather continue his amorous activities than pursue the topic further. With a delighted growl, he moved his head to her other breast, teasing it until it reached the same state of arousal as the first. "You like that, do you?" he murmured, hearing her little whimpers of pleasure. Feeling an overwhelming sense of pure affection for her, he moved back up and nuzzled her nose. "Did I remember to tell you in the last five minutes that I love you?"

Unable to suppress a smile, she shook her head.

"I love you."

"I love you, too, but . . ." Her words trailed off, and she looked embarrassed.

"But what?" He touched her cheek, moving her face slightly so that she could not avoid looking him in the eye.

"I was just wondering . . . that is . . ." She stopped and bit her lip before continuing with, "I just want to know if there is anything I can, that is to say—"

"Out with it, minx."

"Anything I can do for *you,*" she finished, closing her eyes since he would not allow her to look away.

His body tightened. Her shy, unpracticed words aroused his desire like nothing he could have imagined. "You'd better not," he said hoarsely. At her look of rejection, he continued, "*Later,* though. Definitely later."

She nodded, seeming to understand. "Then would you kiss me again?" she whispered.

She was half dressed, flushed with desire, and under him, and he was madly in love with her. There was no way he could deny her request. He kissed her again with all the emotion pulsing through his soul, one hand gently teasing her breasts and the other twisting through her hair. He kissed her endlessly, barely able to believe that one set of lips could be so fascinating, that he didn't need to move back to her neck or ears or breasts.

But his hands were another story, and he could feel one of them dipping ever lower, past the smooth, flat planes of her abdomen to the soft, curly thatch that covered her womanhood. She stiffened, but not very much; he had already torn down most of her restraint by making love to her breasts. "Shhh, my love," he whispered. "I just want to touch. God, I *need* to touch you."

Henry responded to the fierce emotion in his voice; she felt the same passion flowing through her own body. She was telling herself to relax when he lifted his head, stared deeply into her eyes, and said, "May I?"

His voice was so achingly humble and full of respect she thought she might shatter. Jerkily she nodded, thinking that, of course, this would feel nice. It was Dunford, and he would never do anything to hurt her. It would be nice. It would be nice.

She was wrong.

She nearly screamed from the spasms of pleasure that shot through her at his touch. "Oh my *God,*" she gasped. "Nice" could not even begin to describe what he was doing to her. It was too good, too much. Her body couldn't take it. She began to scoot away from him, thinking she would surely explode if he continued this sweet torture.

Dunford chuckled at her squirmings. "You're going to get a burn from the carpet," he teased.

Henry looked at him blankly, her brain so hazy with

passion it took her a few moments to process his words. He laughed again and rolled off her, scooping her up into his arms and carrying her to the plush bed. "I know I said the bed would be a big mistake," he murmured, "but I can't have you rubbing your back raw, can I?"

She felt herself sinking into the bed, and then he was on top of her again, the heat of him scorching her skin. His hand immediately stole down her body, back to her womanhood, where it teased and tickled, pushing her further and further toward oblivion. He slipped his finger inside of her, his thumb continuing to pleasure the sensitized nub of flesh. He flicked back and forth, back and forth . . .

"Dunford," Henry gasped. "I . . . you . . ."

His weight was pressing her into the mattress. He was hard and hot, and she couldn't control her body as her legs wrapped around his.

"My God, Henry," he groaned. "You're so ready. So . . . I didn't want to . . . I never intended . . ."

Henry was beyond caring what he had intended. All she wanted was the man in her arms—the man she loved. And she wanted all of him. She pressed her hips upward, cradling his insistent hardness.

Something within him snapped, and his fingers left her as he furiously tore off his breeches. "Hen," he moaned, "I need you. Now." His hands were on her breasts, then her backside, then her hips. They seemed to move with lightning swiftness, driven by a determination to touch every last inch of her silken skin.

He gently gripped her firmly muscled inner thighs and slid them further open. The tip of his manhood touched her, and he groaned at the wet heat of it.

"Henry, I . . . I . . ." His lips couldn't form the rest of the question, but she could see it in his eyes.

She nodded.

He moved gently forward, her soft skin resisting this new invasion.

"Shhhh," he murmured. "Relax."

Henry nodded. She'd never dreamed a man would feel this large within her. It felt good . . . but so very strange.

"Henry," he whispered, his face set into lines of concern. "This may hurt. But only for a moment. If I could—"

She touched his cheek. "I know."

He surged forward, sheathing himself completely within her. Henry stiffened at the sudden flash of pain.

He immediately held himself still, holding his weight off her by supporting himself on his elbows. "Did I hurt you?" he asked urgently.

She shook her head. "Not really. I just . . . It's all better now."

"Are you certain, Henry? Because I could pull out." His face clearly told her that such an option would be the worst sort of torture.

Her lips curved into a small smile. "All I need is for you to kiss me." She watched as his mouth slowly descended. "Just kiss me."

He did. His lips devoured hers as his body began to move—gently at first, then with an increasing rhythm. He was losing control, and he needed her to experience the same abandon. He moved his hand between their bodies and touched her.

She exploded.

The feeling began in her belly, then her body grew stiff as a board. She gasped, thinking that her muscles could not take this tension, that they would surely splinter—and then, miraculously, she went limp, her entire body warm and tingly yet utterly relaxed.

Her head lolled to the side and her eyelids drooped shut, but she could feel Dunford's intent gaze on her face. He was looking at her—she knew that as surely as she knew her name—and his eyes were telling her how much he loved her. "I love you, too," she sighed.

Dunford hadn't thought he could possibly feel any more tender toward her than he already did, but her soft declaration of love was like a warm kiss placed directly on his heart. He wasn't sure what precisely he had intended when he came to her room. He supposed subconsciously he had wanted to make love to her, but he had never dreamed he would feel this much happiness from pleasuring her.

He held himself above her, content for the moment just to watch her as her soul floated back down to earth. And then slowly—and with great regret—he pulled himself from her body.

Her eyes flew open.

"I don't want to get you with child," he whispered. "At least not yet. When the time comes, I shall derive the utmost satisfaction from seeing you heavy and round."

Henry shuddered, his words strangely erotic.

He leaned down, kissed her nose, and reached for his clothing.

She reached for him. "Please don't go."

He touched her forehead, brushing aside a silky lock of hair. "I wish I didn't have to," he murmured. "I hadn't really intended to do this, although"—he smiled wryly—"I can't say I'm sorry I did."

"But you didn't—"

"It'll have to wait, darling." He kissed her gently, unable to help himself. "For our wedding night. I want it to be perfect."

She was so languid she could barely move, yet

somehow she managed a small yet cheeky grin. "It would be perfect no matter what."

"Mmm, I know, but I'd also like to make certain that any new arrivals to our family don't arrive any sooner than nine months after our wedding. I won't have your reputation besmirched."

She didn't much care about her reputation at that moment, but for his sake she nodded understandingly. "Will you be all right?"

He closed his eyes for a moment. "In a few hours perhaps."

She reached out to touch him in sympathy but pulled her hand away when he shook his head and said, "Better not."

"I'm sorry."

"Please don't apologize." He stood. "I . . . ah . . . I think I might slip out of the house and go for a swim. There is a pond not too far away, and I hear it is very cold."

Much to her horror, she giggled.

He tried to look stern but didn't quite manage it. He leaned down and kissed her one last time, his lips gently brushing against her brow. Then he walked to the door and placed his hand on the knob. "Ah, Henry?"

"Hmmm?"

"We'd better make that *four* weeks."

Chapter 19

Dunford sent a messenger to London the next day to place an announcement in the *Times.* Henry was inordinately pleased by his haste to announce the engagement; it seemed yet another sign he loved her with the same devotion she felt for him.

Belle and John arrived the next morning in time to join the two couples for a late breakfast. Belle was very pleased although not terribly surprised at Dunford and Henry's announcement. She had known, after all, that he was planning to propose, and anyone who had ever seen Henry so much as look at him would have known she would accept.

After lunch the three ladies were sitting in the appropriately named sitting room, discussing Henry's new status as a betrothed woman.

"I hope he did something terribly romantic," Belle said, taking a sip of tea.

Henry delighted them both by blushing. "It was, ah, sufficiently romantic."

"What I don't understand," Emma said, "is when he had the opportunity to propose. He hadn't done so before dinner last night, unless you were keeping a secret, which I don't think you were because, frankly, I do not see how you would be able to keep so large a secret."

Henry coughed.

"And then the two of us retired to the parlor, and then we all went to bed." Emma's eyes narrowed. "Didn't we?"

Henry coughed again. "Do you know, I think I really could use a bit more tea."

Emma smiled wickedly and poured. "Have a sip, Hen."

Henry's eyes slid warily from cousin to cousin as she raised the cup to her lips.

"Has your throat recovered?" Belle inquired sweetly.

"A bit more tea, I think," Henry hedged, holding the cup out to her hostess. "With a bit more milk." Emma picked up the milk and splashed some into Henry's teacup. Henry took yet another sip and then, glancing up at the two pairs of eyes regarding her with devilish purpose, drained the cup. "I don't suppose you have any brandy."

"Out with it, Henry," Emma ordered.

"I . . . ah . . . it's a bit personal, don't you think? Really, I don't see either one of you telling me how your husbands proposed."

To Henry's surprise, Emma flushed. "Very well," the duchess said. "I won't ask you any more questions. But I have to tell you . . ." Her words trailed off, and she looked as if she were trying to figure out how to say something extremely indelicate.

"What?" Henry asked, unapologetically enjoying

Emma's discomfort. The duchess had, after all, been enjoying Henry's discomfort not two minutes earlier.

"I realize," Emma said slowly, "that part of the reason Dunford asked us to host you in a house party was because he realized we would not be the most stern of chaperones."

Belle let out a little snort of laughter.

Emma glared at her cousin before turning back to Henry. "I am sure he supposed he would find a way to get you alone, and I certainly understand that he would want some time alone with you. After all, he does love you." She paused and looked up. "He does love you, doesn't he? I mean, of course he does, but he *has* told you? Men can be such beasts about that."

Henry's cheeks pinkened a touch, and she nodded.

"Right," Emma said crisply. She cleared her throat and then continued, "As I was saying, I do understand your desire, er, perhaps that is the wrong word—"

" 'Desire' is probably quite appropriate," Belle said, her lips twitching with barely restrained laughter.

Emma shot another dagger-like glare at her cousin. Belle smirked back at her, and the two ladies continued this rather unladylike behavior until Henry cleared her throat. Emma immediately straightened, looked at Henry, and then, unable to resist, shot Belle one last glare. Belle responded in kind with her cheekiest of smirks.

"You were saying?" Henry said.

"Right," Emma said, not quite as crisply as before. "All I was going to say was that it is certainly all right to want to be alone with him, and"—she blushed, the effect almost comical against her bright red hair—"it is probably all right to actually *be* alone with him from time to time, but I have to ask you to please contrive not to be *very* alone with him, if you know what I mean."

Henry hadn't known what she meant until the night before, but now she did, and she blushed hard, much harder than Emma.

Emma's expression revealed she had a feeling her message was coming too late. "These things just seem to have a way of getting back to Aunt Caroline," she mumbled.

Henry started to feel embarrassed, but then she remembered that Belle and Emma were her friends. And although she hadn't much experience with female friends, she knew that if they teased, it was only because they cared. She looked up jauntily, first into Emma's violet eyes and then into Belle's blue ones, and said, "I won't tell if you don't."

The rest of the time in the country passed very quickly for Henry. She and her new friends made outings into the nearby village, played cards until the wee hours of the morning, and laughed and teased until their sides ached. But the most special times were when Dunford managed to sneak her away, and they were able to enjoy a few stolen moments together.

These clandestine meetings always seemed to begin with a passionate kiss, although Dunford insisted that was never his intention. "I see you and get carried away," he would say, always with an unrepentant shrug.

Henry tried to scold him, but her heart clearly wasn't in it.

All too soon, however, she found herself back in London, deluged by curious callers who insisted they just wanted to offer their congratulations on her upcoming marriage. Henry was a bit bewildered by all the attention as she hadn't even met the majority of the well-wishers.

The Earl of Billington stopped by, good-naturedly

complaining that he hadn't even been given a chance to court her. "Dunford stole quite a march on us all," he said with a lazy smile.

Henry smiled and shrugged humbly, not at all certain how to respond.

"I suppose I shall have to nurse my broken heart tonight and brave another ball."

"Oh, please," she scoffed. "Your heart isn't the least bit broken."

He grinned, delighted with her forthrightness. "It would have been, had I been given the chance to get to know you better."

"How lucky for me you weren't," drawled a deep voice.

Henry turned to see Dunford filling up the doorway to Caroline's favorite salon. He looked big and tall and so very masculine in his blue coat and tan breeches. He gazed at her and quirked a very small, one-sided smile that was meant for her alone. Her eyes immediately turned to dreamy pools of silvery satin, and she let out a tiny sigh.

"I can see I didn't have a prayer," Billington murmured.

"Not a one," Dunford said affably, crossing the room and sitting down next to Henry. Now that she was safely engaged to him, he finally remembered that he had always rather liked Billington.

"What brings you by?" Henry asked him.

"Just wanted to see you. Has your day been pleasant thus far?"

"Too many callers, I'm afraid." Henry suddenly realized her tremendous faux pas and turned to Billington, stammering, "Present company excluded, of course."

"Of course."

"Oh, please do not think me boorish, my lord. It's just that nearly a hundred people I do not know have come to see me today. I was really quite relieved when you came to call. I actually know you, and more importantly, I rather like you."

"A lovely apology, my dear." Dunford patted her hand as if to say that she needn't go on any further. At the rate she was going, she'd be professing her love for the earl any minute.

Billington caught Dunford's vaguely irritated expression and stood, a knowing smile on his face. "I have always prided myself on recognizing when I am *de trop*."

Dunford stood as well and escorted Billington to the door, where he gave the man a hearty slap on the back. "I have always admired that quality in you myself, Billington."

Billington's lips twitched, and he executed a smart bow in Henry's direction. "Miss Barrett."

A few seconds later she and Dunford were alone.

"I thought he would never leave," he said with a dramatic sigh, shutting the door behind him.

"You fiend. You all but chased him out. And don't think the door is going to remain closed for more than two minutes before Lady Worth gets wind of it and sends over a fleet of servants to chaperone us."

He sighed again. "A man can hope."

Henry's lips curved into a feminine smile. "So can a woman."

"Really?" He leaned toward her until she could feel his breath on her skin. "What were you hoping for?"

"Oh, this and that," she said breathily.

"This?" He kissed one corner of her mouth. "Or that?" He kissed the other.

"I-I believe I said this *and* that."

"So you did." He repeated both kisses. Henry sighed with contentment and allowed herself to sink into his side. His arms stole around her in a platonic embrace, and he nuzzled the back of her neck with his face. He allowed himself this pleasure for a few moments and then lifted his face to ask, "How much longer do you think we have before Caroline releases the hounds?"

"About thirty seconds, I should think."

He reluctantly loosened his hold, moved to the chair opposite her, and pulled out his pocket watch. "What are you doing?" Henry asked, shaking with silent laughter.

"Testing you, my dear." There was silence for about twenty seconds, then he clucked and shook his head. "You're off, minx. It appears I could have had a few more seconds of holding you."

Henry rolled her eyes and shook her head. The man was incorrigible. Then the door was abruptly opened. Neither of them could see who had done it. A liveried arm merely pushed it open, then disappeared. Both of them burst out laughing. "I have been vindicated!" Henry exclaimed triumphantly. "Tell me, how close was I?"

He nodded in reluctant admiration. "You were off by only six seconds, minx."

She gave him a self-satisfied smile and sat back.

He stood. "It appears our time alone has come to an end. What do we have now—just two more weeks?"

She nodded. "Aren't you glad I talked you into a four-week engagement instead of five?"

"Beyond words, my love." He leaned down and kissed her hand. "I trust I shall see you this evening at Lady Hampton's ball."

"If you are there, then so shall I be."

"I wish you were always this biddable."

"I can be quite biddable when it suits my purposes."

"Ah, yes. Then I suppose I shall have to ask you to contrive to find purposes that match my own."

"I believe we are in agreement just now, my lord."

He laughed. "I'm going to have to leave. You have by far surpassed me in the art of flirtation. I'm in serious danger of losing my heart."

"I should hope you have already lost it," she called out, watching him walk to the open door.

He turned around, his eyes burning with emotion. "I haven't lost it. But I did give it to a woman for safe-keeping."

"And is she keeping it safe?" she asked, unable to keep a quaver out of her voice.

"Yes, she is, and I would guard hers with my life."

"I hope it does not come to that."

"As do I. But that does not mean I would not give it." He turned but paused before leaving the room. "Sometimes, Hen," he said, not turning back around to face her, "I think I would give my life just for one of your smiles."

A few hours later Henry was finishing her preparations for that evening's ball. As always, she felt a little shiver of excitement at the thought of seeing Dunford that evening. It was strange how, now that they had professed their love for each other, their time together had grown even more thrilling. Every look, every touch was so infused with meaning; he had only to glance at her a certain way, Henry thought wryly, and she forgot how to breathe.

There was a chill in the night air, so she donned a gown of midnight-blue velvet. Dunford came by to escort her, as did Belle and John, who arrived in their own carriage. "Perfect," Caroline declared, clapping her hands together. "With two carriages already here, there is no reason to have mine brought round. I'll, ah, I'll just ride with Dunford and Henrietta."

Dunford's face fell visibly.

"And Henry—that is to say *my* Henry," Caroline explained, "shall ride with Belle and John."

Belle muttered something about not needing a chaperone when she was married, but Henry was the only one close enough to hear.

The ride to Hampton House was fairly uneventful, as Henry had expected it would be. There certainly wasn't much opportunity for an "event" to arise with Caroline in the carriage. Once at the ball Henry was immediately swept away by the crush of the crowd, most of whom already had decided she must be quite the most interesting young woman of the year if she had managed to land Dunford with such apparent ease.

Dunford watched her parry comments with nosy dowagers and equally nosy young debutantes, decided she was handling herself just fine, and went off to get some fresh air. Much as he wanted to spend every waking minute with her, it wouldn't do to spend too much time by her side. They were engaged, that was true, so people would expect him to pay her a bit more attention than usual, but there was also some less-than-pleasant gossip concerning how exactly they had met. They had, after all, become engaged only two weeks after her arrival in London. Dunford didn't think any of the gossip had reached Henry's ears yet, but he didn't want to do anything that might fan the flames. He decided to give her a bit of time to socialize with Caroline's friends, all highly influential and with unimpeachable reputations, then he'd return to claim her for a waltz. No one could fault him one dance.

He wandered over to the French doors leading out onto the garden. Lady Hampton had had the area lit with Chinese lanterns, and it was nearly as bright outside as it was inside. He leaned lazily against a pillar and was contemplating his tremendous good fortune when he heard someone calling his name. He turned his head.

The Earl of Billington was walking toward him, a smile on his face that was mocking and self-deprecating at the same time. "I just wanted to offer you my congratulations once again," he said. "I don't know quite how you managed it, but you do deserve the best of wishes."

Dunford nodded graciously. "You'll find someone else."

"Not this year. Crop's pitifully thin. Your Henry was the only one with half a brain."

Dunford arched his brow. "*Half* a brain?"

"Imagine my delight when I discovered that the only debutante with half a brain actually had one in its entirety." Billington shook his head. "I'll have to wait until next year."

"Why the rush?"

"Believe me, Dunford, you don't want to know."

Dunford found that comment quite cryptic but pressed no further, respecting the other man's privacy.

"Although," Billington continued, "since it appears I will not be getting myself leg-shackled this season, I most probably will be looking for a companion."

"A companion, you say?"

"Mmm-hmm. Charise returned to Paris a few weeks ago. Said it was too rainy here."

Dunford pushed away from the pillar. "I just might be able to help you out."

Billington motioned with his hand to the darker recesses of the lawn. "I had a feeling you might."

* * *

Lady Sarah-Jane Wolcott saw the two men walking toward the back of the garden, and her interest was immediately piqued. They had been conversing already for several minutes; what else could they need to talk about that would require even greater privacy? Mentally blessing the fact that she had chosen to wear a dark green dress that evening, she slipped into the shadows, moving quietly toward them until she found a spot where she could hide behind a large shrub. If she leaned forward, she could catch most of the gentlemen's conversation.

". . . going to have to get rid of Christine of course." That sounded like Dunford.

"I certainly didn't think you'd want to keep supporting a mistress with such a lovely wife."

"I should have cut her loose weeks ago. Haven't been to see her since I returned to London. One must be delicate about these things, though. I really don't want to hurt her feelings."

"Of course not."

"The lease isn't up on her house for a few months. That ought to give her time enough to find another protector."

"I was thinking about offering myself for that role."

That earned a chuckle from Dunford.

"I've had my eye on her for a few months now. Just been waiting until you tired of her."

"I was planning to meet with her Friday evening at midnight, to tell her I'm getting married, although she's bound to have heard already. I'll put in a good word for you."

Billington smiled as he took a sip of the drink he'd been holding in his hand. "You do that."

"I must confess, I'm glad you've taken an interest in

her. She's a nice woman. I shouldn't like to think of her set adrift."

"Good." Billington slapped Dunford on the back. "I'd best be getting back to the party. One never knows when a debutante with a brain might show up. I'll talk to you next week, after you've had a chance to deal with Christine."

Dunford nodded and watched Billington stride back across the terrace. After a few moments he did the same.

Sarah-Jane's lips curved into a smile as she pondered what she had just overheard and what use she could make of the tidbit. She wasn't exactly certain what it was about Miss Henrietta Barrett that so rankled her, but rankle she did. Perhaps it was simply the fact that Dunford was quite obviously besotted with the girl when she, Sarah-Jane, had been angling after him for nearly a year. And little Miss Henry obviously felt the same way. Every time she looked at the chit, she was looking at Dunford as if he were a god.

Sarah-Jane supposed that was what irritated her most about the girl—she was so damned innocent and unaffected, rather like Sarah-Jane had been at that age, before her parents married her off to Lord Wolcott, a notorious lecher three times her age. Sarah-Jane had consoled herself with a string of affairs, mostly with married men. Henry was going to be in for a rude awakening when she realized that married men did not remain faithful to their wives for very long.

Her head snapped up. Why not teach Henry that little lesson early? It wasn't as if she were doing anything evil, Sarah-Jane rationalized. Henry was going to have to learn the sad truth about *ton* marriages sooner or later. And perhaps sooner was better. Approached from that angle, it was obvious that she was actually doing

Henry a favor. Better that the chit enter her marriage with open eyes than become horribly disillusioned a few months later.

Sarah-Jane was smiling as she made her way back to the party.

Henry tried hard not to crane her neck as she scanned the crowds for Dunford. Where on earth had the man gone? She had spent the last half hour answering questions about their upcoming nuptials and thought it was high time he did his fair share.

"May I congratulate you on your upcoming marriage?"

Henry sighed and turned to the latest well-wisher, then opened her eyes a little wider when she saw it was Sarah-Jane Wolcott. "Lady Wolcott," she said, unable to keep a touch of frost from her voice. The lady had, after all, practically thrown herself on Dunford the last time they had met. "What a surprise."

"Why a surprise?" Sarah-Jane replied with a tilt of her head. "Surely you do not think I would begrudge another lady the happiness of wedded bliss."

Henry wanted to tell her she had no idea what she would or would not do, but mindful of the curious eyes and ears around her, she merely smiled and said, "Thank you."

"I assure you, I have nothing but the fondest wishes for you and your fiancé."

"I believe you," Henry said through clenched teeth, wishing that the other lady would just disappear.

"Good, but I would like to give you a bit of advice. From one woman to another, of course."

Henry did not have a good feeling about this. "That is very kind of you, Lady Wolcott, but Lady Worth, Lady Blackwood, and the Duchess of Ashbourne have all been most kind in giving me all sorts of necessary advice as pertains to the married state."

"That is very good of them, I am sure. I would expect no less from such gracious ladies."

Henry swallowed down the bad taste in her mouth and refrained from saying that the three ladies in question did not view Lady Wolcott with equal admiration.

"The advice I have for you," Sarah-Jane continued with an affected twist of her wrist, "is something no one else could tell you."

Pasting a bright, unnatural smile on her face, Henry leaned forward and said, "I am breathless with anticipation."

"Of course you are," Sarah-Jane murmured. "But here, let us step back from the crowds for a moment. What I have to say is for your ears alone."

Eager now to do anything to get rid of the woman, Henry obligingly took a few paces back.

"Please believe that I would do nothing to hurt you," Sarah-Jane said in a low voice, "and I tell you this only because I do not believe that any woman should enter into marriage without her eyes widely opened. I was not given that privilege."

"What *is it,* Lady Wolcott?" Henry ground out.

"My dear, I just thought you should know that Dunford has a mistress."

Chapter 20

"Is that all, Lady Wolcott?" Henry said frigidly.

Sarah-Jane did not have to feign surprise. "Then you already knew. You must be an exceptional young woman to dote on him so when there is another woman in his life."

"I do not believe you, Lady Wolcott. I think you are malicious in the extreme. Now, if you will excuse me—"

Sarah-Jane caught hold of Henry's sleeve before she could make her escape. "I can understand your reluctance to accept that what I say is true. You probably fancy yourself in love with him."

Henry almost blurted out that she didn't "fancy" anything—she *was* in love with Dunford—but not wanting to give Lady Wolcott the satisfaction of seeing that her emotions had been roused, she simply clamped her mouth shut. Sarah-Jane cocked her head in an extremely condescending manner, and Henry, unable to take any more, tugged at her sleeve and said coldly, "Please let go of me."

"Her name is Christine Fowler. He is going to see her on Friday. At midnight."

"I said, 'Let go of me,' Lady Wolcott."

"Have it your own way, then, Miss Barrett. But think about this: if I am lying, how could I possibly give you the specific time of his next assignation? You could simply go to her house at midnight, see I am wrong, and declare me a liar." Abruptly, she let go of Henry's sleeve. "But I am not a liar."

Henry, who had been poised for flight just moments earlier, found herself rooted to the spot. Lady Wolcott's words held more than a grain of sense.

"Here." Sarah-Jane held out a piece of paper. "This is her address. Miss Fowler is rather well-known. Even I know where she lives."

Henry stared at the slip of paper as if it were a monster.

"Take it, Miss Barrett. What you choose to do with it is up to you."

Henry still stared, unable to identify the awful emotions coursing through her. Lady Wolcott finally picked up her hand, uncurled her fingers, and tucked the paper into her palm. "In case you don't read it, Miss Barrett, I will tell you the address. She lives at number fourteen, Russell Square, in Bloomsbury. It is quite a nice little house. I believe your husband-to-be acquired it for her."

"Please go away," Henry said, her voice flat.

"As you wish."

"Now."

Lady Wolcott inclined her head gracefully and disappeared into the crowd.

"Oh, there you are, Henry!"

Henry looked up and saw Belle approaching.

"What are you doing off in the corner?"

Henry swallowed. "Just trying to escape the crowds for a moment."

"I certainly cannot blame you. It can be rather wearisome being the latest rage, can it not? But have no fear, Dunford surely will be along shortly to save you."

"No!" Henry said wildly. "That is, I don't feel well. Would I be terribly rude if I went home now?"

Belle looked at her with concern in her eyes. "Of course not. You do look a trifle flushed. I hope you do not have the fever."

"No, I just . . . I just want to lie down."

"Of course. Why don't you make your way to the door? I'll find Dunford and have him escort you home."

"No." The word came out quickly and with more force than Henry intended. "That's not necessary. He's probably with his friends, and I don't want to interrupt him."

"I'm certain he won't mind. In fact he would be most upset with me for not informing him you are ill. He'll be very concerned."

"But I really want to go *now.*" Henry could hear a note of hysteria creeping into her voice. "I really would like to lie down, and it may take you ages to locate him."

"All right," Belle said slowly. "Come with me. I'll have my carriage bring you home. No, I'll escort you. You don't look very steady on your feet."

Henry wasn't surprised. She certainly didn't feel very steady, either on her feet or otherwise. "That's not necessary, Belle. I'll be all right once I lie down."

"It's absolutely necessary," Belle replied firmly. "And it is no trouble at all. I'll see you to bed and then return to the party."

Henry nodded, not even noticing when the hated piece of paper slipped from her fingers.

They made their way outside, stopping to ask a friend to inform John and Dunford that they had left. When they reached the carriage, Henry realized she was trembling; the shaking stayed with her the entire way home.

Belle's eyes grew more and more worried, and she reached to touch Henry's forehead. "Are you certain you do not have the fever? I had one once. It was dreadful, but we can treat you more effectively if we detect it early."

"No," Henry said, clutching her arms to her chest. "It's just fatigue. I'm sure of it."

Belle did not look convinced, and when they arrived at the Blydon mansion, she prodded Henry quickly up the stairs and into bed. "I don't think I should leave," she said, sitting down in the chair next to Henry's bed. "You don't look at all well, and I shouldn't like you to be alone if you take a turn for the worse."

"Please don't stay," Henry begged, thinking that somehow she needed to be alone in her misery and confusion. "I shan't be alone. Your parents employ an army of servants. And I don't intend to do anything other than lie down and go to sleep. Besides, John will be expecting you back at the ball. You did leave word that you planned to return."

"You're certain you'll go right to sleep?"

"I'm certain I'll try." With all the thoughts swimming in her head, Henry wasn't sure she'd ever be able to sleep peacefully again.

"All right, then. But don't think I'm going to enjoy myself." Belle smiled as she tried to tease some good humor into her friend.

Henry managed a feeble smile in return. "Would you please blow out the candle when you leave?"

Belle nodded, did as she was asked, and walked out.

Henry laid awake in the dark for several hours. She stared up at a ceiling she could not see, her mind whirling around in a maze that always seemed to take her back to the same spot.

Surely Lady Wolcott had to be lying. She was obviously malicious, and Henry had been made very aware that she wanted—or at least once had wanted—Dunford for herself. She had every motive for trying to destroy Henry's happiness.

Furthermore, Dunford loved her. He had said he did, and Henry believed him. No man could have gazed upon her with such tenderness, made love to her with such exquisite devotion, if he did not love her.

Unless—what if she hadn't pleased him? When they had made love, Dunford had stopped short of completion. He had told her it was because he hadn't wanted her to become pregnant. At the time she had marveled at his control.

But would a man in love possess that kind of control? Maybe he hadn't felt the same sort of urgency she had. Maybe he would have found a sophisticated woman more desirable. Maybe she was still too much of a green, country-bred girl. No, a tomboy. Maybe she wasn't enough of a girl at all.

When it came right down to it, she still knew very little about being a woman. She had to consult Belle on nearly every matter of importance.

Henry curled into a ball, pressing her hands against her ears as if this could shut out the pessimistic voice inside her. She wouldn't let herself doubt him. He loved her. He'd said so, and she believed him.

Only a man in love could have said in such intense,

grave tones, *Sometimes I think I would give my life just for one of your smiles.*

If Dunford loved her, and she was certain he did, then he couldn't possibly want to keep a mistress. He would never do anything to hurt her so viciously.

But then why would Lady Wolcott have offered a specific time and place for his supposed meeting with this Christine Fowler? As she had said, if she was lying, it would certainly be easy for Henry to find her out. All she would have to do is lurk outside Christine Fowler's house at the appointed time and see if Dunford arrived. If Lady Wolcott was lying, Dunford would never show.

So there must be some sort of truth in Lady Wolcott's story, Henry decided. She didn't know how she could have acquired this information, but she would not put it past the woman to eavesdrop or to read other people's missives. But regardless of Lady Wolcott's treachery, one thing was certain: something was going to happen at midnight on Friday.

All at once Henry felt a wrenching wave of guilt. How could she doubt Dunford like this? She would be furious with him if he displayed a similar lack of trust in her. She knew she shouldn't doubt him. She didn't want to doubt him, but she couldn't very well go up to Dunford and question him about the matter. Then he would know she had doubted him. She didn't know if he would react with fury or cold disappointment, but she didn't think she could bear either one.

She was running in circles. She couldn't confront him because he would be angry that she thought there might be even a kernel of truth in Lady Wolcott's words. And if she didn't do anything, she'd spend the rest of her life with this cloud of doubt over her head. She didn't *really* think he kept a mistress, and to accuse him would be provoking in the extreme. But if she didn't confront him, she would never know for certain.

Henry squeezed her eyes shut, wishing she would start to cry. Tears would exhaust her, and then maybe she'd be able to sleep.

"What do you mean she's ill?" Dunford took a menacing step toward Belle.

"Just that, Dunford. She wasn't feeling well, so I took her home and put her to bed. It's been a most tiring fortnight for her, in case you hadn't noticed. Half of London decided they simply had to make her acquaintance in the last two weeks. And then you practically abandoned her to the wolves the moment we got here."

Dunford winced at the note of reproach in Belle's voice. "I am trying to keep gossip to a minimum. If I pay too much public attention to her, the tongues will begin to wag anew."

"Will you cease about the gossip!" Belle snapped. "I know you say you're doing it all for Henry, but she doesn't care a fig about it. All she cares about is you, and you disappeared this evening."

His eyes burned, and he started to walk past her. "I am going to see her."

"Oh, no you don't," Belle said, catching him by the sleeve. "The poor girl is exhausted; let her sleep. And when I said to stop worrying about the gossip, I did not mean to imply that it was acceptable to storm into her room—in my mother's house, no less—in the middle of the night."

Dunford stilled, but he clenched his jaw against the strength of his self-loathing and impotence. He'd never felt this way; it was as if something were eating him from the inside out. Just knowing that Henry was ill, and if not alone at least not with him, made him shiver with cold and hot and fear and God knew what else. "Is she going to be all right?" he finally got out, his tone carefully even.

"She's going to be just fine," Belle said softly, laying a hand on his arm. "She just needs a bit of sleep. I will make certain to ask my mother to look in on her later this evening."

He nodded curtly. "Do that. I'll be by to see her tomorrow."

"I'm sure she'll appreciate that. I'll stop by as well." She started to walk away, but he called out her name. Turning back around, she said, "Yes?"

"I just want to thank you, Belle." He paused, a muscle working in his throat. "For befriending her. You have no idea how badly she needed a friend. It has meant a great deal to her. And to me."

"Oh, Dunford. You don't have to thank me. She makes it so very easy to be her friend."

Dunford sighed as he left the ball. The party had been tolerable only because he had known that he would soon claim his fiancée in a waltz. Now that she was gone, there was nothing left to look forward to. It was amazing to think how bleak life looked without her.

What was he thinking? With a shake of his head, he banished the thought from his mind. There was no reason even to contemplate life without Henry. He loved her, and she loved him. What more could he need?

"You have a visitor, Miss Barrett."

Henry looked up from her bed at the maid who had just made that announcement. Belle had come by that morning to keep her company, and the two of them were presently leafing through fashion plates.

"Who is it, Sally?" Belle asked.

"It's Lord Stannage, my lady. He said he wants to see how his fiancée is faring."

Belle frowned. "It's not really proper for him to come up here, but you *are* ill, and I *am* here to chaperone you."

Henry didn't have time to say that she wasn't certain if she wanted to see him before Belle added, "I'm sure you're just dying to see him. It will be all right for just a moment." She nodded at the maid, who went downstairs to fetch Dunford.

He appeared so quickly that Henry thought he must have taken the steps two at a time. "How are you?" he asked huskily, moving quickly to her side.

She swallowed spasmodically, trying to get rid of the lump in her throat. He was looking at her with such love in his eyes, she felt like a traitor for ever having thought, however briefly, that Lady Wolcott was telling the truth. "A—a bit better."

He took her hand and held it between his. "I cannot tell you how glad I am to hear that."

Belle cleared her throat. "I'll just wait outside the door." She leaned down and said to Dunford, "Only two minutes."

He nodded. Belle left the room but did not close the door. "How are you really feeling?" he asked.

"Much better," Henry said truthfully. She did feel much better now that she'd seen him again. She felt like a fool for ever thinking he'd betray her. "I think it was mostly fatigue."

"You do look a bit tired." He frowned. "There are shadows under your eyes."

The shadows were probably entirely due to her inability to sleep the night before, Henry thought ruefully. "I think I shall spend the rest of today in bed," she said. "I cannot remember the last time I did so. I feel sinfully lazy."

He touched her chin. "You deserve it."

"Do I?"

"Mmm-hmm. I want you well rested when we get married." He grinned wickedly. "Then I intend to tire you out."

A hint of a blush crept across her cheeks, but she was not too embarrassed to say, "I wish we were married right now."

"As do I, my love." He leaned forward, his heavy-lidded gaze dropping to her lips.

"Hello!" Belle poked her head into the room.

Dunford cursed rather fluently under his breath. "Your timing is, as always, impeccable."

Belle shrugged. "It's a talent I cultivate."

"I wish you'd cultivate it a bit less," Henry muttered.

Dunford lifted one of Henry's hands to his lips and kissed it before rising to his feet. "I shall call tomorrow to see how you are doing. Perhaps we can go for a walk if you feel up to it."

"I'd like that."

He took a step as if to leave, then turned back to her, bending his knees slightly so his face was more on a level with her own. "Would you do me a favor?"

Henry nodded, startled by the serious look in his eyes.

"Will you promise me that if you feel the slightest bit worse, you will consult a physician immediately?"

She nodded again.

"I also want you to see one if you don't begin to feel better by tomorrow."

"I already feel much better. Thank you for coming."

He smiled, one of those secret smiles that never

failed to turn her knees to butter. Then, with a slight bow, he left the room.

"Did you have a nice visit?" Belle asked. "No, don't even bother answering. I can see for myself. You're positively radiant."

"I know that ladies aren't supposed to go into trade, Belle, but if we could bottle one of his smiles as medicine, we'd make a fortune."

Belle smiled indulgently as she straightened her skirts. "Much as I adore Dunford, I feel obligated to point out that his smiles are not nearly as special as those of my husband."

"Bah," Henry scoffed. "Speaking from a purely objective standpoint, anyone can see that Dunford's smiles are clearly superior."

"Objective standpoint, my foot."

Henry grinned. "What we need is an impartial observer. We could ask Emma, but I have a feeling she'd simply say that both of us are mad in the head and that Alex has the nicest smile."

"I imagine that is the way it should be," Belle said.

"Mmm-hmm." Henry plucked at her blankets for a few moments before saying, "Belle? Might I ask you a question?"

"Of course."

"It pertains to married life."

"Oh," Belle said knowingly. "I thought you might want to talk to me about that. Since you don't have a mother, I didn't know whom you'd turn to with questions."

"Oh, no, not *that,*" Henry said quickly, feeling the now-familiar blush stain her cheeks. "I know all about *that.*"

Belle coughed, hiding a bit of her face behind her hand.

"Not from firsthand experience," Henry lied. "But remember I grew up on a farm. We did a fair amount of animal breeding."

"I . . . ah . . . I feel I must interject here for a moment." Belle paused, looking as if she were trying to figure out the best way to proceed. "I did not grow up on a farm, but I am not wholly unfamiliar with animal husbandry, and I have to say that although the mechanics are the same . . ."

Henry had never seen Belle blush this much. She decided to take pity on her friend and quickly said, "The matter I wanted to talk to you about is slightly different."

"Oh?"

"I understand—that is to say, I've heard that many men keep mistresses."

Belle slowly nodded. "That is true."

"And that many of them continue to keep their mistresses after they are wed."

"Oh, Henry, is that what this is about? Are you afraid Dunford is going to keep a mistress? I can assure you he won't, not when he loves you so much. I imagine you'll keep him so busy he won't have time for a mistress."

"But does he have one now?" Henry persisted. "I know I cannot expect that he has led the life of a monk before meeting me. I'm not even jealous of any women with whom he might have had liaisons before he met me. I certainly cannot hold it against him if he didn't even know me at the time. But what if he still has a mistress now?"

Belle swallowed uncomfortably. "I cannot give you anything less than complete honesty, Henry. I know that Dunford was keeping a mistress when he left for Cornwall, but I don't think he has seen her since he returned. I swear it. I'm sure he's broken it off with her by now. Or if he hasn't, he's going to."

Henry licked her lips thoughtfully, relief sinking into her bones. Of course, that was it. He was planning to see this Christine Fowler woman on Friday night to tell her she would need to seek another protector. She'd rather that he had taken care of the task when they first arrived in London, but she couldn't censure him for putting off what was probably an unpleasant chore. Henry was sure that his mistress wouldn't want to part with him. She couldn't imagine any woman wanting to part with him.

"Did John keep a mistress before he met you?" Henry asked curiously. "Oh, I'm sorry. That was frightfully personal."

"It's all right," Belle assured her. "Actually, John was not keeping a mistress, but he also wasn't living in London. It's quite a common practice here. I know Alex kept one, though, and he stopped seeing her the minute he met Emma. I'm sure it's the same for you and Dunford."

Belle sounded so convinced that Henry couldn't help but believe her. It was, after all, what she wanted to believe. And in her heart she knew it was true.

For all her certainty in Dunford's innocence, Henry still found herself oddly jittery on Friday. She was startled every time someone spoke to her, and the slightest noise made her jump. She spent three hours reading the same page of Shakespeare, and the thought of food made her sick.

Dunford collected her for their daily walk at three in the afternoon, and the sight of him left her tongue-tied. All she could think about was that he would be seeing HER that evening. She wondered what they would say to each other. What did SHE look like? Was she beautiful? Did she look like Henry? *Please, God, don't let her look like me,* Henry thought. She wasn't entirely certain why this meant so much to her, but she thought she might be ill if she found out she resembled Christine Fowler in any way.

"What has you so preoccupied?" Dunford asked, smiling down at her indulgently.

Henry started. "Just wool-gathering, I'm afraid."

"Penny for your thoughts."

"Oh, they're not worth it," she said with unnecessary force. "Believe me."

He looked at her oddly. They walked on for a few paces before he said, "I hear you have been making use of Lord Worth's library."

"Oh, yes," Henry said with relief, hoping that a benign topic would help to take her mind off Christine Fowler. "Belle has been recommending some of Shakespeare's plays to me. She has read them all, you know."

"I know," he murmured. "She did it in alphabetical order, I believe."

"Did she? How odd." Another silence, and Henry's thoughts were back to precisely where she did not want them. Finally, knowing she was absolutely, positively doing the wrong thing but unable to help herself, she turned to him and asked, "Do you have any special plans for this evening?"

The tips of his ears grew red; a sure sign of guilt, Henry thought. "Ah, no," he said. "I was just planning to meet some friends at White's for a game of whist."

"I'm sure you'll have a lovely time."

"Why do you ask?"

She shrugged. "Curiosity, I suppose. Tonight is the first night in weeks that our plans for the evening don't coincide. Except, of course, for when I was ill."

"Well, I don't expect to be seeing quite as much of my friends once we're married, so I'm rather obligated to join them in a card game now."

I'll just bet you are, she thought sarcastically. Then she berated herself for thinking so badly of him. He was going to his mistress's house that evening to break it off. She should be happy. And if he was lying to her about it, well that was only natural. Why would he want her to know he was going there at all?

"What are your plans?" he asked her.

She grimaced. "Lady Worth is forcing me to attend a musicale."

Horror slid across his face. "Not . . ."

"I'm afraid so. Your Smythe-Smith cousins. She feels I ought to meet some of your relations."

"Yes, but doesn't she understand . . . ? Henry, this is too cruel. Never in the history of the British Isles have there been four females less gifted with musical talent."

"So I've heard. Belle has flatly refused to accompany us."

"I'm afraid I dragged her to one last year. I don't even think she'll walk down their street anymore for fear she might hear them practicing."

Henry smiled. "Now I'm growing curious."

"Don't," he said, very seriously. "If I were you, I would endeavor to have a serious relapse this evening.

"Really, Dunford, they can't be that bad."

"Yes," he said darkly, "they can."

"I don't suppose you could swoop down and save me this evening?" she asked, giving him a sideways glance.

"I wish I could. Truly, I do. As your future husband, it is my duty to shield you from all unpleasantness, and believe me, the Smythe-Smith string quartet is beyond unpleasant. But my engagements this evening are most pressing. I cannot break them."

Henry now was certain that he was going to see Christine Fowler at midnight. *He's breaking it off,* she repeated to herself. *He's breaking it off.* That was the only explanation.

Chapter 21

That may have been the only explanation, but it didn't mean Henry felt particularly chipper about it. As midnight grew near, her thoughts became increasingly fixed on Dunford's upcoming meeting with Christine Fowler. Even the Smythe-Smith musicale, dreadful as it was, failed to distract her.

On the other hand, perhaps Dunford's meeting with Christine Fowler was a blessing in disguise; at least it was distracting her from the Smythe-Smith string quartet.

Dunford had not underestimated their musical skill.

To her credit, Henry managed to sit still throughout the performance, concentrating on discovering a method to somehow close up her ears from the inside out. She looked discreetly up at the clock. It was quarter past ten. She wondered if he was at White's now, enjoying a game of cards before his meeting.

The concert finally drew to its last discordant note, and the audience breathed a collective sigh of relief. As she stood, Henry heard someone say, "Thank goodness they didn't perform an original composition."

Henry almost laughed, but then she saw that one of the Smythe-Smith girls had heard the comment, too. To her surprise, the girl did not look ready to burst into tears. She looked furious. Henry found herself nodding approvingly. At least the girl had spirit. Then she realized that the seething glare was not directed at the rude guest but at the girl's mother. Curious, Henry immediately decided to introduce herself. She made her way through the crowd and onto the makeshift stage. The other three Smythe-Smith daughters had begun to mingle in the crowd, but the one with the forbidding expression on her face played the cello, which she couldn't very well carry around with her. She seemed reluctant to leave it unattended.

"Hello," Henry said, holding out her hand. "I am Miss Henrietta Barrett. I know that it is forward of me to introduce myself, but I thought we might make an exception as we are soon to be cousins."

The girl stared at her blankly for a moment and then said, "Oh, yes. You must be betrothed to Dunford. Is he here?"

"No, he was otherwise engaged. He has a very busy schedule this evening."

"Please, you don't have to make excuses for him. This"—she waved her hand at the chairs and music stands still in place—"is hideous. He's a very kind man and has come to three of these already. Actually, I'm quite glad he didn't come. I shouldn't want to be responsible for his deafness, which is sure to ensue if he attends too many of our musicales."

Henry smothered a giggle.

"No, please go ahead and laugh," the girl said. "I'd much rather you did that than compliment me as all these people are bound to do soon."

"But tell me," Henry said, leaning forward. "Why does everyone keep coming?"

The girl looked bewildered. "I don't know. I think it must be out of respect for my late papa. Oh, but I am sorry, I have not even told you my name. I am Charlotte Smythe-Smith."

"I know." Henry motioned to her program, which listed the daughters' names and their respective instruments.

Charlotte rolled her eyes. "It has been lovely meeting you, Miss Barrett. I hope we will have a chance to do so again soon. But please, I beg of you, do not attend another one of our performances. I should not like to be responsible for the loss of your sanity, which is sure to occur if you do not find yourself deaf first."

Henry bit back a smile. "It's not as bad as that."

"Oh, but I know that it is."

"Well, it certainly is not *good,*" Henry admitted. "But I am glad I came. You're the first of Dunford's relatives I have met."

"And *you* are the first of his fiancées *I* have met."

Henry's heart skipped a beat. "I beg your pardon."

"Oh, dear," Charlotte said quickly, her face growing pink. "I have gone and done it again. Somehow the things I say sound so much different in my head than they do aloud."

Henry smiled, seeing quite a bit of herself in Dunford's cousin.

"You are, of course, his first—and one would hope only—fiancée. It is just that it is most exciting to hear that he is betrothed. He has always been such a rake, and—Oh, dear, you didn't really want to hear that, did you?"

Henry tried to smile again but just couldn't manage it. The last thing she wanted to hear tonight were tales of Dunford's rakehell days.

* * *

Caroline and Henry took their leave soon thereafter, Caroline fanning herself vigorously in the coach and declaring, "I swear I will never attend one of those recitals again."

"How many have you attended?"

"This is my third."

"One would think you would have learned your lesson by now."

"Yes." Caroline sighed. "One would."

"Why do you go?"

"I don't know. The girls are really quite sweet, and I shouldn't want to hurt their feelings."

"At least we may make an early evening of it. All of that noise exhausted me."

"Myself as well. With any luck I'll be in bed before midnight."

Midnight. Henry cleared her throat. "What time is it now?"

"It is probably near to half past eleven. The clock said fifteen minutes past the hour when we left."

Henry wished there was some way to stop her heart from beating quite so fast. Dunford was probably preparing to leave his club at that very minute. Soon he would be on his way to Bloomsbury, to number fourteen, Russell Square. Silently, she cursed Lady Wolcott for having given her the address. She hadn't been able to stop herself from looking it up on a map. It made it all the more difficult, knowing precisely where he was going.

The carriage drew to a halt in front of the Blydon mansion, and a footman immediately came out to help the two ladies down. As they entered the front hall, Caroline wearily pulled off her gloves and said, "I'm going directly to bed, Henry. I don't know why, but I am exhausted. Would you please be so kind as to ask the staff not to disturb me?"

Henry nodded. "I think I shall browse the library for something to read. I'll see you in the morning."

Caroline yawned. "If I wake up by then."

Henry watched her climb the stairs and then wandered down the hall to the library. She picked a candelabra up off of a side table and entered the room, nosing the flames closer to the books so she could read the titles. No, she mused, she didn't much feel like another Shakespeare. Richardson's *Pamela* was much too long. The tome looked to be over a thousand pages.

She glanced at the grandfather clock in the corner. Moonlight spilled through the windows onto its face, making it very easy for Henry to see the time. Half past eleven. She gritted her teeth. There was no way she was going to be able to sleep that night.

The minute hand moved lazily to the left. Henry stared at the clock until it was thirty-three minutes past the hour. This was insane. She couldn't just sit there and watch the clock all night. She had to do something.

She raced upstairs to her room, not quite certain what she was planning to do until she threw open her closet and saw her men's breeches and jacket folded up in a corner. It looked as if the maid had been trying to hide them. Henry picked up the garments and fingered them thoughtfully. The jacket was dark blue and the breeches, charcoal gray. Both would blend well into the night.

Her decision made, she hastily shrugged off her evening gown and pulled on the masculine attire, slipping a key to the house into the pocket of her breeches. She pulled her hair back like a pony's tail and then tucked the end into the collar of the jacket. No one who got a good look at her would mistake her for a boy, but she wouldn't attract attention from afar.

She put her hand on the doorknob, then remembered how she had been mesmerized by the ticking of the clock in the library. She dashed back across the room, picked up the very small clock that sat on her dressing table, and ran back to the door. Poking her head out into the hallway, she ascertained that it was empty and hurried out. She made it downstairs and out the door without being noticed. She took off at a brisk pace, making sure she walked as if she knew where she was going. Mayfair was the safest part of town, but a woman still couldn't be too careful. There was a spot where hacks queued up only a few blocks away. She'd get one to take her to Bloomsbury, wait with her while she spied on Christine Fowler's house, and then return her to Mayfair.

She reached her destination quickly, her hand still clutching the clock. Glancing down, she saw it was 11:44. She'd have to get across town quickly.

There were several hacks queued up, and Henry hopped into the first one, giving the driver Christine Fowler's address. "And step lively about it," she said crisply, trying to imitate Dunford's tones when he wanted to get something done immediately.

The driver turned onto Oxford Street, then headed along that road for several minutes until he made a series of twists and turns that led them to Russell Square.

"Here you are," he said, obviously expecting her to step down.

Henry glanced at the clock. 11:56. Dunford wouldn't have arrived yet. He was extremely punctual but not the sort who inconvenienced hosts by arriving early. "Er, I'll just wait a moment," she called out. "I'm meeting someone, and he's not here yet."

"It'll cost you extra."

"I'll make it worth your while."

The driver took a good look at her, decided that only someone with money to burn would be dressed in such an outrageous getup, and sat back, figuring that sitting still in Bloomsbury was a hell of a lot easier than looking around for another fare.

Henry stared at her little clock, watching the minute hand slowly sweep toward the twelve. Finally she heard the clip-clop of horses' hooves, and looking up, she recognized the carriage coming down the street as Dunford's.

She held her breath. He stepped down, looking very elegant and, as always, extremely handsome. She exhaled with an irritated sigh. His mistress wasn't going to want to let him go when he looked like that.

"Is that the person yer waitin' for?" the driver asked.

"Not really," she hedged. "I'm going to have to wait a bit longer."

He shrugged. "It's yer money."

Dunford ascended the steps and rapped on the door. The sound of the heavy brass knocker echoed down the street, straining Henry's already jangled nerves. She pressed her face to the window. Christine Fowler would probably have a manservant to answer the door, but Henry wanted to get a good look just in case.

The door opened to reveal a startlingly lovely woman with thick, black hair that cascaded down her back in rippling curls. She obviously wasn't dressed to receive ordinary visitors. Henry looked down, taking in her own decidedly unfeminine attire, and tried to ignore the sick feeling in her stomach.

Just before the door shut, Christine placed her hand at the back of Dunford's head, pulling his lips down to hers. Henry's fists clenched. The door shut before she could see just how deeply they kissed.

She looked down at her hands. Her fingernails had drawn blood on her palms.

"It wasn't his fault," she muttered under her breath. "He didn't initiate the kiss. It wasn't his fault."

"Did you say something?" the driver called.

"No!"

He sat back, obviously deciding all his theories about the general dim-wittedness of women had been confirmed.

Henry tapped her hand nervously against her seat. How long would it take him to tell Christine she had to find a new protector? Fifteen minutes? A half hour? Surely not longer than that. Forty-five minutes, perhaps, just to be generous, in case he had to make monetary arrangements with her. Henry didn't particularly care how much gold he gave her, just as long as he got rid of her. For good.

Taking deep breaths to try to control the tension racing through her, Henry perched the clock on her lap. She stared at it until she saw double, until her eyes watered. She watched the minute hand sweep down to the three and then told herself sternly that she had been far too optimistic; he couldn't possibly conduct his business in only fifteen minutes.

She watched as the minute hand fell ever lower, resting at the six. She swallowed uncomfortably, telling herself that since her fiancé was such a nice man, he'd want to break the news to his mistress gently. That must be what was taking so long.

Another fifteen minutes passed, and she choked back a sob. Even the kindest of men could have gotten rid of a mistress in forty-five minutes.

Somewhere in the distance a clock struck one.

Then it struck two.

And then, unbelievably, three chimes were heard.

Henry finally gave in to her despair, poked the sleeping driver in the back, and said, "Grosvenor Square, please."

He nodded, and they were off.

She stared straight ahead the entire way home, her eyes glazing over with utter emptiness. There could be only one reason why a man spent so long with his mistress. He hadn't emerged even after three hours. She thought back to their few stolen moments in her bedroom at Westonbirt. He certainly hadn't been with her for three hours.

After all this, all these lessons in how to behave with poise and propriety and feminine grace, she still wasn't woman enough to keep his interest. She could never be more than what she was. She'd been insane to think she could even try.

At Henry's instruction, the hack pulled up a few houses away from the Blydon mansion. She gave the driver more coins than was necessary and walked blindly home. She slipped noiselessly inside and up to her room, where she peeled off her clothes, kicked them under the bed, and pulled on a nightgown. The first one she grabbed was the one she'd worn when she and Dunford had . . . No, she couldn't wear that again. It seemed sullied somehow. She balled it up and threw it into the fireplace, grabbing another.

Her room was warm, but she was shivering as she crawled beneath the sheets.

Dunford finally staggered down Christine's front steps at half past four in the morning. He had always thought of her as a reasonable woman; he supposed that was why he'd been with her for so long. But tonight he'd almost had to revise his opinion. First she'd cried, and he'd never been the sort of man who could walk out on a woman when she was crying.

Then she'd offered him a drink, and when he'd finished that, she'd offered him several more. He'd refused, smiling mockingly at her and saying that although she was an exceptionally lovely woman, alcohol didn't tend to seduce him when he didn't want to be seduced.

Then she'd started to express her worries. She had tucked away some money, but what if she couldn't find another protector? Dunford had told her about the Earl of Billington and then spent the next hour assuring her he would forward some funds and that she could remain in the house until the lease expired.

Finally she'd just sighed, accepting her fate. He'd prepared to leave, but she had put her hand on his arm and asked him if he'd like a cup of tea. They had been friends as well as lovers, she had said. She didn't have many friends, her line of work didn't encourage it. Tea and conversation were all she wanted. Just someone to talk to.

Dunford had looked into her black eyes. She had been telling the truth. If there was one thing you could say for Christine, she was honest. And so, since he'd always liked her, he stayed and talked. They gossiped; they talked politics. She told him about her brother in the army, and he told her about Henry. She didn't seem the least bit bitter about his betrothed; in fact, she'd smiled when he told her about the pigpen incident and told him she was happy for him.

Finally he'd dropped a light, brotherly kiss on her lips. "You'll be happy with Billington," he'd told her. "He's a good man."

Her lips curved into a small, sad smile. "If you say so, then it must be true."

He looked at his pocket watch when he reached his carriage and swore. He hadn't meant to stay so late. He was going to be tired the next day. Ah well, he supposed he could sleep in past noon if he was so inclined.

He didn't have any plans before his daily afternoon jaunt with Henry.

Henry.

Just the thought of her made him smile.

When Henry woke the next morning, her pillowcase was soaked through with tears. She stared at it uncomprehendingly. She hadn't cried herself to sleep the night before; in fact, she'd felt strangely hollow and dry. She had never heard of sorrow so great that one actually cried while asleep.

Still, she couldn't imagine a sorrow greater than hers.

She couldn't marry him. That was the only clear thought in her head. She knew most marriages were not based upon love, but how could she commit herself to a man who was so dishonest he could profess his love for her and then make love to his mistress only two weeks before their wedding?

He must have proposed out of pity, that and his blasted sense of responsibility. Why else would he shackle himself to a tomboyish freak who hadn't even known the difference between a day dress and an evening gown?

He had said he loved her. She had believed him. What an utter fool she was. Unless . . .

Henry choked on a sob.

Maybe he did love her. Maybe she hadn't misread him. Maybe she simply wasn't womanly enough to satisfy him. Maybe he needed more than she could ever be.

Or maybe he had simply lied. She didn't know which she preferred to believe.

The astounding part was that she didn't hate him. He had done too much for her, showed her too much kindness for her ever to hate him. She didn't think he had slept with Christine out of any sense of malice toward her. And she didn't think he'd done it for some perverse thrill.

No, he'd probably slept with her just because he'd thought it his right. He was a man, and men did things like that.

It wouldn't have hurt so much if he hadn't told her he loved her. She even might have been able to go through with the marriage.

But how was she to break it off? All of London was abuzz about their engagement; to cry off now would be the height of embarrassment. She didn't particularly mind the thought of the gossip for herself. She'd head back to the country—although not to Stannage Park, she thought painfully. He probably wouldn't allow her to return. But she could go somewhere where the *ton* couldn't reach her.

He, however, couldn't. His life was here in London.

"Oh, God!" she burst out. "Why can't you just hurt him?"

She loved him still. Somewhere someone had to be laughing about this.

He was going to have to be the one to call off the engagement. That way he wouldn't suffer the embarrassment of being jilted. But how to make him do it? How?

She laid on her bed for over an hour, her eyes focusing on a tiny crack in the ceiling. What could she do to make him hate her so much he'd break off the engagement? None of her schemes seemed plausible, until . . . Yes, that was it. That was exactly it.

With a heavy heart she walked over to her desk and pulled open the drawer Caroline had thoughtfully stocked with writing paper, ink, and a quill. Out of nowhere she remembered the imaginary friend she'd had as a child. Rosalind. That name would do as well as any.

Blydon House
London
2 May 1817

My dear Rosalind,

I am sorry that I have not written in such a long time. My only excuse is that my life has changed so dramatically in the last few months that I have barely had time to think.

I am to be married! I can imagine you are surprised. Carlyle passed away not so very long ago, and a new Lord Stannage came to Stannage Park. He was a very distant cousin of Carlyle's. They didn't even know each other. I haven't the time to expound upon the details, but we have become engaged to be married. I am very excited, as I'm sure you can imagine, as this means I may stay at Stannage Park for the rest of my life. You know how much I love it there.

His name is Dunford. That is his family name, but no one calls him by his given name. He is very nice and treats me kindly. He has told me he loves me. Naturally, I answered similarly. I thought it only polite. Of course I am marrying him for my dear, dear Stannage Park, but I do like him well enough and didn't want to hurt his feelings. I think we shall deal well together.

I haven't time to write more. I am staying in London with some of Dunford's friends and shall be here for another two weeks. After that you may send correspondence to Stannage Park; I am cer-

tain I can convince him to retire there immediately following the marriage. We shall honeymoon for a bit, I suppose, and then he will probably want to return to London. I don't particularly mind if he stays; he is, as I mentioned, a nice enough fellow. But I imagine he'll soon grow bored of country life. That will suit me well. I will be able to go back to my old life without fear of ending up someone's governess or companion. I remain

Your dear friend,
Henrietta Barrett

With quivering hands, Henry folded the letter and slid it into an envelope addressed "Lord Stannage." Before she had a chance to rethink her actions, she dashed down the stairs and placed it in the hands of a footman with instructions to see it delivered immediately.

Then she turned around and made her way back up the stairs, each step requiring a staggering amount of energy to ascend. She made her way to her room, shut and locked her door, and laid upon her bed.

She curled up into a tight ball and stayed that way for hours.

Dunford smiled when his butler handed him the white envelope. As he picked it up off the silver tray, he recognized Henry's handwriting. It was rather like her, he thought, neat and direct with no flowery decoration.

He slit the envelope open and unfolded the note.

My dear Rosalind . . .

The silly girl had gone and mixed up her letters and envelopes. Dunford hoped he was the reason for her uncharacteristic absentmindedness. He started to refold the letter, but then he caught sight of his name. Curiosity won out over scruples, and he smoothed out the sheet of paper.

A few moments later it slipped from his numb fingers and drifted to the ground.

Of course I am marrying him for Stannage Park . . .

Of course I am marrying him for Stannage Park . . .

Of course I am marrying him for Stannage Park . . .

Dear God, what had he done? She didn't love him. She had never loved him. She probably never would.

How she must have laughed. He sank back into a chair. No, she wouldn't have laughed. Despite her calculating behavior, she wasn't cruel. She simply loved Stannage Park more than she could ever love anything—or anyone—else.

His was a love that could never be returned.

God, it was ironic. He still loved her. Even after this, he still loved her. He was so furious with her he damn near hated her, but still he loved her. What the hell was he going to do?

He staggered to his feet and poured himself a drink, oblivious to the fact that the hour had not yet slipped from morning to afternoon. His fingers clutched the glass so tightly it was a wonder it didn't break. He downed the drink, and when it did nothing to ease his pain, he drank another.

He pictured her face, his mind drawing the delicately winged eyebrows that hung over those spectacular silver eyes. He could see her hair, could detect each one of the myriad colors that made up that mane which was rather insufficiently called light brown. And then her mouth—it was always in motion, smiling, laughing, pouting.

Kissing.

He could feel her lips under his. They had been soft

and full and so eager to respond. His body hardened as he remembered the sheer ecstasy of her touch. She was an innocent, yet she instinctively knew how to bind him to her with passion.

He wanted her.

He wanted her with an intensity that threatened to engulf him.

He couldn't break the engagement yet. He had to see her one last time. He had to touch her and see if he could withstand the torture of it.

Did he love her enough to go through with this marriage, knowing what he did about her?

Did he hate her enough to marry her just to control her and punish her for what she'd made him feel?

Just one more time.

He had to see her just one more time. Then he would know.

Chapter 22

"Lord Stannage is here to see you, Miss Barrett."

Henry's heart slammed in her chest at the butler's announcement.

"Shall I tell him you're not at home?" the butler asked, noting her hesitation.

"No, no," she replied, nervously wetting her lips. "I'll be right down." Henry set down the letter she'd been penning to Emma. The Duchess of Ashbourne would probably withdraw her friendship from Henry once news of the broken engagement got out. Henry had decided she'd like to send one last piece of correspondence while she still could count Emma among her friends.

This is it, she said to herself, trying to fight the choking feeling in her throat. *He hates you now.* She knew she'd hurt him, perhaps just as much as he'd hurt her.

She stood, smoothing down the folds of her pale yellow morning dress. It was the one he had bought her back in Truro. She wasn't sure why she'd instructed her maid to take that one out of the closet that morning. Perhaps it was a desperate attempt to hold on to a tiny piece of her happiness.

Now she only felt foolish. As if a dress could mend her broken heart.

Squaring her shoulders, she walked out into the hall and carefully shut the door behind her. She had to act normally. It was going to be the hardest thing she'd ever done, but she was going to have to behave as if nothing were wrong. She wasn't supposed to know that Dunford had received a note meant for Rosalind, and he would be suspicious if she acted otherwise.

She reached the top of the staircase, and her foot hovered over the first step. Oh, God, she could feel the pain already. It would be so easy to turn around and flee to her room. The butler could say she was ill. Dunford had believed her to be ill the previous week; a relapse was plausible.

You have to see him, Henry.

Henry swore at her conscience and finally stepped onto the staircase.

Dunford stared out a window in the Blydons' sitting room as he waited for his fiancée to greet him.

Fiancée. What a joke.

If she hadn't told him she loved him . . . He swallowed convulsively. He might have been able to bear it if she hadn't lied to him.

Was he so naive to want what his friends had? Was he crazy to think a member of the *ton* could find a love match? Alex's and Belle's successes in that endeavor had made him hopeful. Henry's arrival in his life had made him ecstatic.

And now her betrayal had ravaged him.

He heard her walk into the room but didn't turn

around, unable to trust himself until he had a stronger hold on his emotions. He kept his gaze firmly on the window. A nanny was pushing a pram down the street.

He took a ragged breath. He'd wanted her children . . .

"Dunford?" She sounded oddly hesitant.

"Close the door, Henry." He still didn't turn to face her.

"But Caroline . . .

"I said, 'Close the door.' "

Henry opened her mouth, but no words came out. She stepped back to the door and closed it. She took no further steps into the center of the room, leaving herself poised to flee if necessary. She was a coward and she knew it, but just then she didn't much care. She clasped her hands in front of her body and waited for him to turn around. When a full minute passed without a sound or movement from him, she forced herself to say his name again.

He whirled around abruptly, surprising her with a smile on his face.

"Dunford?" She hadn't meant to whisper.

"Henry. My love." He took a step toward her.

Her eyes widened. His smile was the same one she'd always seen, the same curve on his finely molded lips and the same gleam of even, white teeth. But his eyes . . . oh, they were hard.

She forced herself not to step back and pasted her signature cheeky grin on her face. "What did you need to tell me, Dunford?"

"I need a specific reason to visit my fiancée?"

Surely it was her imagination that heard that slight stress on the word "fiancée."

He began to walk toward her, his long, even paces reminding her of a predatory cat. She took a few steps to the side, which was just as well, for he brushed right past her. Her head whipped up in surprise.

Dunford took two more steps to reach the door, then he turned the key in the lock.

Henry's mouth went dry. "But Dunford . . . My reputation . . . it will be in tatters."

"They'll indulge me."

"They?" she said stupidly.

He shrugged with supreme nonchalance. "Whoever it is who shreds reputations. Surely I'm allowed a little license. We're going to be married in a fortnight."

We are? her mind screamed. He was supposed to hate her. What had happened? Surely he had received her letter. He was acting so oddly. He wouldn't be looking at her with that hard expression in his eyes if he hadn't come here to break off the engagement.

"Dunford?" It seemed the only word she could make herself say. She knew she wasn't acting as she ought; she should be cheeky and flippant and everything he expected from her. But he was behaving so strangely, she didn't know what to do. She'd expected him to lose his temper, to come storming in and break off the engagement. Instead, he was quietly stalking her.

And she felt very much like a cornered fox.

"Perhaps I just want to kiss you," he said, absently brushing the cuff of his jacket.

Henry swallowed nervously and then blinked before saying, "I don't think so. If you wanted to kiss me, you wouldn't be picking lint from your jacket."

His hand stilled, hovering over the sleeve. "Perhaps you're right," he murmured.

"I—I am?" Good Lord, this wasn't going at all how it was supposed to.

"Mmmm. If I really wanted to kiss you—*really,* mind you—I would probably reach out, grab your hand, and pull you into my arms. That would probably be an appropriate show of affection, don't you think?"

"Appropriate," she replied, hoping her voice sounded natural, "if you really wanted to marry me." She'd given him the perfect opening. If he was going to jilt her, he'd do it now.

But he didn't. Instead, he arched a mocking brow and began to move toward her. "If I want to marry you," he murmured. "An interesting question."

Henry took a step back. She didn't mean to, but she couldn't help herself.

"Surely you're not afraid of me, Hen?" He stepped forward.

Frantically, she shook her head. This was wrong, terribly wrong. *Dear Lord,* she prayed, *make him love me or make him hate me, but not this. Oh, not this . . .*

"Is something wrong, minx?" He didn't sound as if he particularly cared.

"D–don't toy with me, my lord."

His eyes narrowed. "Don't *toy* with you? What an odd choice of words." He took another step toward her, trying to read the expression in her eyes. He didn't understand her this afternoon. He had expected her to come bounding into the room, all smiles and laughter as she usually was when he came to visit. Instead she was nervous and withdrawn, almost as if she were *expecting* bad news.

Which was preposterous. She couldn't have realized she'd accidentally sent him the letter meant for her dear friend Rosalind. Whoever this Rosalind person was, she didn't live in London or Dunford would have heard about her. And there was no way she could have received Henry's missive and replied in the space of one day.

"Toy with you?" he repeated. "Why do you think I would want to toy with you, Henry?"

"I—I don't know," she stammered.

She was lying. He could see it in her eyes. But for

the life of him, he couldn't imagine why she would lie. What did she have to lie about? He closed his eyes for a second, taking a deep breath. Perhaps he was misreading her. He was so furious and still so much in love he didn't know *what* to think.

He opened his eyes. She was looking away, her gaze focused on a painting across the room. He could see the elegant, sensuous line of her throat . . . and the way one silken curl rested on the bodice of her gown. "I think I do want to kiss you, Henry," he murmured.

Her eyes flew back to his face. "I don't think you do," she said quickly.

"I think you're wrong."

"No. If you wanted to kiss me, you wouldn't be looking at me like that." She backed up a step and then scooted around a chair, trying to put some furniture between them.

"Oh? And how would I be looking at you?"

"Like . . . like . . ."

"Like what, Henry?" He rested his hands on the arms of the chair and leaned forward, his face dangerously close to hers.

"Like you want me," she said, her voice barely a whisper.

"Ah, but Henry, I do want you."

"No. You don't." She wanted to flee, wanted to hide, but she couldn't tear her eyes away from his. "You want to hurt me."

His hand closed around her upper arm, holding her in place as he circumnavigated the chair. "Maybe there's a little of that, too," he said with chilling softness.

His lips captured hers. It was a hard, cruel kiss, unlike any other he'd given her, and she clearly was not enjoying it. "Why so resistant, Hen? Don't you want to marry me?"

She twisted her head away from him.

"Don't you want to marry me?" he repeated, his voice a cold singsong. "Don't you want all I have to offer you? Don't you want security, a comfortable life, and a home? Ah, yes, a home. Don't you want that?"

He felt her struggle in his arms, then go still, and he knew he should release her. He should let her go, turn around, and walk out of the room and out of her life. But he wanted her so much . . .

Lord, he wanted her, and that lust overtook him, turning his fury into desire. His lips grew softer, demanding only pleasure. He trailed kisses along her jawline to her ear, down her neck to the tender skin ringed by her pale yellow bodice. "Tell me you can't feel this," he whispered, his words a dare. "Tell me."

Henry only shook her head, not sure whether she was signaling him to stop or admitting the sense of need he whipped up in her.

Dunford heard her whimper with desire, and for a split second he didn't know whether he'd lost or won. Then he realized it really didn't matter.

"God, I'm an ass," he whispered harshly, furious with himself for letting his desire take over his body. She had betrayed him—*betrayed him*—and still he couldn't keep his hands off her.

"What did you just say?"

Dunford saw no reason to answer her. It wasn't really necessary to expound at length on how much he wanted her and, damn it, still loved her despite her lies. All he did was murmur, "Shut up, Hen," and lower her onto the sofa.

Henry stiffened. His tone had been soft, but his words had not. Still, this was probably the last time she would be able to hold him like this, the last time she could pretend he still loved her.

She felt herself sinking into the plush cushions, felt the heat of his body as it covered hers. His hands cupped her bottom, pulling her toward his obvious desire. His lips were on her earlobe, then her neck, then her collarbone. He was traveling lower, lower.

Henry couldn't quite make her arms encircle him, but neither did she possess the fortitude to pull herself away. Did he love her? His mouth loved her. It was loving her with startling intensity, circling around her taut nipple through the thin muslin of her gown.

She stared down, her mind strangely detached from her burning body. His kisses had left an indecent stain on her bodice. Not that he would care. He was doing this to punish her. He would—

"No!" she cried out, pushing at him so violently that he fell to the floor in surprise.

He was silent as he slowly rose to his feet. When he finally leveled his gaze at her face, Henry knew panic like none she had ever imagined. His eyes were slits.

"Suddenly worried about our virtue, are we?" he asked rudely. "It's a bit late for that, don't you think?"

Henry hastily scrambled into an upright position, refusing to reply.

"Rather an about-face for the girl who told me she didn't care two figs for her reputation."

"That was before," she said in a low voice.

"Before what, Hen? Before you came to London? Before you learned what women are supposed to want from marriage?"

"I—I don't know what you're talking about." She awkwardly rose to her feet.

Dunford let out a short bark of angry laughter. God, she wasn't even a good liar. She stumbled over her words, her eyes refused to meet his, and her cheeks were flushed pink.

Of course that might only be passion. He could still make her feel passion. It might be the only thing he could make her feel, but he knew he could raise her body to fever pitch. He could make her need him, bind her to him with lips, hands, the heat of his skin.

His body grew aroused as his thoughts grew more erotic. He could see her as she had been at Westonbirt, her soft skin glowing in the candlelight. She had moaned with desire, arched her body toward his. She had cried out in rapture. *He* had given her that.

Dunford took a step forward. "You want me, Henry."

She stood utterly still, unable to deny it.

"You want me now."

Somehow she managed to shake her head. He could tell it took all her fortitude to do it.

"Yes," he said silkily. "You do."

"No, Dunford. I don't. I don—"

But her words were cut off by the pressure of his lips on hers. They were cruel, demanding. Henry felt as if she were suffocating, smothered by the weight of both his anger and her own insensible desire for him.

She couldn't let him do this. She couldn't let him use his fury to make her want him. With a wrench of her head she tore her lips from his.

"That's all right," he murmured, cupping her breast with his hand. "Your lying mouth is not the part of you that most interests me."

"Stop!" She pushed against his chest, but his arms were closed around her like a vise. "You can't do this!"

One corner of his mouth tilted up in a mockery of a smile. "Can't I?"

"You are not my husband," she said, her voice shaking with fury as she wiped her mouth with the back of her hand. "You have no rights over my person."

He let her go and leaned back against the doorjamb, his posture deceptively lazy. "Are you telling me you wish to call off the wedding?"

"Wh-why would you think I want to do that?" she asked, knowing he thought she wanted to marry him for Stannage Park.

"I can't fathom even a single reason," he said in a very hard voice. "In fact, I seem to have *everything* you require in a husband."

"We're feeling a bit superior today, aren't we?" she retorted.

He moved like lightning, pinning her against the wall, his hands planted firmly on either side of her shoulders. "*We,*" he said with unconcealed sarcasm, "are feeling just a bit confused. *We* are wondering why our fiancée is acting so oddly. We are wondering if perhaps there is something she wants to say."

Henry felt all the breath leave her body. Wasn't this what she wanted? Why did she feel so utterly wretched?

"Henry?"

She stared at his face, remembering all of his kindnesses toward her. He had bought her a dress when no one else had thought to. He had badgered her into coming to London and then made sure she had a lovely time once she arrived. And he had smiled the entire time.

It was difficult to reconcile this image with the cruel, mocking man standing before her. But still, she couldn't bring herself to humiliate him publicly. "*I* won't call off the wedding, my lord."

He tilted his head. "I can only surmise from your inflection that you wish me to do so."

She said nothing.

"Surely you realize that, as a gentleman of honor, I cannot do so."

Her lips parted slightly. It was several seconds before she was able to say, "What do you mean?"

Dunford regarded her closely. Why the hell was she so interested in whether or not he could jilt her? That was the one thing he was certain she didn't want him to do. If he did, she would lose Stannage Park forever.

"Why can't you cry off?" she pressed. "Why?"

"I see we have not educated you in the ways of society as well as we thought. A gentleman of honor *never* jilts a lady. Not unless she has proven herself unfaithful, and perhaps not even then."

"I have never betrayed you," she blurted out.

Not with your body, he thought. *Only with your soul.* How could she ever love him as much as she loved her land? No one's heart was that big. He sighed. "I know you haven't."

Again she said nothing, just stood there looking pained. How baffled she must be at his anger, he thought. She couldn't know that he knew her true motives for marrying him. "Well," he said wearily, dreading her reply. "Are you going to jilt me?"

"Do you want me to?" she whispered.

"It is not my decision," he said stiffly, unable to say the words that would force her to let him go. "If you're going to call it off, do it."

"I can't," she said, wringing her hands. Her words sounded as if they were wrenched from her very soul.

"Let it be on your head then," he said flatly. He left the room without a backward glance.

Henry was aware of very little during the next two weeks, aside from the dull pain wrapped around her heart like a shroud. Nothing seemed to bring her joy. She supposed her friends attributed her strange mood to prenuptial nerves.

Luckily she saw Dunford infrequently. He seemed to know exactly how to cross paths with hers at parties for only the shortest of times. He would arrive with time enough for only one dance before she left. They never waltzed.

Her wedding day loomed closer and closer, until finally she woke up one morning with the most intense feeling of dread. This was the day on which she would bind herself forever to a man she couldn't satisfy.

A man who now hated her.

With slow movements she rose from her bed and pulled on her dressing gown. The only consolation in all of this was that at least she would get to live at her beloved Stannage Park.

Although it no longer seemed quite so precious.

The wedding was agony.

Henry had thought a small ceremony would be easier, but she discovered that it was harder to maintain a cheerful facade in front of a dozen good friends than it would have been in front of three hundred passing acquaintances.

Henry did her bit, said, "I will," when it was time, but only one thought was running through her mind.

Why was he doing this?

But by the time she mustered up the nerve to ask him, the priest was telling Dunford he could kiss his bride. Henry barely had time to turn her head before his lips descended onto hers in a passionless kiss.

"Why?" she whispered against his mouth. "Why?"

If he heard her, he didn't reply. All he did was grab her hand and practically drag her back up the aisle of the church.

Henry hoped her friends didn't see her stumble as she tried to keep up with her new husband.

* * *

The next evening, Henry found herself on the doorstep of Stannage Park, a gold band now joining her engagement ring on her left hand. None of the servants were out to greet them; it was well past eleven, so she thought they must all be in bed.

Besides, she had written that they were to arrive the next day. She had never dreamed that Dunford would insist they leave for Cornwall directly following their wedding. They had stayed at their reception a mere thirty minutes before she was hustled into a waiting carriage.

Her ride across England had been silent and uncomfortable. Dunford had brought along a book and ignored her the entire way. By the time they arrived at the inn—the same one they had visited on their earlier journey—her nerves were utterly shot. She had spent the entire day dreading the night. What would it be like to be made love to in anger? She couldn't bear to find out.

And then he had completely stunned her by putting her in a room clear down the hall from his, saying, "I think our wedding night ought to be at Stannage Park. It seems so . . . *appropriate,* don't you think?"

She had nodded gratefully and fled to her room.

But now she was here, and he would demand his wedding night. The fire burning in his eyes was proof enough of his intentions.

She stared out over the front gardens. There wasn't very much light coming from the house, but Henry knew every inch of the landscape so well that she could picture every last tree branch. She could feel Dunford watching her as she watched the chilly wind rustle the leaves.

"Does it feel good to be back, Henry?"

She nodded jerkily, lacking the courage to face him.

"I thought it might," he muttered.

She turned around. "Are *you* glad to be back?"

There was a long pause before he replied, "I don't know yet." And then he added more curtly, "Come inside, Henry."

She stiffened at his tone but walked into the house nonetheless.

Dunford lit several tapers in a candelabra. "It's time to go upstairs."

Henry looked back through the open door at the still-full carriage, searching for anything that would delay the inevitable. "My things . . ."

"The footmen will bring them up in the morning. It's time for bed."

She swallowed and nodded, dreading what was ahead. She ached for the closeness they had shared at Westonbirt, that all-encompassing feeling of love and contentment she had found in his arms. But that had been a lie. It had to have been a lie, or he wouldn't have needed a night of additional sport in his mistress's bed.

Henry ascended the stairs, making her way toward her old bedroom.

"No." Dunford's hands descended upon her shoulders. "I sent word to have your belongings moved to the master suite."

She whirled around. "You had no right."

"I had every right," he bit out, half dragging her into his bedroom. "I still have every right." He paused, then continued in a softer tone, as if realizing he had overreacted. "At the time I thought you would be in favor of the idea."

"I could move back," she offered, somewhat hopefully. "If you don't want me here, I don't need to stay."

He let out a ragged laugh. "Oh, I *want* you, Henry. I have always wanted you. It kills me how much I want you."

Tears pooled in her eyes. "It shouldn't be this way, Dunford."

He stared at her for several moments, his eyes filled with rage and hurt and disbelief. Then he turned and stalked to the door. "Make yourself ready in twenty minutes," he said curtly. He didn't look back.

Chapter 23

Henry's fingers shook as she changed out of her traveling dress. Both Belle and Emma had contributed to her trousseau, and as a result she now had a valise full of ultrasheer nightgowns. They all seemed vaguely indecent to a young woman who had never worn anything other than thick, white cotton to bed before, but somehow feeling it was her duty to wear these now that she was married, she slipped one over her head.

She glanced down at her body, gasped, and jumped into bed. The pale pink silk did not even pretend to hide the contours of her body or the dark rosiness of her nipples. Henry quickly pulled the covers up to her chin.

When Dunford returned he was clad in only a dark green robe that fell to his knees. Henry swallowed and looked away.

"Why so nervous, Hen?" he asked flatly. "It isn't as if we haven't done this before."

"It was different then."

"Why?" Dunford looked at her intently, his thoughts racing in the most depressing of directions. Was it different because she no longer had to pretend she loved him? Stannage Park was safely hers now; she was probably trying to figure out how to scare him off the premises most quickly.

She was silent for a full minute before she finally said, "I don't know."

He regarded her, saw insincerity in her eyes, and felt anger rising within him. "Well, I don't care," he all but snarled. "I don't care if it's different." He tore off his robe and moved onto the bed with feral grace. He hovered above her on his hands and knees, watching as her eyes grew wide with apprehension.

"I can make you want me," he whispered. "I know I can do *that.*" He slid down until he was lying on his side, still atop the covers beneath which she had burrowed. One of his hands snaked out behind her neck, pulling her toward him.

Henry felt his hot breath on her mouth a split second before his lips touched hers. As he coaxed her response, she wildly tried to make sense of his behavior. He certainly *acted* as if he wanted her.

And yet she knew he didn't, at least not enough for him to forsake all other women.

Something within her was lacking, but she didn't know what. Suddenly self-conscious, she pulled away, her fingers rising to cover her swollen lips.

He raised a sardonic brow.

"I'm not good at kissing," she blurted out.

That made him laugh. "I taught you, Hen. You're quite proficient." And then, as if to prove it, he kissed her anew, his mouth hot and demanding.

She was unable to stifle her response, and heat rose within her, licking her skin from the inside out. Her brain, however, remained curiously detached, and as she felt his tongue explore the contours of her face, she hastily inventoried her body, trying to figure out what it was about her that wasn't enough to keep his interest.

Dunford didn't seem to notice her lack of concentration, and his hands fanned the warmth of her body, burning through the thin silk of her gown. The fastenings slid open, baring her skin to the cool night air. He traveled upward, along the flat plane of her stomach, until he reached her—

Breast!

"Oh, God!" Henry blurted out. "Don't!"

Dunford lifted his head so he could see into her face. "What the hell is wrong now, Henry?"

"You can't. I can't."

"You *can,*" he ground out.

"No, they're too—" She looked down, objectivity unexpectedly piercing her pain. Wait a second, they *weren't* too small. What the hell was wrong with him that he couldn't enjoy a perfectly good pair of breasts? She tilted her head, trying to analyze their shape.

Dunford blinked. The girl—his *wife*—was twisting her neck in what appeared to be an extremely uncomfortable manner and staring at her breasts as if she'd never seen anything like them in the world.

"What are you doing?" he asked, too baffled to maintain his anger.

"I don't know." She looked up at him, her eyes filled with an odd combination of hesitation and annoyance. "They're wrong somehow."

Exasperated, he bit out, "*What* is wrong?"

"My breasts."

If she had begun a lecture on the comparative differences between Judaism and Islam he would not have been more surprised. "Your *breasts?*" he echoed, his voice coming out a bit more sternly that he'd intended. "For Christ's sake, Henry, they're fine."

Fine? *Fine?* She didn't want them to be fine. She wanted them to be perfect, spectacular, utterly ravishing. She wanted him to want her so much that he'd think her the most beautiful woman in the world, even if she weighed fifteen stone and had a wart on her nose. She wanted him to want her so much that he lost all sense of himself.

Most of all she wanted him to want her so much that he would never need another woman.

"Fine" was something she couldn't tolerate, and even as his mouth captured one of her nipples in a hot kiss, she twisted herself out of his grasp and scrambled out of bed, frantically clutching her open nightgown against her body.

Dunford's breath came in short pants. He was painfully hard, and he was clearly losing patience with his new wife. "Henry," he ordered. "Get back into bed *now*."

She shook her head, hating herself for cowering in the corner, but doing it all the same.

He jumped out of bed, unconcerned with the way his erection jutted out from his naked body. Henry stared at him with both fright and wonder—fright because he was advancing toward her like a menacing god, and wonder because it was plainly clear there was *something* about her he liked. The man definitely wanted her.

Dunford grabbed her by the shoulders and shook. When that failed to shake words from her mouth, he shook again. "What the *hell* is wrong with you?"

"I don't know," she cried out, surprised by the volume of her reply. "I don't know, and it's killing me."

Whatever thread had been keeping Dunford's fury

in check snapped. How *dare* she try to make herself out to be the victim in this sordid union? "I'll tell you what the hell is wrong with you," he said in a low, menacing voice. "I'll tell you *exactly* what is wrong. You—"

He stumbled over his words, unprepared for the look of total desolation that washed over her face. No. *No.* He would not let himself feel sorry for her. Forcing himself to ignore the stark pain in her eyes, he continued, "You know that your little game is up, don't you? You heard back from Rosalind, and now you know I'm on to you."

Henry stared at him, barely able to breathe.

"I know all about you," he said with a ragged laugh. "I know you think I'm a *nice enough fellow.* I know you married me for Stannage Park. Well, you did it. You got your precious Stannage Park. *But I got you.*"

"Why did you marry me?" she whispered.

He snorted. "A gentleman doesn't jilt a lady. Remember? Lesson number 363 in how to comport oneself in—"

"No!" she burst out. "That wouldn't have stopped you. Why did you marry me?"

Her eyes seemed to be begging him for an answer, but he didn't know what she wanted to hear. Hell, he didn't even know if he wanted to tell her anything. Let her squirm for a little while. Let her suffer as he had suffered. "Do you know something, Henry?" he said in an awful voice. "I haven't the slightest idea."

He watched as the fire flickered out of her eyes, disgusted with himself for so enjoying her distress but too furious and, yes, aroused to do anything other than yank her into his arms and crush her mouth with his. He tore at her gown until she was as bare as he, her skin hot and flushed against his own.

"But you're mine now," he whispered hotly, his words caressing her neck. "Mine forever."

He kissed her with a fervor born of fury and desperation, and he felt the instant when desire overtook her. Her lips began to move against his temple, her hands roved the corded muscles of his back, and her hips pressed urgently against his.

It was utter torture, and he couldn't get enough.

He wanted to surround himself with her, bury himself within her and never leave. Mindless in his desire, he wasn't certain how he maneuvered them back to bed, but he must have done so, for he soon found himself over her, pressing his body primitively into hers.

"You're mine, Henry," he whispered. "Mine."

She moaned incoherently in reply.

He rolled over onto his side, pulling her with him. His hand tugged at her ankle, draping her leg over his hip.

"Oh, Dunford," she sighed.

"Oh, Dunford, what?" he murmured, nipping her earlobe softly with his teeth.

"I—" She gasped as he squeezed her buttocks.

"Do you need me, Henry?"

"I don—" She couldn't finish the sentence. Her breaths were coming on top of each other now, and she could barely speak.

He smoothed his hand further down her backside until it curved under her and touched her intimately. *"Do you need me?"*

"Yes! Yes!" Then she opened her eyes and stared into his. "Please."

Thoughts of anger and revenge slipped from his mind as he stared into the clear, gray depths of her eyes. He could feel only love, remember only the laughter and intimacy they had shared. He kissed her lips and remembered the first time he had seen her smile—that saucy, cheeky grin. He ran his hands along her supple arms and remembered how she had stubbornly hefted rocks onto the pigpen's stone wall as he sat and watched.

She was Henry, and he loved her. He couldn't help himself.

"Tell me what you want, Henry," he whispered.

She stared at him blindly, unable to form words.

"Do you want this?" He rolled her nipple between his thumb and middle finger, watching it harden and peak.

With a strangled gasp, she nodded.

"Do you want this?" He leaned down and treated her other breast to the pleasure of his tongue.

"Oh, my God," she moaned. "Oh, Lord."

"What about this?" He gently laid her on her back and placed one hand on each of her thighs. He slowly pushed them apart, meeting no resistance. With an arrogant smile, he leaned forward and kissed her softly on the mouth as his fingers tickled the hot folds of her womanhood.

Her leaping pulse was answer enough.

He smiled devilishly. "Tell me, minx, do you want *this?*" He kissed a fiery trail down through the valley between her breasts, along the flat planes of her midriff, until his mouth met his fingers.

"Oh, Dunford," Henry gasped. "Oh, my God."

He could have spent hours loving her in that way. She was sweet and mysterious and pure woman. But he could feel her inching toward completion, and he wanted to be joined with her when she climaxed. He needed to feel her body tighten around him.

He slid himself up along the length of her until they were face-to-face again. "Do you want me, Henry?" he whispered. "I won't do this unless you want me."

Henry looked up at him through passion-clouded eyes. "Dunford. Yes."

He nearly shuddered with relief, not knowing how he would have had the power to keep his word had she refused him. He was heavy and hard, and his body was crying for release. He pushed upward, entering her slightly. She was warm and wet, but her body was tight with inexperience, and he had to force himself to go slowly.

But Henry would have none of that. She was straining against him, arching her hips to receive his entire length. It was more than Dunford could take, and he thrust forward, sheathing himself completely within her.

It was like coming home, and he lifted himself up on his elbows so he could watch her. Suddenly he couldn't remember why he was so angry with her. He looked at her and all he could see was her face—laughing, grinning, her mouth quivering in sympathy for the baby who had died in the abandoned cottage.

"Henry," he groaned. He loved her. He pushed forward again, losing himself in a primitive rhythm. He loved her. He moved. He loved her. He kissed her brow in a desperate attempt to move ever closer to her soul.

He loved her.

He could feel her quickening beneath him. She began to twist, and odd little sounds were escaping her mouth. Then she cried out his name, every ounce of her energy in that single word.

The sensation of her clenching around him pushed him over the edge. "Oh, my God, Henry!" he shouted, unable to control his thoughts, his actions, or his words. "I love you!"

Henry went utterly still, a thousand thoughts racing through her mind in the space of a second.

He said he loved her.

She could see him at the dress shop, gently insisting she try on gowns for his nonexistent sister.

Could he mean it?

She remembered him in London, overcome with jealousy because she had taken a stroll with Ned Blydon, of all people.

Could he love her and still need other women?

She saw his face, filled with intense tenderness as he asked her if she wanted him. *I won't do this unless you want me,* he'd said.

Could those possibly be the words of a man who wasn't in love?

He loved her. She no longer doubted it. He loved her, but she still wasn't enough of a woman for him. Lord, it was almost more painful than thinking he didn't love her at all.

"Henry?" Dunford's voice was hoarse, still raw with spent passion.

She touched his cheek. "I believe you," she said softly.

He blinked. "What do you believe?"

"You." A tear welled up in her eye and slid down her temple to disappear in the pillows beneath her. "I believe you love me."

He stared at her, dumbfounded. *She believed him?* What the hell did that mean?

She had turned her head so she didn't have to look at his face. "I wish . . ." she began.

"What do you wish, Henry?" Dunford asked. His heart thudded in his chest, somehow recognizing that its very fate hung in the balance.

"I wish . . . I wish I could . . ." She choked on her words, wanting to say, "I wish I could be the woman you need," but unable to admit her shortcomings in so vulnerable a position.

It mattered not, anyway. Dunford never would have

heard her completed sentence, for he was already on his feet and halfway out the door, not wanting to hear her pity as she said, "I wish I could love you, too."

Henry awoke the next morning with a fierce pounding in her temples. Her eyes ached, probably from a night of crying. She staggered over to the washstand and splashed some water on her face, but it did little to ease her pain.

Somehow she had managed to botch up her wedding night. She supposed she shouldn't be surprised. Some women were born knowing the womanly graces, and it was time she accepted that she wasn't one of them. It had been foolish of her even to try. She thought wistfully of Belle, who always seemed to know what to say and how to dress. But it went deeper than that. Belle had some inborn sense of femininity that, no matter how hard the lovely baroness tried, she couldn't teach to Henry. Oh, Belle had told Henry that she had made great strides, but Henry knew that Belle was simply too kind to say anything else.

Henry walked slowly to the dressing room that connected the two larger bedrooms of the master suite. Carlyle and Viola had not preferred separate bedrooms, so one of the rooms had been converted into a sitting room. Henry supposed that if she didn't want to spend every night with Dunford she would have to have another bed moved into the suite.

She sighed, knowing she *did* want to spend her nights with her husband and hating herself for it.

She stepped into the dressing room, noting that someone had already unpacked the dresses she'd brought back from London. She supposed she would have to hire a lady's maid now; many of the dresses were nearly impossible to don without assistance.

She pushed past the dresses to the small pile of men's clothing that had been neatly folded and left on a shelf. She picked up a pair of breeches. Too small for Dunford—they must be one of the pairs she had left behind.

Henry fingered the breeches, then looked up longingly at her new dresses. They were lovely—every shade of the rainbow and fashioned of the softest materials imaginable. Still, they had been made for the woman she had hoped to be, not the woman she was.

With a painful swallow, Henry turned her back on the dresses and stepped into her breeches.

Dunford glanced impatiently at the clock as he ate his breakfast. Where the hell was Henry? He'd been down for nearly an hour.

He put another forkful of his now cold eggs into his mouth. They tasted dreadful, but he didn't notice. He kept hearing Henry's voice; it was so loud it seemed to obliterate his other senses.

I wish I could . . . I wish I could . . . I wish I could love you.

It wasn't difficult to complete her sentence for her.

He heard the sound of her footsteps on the stairs and stood before she even appeared in the doorway. When she did appear she looked tired, her face pinched and drawn. He looked her up and down insolently; she was wearing her old attire, her hair pulled back like a pony's tail.

"Couldn't wait to get back to work, eh, Henry?" he heard himself say.

She nodded jerkily.

"Just don't wear those things off the property. You are my wife now, and your behavior reflects upon me." Dunford heard the derision in his voice and hated himself for it. He had always loved Henry's independent spirit, had always admired that sense of practicality that led her to wear men's clothing while working on the farm. Now he was trying to hurt her, trying to make her feel the same pain she'd squeezed around his heart. He knew that, and it disgusted him.

"I will try to comport myself appropriately," she said in a cold voice. She looked down at the plate of food that had been set in front of her, sighed, and pushed it away.

Dunford raised a brow in question.

"I'm not hungry."

"Not hungry? Oh, come now, Henry, you eat like a horse."

She flinched. "How kind of you to point out one of my many feminine attributes."

"You're not exactly dressed for the part of lady of the manor."

"I happen to like these garments."

Dear God, was that a tear he saw forming in her eye? "For God's sake, Henry, I—" He raked his hand through his hair. What was happening to him? He was becoming a man he didn't much like. He had to get out of here.

Dunford stood. "I'm leaving for London," he said abruptly.

Henry's head whipped up. "What?"

"Today. This morning."

"This morning?" she whispered, so softly that there was no way he possibly could have heard her. "The day after our wedding night?"

He strode from the room, and that was that.

The next few weeks were lonelier than Henry ever could have imagined. Her life was much the same as it had been before Dunford had entered it—with one colossal exception. She had tasted love, held it fleetingly in her hands, and for one second had touched pure happiness.

Now all she had were her big, empty bed and the memory of the man who had spent one night there.

The servants treated her with exceptional kindness—so exceptional that Henry thought she might break under the weight of their solicitousness. She wished they would stop treading on eggshells and start treating her like the old Henry, the one who had romped about Stannage Park in breeches without a care, the one who hadn't known what she was missing by burying herself in Cornwall.

She heard what they said: "God rot his soul for leaving poor Henry alone" and "a body shouldn't be that lonely." Only Mrs. Simpson was forthright enough actually to pat Henry on the arm and murmur, "Poor ducky."

A lump had formed in Henry's throat at Simpy's consoling words, and she ran off to hide her tears. And when she had no more tears she threw herself into her work at Stannage Park.

The estate, she said to herself with pride but not much contentment a month after Dunford left her, had never looked better.

"I'm giving this back."

Dunford looked from his glass of whiskey to Belle to the pile of money she had dumped in front of him and back to Belle. He raised an eyebrow.

"It's the thousand pounds I won from you," she explained, irritation with him written clearly on her face. "I believe the wager called for you to be 'tied up, leg-shackled, and loving it.' "

This time he raised both eyebrows.

"You are clearly not 'loving it,' " Belle all but snapped.

Dunford took another sip of his whiskey.

"Will you say something!"

He shrugged. "No. Clearly, I am not."

Belle planted her hands on her hips. "Have you anything to say? Anything that might explain your atrocious behavior?"

His expression turned to ice. "I fail to see how you might be in any position to demand explanations from me."

Belle stepped back, her hand covering her mouth. "What have you become?" she whispered.

"A better question," he bit off, "would be: 'What has she made me?' "

"Henry couldn't have done this. What could she possibly have done to have made you so cold? Henry is the sweetest, most—"

"—*mercenary* woman in my acquaintance."

Belle let out a sound that was half laugh, half exhalation, and pure disbelief. "Henry? Mercenary? Surely you're jesting."

Dunford sighed, aware that he'd been somewhat unfair to his wife. "Perhaps 'mercenary' is not quite the most appropriate word. My wife . . . She . . ." He held out his hands in a gesture of accepted defeat. "Henry will never be able to love anything or *anyone* as much as she loves Stannage Park. It doesn't make her a bad person, it just makes her . . . it makes her . . ."

"Dunford, what are you talking about?"

He shrugged. "Have you ever experienced unrequited love, Belle? Other than being on the receiving end of it, I mean."

"Henry loves you, Dunford. I know she does."

Wordlessly, he shook his head.

"It was so obvious. We all knew she loved you."

"I have a letter written in her own hand that would attest otherwise."

"There must be some mistake."

"There is no mistake, Belle." He let out a harsh, self-deprecating laugh. "Other than the one I made when I said, 'I will.' "

Belle paid Dunford another visit after he'd been in London for a month. He wished he could have said he was delighted to see her, but the truth was there wasn't anything that could have lifted him out of his melancholy.

He saw Henry everywhere. The sound of her voice echoed in his head. He missed her with a fierceness that was painful. He despised himself for wanting her, for being so pitiful that he loved a woman who would never return his feelings.

"Good afternoon, Dunford," Belle said in crisp greeting as she was shown into his study.

"Belle." He inclined his head.

"I thought you might like to know that Emma was safely delivered of a baby boy two days ago. I thought *Henry* might like to know," she said pointedly.

Dunford smiled for the first time in a month. "A boy, eh? Ashbourne had his heart set on a girl."

Belle softened. "Yes, he's been muttering that Emma always manages to get what she wants, but he's as proud as a papa can be."

"The baby is healthy, then?"

"Big and pink, with a thick patch of black hair."

"He'll be a terror, I'm sure."

"Dunford," Belle said softly, "someone should tell Henry. She'll want to know."

He looked at her blankly. "I'll write her a note."

"No," Belle said, her voice stern. "She should be told in person. She'll be very happy; she'll want to celebrate with someone."

Dunford swallowed. He wanted to see his wife so very badly. He wanted to touch her, to hold her in his arms and inhale the scent of her hair. He wanted to hold his hand over her mouth, so she couldn't say any more damning words, and make love to her, pretending all the while that she loved him back.

He was pathetic, he knew, and Belle had just come up with a way for him to go to Cornwall without sacrificing what was left of his pride. He stood.

"I'll tell her."

Belle's relief was so obvious it was almost as if she deflated on her chair.

"I'll go to Cornwall. She needs to be told about the baby. She'll want to know," he reasoned. "If I don't go and tell her, I don't know who will." He looked over at Belle, almost as if asking for her approval.

"Oh, yes," she said quickly. "If you don't go, I don't see how she'll find out. You really must go."

"Yes, yes," he said distractedly. "I really must. I have to go see her. I really don't have a choice."

Belle smiled knowingly. "Oh, Dunford, don't you even want to know the baby's name?"

His expression was sheepish. "Yes, that would be helpful."

"They named him William. After you."

Chapter 24

Henry was shoveling slop.

Not that she much liked shoveling slop. She never had. She had always felt that, as the person in charge of Stannage Park, she should take part in the day-to-day chores of the estate. But she had never before been so democratic as to force herself to do the messiest tasks.

But now she didn't mind it so much. The physical activity kept her mind blessedly blank. And when she tumbled into bed in the evening, her muscles were so sore she fell right asleep. It was a blessing, that. Before she'd decided upon exhaustion as a cure for heartbreak, she'd lain awake for hours, staring at the ceiling. Staring, staring, staring—but seeing nothing aside from her failed life.

She thrust her shovel into the mess, trying to ignore the clumps that splattered onto her boots. She focused her mind on how nice a bath would feel that afternoon. Yes, a bath. A bath with . . . lavender. No, rose petals would smell nice. Did she want to smell like roses?

Henry spent most of her afternoons like this, desperately trying to think about anything besides Dunford.

She finished her chores, put the shovel away, and walked slowly back to the house, heading for the servants' entrance. She was a mess, and if she tracked any of the slop on the front hall carpet, they'd never be able to get the stench out.

A maid was standing on the steps, feeding a carrot to Rufus. Henry asked her to see to her bath, leaning down to give the rabbit a pat on the head. She then pushed open the door, unable to muster the energy to call out her customary hello to Mrs. Simpson. She smiled faintly at the housekeeper, reached for an apple, took a bite, then looked back at the housekeeper. Simpy's expression was rather odd, almost strained.

"Is something amiss, Simpy?" Henry inquired before lifting the apple to her mouth for another bite.

"He's back."

Henry froze, her teeth lodged in the apple. She slowly removed the fruit from her mouth, leaving perfect little toothprints. "I assume you mean my husband?" she said carefully.

Mrs. Simpson nodded as she let loose a torrent of words. "I would've told him what I think of him, too, and hang the consequences. He'd have to be a monster to leave you the way he did. He . . ."

Henry didn't hear the rest of her words. Her feet, acting with no direction from her brain, were already carrying her out of the kitchen and up the side stairs. She didn't know if she was fleeing to him or away from him. She had no idea where he was. He could be in the study, the sitting room, or the bedroom.

She gulped, hoping he wasn't in the bedroom.

She pushed open the door.

She swallowed. She'd never been an exceptionally lucky person.

He was standing by the window, looking unbearably handsome. He'd taken off his coat and loosened his cravat. He inclined his head. "Henry."

"You're home," she said dumbly.

He shrugged.

"I . . . I need a bath."

A glimmer of a smile touched his face. "So you do." He walked over to the bellpull.

"I already ordered one drawn. The maids should be here any minute to fill it."

Dunford lowered his hand and turned around. "I suppose you're wondering why I'm back."

"I . . . well, yes. I don't suppose it had anything to do with me."

He winced. "Emma had a baby boy. I thought you'd like to know." He watched her expression change from forlorn distrust to complete joy.

"Oh, but that's wonderful!" she exclaimed. "Have they named him?"

"William," he said sheepishly. "After me."

"You must be so very proud."

"I am quite. I'm to be godfather. It's quite an honor."

"Oh, yes. You must be delighted. They must be delighted."

"They are quite."

It was at that point that they ran out of things to say. Henry stared at Dunford's feet, he stared at her forehead. Finally she blurted out, "I really need to bathe."

A knock sounded on the door, and two maids entered with steaming buckets of water. They pulled the bath out of its storage space in the dressing room and began to fill it.

Henry stared at the bath.

Dunford stared at Henry, imagining her in the bath. Finally he swore and left the room.

When Henry next encountered her husband, she was smelling a bit more like flowers and less like a pigpen. She even donned one of her gowns, lest he think she was wearing her mannish clothing just to annoy him. She didn't want to give him the satisfaction of knowing he was so frequently in her thoughts.

He was waiting for her in the sitting room before dinner, a glass of whiskey next to him on an end table. He rose when she entered, his eyes resting on her face with an expression that could only be called tortured.

"You look lovely, Hen." He sounded as if he wished she didn't.

"Thank you. You look nice, too. You always look nice."

"Would you like a drink?"

"I . . . yes. No. No. I mean yes. Yes, I would."

He turned his back to her as he fussed with the decanter so she wouldn't see him smile. "What would you like?"

"Anything," she said weakly, sitting down. "Anything would be fine."

Dunford poured her a glass of sherry. "Here you are."

She took the glass from his outstretched hand, making sure her hand never touched his. She took a sip, let the wine fortify her, and asked, "How long do you plan to stay?"

His lips twisted. "That anxious to be rid of me, eh, Hen?"

"No," she said quickly. "Although I rather thought *you* wouldn't want to remain overlong with *me*. I'm perfectly happy to have you stay." And then she added, just for pride, "You won't interrupt my routine."

"Ah, yes, of course not. I'm a nice enough fellow. I'd almost forgotten."

Henry cringed at the bitterness laced in his words. "I wouldn't want to go to London and interrupt *your* routine," she shot back. "Heaven forbid I pull you away from your *social* life."

He stared at her blankly. "I have no idea what you're talking about."

"That's because you're too polite to discuss it," she muttered, almost wishing he *would* discuss his mistress. "Or maybe you think I'm too polite."

He stood. "I've traveled all day, and I'm far too weary to waste my energy trying to solve your little riddles. If you'll excuse me, I'm going in to supper. Join me if you like." He walked off.

Henry now knew enough about society to know he'd just been unforgivably rude to her. And she knew enough about him to know he'd done it on purpose. She stamped out of the room after him, turned toward his retreating form, and yelled, "I'm not hungry!"

Then she ran up the stairs to her room, ignoring the rumblings of her stomach.

Supper tasted like sawdust. Dunford stared straight ahead as he ate, ignoring the servants as they motioned to the empty place setting across from him, obviously wondering if they should clear it away.

He finished his meal in ten minutes, eating the first course and ignoring the rest. It was a damning feeling, sitting there across from where Henry should have been, under the hostile regard of the servants, all of whom loved her to distraction.

With a shove of his chair, he rose and retired to his study, where he poured himself a glass of whiskey. And another. And another. Not enough to get stinking drunk, just enough to make him overly contemplative. And enough to pass the time until he could be sure Henry had fallen asleep.

He made his way up to his bedroom, weaving ever so slightly as he walked. What was he going to do with his wife? God, what a mess. He loved her but he didn't want to love her. He wanted to hate her but he couldn't—despite her lack of love for him, she was still as nice a woman as they came, and no one could find fault with her love and devotion for the land. He wanted her and he despised himself for the weakness. And who the hell knew what *she* thought?

Besides the fact that she didn't love him. That much was clear.

I wish I could . . . I wish I could love you.

Well, you couldn't fault the girl for lack of trying.

He turned the doorknob and stumbled into the room. His eyes fell on the bed. Henry!

He caught his breath. Had she waited for him? Did this mean she wanted him?

No, he thought perversely, it just meant there wasn't a bed in the other bedroom.

She was lying there, asleep, her chest gently moving with the rhythm of her breaths. The moon was nearly full, and its light shone through the open windows. She looked perfect—everything he had ever wanted. He sank down into a cushioned chair, his eyes never leaving her sleeping form.

For now this would be enough. Just to watch her as she slept.

Henry blinked herself awake the next morning. She'd slept uncommonly well, a surprise considering the stress of the evening before.

She yawned, stretched, and sat up.

And then she saw him.

He'd fallen asleep in the chair across the room. He was still fully clothed and looked frightfully uncomfortable. Why had he done that? Had he thought she would not want to receive him in the bed? Or was he so repulsed by her that he couldn't bear the thought himself?

With a silent sigh, she slipped out of bed and made her way to the dressing room. She pulled on her breeches and shirt and crept back into the bedroom.

Dunford hadn't moved. His dark hair was still in his eyes, his lips looked just as kissable, and his large frame was still lodged most awkwardly in the small chair.

Henry couldn't bear it. She didn't care that he'd left her the day after they'd returned to Cornwall. She didn't care that he'd been unbelievably rude to her the night before. She didn't even care that he didn't desire her enough to give up his mistress.

The only thought in her heart was that she still loved him despite all that, and she couldn't bear to see him so uncomfortable. She padded over to where he sat, put her hands under his arms, and tugged. "Up with you, Dunford," she murmured, trying to heave him onto his feet.

His eyes gave a few sleepy blinks. "Hen?"

"Time for bed, Dunford."

He grinned sloppily. "You coming?"

Her heart lurched. "I . . . Ah . . . No, Dunford, I'm all dressed. I . . . Ah . . . have chores to do. Yes, chores." *Keep talking, Hen, lest you get tempted to jump in right after him.*

He looked utterly crestfallen, and leaned forward drunkenly. "Can I kiss you?"

Henry swallowed, not at all certain he was awake.

He'd kissed her once before in his sleep; what harm could there be in doing it one more time? And she wanted it so badly . . . wanted *him* so badly.

She leaned up and brushed her lips against his. She heard him groan, then felt his arms come around her, his hands searching the planes of her back.

"Oh, minx," he moaned. If he was still asleep, she thought, at least he had the right person this time. At least he wanted her. Right now, at least, he wanted her. Only her.

They tumbled onto the bed, arms and legs tangling on the way down, fairly tearing each other's clothes off as they went. He kissed her desperately, tasting her skin like a starving man. She was just as frantic, wrapping her legs around him, trying to pull him closer and closer to her—right to the point where they could be one person.

Before she knew it, he was inside her, and it felt as if heaven itself had descended into their bedroom and wrapped them in its perfect embrace.

"Oh, Dunford, I love you I love you I love you." The words flew straight from her heart to her mouth, her pride be damned. She no longer cared that she wasn't enough of a woman for him. She loved him, and he loved her in his own way, and she'd say anything, do whatever it took to keep him by her side. She'd swallow her pride, she'd humble herself—anything to avoid the aching loneliness of the previous month.

He didn't seem to have heard her, so violent were his physical needs. He plunged into her, groans being ripped from his mouth with each thrust. Henry couldn't tell from his face whether he was in agony or ecstasy—perhaps it was a bit of both. Finally, just as her muscles began to quiver around him, he surged forward with stunning power, shouting her name as he poured his very life into her.

Henry's breath stopped as she was overcome by the power of her own release. She welcomed Dunford's weight as he collapsed upon her, savoring the jerky movements that accompanied his ragged breathing. They lay that way for several minutes, silent and content, until Dunford groaned and rolled off of her.

They were side by side now, facing each other, and Henry couldn't take her eyes off him as he leaned forward and kissed her.

"Did you say you loved me?" he whispered.

Henry said nothing, feeling utterly trapped.

His hand clutched her hip. "Did you?"

She tried to say yes, she tried to say no, but neither came out. Choking on her words, she wrenched herself out of his grasp and scrambled off the bed.

"Henry." His voice was low and demanded an answer.

"I *can't* love you!" she cried out, thrusting her arms into the shirt she recently had torn off her body.

Dunford stared at her in shock for several seconds before finally saying, "What do you mean?"

By now she was tucking the shirt into her breeches. "You need more than I can give you," she said, gasping back her sobs. "And because of that, you can never be what *I* need."

Dunford's bruised heart skimmed over her first sentence and focused only on the second. His expression turned to granite, and he stalked out of bed to retrieve his own clothing. "Very well then," he said in the clipped tones of one who is trying very hard not to show emotion. "I will leave for London posthaste. This afternoon, if I can manage it."

Henry swallowed convulsively.

"Is that soon enough for you?"

"You—you're going?" she asked, her voice very small.

"Isn't that what you want?" he bit out, looming over her like a dangerous—and naked—god. "Isn't it?"

She shook her head. It was a tiny movement, but he caught it. "Then what the hell *do* you want?" he snapped. "Do you even know?"

She stared at him mutely.

Dunford swore viciously. "I have had enough of your little games, Henry. When you decide just what it is you want out of marriage, pen me a note. I'll be in London, where my acquaintances *don't* try to rip my soul to shreds."

Henry didn't feel the rage coming on. It descended on her like a fury, and before she realized what was happening, she was screaming. "Go then! Go! Go to London and have your women! Go and sleep with Christine!"

Dunford went utterly still, his face pinched and white. "What," he whispered, "are you talking about?"

"I know you still keep a mistress," she choked out. "I know you slept with her even while we were engaged, even when you professed your love for *me*. You said you were playing cards with friends, be-because you wouldn't be seeing very much of them after we married. But I followed you. I saw you, Dunford. *I saw you!*"

He took a step toward her, his clothing slipping from his fingers. "There has been a terrible mistake."

"Yes, there has," she said, her entire body shaking with emotion. "I was mistaken to think I could ever be enough of a woman to please you, to ever think that I could learn what it means to be anyone else but me."

"Henry," he whispered raggedly, "I don't want anyone else but you."

"Don't lie to me!" she cried out. "I don't care what you say, as long as you don't lie. I can't please you. I tried so hard. I tried to learn the rules, and I wore dresses, and I even liked wearing them, and still it wasn't enough. I can't do it. I know I can't, but I— Oh, God." She crumpled into a chair, overcome by the force of her tears. Her entire body shook with sobs, and she clutched herself, trying to keep from going to pieces. "All I wanted was to be the only one," she gasped. "That's all."

Dunford knelt in front of her, took both of her hands in his, and raised them to his lips in a reverent kiss. "Henry, minx, my love, you're all I want. *All* I want. I haven't even looked at another woman since I met you."

She looked up at him, tears streaming from her eyes.

"I don't know what you thought you saw in London," he continued. "I can only deduce it was the night I told Christine she would need to find another protector."

"You were there so long."

"Henry, I did not betray you." His hands tightened around hers. "You must believe me. *I love you.*"

She stared into those liquid brown eyes and felt her world come crashing down around her. "Oh, my God," she whispered, shock squeezing her heart. She jerkily rose to her feet. "Oh, my God. What have I done? What have I done?"

Dunford watched the blood drain from her face. "Henry?" he said hesitantly.

"What have I done?" Her voice grew progressively stronger. "Oh, my *God!*" And then she bolted from the room.

Dunford, unfortunately, was a bit too naked to follow her.

* * *

Henry ran down the front steps and into the fog. She kept going until she was shielded by trees, until she was sure not a living soul could hear her.

And then she cried.

She sank into the damp earth and sobbed. She had been given a chance at the purest joy on earth, and she had ruined it with lies and distrust. He would never forgive her. How could he, when she could not forgive herself?

Four hours later Dunford was ready to claw the paint from the walls with his fingernails. Where could she be?

He hadn't considered sending out a search party; Henry knew the land better than anyone. It was unlikely she'd had an accident, but it was starting to rain, damn it, and she'd been so distraught.

Half an hour. He'd give her half an hour more.

His heart twisted as he relived the agonized expression on her face that morning. Never had he seen such a look of pure torture—unless, of course, one counted the times he'd looked in the mirror this past month.

Suddenly he had no idea why their marriage was such a shambles. He loved her, and it was becoming increasingly apparent that she returned his love.

But there were so many unanswered questions. And the only person who could answer them was nowhere to be found.

Henry stumbled home in a daze. The rain pelted her, but she barely felt its sting. She looked straight ahead, repeating to herself, "I must make him understand. I must."

She had sat at the base of a tree for hours, sobbing until her tears ran out. And then, when her breathing had quieted, she wondered if perhaps she didn't deserve a second chance. People were allowed to learn from their mistakes and move on, weren't they?

And, above all, she owed her husband the truth.

When she reached the front steps of Stannage Park, the door was savagely wrenched open before she could even grasp the knob.

Dunford.

He looked like an avenging, if slightly disheveled, god. His brows were pulled into a firm line, his color was high, his pulse was beating rapidly in his neck, and . . . and his shirt wasn't buttoned properly.

He hauled her unceremoniously into the front hall. "Do you have any idea what has gone through my mind in the last few hours?" he thundered.

Wordlessly, she shook her head.

He began to tick off his fingers. "A ditch," he bit out. "You could have fallen into a ditch. No, don't say it, I know you know the lay of the land, but you could have fallen into a ditch. An animal could have bitten you. A tree branch could have fallen on you. It's storming, you know."

Henry stared at him, thinking that the windy shower hardly constituted a storm.

"There are criminals," he continued. "I know it's Cornwall. I know it's the end of the earth, but there are criminals. Criminals who wouldn't think twice about . . . about . . . Christ, Henry, I don't even want to think about it."

She watched as he raked his hand through his already mussed hair.

"I am going to lock you in your room."

Hope began to flare in her heart.

"I am going to lock you in your room and tie you up and— Oh, for love of God, will you *say something?*"

Henry opened her mouth. "I don't have a friend named Rosalind."

He stared at her blankly. "What?"

"Rosalind. She doesn't exist. I—" She looked away, too ashamed to meet his gaze. "I wrote the letter knowing you would get it. I wrote the letter to try to goad you into breaking off the engagement."

He touched her chin, forcing her gaze back to his. "Why, Henry?" he asked, his voice a hoarse whisper. *"Why?"*

She swallowed nervously. "Because I thought you'd been with your mistress. I couldn't understand how you could be with me, then be with her, and—"

"I didn't betray you," he said fiercely.

"I know. I know now. I'm sorry. I'm so sorry." She threw her arms around him, burying herself in the haven of his chest. "Can you forgive me?"

"But, Hen, why didn't you trust me?"

Henry swallowed uncomfortably, shame coloring her cheeks pink. Finally she told him about Lady Wolcott's lies. But she couldn't blame Lady Wolcott for everything; if she had been truly secure in Dunford's love, she wouldn't have fallen for her lies.

Dunford looked at her in disbelief. "And you believed her?"

"Yes. No. Not at first. Then I followed you." Henry paused, forcing herself to look him in the eye. She owed him that measure of honesty. "You were in there so long. I didn't know what to think."

"Henry, why would you think I would want another woman? I love you. You knew I loved you. Didn't I tell you enough?" He leaned down and rested his chin against the top of her head, breathing in the heady fragrance of her wet hair.

"I suppose I thought I didn't please you," she said.

"That I wasn't pretty enough or feminine enough. I tried so hard to learn how to be a proper lady. I even enjoyed learning. London was so lovely. But deep down I'm always going to be the same person. The mannish freak—"

His hands grew fierce around her upper arms. "I believe I told you once before never to refer to yourself that way."

"But I'm never going to be like Belle. I'm never going to—"

"If I wanted Belle," he cut in, "I would have asked *her* to marry me." He pulled her more tightly against him. "Henry, I love *you.* I'd love you if you wore a sackcloth. I'd love you if you had a mustache." He paused and tweaked her nose. "Well, the mustache would be difficult. Please promise me you won't grow one."

Henry giggled despite herself. "You truly don't want me to change?"

He smiled. "Do you want *me* to change?"

"No!" she said, very quickly. "I mean, I very much like you the way you are."

This time he grinned—that familiar deadly grin that always made her go limp. "You only *like* me?"

"Well," she said coyly, "I believe I said I *very much* like you."

He tangled his hand in her hair and gave it a tug to tip her face up toward his. "Not good enough, minx," he murmured.

She touched his cheek. "I love you. I'm so sorry for making a muck of everything. How can I make it up to you?"

"You could tell me you love me again."

"I love you."

"You could tell me tomorrow."

She grinned. "I won't need even the tiniest reminder. I could even tell you twice."

"And the next day."

"I could probably manage that."

"And the next . . ."

Epilogue

"I'm going to *kiiiiiillllll* him!"

Emma touched Dunford's arm. "I don't think she meant it," she whispered.

Dunford swallowed, his face pinched and white with worry. "She's been in there so long."

Emma wrapped her hand around his wrist and pulled him away from the sickroom door. "I was even longer with William," she said, "and I emerged healthy as a horse. Now, come with me. *You* shouldn't have come to the door. You'll make yourself sick, listening to her screams."

Dunford let the duchess lead him away. It had taken him and Henry over five years to conceive. They had wanted a baby so desperately; it had seemed a miracle. But now that Henry was actually giving birth, a baby no longer seemed quite as necessary.

Henry was in *pain.* And he couldn't do anything about it.

It ripped his heart apart.

He and Emma made their way back down to the sitting room, where Alex was playing with his children. Six-year-old William had engaged the duke in a mock duel and was soundly trouncing his father, who was somewhat handicapped by the presence of four-year-old Julian on his back. Not to mention two-year-old Claire, happily wrapped around his left ankle.

"Did she have it yet?" Alex asked, a bit too flippantly for Dunford's taste.

Dunford made a growling sort of sound.

"I believe that was a no," Emma said.

"I've killed you now!" William screamed gleefully, stabbing his sword into Alex's midsection.

Alex shot his best friend a sidelong glance. "And you're sure you want one of these?"

Dunford sank into a chair. "Just so long as she's all right," he sighed. "That's all I care about."

"She'll be fine," Emma said soothingly. "You'll see— Oh, Belle!"

Belle stood in the doorway, a bit sweaty and disheveled.

Dunford sprang to his feet. "How is she?"

"Henry? Oh, she's—" Belle blinked. "Where is John?"

"Out in the garden rocking Letitia," Emma replied. "How is Henry?"

"All done," Belle said with a big smile. "It's a— I say, what happened to Dunford?"

The new father had already run out of the room.

Dunford paused briefly when he reached Henry's bedroom door. What was he meant to do now? Was he supposed to go in? He stood there for a moment, a blank expression on his face, until Belle and Emma rounded the corner, both out of breath from running up the stairs after him.

"What are you waiting for?" Emma demanded.

"I can just go in there?" Dunford asked doubtfully.

"Well, you might want to knock first," Belle suggested.

"It won't be too . . . female?"

Belle choked on a laugh. Emma took the initiative and knocked on the door. "There," she said firmly. "Now you *have* to go in."

The midwife opened the door, but Dunford didn't see her. He didn't see anything other than Henry—and the tiny bundle she held in her arms.

"Henry?" he breathed. "Are you all right?"

She smiled. "I'm perfect. Come sit with me."

Dunford crossed the room and perched next to her on the bed. "You're certain you're not ill? I heard you calling out quite vehemently for my demise."

Henry turned her head sideways and dropped a kiss on his shoulder. "I'd rather not endure childbirth every day, but I think it was worth it, don't you?" She held out the baby. "William Dunford, meet your daughter."

"A daughter?" he whispered. "A daughter. We have a girl?"

Henry nodded. "I checked very closely. She's definitely a girl."

"A girl," he repeated, unable to keep the wonder out of his voice. He gently pushed back the blanket so he could see her face. "She's beautiful."

"I think she looks like you."

"No, no, she definitely looks like you."

Henry looked down at the baby. "I think perhaps she looks like herself."

Dunford kissed his wife's cheek. And then he leaned down and ever so gently did the same to his new daughter.

"I hadn't considered a girl," Henry said. "I don't

know why, but I was so certain it would be a boy. Perhaps it was because she kicked so very much."

Dunford kissed his daughter again, as if suddenly realizing how very pleasant that endeavor was.

"I really only thought about boys' names," Henry continued. "I hadn't thought about girls'."

Dunford smiled smugly. "I did."

"Did you?"

"Mmm-hmm. I know exactly what we're going to name her."

"Do you now? And do I get any say?"

"Not a bit."

"I see. Well, are you going to share this name with me?"

"Georgiana."

"Georgiana?!" Henry repeated. "Why, that's almost as bad as Henrietta!"

Dunford smiled lazily. "I know."

"We couldn't possibly burden her with such a name. When I think of what I've endured . . ."

"I couldn't imagine anything that would have suited you better, *Henry.*" Dunford leaned down and kissed his daughter again. And then, for good measure, he kissed his wife. "And I don't see how someone like you could have a daughter named anything but Georgie."

"Georgie, eh?" Henry looked down at her daughter assessingly. "What if she wants to wear trousers?"

"What if she wants to wear dresses?"

Henry tilted her head to the side. "Point taken." She touched the baby's nose. "Well, little one, what do *you* think? It's your name, after all."

The baby gurgled happily.

Dunford reached to take the precious bundle. "May I?"

Henry smiled and released the baby into her father's arms.

He rocked her for a moment, testing the weight and feel of her, then leaned down, his lips finding her tiny ear. "Welcome to the world, little Georgie," he whispered. "I think you're going to like it here."

SPLENDID

American heiress Emma Dunster has always been fun-loving and independent with no wish to settle into marriage. She plans to enjoy her Season in London in more unconventional ways than husband-hunting. But this time Emma's high-jinks lead her into dangerous temptation.

Alexander Ridgely, the Duke of Ashbourne, is a notorious rake who carefully avoids the risk of love – until he plants one reckless kiss on the sensuous lips of this high-spirited innocent. For Emma's British cousins are just as determined to see her settle in England and soon sparks – and laughter – fly when all these terribly determined people cross paths during one very splendid London spring.

978-0-7499-3912-0